C000115670

Books by Russ

FICTIC

Siege: A Novel of the Eastern Front, 1942

Madness Without End:
Tales of Horror from the Russian Wilderness 1941-45

Demyansk: More Tales from the Russian Wilderness 1941-45

NON-FICTION

Gotterdammerung 1945: Germany's Last Stand in the East

Praise for *Siege*

"Russ Schneider's *Siege* is in the same league as Theodor Plievier's classic Stalingrad—haunting, mesmerizing, and spellbinding."
—*Nelson DeMille*

"While this novel only deals with two small cities under siege by the Russians on the Eastern Front during World War II, it manages to give us the face of all war, the horror, blood, exhaustion, hunger, and sacrifice of human conflict wherever it has raged over the face of the world. This darkly painful narrative by a writer himself too early dead will change you forever. Such is art on its highest level."
—*Harry Crews*

About *Madness Without End*

"A fascinating new release containing fictionalized accounts and small-unit actions based on fact from the Russian Front. These stories help illustrate the bewilderment and horror experienced by German soldiers as they entered into bitter combat in a dark and largely unknown country."
—*Eastern Front Books*

Russ Schneider's out-of-print books are widely sought after and highly praised on the internet. This printing of Demyansk will be followed by *Madness Without End* and his other out-of-print books.
See russschneider.net

DEMYANSK

More Tales from the Russian Wilderness 1941-45

Russ Schneider

Neue Paradies / NPV

Gainesville, Florida

Demyansk: More Tales from the Russian Wilderness 1941-45, is a work of fiction. Although based in history, names, characters, and incidents are used fictitiously.

Second Edition, second printing, 2011. 1st printing 1995 by Neue Paradies / NPV.

Library of Congress Cataloging in Publication Data: 95-069563

ISBN: 0-9642389-1-8

www.russschneider.net

Neue Paradies / NPV

Gainesville, FL 32605

Manuscript and cover prepared by Prairie Publication Services, Gainesville, FL.

CONTENTS

Illustrations and Photographs

Frontispiece. Demyansk Campaign Shield by Carol MacDonald

Page viii. Munin Verlag.

Page 9. Munin Verlag.

Page 69. Podzun Pallas Verlag.

Page 229. Aurora Art Publishers, Leningrad.

Page 287. Soviet Archives.

Maps and other illustrations by the author.

Cover design by the author.

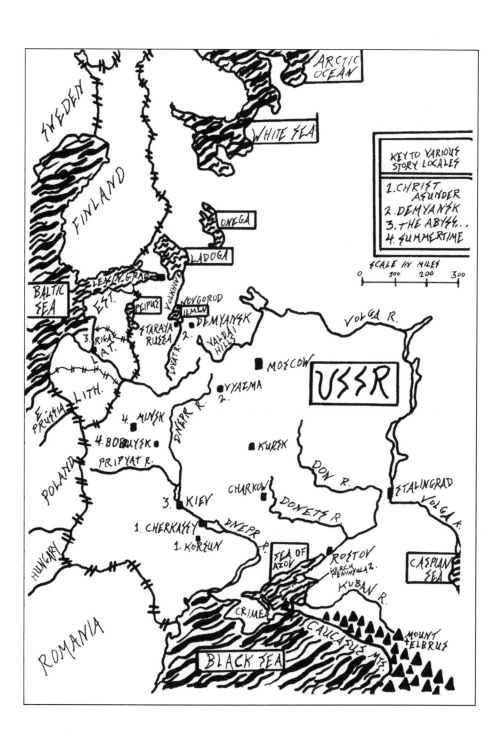

Theodor Eicke in Russia, 1941 (Standing in Vehicle)

INTRODUCTION

I

In 1941, German newsreels and other propaganda outlets referred to the Soviet Union as "a new German paradise." *Ein neue deutsche Paradies.*

Years later, one writer likened the campaign in Russia to a battle of mutual extermination between different species of insects, or between beings from neighboring planets engaged in a war to the death.

This is a striking remark. I was sure I had read it in the preface to one of the large overall histories of the war, perhaps by Alan Clark or Albert Seaton. Yet search as I might, through those books and many others lining my bookshelves, I have never been able to find the source of this quote again. Perhaps the author or someone else will call it to my attention one day. In the meantime the image emerges and re-emerges like something from a dream.

II

One finds strange examples of how the war against the Soviet Union has been impressed on German memories, particularly on the memories of the soldiers. For most of World War II, the war against Russia was *the* war.

The many campaign histories of individual divisions published after the war focus almost exclusively on the struggle with the Soviet Union. One would be surprised to find that there are no individual unit histories of the divisions that comprised Rommel's Afrika Korps. The Afrika Korps was a corps in a quite literal sense; it was a relatively small body of troops that for most of its existence contained only two divisions, less than fifty thousand men. This, as opposed to the three million men fighting in Russia.

Rommel was a glamorous figure and in many ways Africa was a glamorous, or at least exotic, theater of war. But to the German public and to the German leadership it was never more than a sideshow.

It is also arresting to leaf through photographic histories of units that fought both in Russia and on the Western Front after the Normandy invasion. Divisions of the Waffen-SS were heavily represented in France after D-Day. Yet if one were to look through the photo history of the SS Division Das Reich, for example, one would find less than twenty out of four hundred pages devoted to the Normandy campaign. Das Reich also took part in the Battle of the Bulge; this battle is covered by a grand total of two pages.

Almost the entire book deals with Russia. Russia. Russia. Russia.

The proportions are similar in the large photo history of the entire Waffen-SS, *Wenn Alle Bruder Schweigen*. Out of over six hundred pages, only a handful deal with the Western Front. The book is fundamentally a history of the war against the Soviet Union.

Part of the reason for this disparity is that by 1944 the German struggle on all fronts was so desperate that war correspondents, and individual soldiers, had less time to spend taking pictures. The German publications state this plainly. Yet even during the later years of the war there remains a greater emphasis on the Eastern Front. After their abortive, and relatively short-lived, offensive in the Ardennes, almost all of the Waffen-SS divisions were transferred back to the east. The fighting in eastern Germany and Hungary in 1945 is, by and large, given more attention than the Battle of the Bulge.

As for the regular army, there are very few unit histories of divisions that fought exclusively in the west—in Italy, France,

Belgium, Holland, western Germany. It would be an injustice to call these units second-rate, but many of them were raised late in the war and had little or no previous combat experience. Contrary to what one might expect, there was no large-scale transfusion of combat divisions from Russia to the west after D-Day. Almost all of the army divisions that entered Russia in 1941, whose soldiers quickly became the most hardened veterans in the German military, remained to fight on the Eastern Front for the duration of their existence; until they were destroyed, or until the war ended.

The number of army divisions transferred to the west from Russia can very nearly be counted on the fingers of one hand. Of these, several had been wiped out in the east, particularly at Stalingrad; upon being re-formed to fight in the west, they were basically composed of inexperienced recruits with a small cadre of surviving veterans.

Fifty years after the fact, it is still necessary to call attention to the enormity of the Russo-German War. In many ways, it would be a distortion to look on this struggle as merely "a theater of war," one out of the many theaters of war that made up the entirety of World War Two. One could almost invert the normal hierarchy of events, and describe much of World War Two as a secondary theater, or subset, to the war between Germany and the Soviet Union.

When the end came in 1945, Russian and German losses on the Eastern Front exceeded total human losses throughout the rest of the globe.

On the other hand, war is war. Terror is terror. Death is death. It is not the intention here to trivialize or diminish events that took place elsewhere in the 1940s. Human loss was terrible everywhere.

Even in German accounts, one does not necessarily perceive an intent to diminish the struggle against the Western Allies. Losses among U-Boat crews in the Atlantic reached nearly ninety percent by war's end. The air war over Germany saw high casualties among pilots and fantastic casualties among civilians. The ground war was a brutal and killing business.

Perhaps the impression one really gets from German accounts is that Russia was more than just a war. In the same sense that the Trojan War was more than just a war. It was also an epic, an epic nightmare, fought with unbelievable savagery in a terrain and climate that was, as often as not, also unbelievably savage.

There is also the element of hubris, in the old Greek sense of the word. Perhaps in Russia a term like anti-hubris might be more appropriate, in the sense that Russia and Germany during this era could almost be called anti-nations. One would have to think hard, and perhaps play up the role of devil's advocate, to propose any government in recent human history to compare with the regime of either Hitler or Stalin, especially if one considers the sheer scale of their crimes. To look back on these two regimes engaged in a war to the death must have, and continue to have, its own epic qualities.

III

Over half of what is now Poland was German territory that was taken—one might reasonably say stolen—after World War One. Much has been made of the unfair humiliations imposed on Germany by the Versailles Treaty. Yet even now surprisingly little emphasis is placed upon the forced dissolution of a large part of the German nation. German anger over the creation of the Polish state— primarily the doing of Britain and France—was justified. A German might argue that Britain had no more business declaring war over the issue of Poland in September of 1939, than Germany would have had in declaring war over the issue of Northern Ireland. There was more to World War Two than naked aggression; this too has been acknowledged, but perhaps not to the extent that is merited.

All of the events leading up to the invasion of Poland involved not only German aggression but a persistent meddling in other peoples' affairs on the part of the Allied nations. The British in particular had long made a habit out of a certain politely arrogant meddling which was deeply resented by many Germans. After the conquest of Poland Hitler attempted to make peace with the western nations; he had no interest in fighting them. Britain and France turned him down. The war was on for good.

Unfortunately, to attempt to make any objective or "reasonable" analysis of this kind is to leave certain "unreasonable" factors out of the equation—in particular, the factor of Hitler himself, and of the whole phenomenon of Nazism. Murder, debasement, and enslavement of Polish Jews, and also of other Poles, began even before the Blitzkrieg of 1939 was finished. This was only a foreshadowing of other activities that were to take place later in eastern Europe and the Soviet Union.

Did France and Britain go to war because they saw all this coming? To some extent, clearly, they did. Those still alive today may recall their gut reactions to the situation brewing in Nazi Germany in the 1930s. A German may recall the explosive anger that is fed by the interference and intrusions of other nations. The Germans, of course, had by no means been innocent on this account in the past either.

There is more to be said about all this, more that has already been said, more to be said in the future.

I have sometimes wondered how the United States would have dealt with the presence of a large and powerful Communist nation—indeed, *the* Communist nation—if such a nation had bordered America over a period of decades. It is not a pretty situation to think about. It is disturbing to imagine what kind of belligerence, treachery, and aggression this might have led to, by both sides, by either side, by any side.

It is hard to write about the war in Russia and maintain a neutral stance, or even an objective stance. For such a stance becomes itself a kind of opinion. The temptation to point fingers at the guilty is powerful; the feeling that one may also be pointing fingers at the innocent is disturbing. The feeling that any accuser may be guilty of a certain degree of hypocrisy is also disturbing.

5

DEMYANSK

Even so, the nightmares unleashed by Hitler and Stalin had a unique force to them, a force which seems to continually destabilize attempts to make comparisons with the acknowledged crimes of other nations at other times. There are reports that not only the SS but the German army as a whole became the purposeful instrument of Hitler's crimes in Russia. And it is clear that army leaders contributed to or at least condoned a great deal of murderous conduct. Yet it also seems clear that the average German soldier was as lost and terrified as other soldiers in other wars; reports that the entire German army in the East was imbued with National Socialist bestiality are not very convincing. The soldiers of Stalin's army also fought in the service of a depraved and criminal government, yet like their German counterparts, most of them fought under duress, without any great enthusiasm, dying by the thousands and millions.

All of this . . .very disturbing, very disturbing. . . . I did not set out to stimulate this disturbance in myself or in any reader of these stories, yet perhaps it is inevitable that this should happen. It has already been happening for a long time. My own interest in Russia stemmed primarily from strange visions of terrible combat in a strange and enormous land.

German soldiers took a lot of pictures in Russia. It was a strange country, probably the strangest any of them had ever seen. They made much of the foreignness of the place, and often medieval comparisons would come to their minds; probably because, to a European, the Middle Ages epitomize a time and place that seems from another world.

An American might recognize something different though. Many scenes from Russian rural settlements bear a curious resemblance to photographs of the American frontier in the 1800s. The more I look at scenes from the Russian wilderness the more I think of this, and not of anything medieval. The crude wooden houses, the rickety fences, the muddy thoroughfare that formed the single street through a town. The immensity of the landscape, and of the sky overhead. Sometimes tidy and solidly constructed dwellings standing next to others that are slipshod and falling apart. The lack of even the most basic modern conveniences and consumer goods, mixed with occasional modern intrusions such as telegraph lines or distant railroad embankments.

The people too, surprisingly, start to look familiar in this way. They clearly bear the stamp of another culture. But they also have a hardy look about them, the look of people for whom the hardships of nature form as much a part of their lives as the brutalities of their rulers. They frequently bear the expressions of people cowed by vague or immediate terrors; yet it is also interesting to see how frequently such expressions are absent from their faces.

Another world. Sometimes even Germans would remark that certain villages reminded them of American frontier towns, such as they had seen in books or films, or in their own imaginings.

SS Regiment Deutschland on the Ukrainian Steppes, Winter 1943-44

DEMYANSK

After the fall of Stalingrad in February 1943, the Germans retreated from the far-flung areas of the Volga and the Caucasus, returning to nearly the same positions they had held a year earlier. The territory they occupied still included almost all of western Russia. If they had adopted a defensive posture, they might have held out here indefinitely.

Yet, as has frequently been noted, a purely defensive attitude did not sit well with Hitler's mentality. In July of 1943 he launched an offensive against the Kursk bulge in the Ukraine. Despite having amassed one of the largest armored concentrations in history in a fairly small area, the attack was stopped cold in only a week. Losses on both sides were about equal, but in strategic terms Kursk was, along with Stalingrad, one of the great German defeats of the war. Having brought disorder and exhaustion to the German armored reserves, the Red Army launched a massive counterattack whose momentum was not stopped until nearly a year later.

For the Germans this was a period of constant retreat and constant, desperate fighting. Large German units were in continuous danger of encirclement and destruction in the so-called "cauldron battles," a phrase which gained a notorious standing in the German military lexicon. Early in the war it was the Red Army which had been nearly wrecked by these vast battles of encirclement. Now it was the Germans' turn. One of the most infamous of these cauldrons began to take shape in the neighborhood of Cherkassy, on the west bank of the Dnepr River, in the early months of 1944. . . .

CHRIST ASUNDER

The Disaster at Cherkassy, February 1944

The third winter had come. As usual it seemed to have lasted forever, even though it was not yet the end of December.

The muddy season lasted a long time, almost like a separate winter by itself. Then finally it grew cold. Snowstorms blew. We were on the steppe, in a little village, or else camped in positions outside of it that seemed truly in the middle of nowhere. There was nothing to be seen. It was like a desert, a white desert. On clear days men suffered from sunburn, or else greased their faces to get some relief from the glare.

Then the snowstorms closed in again. Snow piled up everywhere. It piled up so high that when the sun returned it seemed the very surface of the earth was markedly closer to the sky. As if you might stand on the roof of one of the isbas and raise your head up through the rim of the sky. The winter landscape was always full of strange illusions. They helped alleviate the endless tedium and fatigue, if only slightly.

January came. The Russians had surrounded the garrison at Cherkassy, but they had managed to fight their way free. The weather grew colder. Terrible cold. There was more clear weather and fewer snowstorms. But the snow was already heaped so high, shining into infinity under the sun. All that space could get on your nerves. Sometimes you would welcome a snowstorm, just to have everything close in around you for a while. It was a kind of relief.

DEMYANSK

But mostly the sky remained clear, through January, into February. The cold was so bad that you began to fret about certain parts of your body. More than just fret—sometimes you began to despise certain of your digits and organs, wishing you had not been born with them, for all the pain they caused you. The nose was the worst. You felt like the wind might just saw it off one day, or that you might accidentally break it off with your finger trying to rub a piece of snot off your lip before it froze there. The thought of this would give you a queasy feeling in your stomach.

No, it was not as bad as the first winter. How we had endured that no one knew anymore. We were no longer dressed in rags. We had good clothing now, parkas with hoods and thick coveralls like a real Arctic get-up, thick boots that looked like they had been shorn off the lower legs of elephants. All of this rig was bulky and sometimes we looked quite strange in it. Beneath our hoods we often wore tight-fitting padded caps that resembled aviators' leather flight helmets more than anything else—except they were white, so maybe they made us look like some strange order of monks I might have seen in picturebooks somewhere.

Maybe we just couldn't stand these winters anymore. In a way we had built up a tolerance for them, after three years, but maybe we were also just worn out, fed up with it all. The new recruits knew all about the first winter. Everyone knew about it. But they could not conceive of how it had been. They would say as much. After a few months out here, they would be depressed and half crazy from the cold. How had we endured it back then, they would ask, without warm clothing, without any experience in how to do anything? How had we done it?

But none of us even knew anymore. The fact was, there were not too many of us left from that first winter. We could not even describe what it had been like back then. Words failed us. We might try and say something if some youngster pestered us enough. Indeed, we didn't really mean to be disagreeable. We didn't know what to say. We just didn't know anymore.

The hell with it. Eventually the new recruits lost interest, engrossed in their own miseries, which we all shared. There was no need to think about the past. Each month out here seemed to last a lifetime. That was all the past we needed.

•   •   •

Sometimes when things were quiet we would make ski-jour-neys out into the emptiness. Sunny weather. There were a few beautiful days from that war.

•   •   •

We were in a village called Schanderowka. It was hard to remember the names of these places. We had passed through so many of them. They all looked so much alike. The strange squalor of these Russians shacks, isbas. Vermin-infested, flea-infested, lice-infested. In a way it was worse than the cold, because it was so much more disgusting. The itching under all your garments, night and day. The rashes, the running sores, itching, itching. You had to suppress the urge to strip whole layers of your skin away with your fingernails. But at night you would dream about it, where nothing could stop you from clawing at your flesh.

Schanderowka. It could have been anyplace. There had never been any signboards on the outskirts of Russian villages, to say what the name of such and such a place might be. Naming places in any intelligible fashion was simply foreign to them. If you were out on patrol in the wastes, looking for a certain vil-lage, trying to link up with some other unit or whatever, you could never be sure you had come to the right place. You would be disoriented, knowing your map was of little use, yet never very comfortable navigating by compass alone, dead reckoning, even though we were forced to resort to this time and again. You would arrive at last at some cluster of shacks out in the steppe, checking it against your map, asking the inhabitants (if any were still living there) if this place was Novo-Archangelsk or Malo-Wissera or wherever. The peasants were usually too naive to even try to deceive you, yet often enough you would wind up lost all the same. Why? Because within a thirty mile radius there might be ten villages named Novo-Archangelsk, or Bol-Archangelsk or Sstary-Archangelsk or plain and simple Archangelsk. As often as not the peasants themselves seemed unsure which Archangelsk they lived in. As if the whole idea of what name their town had was stupid, something only stupid German bastards would worry about. At times our officers would be convinced they were trying to deceive us, throw us off the track, guide us into the arms of the partisans or a Russian ambush. We would try to beat the truth out of them sometimes. You could never tell what went through the minds of these peasants. Mostly it was just ignorance, idiocy, not even knowing where they lived.

It had bad consequences sometimes. Once we were holed up for three days at a place called Dogolye. Or at least that's what we thought. We were trying to link up with a battalion of the 72nd Infantry Division, people that had just broken out of the Russian encirclement at Cherkassy. They radioed that they were headed for Dolgoye and we went out to meet them, to help guide them back to the new main line. We knew they would be in bad shape. We weren't in such good shape ourselves, plowing for miles through the snow to reach this damn place. When we arrived there was no one there, no one except for the usual two or three dozen peasants, women, children, old people who looked half-cracked, all the men having long since vanished, except for one or two who might charitably be called village idiots.

Dogolye, Dogolye. Da, da, they said.

We set up our perimeter, fortifying the place as best we could. It was common knowledge that a Russian tank column might show up before any stragglers from the 72nd ever reached us. We had been on any number of these crazy rescue missions over the years. Or had ourselves waited for rescue in just such a miserable scattering of shacks. No matter how much you tried to get used to it, it always wore on your nerves. Stranded out in the wastelands with only a small group of men, never knowing where the Russians were; knowing only that there would be ten times as many of them as your own people.

We sent patrols out to comb the eastern horizon, towards Cherkassy, hoping to make contact with the ones escaping from there.

14

The snow was too deep to go very far. We returned exhausted and frozen, praying we wouldn't become lost out there. We had no more radio contact. We didn't know what was happening to the fugitives trying to get to us.

Maybe you can guess what the upshot of all this was. The battalion of the 72nd did indeed reach Dogolye. The Russians caught up with them there and wiped them out to the last man.

But we had no inkling of it. We waited where we were. After three days another column was sent out to us from the main line. They had received a last radio message from Dogolye and they told us what had happened there. As you might expect, our commander was not quite delighted with this news. His first reaction was to shoot the village head man, but this fellow had conveniently disappeared into the steppes.

We were not in Dogolye after all. The officers pored over the maps, argued, yelled and cursed at each other, interrogated a few peasants, yelled and cursed at them, and at length arrived at some kind of consensus. No, we were not in Dogolye. We were in Malo-Dogolye. Or somewhere. I don't know if anyone ever really knew for sure.

Our commander, perhaps fearing he would be cashiered for this lapse, stormed around the village, looking for someone else to shoot. The headman's wife and children, left behind by that coward, seemed an obvious choice. Somehow our battalion 1a, Hauptman Guisemann, talked him out of this. It was a close thing. A number of our boys were all for it; it wasn't just our commander. We all felt put out by this idiocy, to say nothing of the fact that three hundred men had just been massacred because of it.

But in the end we just left, and headed back to Schanderowka. The little hamlet disappeared into the white emptiness behind us. It was sunset. The wind was vicious. The sky was blue. It was so blue it looked black, long before night ever fell. Maybe the peasants back there were kneeling before their icons, thanking their lice-infested saints that we had not shot every one of them. Or perhaps they still didn't have any idea what all the fuss had been about.

• • •

We marched through the night. An unnerving experience, though in fact the stars were probably a better guide than the sun. We reached Schanderowka at sunrise, a clean and beautiful sunrise, ourselves hating it as usual in the cold. Then we were home again. It was an unpleasant surprise.

"What the hell is this?" said Fritz Petschat, trudging beside me.

"Christ, this isn't Schanderowka," I said. "Where the hell is that bastard taking us to now?"

By "that bastard" I meant Weist, our battalion commander. He wasn't such a bastard. You would just refer to anyone that way.

"The hell it isn't. What are you talking about?" said Fritz.

As soon as I opened my mouth I saw I was wrong. Of course it was Schanderowka. We had just passed any number of the same markers we would pass every time we came in from patrol—the burnt-out T-34, only its turret rising free of the snow, the junked bicycle that had somehow gotten tossed up on top of it, the scraggly line of trees just beyond that led to the edge of town. The obnoxious signpost warning us to stick to the line of trees, where a path had been cleared through the minefields. Minen: Dein Arsch nicht zu verlassen. Mines: Don't leave your ass behind.

But anyway, it was Schanderowka all right. All these little markers were so familiar to us that I'd just walked right by them without even noticing. Everything else was changed though. That was what had confused me for a second.

Our miserable outpost on the steppe had grown overnight into a kind of city. Or at least an enormous vehicle park that looked like a city. And there were tents too, army tents, Finnish tents, new bunkers mounded up everywhere with stovepipes the only thing to distinguish them from another snowdrift. And men, men, lots of men.

Everyone else was also wondering aloud about this new development. The grapevine running back and forth along our exhausted column even before we had a chance to go inside and get warm. The other men, the ones who had marched out to tell us the news about Dogolye, didn't know anything about it either.

"SS," said Fritz, looking around more closely.

"Ja, gut. That explains all the bathroom fixtures," I said. I meant all the vehicles parked everywhere. Even the ones half-buried under snow had their motors running, blue plumes from hundreds of exhaust pipes now making a factory town out of tiny pigshit Schanderowka.

The SS always had more vehicles than was good for them. After three years we in the army still had to make do with horse-drawn wagons, most of the time.

"So. Our friendly homos from the SS," said Fritz.

"So. Our friendly homos from the SS," I repeated mechanically. Savoring the phrase, as if it were a good cigar Fritz had just passed over to me.

"The lovely little cunts."

We weren't too fond of the SS. Though we didn't really think of them as homos either. Granted, some of their more fair-skinned specimens did have that look about them sometimes. No, Fritzie and I just had very foul mouths. Probably that was why we were friends. Of course, with a few exceptions, everyone else had a pretty foul mouth too, so I wouldn't flatter myself about my own repertoire of filth. But Petschat and I had gotten the reputation for being the worst in the battalion. If you could place any stock in such things. But I supposed it was true.

"We've been surrounded," I heard someone say. As we moved along into the village I heard a lot of people saying this. It wasn't our SS friends they were talking about.

We arrived at a row of collapsed isbas that had been our quarters three days before. Our bunkers, as we called them, by which we meant "home." A bunker could be a drafty and stinking isba, or it could be a cozy masterpiece of tight-fitting logs that we'd worked on for weeks to make livable. Or it could be a dirty hole out in the snow with a piece of cardboard pulled over for a roof. They were all our bunkers. Our little homes in Russia. Before us stood three shacks leaning against each other like drunks standing at the side of the road. Our isbas. Our bunkers. I kicked open the front door to the first one and got into a vicious shouting match with the group of SS who had taken over our bunkers.

The other men egged me on. Next thing I knew I had an SS man by the collar and was clouting him in the head with my free hand. But he was no more about to back down than I was. I had a talent for working myself into a rage without any preliminaries, so I'd more or less taken him by surprise. I took advantage of this to deliver him a few good blows but then he started to fight back. Fritzie took up a blocking position to head off any other SS swine that might try to jump me. I couldn't even see how many there were in there; the place seemed black as night after so many days out in the snow-glare.

We were outnumbered. Most of our boys were too exhausted to do anything except sit around outside, laughing and cursing and yelling crazy things. Somehow I was outside in the sun again with several SS morons sprawled on top of me. Petschat had vanished.

They had my arms pinned and I was in the process of getting my face worked over.

"Good, how about another one, you thieving pukes?"

The blood rushed to my head so I thought it would burst my temples. I received a blow that might have broken my nose. This seemed to satisfy them. They kicked me a few times and began to stand up.

I lay there, drained and peaceful. Ah, thank God, I thought. I stared up into the blue infinity of the morning sky and seemed to feel myself vanishing up there. This lasted for two or three seconds. An officer commenced to bark at me.

"Bark, dog," I whispered.

I began to struggle to my feet before one of the SS tried to lay hands on me again. I saluted with one hand while feeling with the other to see that my nose was in one piece.

"Gefreiter George Hake begs to report," I shouted. For that I got a blow to the head from the officer himself.

It was one of the SS. At first I hadn't been sure if it might have been one of our own officers.

"Don't speak. If you provoke me again I'll see you head gets mounted on the roof."

So. An articulate fellow. The other SS seemed to enjoy this little remark. They stood around grinning thinly. Some of our own boys also seemed to enjoy it, for that matter.

"Stand aside," said the officer.

I didn't know where he wanted me to stand. I turned sideways. He glared at me again and then looked at me no more. He stepped past me.

"I'll say this once. We are under a state of emergency. There'll be no talk of court martials or penal battalions. Discipline will be conducted by firing squad only. There will be no more scenes of this kind. Where is your commanding officer?"

He was addressing all of us. Therefore no one answered. Furtively I began looking around myself, looking for Weist or

Guisemann or one of them. A shape appeared from nowhere. Hooded, swaddled in filthy white, unrecognizable.

"Well done," he said to the SS.

He pulled his hood back, shook his hair out a little. It was Leutnant Becker.

The SS officer stared at him with contempt, maybe a little puzzlement.

"Is this the kind of discipline you keep?"

"I'll see to that," said Becker. "All right, get out of here, all of you. If you can't find anyplace to stay then start digging holes in the snow. Los!"

Becker wouldn't bother to look at me either. He gave the SS officer a casual salute and then walked off without a backward glance, washing his hands of us. I supposed we expected him to stand up for us more. But he was probably a little fed up.

The SS officer began to walk after him, as if he had not received satisfaction or something. But Becker was already gone, vanishing the same as he had appeared. The SS stopped in the middle of the street, then walked over to a truck sunk up to its axles in mud and put one boot up on the hood. He broke out a smoke and began staring out into the steppe.

Strange, I thought.

No one moved for a moment or two. We were too tired. The other SS just stood around watching us. Like the show was over.

"What the hell's the matter with you anyway? You expect someone to keep your hotel rooms reserved?"

I shrugged. A hard-bitten young Kerl was looking me over, an NCO. He offered me a smoke. I took it. He lit up, looking over the rest of my crew.

"Who are you?" I said.

"SS Wiking."

"SS Wiking," I muttered.

The smoke felt almost as good as being knocked flat on my back. I stared over at the officer with his leg bent up on the truck. As if he'd forgotten the whole thing already. Petschat stumbled out of the isba, or maybe was thrown out. His face was bloody.

"How about another smoke?" he said.

The Wiking NCO stared at him. His face began to cloud. He started to go into his pocket again but then just looked away. Fritzie's face took on an identical black hue. He shook his head violently.

"All right, all right," he said. "So, little children of the shit. What's going on. Something smells like shit around here."

"Your lieutenant told you to get the hell out of here. So why don't you do that," said the Wikinger. Fritzie's eyes narrowed. After a moment the Wikinger went on, "Our cousins have had us surrounded for the last three days. If you didn't run into them out there, you must really have had pig's luck."

•   •   •

Maybe so.

At last it began to sink in. What we'd heard from every passing mouth on our way back into town. How we'd managed to walk back from Dogolye without seeing a single other soul was a mystery. The Ivans had broken through everywhere. Pig's luck, yeah. Maybe we'd just marched right through them in the middle of the night. Stranger things had happened in these wastelands.

Schanderowka was like an enormous bundle of nerves. We felt that way too, once we understood what had happened. The fiasco with the men from the 72nd was still fresh on our minds. But that had only been one battalion. There must have been ten thousand men crammed into Schanderowka by now. Maybe more. We began hearing that the Russians had us surrounded to a depth of thirty miles. Or forty miles, or fifty miles. We all started getting nervous.

Even though there was not a sign of anyone out there. Out there beyond the last isbas, beyond the last fortified posts filled with men armed to the teeth. Beyond the barbed wire. Nothing. Snow. The ocean. The desert. Space.

Nothing.

We weren't about to just start digging holes out in the snow, as Becker had told us to do. We began looking around for some other shacks to shelter in. But this didn't last long. Every nook and cranny was already occupied. Even to push in and share quarters with some other bunch was impossible; there was simply no room. Heidemann's platoon finally holed up in one of the stables, shoulder to shoulder with the horses in there. But everyone else had to start digging in the snow, throwing up tents, mounding them up with snow and broken boards to keep the cold out. Petschat and myself and some others from our company got ourselves set up in a kind of yard in the middle of three or four isbas. Probably a vegetable plot in the summertime, patch of weeds, something; there was a rickety fence around it to catch the snow drifts. The isbas were set up senselessly in the typical Russian style, facing at random in any direction at all. But they also provided a kind of enclosure from the wind.

After we had finished bitching about our bad luck we changed tack and started congratulating ourselves on not having to hole up again in one of the stinking lice-infested isbas. It was just a slight change in tone, so to speak, this optimism, as the filth that issued from our mouths remained entirely unchanged. The tents were warm enough, once you got them insulated with enough snow. And we knew how to light a fire with a stovepipe sticking up through everything so we wouldn't burn the whole place down. It was too crowded though. Everyone got on everyone else's nerves, night and day.

So it was a kind of relief to take our turn out on the perimeter, out in the forward posts at the edge of town. We were allowed to rest on the day we came in; after that we took our turn out in the defensive perimeter, shoulder to shoulder with the SS and scattered groups from half a dozen other army divisions. New rumors went up and down the line almost like clockwork, every hour on the hour. It was always like that in these situations. Because there was really nothing else to talk about. The steppe did not stay empty for long. It wasn't our cousins out there, at least not yet. It was other groups of men retreating into Schanderowka, columns of trucks following behind prime movers rigged up with snowplows, or miserable columns of panje-wagons with horses driven almost to collapse, or just men marching, marching in from everywhere.

They all had that peculiar bad look that you only see when everything has gone to hell, when the situation has turned into a rout and everyone knows it. A lot of them had bad stories to tell. Groups scattered everywhere, split up, overrun by T-34s, mounted Cossacks appearing out of nowhere and sabreing everyone in sight, then disappearing back into the waste. The same stories, over and over again. Cherkassy overrun, Korsun overrun, towns twenty miles back in the rear areas only a week ago.

DEMYANSK

It was that peculiar fucked-up atmosphere that would hang over everything, which I remembered very well from in front of Moscow during that first winter, and in a number of places since then. There was never any panic. Or almost never. Men took it calmly, used to it by now, their nerves on edge, but trying to stay calm and let things take their course; waiting to see how we would get out of it this time. Another Schweinerei. All of these men packed into Schanderowka, exhausted, calm, fucked-up, and waiting.

● ● ●

The Russians showed up.

They showed up first at a few outlying villages. Like suburbs, as it seemed to us, though of course they were nothing but other filthy little places out there somewhere, no smaller than Schanderowka, no bigger. Nameless because we could never remember their names. They were outposts trying to cover the overall retreat. Our battalion marched out to one of those places, three or four miles away. Another straggle of shacks on either side of a single road buried in the snow. The Russian tanks showed up in the middle of the night, driving right through the middle of the village, shooting up everything in sight, knocking walls down, setting everything on fire, the crazy daylight of a village burning at midnight in the snow-wastes. A T-34 burned like a torch right in the middle of everything, an evil illumination that flared out into the blackness and then sucked the blackness in closer. It was Becker who had climbed on and knocked it out with a Teller mine. The rest of them kept milling about for an hour or so, accomplishing little with their typical Russian craziness, then vanishing into the night. We had a few wounded and a few dead. Becker was dead. Several men, including Fritz, swore they had seen Becker alive and whole for quite some time after he took on the T-34. So no one knew when he had gotten it. A headshot. He was a decent officer.

Morning. We waited to be relieved. Like Dogolye again. Or like anywhere. Orders were delivered by radio. No relief. The pocket—the "cauldron"—was shrinking. There were no more stragglers out there for us to shepherd back to Schanderowka. We were told to return.

"Thank Christ," said Fritz.

"Count your blessings," I said. "Those tanks are probably standing square in our way."

"No, they're not."

"How the hell do you know?"

"I don't know a damn thing," he snapped. "Kiss my ass and hope for the best. It's only a couple of miles to get back there."

I let loose with a stream of filth, speaking with stone-dead calm as I did nine times out of ten. We looked out over the snowfields in the direction of Schanderowka. The morning was pure. No such clarity existed in any other place I had ever been, outside Russia.

We buried Becker and the other dead beneath the floor of an isba. If we buried them outside then the snowmelt would uncover them in the spring, and we all knew how the Russians liked to amuse themselves with our dead. Birchbark crosses marked our dead for two thousand miles. But we erected no crosses any more, unless we knew for sure we would be sticking around to protect them. They only served as further invitations for our cousins to behave like pigs. It pained us. Almost as if we were performing some kind of sacrilege, to have to just dump them in a pit like that and wipe away any trace of their earthly existence.

Weist said a few words. Standing outside the isba, where there was room for the rest of us to gather. Becker would receive the Iron Cross, or the German Cross, or some other decoration. We knew as much without being told. It would be too cynical to say we didn't care, as we respected Becker. But no one really cared, probably Weist included. He looked less put out than he'd been at Dogolye. Maybe he was the only person in the whole stinking cauldron who had anything to be satisfied about. In the big fuckup in which we found ourselves smaller fuckups tended to get lost in the shuffle. Though you could never know for sure. But Weist looked a little more collected now. As if if he were thinking maybe that his stupid mistake at Dogolye might be overlooked in all the chaos. Maybe so. It had hardly been his fault, anyway.

I found myself thinking of Becker, regretting that I had liked him. I shut my eyes, ran my fingers in my hair, clutching at my scalp. Only yesterday he had been getting on my case about my little disturbance of the peace with the Wikingers. A couple of days had passed since that little fight and I was hoping he'd forgotten about it. Indeed, he seemed distracted, as if he were only reminding himself to cuss me out in case he forgot about it later. I said I was sorry, as I'd said to him on several similar occasions in the past.

"You're a gentleman, Hake," he said.

"What do you mean?" I asked, a bit thickly.

He stared at me as if my dim-wittedness had caught him off guard. We were standing at the side of the shitty little road that passed through this nameless village, only a few feet from where the T-34 would be torched later that night.

That was the last chance I had to speak with him.

• • •

Back to Schanderowka once again. Only a couple of miles, Petschat had said. Like a prayer. The T-34s from the night before were nowhere to be seen. We trudged in through the drifts and made it back while it was still full daylight. If anything the place looked even more crowded now.

We marched in through the outposts and the barbed wire. Artillery came in at that moment. We went to ground in the perimeter dugouts, which were probably safer than being in town. Even from the outskirts the place looked like an anthill. I shuddered to think of shells exploding in the middle of all that. The barrage lasted about half an hour. We crawled out of our holes and continued into town. Terrible sights greeted us.

We ignored them as best we could. It was like being in a city after some disaster has happened. There were the usual human bodies painted onto the walls by the force of the explosions. A headless traffic policeman pointed the way back to our little yard in the snow. But it had already been like this for days, with so many wounded being brought into town, dying and screaming in the midst of crowds of other men milling about, as aimless looking as a great throng of people in a city. You would just shuffle on past horrible sights, as if you could disappear into the crowds.

This went on for days. The barrages became more frequent. Heavy caliber stuff. We were terrified that the Russians would bring up Katyushas. The rocket launchers. Stalin Organs. What they would do to so many men in such a small place did not bear thinking about. Still they did not appear. But the thought of them was never very far from our minds.

Groups of men who had been sent out from Schanderowka came back in, abandoning other villages out there like the one where Becker had been killed. The cauldron was growing tighter and tighter. In fact the cauldron was no longer any more than Schanderowka itself. When we first heard about being surrounded the rumor was that we still had a fifty mile perimeter to move about in. That was bad enough. But now our perimeter was no more than a few miles. We had to get out of here. For days men had kept their worries down to a kind of nervous chatter, but now some people started getting more outspoken. We had to get out.

I cursed every conceivable thing that existed, but as that was normal for me no one paid me much attention. Hake and Petschat, the two foul-mouthed louts. Very well. It was the younger recruits who were really starting to get nervous; the young ones, plus a few of the veterans who had been through it all before, who started saying they weren't going to put up with this another time.

Still, there was no panic. No drumhead SS discipline. The Wiking swine mixed with every one else, and as the days passed by they looked not much different from everyone else. The Russians closed in around the perimeter. We could see them out there now. The attacks began, and so they continued, one day after another. The bodies began piling up beyond our guns. When they had exhausted themselves temporarily (for it was never more than temporarily) the loudspeaker broadcasts would begin. German soldiers addressed us. General Seydlitz addressed us, he who had been the saviour of the Demyansk cauldron two years before. The Russians had captured him at Stalingrad, and now he addressed us on a still winter night, imploring us to surrender. Surrender, surrender. . . . Who knows who might have taken him up on his offer? He was as brave a man as any of us, no doubt. Perhaps the Russians would have treated us well, or as well as could be expected after all these years. . . . It was impossible to believe that it was only three years since all this had begun; it seemed more like decades. But we all had our doubts, you see. Whether they would let us surrender peaceably, or whether they would murder us all like dogs. It was difficult to have much confidence in our cousins along those lines. . . .

The bastards kept trying to wear us down, either with psychological warfare or with high explosive, or with those sickening waves of their own men, their own flesh sent out to be murdered in front of our guns. Well, it was succeeding. They were wearing us down. They could not break through, because as of yet there were still too many of us packed in here. There were so many people packed in Schanderowka that the battle lines could not contain us all; the rest of us would wander about inside the town, like thousands of men at loose ends at a bus station. But they were wearing us down. The field hospitals soon came to hold half the population of the entire town, men screaming, or men who had just given up, unattended, staring at nowhere, waiting to die. The release, the release from all of it. . . .

•   •   •

The order to break out was given on the 15th or 16th of February. Stemmerman, who had been placed in overall command of the pocket, relayed the orders to the commanders of the individual units, and then so on down through the ranks, to us, the Landsers. Weist gave us the news. He made the rounds from one company or platoon to the next, as there was no room for the whole battalion to gather in one place.

He came into our yard, accompanied by Leutnant Ord, who had taken over our company after Becker. The divisional chaplain was also with them, Father Barkhorn, the Lutheran pastor. He stood to one side while Weist laid out the situation. All the men crawled out of their tents, or stood in the doorways of the isbas.

"All right, here it is, gentlemen. I suspect you've heard the rumors by now. We're getting out."

A wave of strange expressions passed over the men. It was a relief, to be sure, and a few Landsers shouted things or started forward a few steps.

"Ja, gut. Let's get the hell out."

A dozen voices muttered this. Others said other things or stared fixedly at Weist. Every face had that strange animated look—the breaking of the tension—and yet tension remained. Faces all around the little yard, looking both illuminated all of a sudden and yet still very stiff.

Weist waited for everyone to settle down. He said,

"Panzer Group Bake has been trying to reach us for over a week. Apparently they can go no farther. General Stemmerman received orders from the High Command only an hour ago. We are to break out on our own and link up with Bake's people at Lysyanka. It is a little place about eight miles west of here. I was there myself not too long ago, so I can assure you there will be no unpleasant confusion this time."

A strange glare suddenly burst forth from Weist's eyes, a startling expression. As well as a tiny crook of a smile that seemed paralyzed at one corner of his mouth. For a moment he seemed not to be looking at us, but looking right through us, through the walls of the shacks, through everything. A few of the men laughed nervously. It might have been the closest kinship any of us had felt for Weist.

He said,

"We will leave after sundown. Our chances will be better that way. With luck we should make it to Lysyanka before daylight, or else soon thereafter. We will hope to catch our cousins off guard. Just remember that we have all done this in the past, gentlemen. Keep that in mind."

He paused. He went on,

"It is not possible for everyone to leave at once. You all know the reason for this. Our cousins must not be tipped off by any great crowds marching out into the steppe. The spearhead will depart at 2100 hours. Stemmerman has assigned this task to battlegroups from the Wikings and the 132nd. Do not look unkindly upon your SS neighbors, gentlemen. The rear guard will also be composed of Wiking people.

"The exact hour for our own departure has not been set yet. Stemmerman will be in touch with the unit commanders throughout the day. Either myself or Leutnant Ord will inform you at the earliest possible moment. In the meantime we have things to do. Gasoline will be shared out. The remaining vehicles will be destroyed. The wounded will be organized and transported out with the heaviest possible protection. No one will be left behind."

He continued for a few more minutes. Laying out every last detail, or at least giving us the impression that these had been seen to. It was the most I had heard him say to us at one time. I felt a small twinge of respect for him.

Then he walked off, presumably to say the same things all over again to the next group of men. He could have left all this to the company commanders. But he didn't.

Ord stayed behind, along with Barkhorn the chaplain. The chaplain had been making the rounds for days. Not so much to speak to us, as he knew from experience that that could get on our nerves. But rather to make himself available to anyone who wished to speak to him.

Barkhorn had been the only chaplain in the division for several years. A Lutheran, as I said. The Catholic father, Pellsbach, had been killed in the very first days of the war. I didn't know if it was true, but it had become part of divisional lore that he had been the very first man of our division to die in Russia. No other Catholic chaplain had ever been sent out to replace him. I had never asked any of my Catholic friends if this concerned them. Barkhorn tended to us all. I had never spoken to him myself.

He looked at all of us. He walked through the doorway of the nearest isba. A few men followed him in there.

•　　•　　•

It is strange to speak about what happened next. It was a terrible disappointment. I cursed automatically, hour after hour, yet hardly aware that I was saying anything at all.

Yet the weather grew so warm so suddenly that I felt strange twitches of ecstasy pulsing through me, and I was not alone.

"Ah, God. Ah, God," men said, staring up at the sky.

"Ah, God," men repeated for hours.

"Ah, God. Ah, shit. It feels good," said Fritz. "We're fucked. We're fucked, George."

"No, we're not," I said. "We're getting out. We're getting out tonight. I'm going to wipe my ass with pigshit Schanderowka and then I'm leaving."

I had seen the thaw in Russia before. Most of us had. It would come so quickly that it seemed like a thunderstorm. It is the only comparison that comes to my mind. It would burst upon you like a radiant and beautiful thunderstorm, the air so soft it left you speechless. Men groaned for hours out in the sunlight, groaning with joy and fear.

I had seen the temperature shoot up like this over the course of a few days, or even overnight. But this was a new one. There had been no signs of warming at dawn, or at least I hadn't felt anything. Yet by noon the snow was flowing in rivers down the filthy street, flowing out into everything, into every yard and back alley. There were lakes outside the village and there were lakes inside the village. Vehicles raised spray and left wakes behind them like boats, driving up to any patch of high ground before they were flooded and sucked down into the mud. Men waded everywhere. The dead floated in the streets. The recent dead floated among the dead who had been dead for months and buried under months of snow. They floated like rafts of timber, dead men, dead horses, dead rats and dogs, revolting heaps of dead Russians who had been wiped out earlier in the winter; all of these men—these things—floating up out of their snow-graves.

These corpse-flotillas we mostly ignored, as it was a phenomenon that was not new to us. Men bumped through them like loggers at work, pushing them aside with their knees, wading on in one direction or another. I saw a couple of men singing in the middle of the road. They looked drunk. The thaw would have that effect on people. They sang with happiness and despair, a stinking drunken disgrace. Probably Fritz was right. We were fucked.

Neither Ord nor Weist was anywhere to be seen. Weist was probably with Stemmerman. And Ord was probably hiding somewhere. People had been pestering him all morning, wondering what was going to happen now. He didn't know. After that he had simply disappeared for hours.

"Just remember," I said to Petschat. "It can freeze up again just as fast."

"You stupid bastard," said Fritz. "I suppose next you'll tell me you're going to volunteer for the SS."

"No, I don't think so," I said.

He looked like he was about to cry.

"I've got the fever, George. I can't stand it anymore. I'm leaving tonight. Ah. You know how it is. Next thing the turds will start floating out of the outhouses. Ha ha ha!"

"So what?" I said dully.

"So what? I don't know. I'm heading for Lysyanka or wherever the hell it is. I'd rather drown out in the mud than have to look at all your lousy faces any longer."

"Well, ask around. You can probably find plenty who'll go with you."

"Ah, shit, shit, goddamned shit of Christ. We're done for. Such fine weather, George. I think I'll just shoot myself now while the air feels so good."

He spoke with a hiss and a croak, though I might not explain how those things could combine into one sound.

Listlessly I watched him standing in the mud. We were both standing in the mud. A dull paralysis settled within me. I had felt it on and off for days. Now it was stronger. It was like a kind of sickness and I recognized it the way you would recognize any kind of ordinary ailment that would afflict you from time to time. A cold, a fever. It was fear, but it was more than that. One did not like to speak of it, except in incoherent cursing tirades. The words were not lies exactly, but they hid other things that were beyond naming and to convey them even now fills me with distress, even a kind of self-hatred. Perhaps this is understandable, or perhaps enough people will understand it.

You felt these things before going into combat, but at least then you knew it would be over with soon enough, in one way or another. But at times like this it might last for hours, days; or perhaps only a few minutes. A brief explosion of rage and disgust, and you got it out of your system. Or maybe not. I looked at my friend Fritz Petschat. He was staring at the ground, at the evil mud. Still muttering under his breath. One year to the next. I remembered other times when he had gone on and on like this, as if he had finally done it, worked himself into a nervous breakdown. But nothing had happened. He had gone on, the rest of us had gone on, as if human beings were no different from the days and months going on. The Rudnya Stellung. The Yelnya Stellung. The Wob Stellung. The Desna Stellung. The Samara Stellung. I remembered these places where we had been, some of them fairly quiet for periods of time. In others we had been surrounded, cut off. I remembered Fritz working himself into a state that had gone on for days, though for some reason I could not remember exactly where this had been. If I thought about it for a moment I could remember it. But my thoughts were dull, like some kind of thing that had sunk down from my head into my shoulders and chest.

I was frightened by the mud. The urge to escape this place was dulled by the thought of it. I remembered other days when I had been coated head to foot in freezing mud. Certain things simply made you want to kill yourself. You struggled with the notion that somehow you could pull through, survive; you struggled with the overpowering temptation to put the muzzle against your temple. To remember these things was enough to turn your mind white. In a way it seemed like you were not even capable of remembering it. I was standing in front of Fritz, standing in the mud, in the freezing thaw-water, talking to him, thinking all these things and yet really hardly thinking of anything, looking at his face, looking over his shoulder at things in the ordinary daylight.

"Are you sure you're all right, Fritz?" I said.

"What's the matter? Do I sound peculiar to you?"

I shook my head.

"Maybe I'll go find Ord," I said. "I'll drag him out by the legs."

Birds were singing. They had appeared from nowhere. They sang in the beautiful air. They perched on the roofs, they drank from puddles and little lakes. Bloated horses and ghastly looking Russians floated on by without disturbing them, nor the black churned-up mud that quickly began to befoul everything, nor the familiar turds that just floated on by, frozen little things that began to dissolve into the meltwater.

Find Ord. I changed my mind as soon as the words left my mouth. I had no desire to struggle out into the quagmire to look for the bastard. There was so much fresh water flowing past that it was still not all that disgusting yet; by tomorrow it would be far more disgusting, if the thaw lasted till then. But even so I suddenly felt limp, with no desire to go anywhere.

Our tents were flooded. There was no place to go except into the isbas, crowded as they were. A number of men climbed up on the roofs rather than sit inside in the filthy dark. Taking the sun up there, pulling their hoods back, opening their muddy parkas as if they didn't have a care. It was as good an attitude to take as any other.

But I'd seen too much of this blasted sunlight. There was just too much of it; just as on days when the snowstorms and the dead overcast rolled in there was too much of that. There was never any moderation in anything in Russia—in the weather, in violence, in murder, in soul-sickness, in rage, in anything. The most ordinary man of us had psychotic threads pulled taut into every corner of his body, after three years of this.

I pushed into one isba, into the darkness in there, sitting shoulder to shoulder with other men as if packed into the hold of a ship. Tempers were bad. Bitter arguments and fights broke out. Men cursed and went back outside, unable to resist the warm air even while wading around up to their hips. Yet other men continually wandered in, sopping wet, depressed, hunkering down and holding their heads in their hands. We were all depressed, or else so anxious we could hardly think straight.

Just one more day. Just one more lousy day. If the thaw had held off for that long we would have been able to make our break. Yet this was so obvious to everyone that only a few people actually said as much.

Besides, we had still not received orders one way or another. To try and stage a breakout during the thaw—which was really only another word for mud, the unspeakable Russian mud which seemed to lie all the way to the Earth's core, once you had experienced it a few times—would be foolhardy, if not altogether mad. Yet we wanted to get out so badly. Men were willing to risk almost any kind of foolhardiness. It was under conditions like this that whole units would undertake some senseless course of action, marching off to their destruction. The officers were no different from the men; the fever took everyone.

Ord showed up at last.

He stood in the doorway, black as night silhouetted in the sunlight beyond.

"It's off! It's off, children!"

He shouted this at the top of his lungs.

There was no reaction for a moment. Probably because no one was very surprised.

Somewhat more quietly he said,

"If you want any further news you'll have to come outside. I'm not going to talk to you in this hole."

Two words had given us all the news we needed. Yet almost everyone in there, myself included, stood up and started to squeeze out the doorway. Nervous energy, something. Even if there was nothing more for him to say, we still had to hear the rest of it. There had to be something more.

He climbed up on top of a wagon-bed. The horse was still harnessed to it. The horse stood quietly in water up to its belly, looking at one thing or another.

The rest of us stood in the water and the filth, or else sat down on any little thing that still rose up out of it.

Ord looked fit to be tied. That was about how he looked. He commenced to give us the rest of the details, the situation as it now stood. He tried to speak calmly, as if mindful of how Weist had addressed us only this morning. Yet he looked distracted, as if trying to fight back the urge to scream curses at everything. I imagined him doing this, wandering off by himself a little ways and cursing apoplectically into space; then wandering back to continue talking to us.

Maybe I was just substituting him for myself. But it was only a little daydream, a moment's fancy that passes in and out of your mind along with a thousand other things.

•　　•　　•

So. It was off. The breakout was off.

We would have to wait for cold weather to return, for the ground to freeze up again.

The only good news was that the Russians would be bogged down no different than we were. We could expect a slacking off of their attacks, the probes around our perimeter that had grown more savage with each passing day.

Our own experience had taught us that. In fact they were far more sensible than we were, probably because they knew their own country. They had always had enough sense not to conduct operations in the mud, which could reduce men to lunacy. It had taken us a long time before we had learned to imitate them. Or before Hitler had learned it, or before the rarefied higher-headquarters swine had learned it. And even now we still didn't possess the patience to sit tight like this, even when we knew better. We were strangers in this land. We always would be.

Besides, you could never trust the Russians. They might conduct their operations a thousand times over again in the same obstinate, stone-headed, rigid manner. In fact we had learned to count on this, and it had saved many lives. But all the same you could never trust them. Never. I suppose it was fear. Nothing but fear.

Their attacks did slack off. The tanks, especially, no longer appeared out there, rumbling around. It was the barrages that got worse and worse. Either they already had enough artillery set up or they had managed to drag more pieces through the mud in spite of everything. We waited to hear the first screams of the earth-flatteners. The rockets. But the Katyushas did not appear. Maybe we did hear those awful salvoes over and over again, but as yet it was only in our thoughts. The standard artillery killed men by the dozens. More human timber floating through the streets.

I don't know what to say about those days. It was a gap, a void. Men were there, but they weren't there. As if no one could live in the present moment anymore. Our thoughts were always on the one moment ahead—when the cold would come back, when the freeze would hard up the ground again.

Supply planes flew over dropping canister bombs—food, ammunition. Yet these events caused little excitement. A lot of men seemed too nervous to eat much.

I remember sitting inside one of the isbas, in the dark. If you got tired of looking ahead, you could look back; you would think about your life, daydreaming about anything at all. I was still fed up with the sunlight. The burning naked clarity everywhere out there. I didn't even know why anymore. It wasn't normal. But I didn't care whether it was or not.

I was sitting dully in the dark, back to back with a total stranger with whom I had not exchanged a single word. Foul, lice-scurrying. Unaware of anyone else around me. I might have been alone in there. There was a single window that had not been boarded over, up near the roof. It was like a picture frame containing a single picture of blue light; like a picture that someone had hung up on the black wall of outer space. There was something about this that was strangely soothing. As if some idiot had finally figured out the proper proportions between light and dark that would leave a man in peace for a while. Strange waves and undulations were visible in the window. It was the strange force of the atmosphere in the winter, blue things shifting and intermingling in the light. The small square of the window concentrated this effect. The little shimmering waves seemed almost like some radio frequency that had been made visible to the naked eye; and a time came when I began to hear music passing through my head, that seemed to correspond to these strange blue undulations. Daydreams, more daydreaming . . . it was nothing more than that. I heard beautiful music, old German songs, very sweet music of one kind or another. A time came when I imagined human voices singing, and after a while these voices began singing words of utter filth, though the melodies remained no less beautiful and dreamy for all that. Sweetly they sang the most sickening imaginable obscenities, or else filth that was nothing but childish; childish and disgusting filth.

It was not the first time such curious things had passed through my mind. To be honest, it was a phenomenon that had happened to me more often than I cared to admit. I could not remember when it had started; maybe sometime during the first year in Russia, or maybe sometime in the second year. I did not think I was going mad. I had never thought that. Sometimes I had the urge to ask other people if they heard things like this, had daydreams like this. But I suppose I never quite worked up the nerve, though I never really felt embarrassed by it either. I had always wanted to ask Fritz about it; once or twice I had been on the verge of saying something to him. But I never did.

It was only to my wife that I had mentioned these things, last year when I had been on leave. In a way she was the last person I should have spoken to, for I didn't know how she would react to it. I was afraid that some kind of strange and disgusting thing had begun to permeate my mind; which, in all honesty, I couldn't really give a shit about out here, considering how we lived out here; and even worse, the things we had seen out here; and even worse, the things we had done out here, the things I had done. Fuck it, fuck all that. . . .

Even while on leave I hardly felt embarrassed about it. Strange little daydreams—they were beneath contempt, compared with all the other nightmares we had lived through. I was leery of talking to her about it, but I suppose some urge got the better of me and I just started talking about it one day.

She took it all right. It was a relief somehow, a small relief. Better than relief was the way she treated me after that, the way she looked at me. So it was all right then. She didn't have to say as much, as I could see it in her eyes. It was good. But after that it pained me all the more, when I had to come back out here. The thought of her gave me more comfort than before; yet it also pained me more, as if some little thing had broken down inside me, and I began to wonder more than ever how much more of this I could stand . . . how many more years I could take of this.

It is hard not to exaggerate it, these dreamy songs of filth. The mere mention of it seems like some crazy, demented thing—or at least I thought someone else might take it that way. Even though I hardly paid attention to it myself; it was so ordinary, so matter-of-fact. But she seemed to understand this too. Or even if she didn't, it made no difference. We walked down the Kurfurstendamm on a May evening, winding up eventually in one of the cellar cafes that were still operating at full steam beneath all the rubble of the air raids.

The cellar was a cheerful place, or at least it seemed that way after we had had a number of beers. Being on leave was not always easy. I was glad she liked to drink with me. When I had had a little to drink those strange songs of filth would pass more freely through my mind, though I still paid no more attention to them than at other times. They did not dampen my mood. In fact I began humming quietly to myself, smiling faintly, sitting back in my chair in the comfortable dimness of the place.

These congenial moments were interrupted by the wailing of the air raid sirens. Some people rose to leave, to go to the shelters. Others did not. We did not. I reached out to hold her hand, but her hand was cold and did not move. It lay on the table. I opened my eyes to look at her. She looked overhead, then lowered her head and sat with her eyes closed. She slumped against me, but seemed not to wish me to touch her too closely. The roar of the planes grew louder, a deep droning unlike anything I had heard in Russia. It seemed that we were were safe down here, but I didn't know. Neither did she. After a fairly long time the droning began to go away, and then the sirens sounded again. She raised her head as if she had been asleep. I needed another beer, though she had had enough. We walked home while it was still light out, evenings getting longer towards summertime. She started to perk up again after a while.

•   •   •

Snow was melting all round us, outside in the warm sunlight. Hour after hour these sounds of trickling and dripping water filled my mind, sounds which would give you a strange feeling of peace, in spite of everything. If only for a few moments at a time. The sound of trickling water somehow took you far away from yourself, even though it might pain you all the more that this feeling lasted for only a few moments. Maybe as long as half an hour; I couldn't really say. It was better just sitting here in the dark, the trickling sounds passing through my mind that way. At length I turned my back to the little window, so even that I wouldn't have to look at. Forty or fifty other men sat all around me in here, the nearest heads no more than a few inches from my own head. What was passing through their own minds no one would ever know.

•   •   •

We left in the pitch-dark night of the 18th of February at 2300 hours. The spearheads had gone out at 1900 hours and other units had followed at intervals throughout the night. It was hard to wait but at least we knew nothing could turn us back this time. The night was full of fog, which eased our minds as much as anything could. The ground was rock-hard after the frost but the cold was not bitter. There was no wind.

Meanwhile heavy fighting had broken out on the eastern perimeter, opposite our escape route. I thought maybe this was a diversion to throw our cousins off the scent. I racked my brains but could not remember if Weist had said anything about this. Gustav Bollinger was standing beside me smoking in the dark. I asked him.

"I don't know. I don't remember anything about that either. Ask Ord."

Ord could not have been far off. But it was impossible to see more than a few feet in the dark. I stayed where I was, smoking with Bollinger. He said,

"I hope those Wiking bastards put up a good fight. If the Ivans get any closer someone's going to tell us to go back and help them."

I said nothing. The last three or four tanks operating in the pocket had rumbled past us a few hours before, headed east. Hoping to keep the Russians at bay for a few more hours, before we were all overrun. Wiking tanks. The SS always had more vehicles than was good for them. They would find that out for sure now.

Illumination from shellfire and tracer bullets erupted out in the distance, yet still cast only a faint and intermittent light upon us. The fog grew thicker and the light from gunfire was reflected up in it, so that each man could begin to see his neighbors a little better. It was like waiting in a pitch-black closet with light from some distant well-lit room throwing faint cracks of illumination around the edges of the door. A few vehicles still burned inside the town, adding to the effect.

"You seen Petschat anywhere?"

"No," he said.

I saw Bollinger's face under his hood, a faint reddish thing. Then it disappeared in another moment of total darkness. He said,

"I don't know. The Kerl might only be ten feet away. I think I did see him a couple of hours ago."

I decided to look around for him. After a few minutes I ran into Ord.

"He'll be around somewhere. Don't run off anywhere, Hake. It's almost time."

"What time is it?"

A faint disc of radiation floated up in the darkness between us.

"Eleven minutes."

This time passed by and then Weist's voice was audible from somewhere. The gunfire was loud to the east. It was time. Men stood and picked up their weapons and their other gear. We carried our weapons and ammunition and nothing else. The wounded had been sent off on the sleds and the wagons several hours before. It would not be a good time for anyone else to be wounded, not now. We had already heard the word, that other units had too many wounded men to transport them all to safety, and so they would be left behind for the Russians, along with a few doctors. No doubt some of them were already putting a bullet through their heads, or perhaps some of their comrades were doing the job for them, if they feared the Russians would subject them to a fate still worse. No doubt such scenes were being played out in other darkened isbas all around us; unimaginable scenes which I could imagine very well because I had seen them happen in the past, though I refused to imagine them any longer now. Dear God. I did not even know who had made the decision to carry our own wounded out, though I suspected it was Weist. Men from other units also tried to carry their wounded out, disobeying direct orders, some of them. We walked out. We walked out through the rock-hard streets of Schanderowka.

We passed by the last burning vehicles, passing through this hole of light. The fog rolled above it. The thaw had created small lakes scattered about at random in the ground, now all of them frozen solid once again, skating rinks. We skirted around the edges of them. Abandoned vehicles and carts and every manner of junk was imbedded in these pools, metal and wooden objects sticking out of the ice at every possible angle. The dead too—shoulders rising up from the ice like men caught turning over in their sleep, heads and torsos rising up like old tree stumps, legs bent up at one angle or another like men kicking quietly through a frozen sea, hands raised up in every conceivable gesticulation of goodbye, of hopeless entreaty, of anything at all. German dead, Russian dead, civilians, you could no longer tell who was who. The night hummed with the silence of the dead and we could hear it clearly enough, whether we bothered to listen or whether we didn't. Auf Wiedersehn, Schwein. May one of the Ivan bastards trip over your frozen skull and break his leg in twenty places. See you all very soon, I don't hope.

They were visible in the light from the burning vehicles, and then less so as we passed on further into the dark beyond the town. We passed Weist and a few other regimental and battalion officers. They stood watching us go by in the last dim twilight cast by the fires, a dim borderland between that and the black night beyond. I saw Barkhorn the chaplain standing with them. I'd heard it said that he often knew better than anyone else where people were to be found. I stopped walking for a moment, wondering if he might have seen Fritz anywhere. But somehow it did not seem the right moment to be bothering the high-and-mighties with stupid questions. Probably he did not even know who Petschat was. I hesitated. Where had that damned Stuttgarter cart driver gone off to? A dull feeling of obligation, worry even, weighed me down. I looked around for a few moments, hooded shapes marching past in the dimness. Bollinger, Wertz, Heidemann, Marcks, Grote, Feuersanger, a few others from my company that I thought I recognized but couldn't be sure in the dark. Fritz knew how to take care of himself. I started walking again. A single panje-wagon creaked along in the midst of our group. It was not loaded up too heavily, there was still a bit of room left on it. Anyone else who got wounded from this point on would have to be transported out by some means. It was the way it had to be. No one was going to be left behind.

We marched into the night. There was nothing. Only a faint sensation of the fog rolling by, rolling overhead. Occasionally flares and explosions out on the horizon. We marched up and down little hills, probably only low rises on the steppe but in the dark they seemed steeper. Men slipped on the crusted re-frozen snow or else broke through it. Curses were quiet. Otherwise no one said anything. Our own battalion had marched right through half the Russian army on the way back from Dogolye without seeing a soul. The country was endless, the fog sheltered us. So maybe we would get lucky again. Or maybe we wouldn't. I figured we would do it. There was nothing else to think.

Sometime in the night we caught up with another wagon column. It was one of the convoys with the wounded. Dim shapes of sleds and wagons stood tilted along the contours of the ground. The wounded were quiet. Everyone was quiet. Only a faint mutter of whispering here and there, that seemed hardly louder than your own thoughts.

"How long before dawn?" I said to Bollinger.

"I don't have a watch."

"It's almost four," said Feuersanger.

"How far have we come?" someone said.

"God only knows."

"Keep your voices down, children." It was Guisemann's voice, the 1a. I looked over there. He always knew what was going on. But I couldn't see where he was. We waited. We didn't know what the halt was for. It was good to get a rest. But we didn't need too long. The dull adrenaline of nervousness had been working through us for hours. There was plenty left to burn. Men walked out into the dark a few paces as if to see where we were, or just to see anything at all. There was only the dim impression of the low hills. Sometimes stars were visible through gaps in the fog overhead.

"Be nice if it lasts into the morning," said Bollinger.

"The only thing I want to see in the morning is the reception committee," said Heidemann.

"Ja, gut."

The march continued. We marched on. We could only assume that the officers or whoever was guiding us knew where to go. This somehow seemed highly unlikely and I tried not to think about it. Someone up ahead would be holding a compass in the palm of his hand, looking down at the little radium indicators every few hundred yards. I hated the things. More stars were visible. The fog no longer looked like smoke, only some tattered and shredded stuff drifting on by. Our pace slowed. We had to keep pace with the wounded. It would not be good behavior to march on past them, even though their escort already numbered more men than our own group had. We helped with the wagons and the sleds, pushing them up inclines, then steadying them on the downward slopes so they wouldn't slide out of control. Inevitably some would do so and you had to be ready to jump out of the way in an instant. Or else they would become stuck in some muddy boghole that had stubbornly refused to freeze up again. Sometime during all this pushing and steadying I realized I had injured my shoulder.

A momentary fit of adrenaline at the bottom of one of these slopes, in other words a burst of rage, pushing with all my might against the spokes of a wagon wheel . . . a short time later I noticed that my right shoulder made a cracking noise every time I moved it. I felt to see if I had dislocated it, but my clothes were too bulky. It didn't hurt much. But I couldn't use it to push anymore. I kept on going through the motions of doing so, too embarrassed to just stand aside and do nothing. But after a few more minutes I felt stupid to be going through these fake exertions and I stepped off to one side, irritated, glaring about.

"What are you doing, Hake?"

It sounded like Heidemann, though I wasn't sure. He stood in front of me. How he had recognized me I didn't know. Probably my cursing.

"I think I broke my shoulder. I'm not sure," I said.

He said nothing.

"I'll try with my other shoulder. Just give me a moment."

"All right," he said.

He turned and started to walk off. He knew I was no shirker. He stopped dead in his tracks. An engine roared out in the darkness.

"Ah, dear God," he said.

Several engine roars, and roadwheels creaking. Tanks.

I looked. Blackness. Then flames from exhaust pipes out there. They flickered in the darkness. They might have been a mile away or ten feet away. I felt weak.

"Ah God."

Someone said this. Others repeated it.

A vast and terrible murmuring passed up and down the entire column. No shouting. Everyone knew at once. Officers hissed for silence. All fell silent. There was the clicking noise of several hundred bolts being drawn back.

More engines started up and no other sound was audible. I counted five pairs of exhaust flames. Then what looked like several more, perhaps obscured by fog.

A long line of men detached itself parallel from the column and moved several hundred yards out into the snow, till they were no longer visible. They would be carrying Teller mines or anything else that could be used.

The roar of the tanks gradually diminished, though the sound did not entirely disappear. It seemed that from that point on the sound never disappeared for the rest of the night. The exhaust flames diminished gradually like fires being sucked into deep holes.

It was even possible that they were ours. Some people said as much and everyone thought it. A distress flare sent up into the night and perhaps we would all be rescued, saved. Just like that. But it was unthinkable. We all knew instinctively they were not ours. We all knew that there was a chance we might be wrong, but only a very small chance. We knew.

Terror descended quietly on everyone with the ordinary force of terror that must be endured for hours on end. We continued our march. Throughout the course of the night we had heard the rumble of distant firefights, seen the glows flickering around the horizon. A terrible noise now erupted only a short distance away. Shellfire silhouetted a few intervening hillocks like waves at sea backed by bolts of lightning. The roar of the tank motors seemed louder than the shellfire, carrying through everything.

"Say your prayers, swine."

"So there you are, you miserable little fuck," I blurted out with stone-dead calm. I could hardly hear my own voice in the roar, much less his. The voice had only been a few inches from my ear. But there was no one standing next to me. I looked around wildly, then looked around a second time. There was no one. I forgot about it. I looked back at the firefight, at the illumination and the silhouettes.

We marched on. The light from the gunfire over there was so intense that it lit us up as well, and we struggled in a kind of dim, methodical panic to get all the wagons down into the next depression where we would not be skylined. We descended into shadow. The men with Teller mines scurried back to the column to assist everyone else. Throughout the remainder of the night we saw the twin flickers of exhaust pipes out there, to one side, to the other side. It was hard to keep quiet. If you could not curse or shout or say filthy things to your neighbor then you felt your nerves stretched all the more because you did not know what else to do. The silence among us was hard to bear, even while the roars from all around grew louder and louder, sometimes diminishing beyond the next set of hills, then coming back closer again. We marched on in the darkness through a ring of firefights all around the horizon, horizons both nearby and far away, the distance to each massacre marked out by the intensity of the explosions. It would be a massacre. Because every column out there would look no different from our own. Hopeless people dragging carts of wounded through the snow. Like a disaster at sea where helpless groups of men are scattered for miles across the water, pulled down by sharks one after the other, yourself left only to pray that your turn would not be next. Every moment was a prayer. Whether you actually prayed—as I could hear sometimes around me during strange snatches of quiet—or whether you thought of other things or thought nothing at all. It was all prayer. The ticking of a watch was prayer.

Say your prayers, swine, the stupid bastard would always say. He seemed to like that expression.

The exhaust flames roaming out in the dark were worse than anything else. You could not tell how far away they were. Every time I saw one I felt weak. I was not tired, I didn't really think I was. It was fear draining me out. I was sure I had enough energy to march fifty miles, yet I felt weak all the time. I had to tell myself to keep marching, to not just stand there and stare.

Dawn came gradually with the dim passage of one existence to an entirely different one. The darkness had been lit up in so many different places that I'd forgotten all about the fog, figured that it must have lifted away at some point. No, I'd simply forgotten about it. Yet gradually we began to see that the fog was still there. Perhaps not quite as thick as the day before. At first you could only see that it was growing light. It was too dim to tell anything else. Then we began to make out the hills through the fog nearby and they too looked different from the night. They were no more than small rises here and there, little humps in the steppe. During the night they'd all seemed much steeper, strange hills silhouetted by the light from the explosions, interminable inclines with us pushing the wagons up or down.

The thing that was the most different was that there was no one out there now. The emptiness looked no different from the way it had looked outside Schanderowka. The night was over. It was the usual ugliness of another morning when you had never had enough sleep and everything seemed weary and dull. For a little while I no longer felt weak from fear but only from exhaustion; it wasn't even exhaustion, not yet, it was just dullness and fatigue, the bleary advent of another day without proper sleep. All my senses had gone dim, blurry inside my head; the seriousness of our situation seemed more like a stupid annoyance, the way even the most terrible emergency will seem when you would simply rather go to sleep and forget the whole thing. A man without proper sleep has more contempt for death than a thousand crack-brained heroes. I only felt depressed and tired, fed up with everything. It was a familiar sensation.

We could not, after all, pretend that it was over now. Morning or no morning; empty landscape or not. For we could still hear them out there. Rumbling around in the fog. Motors roaring and an endless shifting up and down of gears and it seemed somehow that we were wandering through some immense construction site, workers marching bleary and mindless through the middle of it all towards the beginning of their morning shift.

The fog began slowly to lift away through murky patches of sunlight. We marched on and before long I started to become more alert again in spite of myself, more aware of everything; all the fear from the previous night was inside me once again, returning with a despairing and unexpected suddenness. There was no sign of Lysyanka or Bake's people and if any of the officers knew anything they were not passing the word along. With the advent of the daylight men could no longer be compelled to keep quiet, or at least not completely quiet. People all around were wondering aloud when we were going to get there and the serious case of nerves that showed in their voices was not well hidden. We began to see black traces of terrible disasters off in the distance to the left and to the right. Officers paused to study these scenes through field glasses and the expressions on their faces were not encouraging. We marched on, the wagons creaking, the sleds creaking, the horses muttering beneath their clouds of vapor, the hundreds of wounded men all strangely silent just as they had been during the night. I caught the eye of a few of them and it was not quite real, the way they looked at me, the way they looked up at the sky, the way they struggled to look out over the edge of the wagon bed for a moment and then lay back down again.

We were marching along the bottom of a small ravine which terminated suddenly in what could hardly be called a cul-de-sac;

it was only another little rise barring our way and dully we began the ascent. More struggling with the wagons, the horses struggling, men struggling to push; the exasperating ordinariness of such hard labor when you felt in your crotch that the Russians could be just beyond the next ridge and still it was impossible to do anything with any urgency; the wagons would only go as fast as they would go, and when they got stuck you simply had to struggle with them till they got free. My shoulder hurt and then I would forget about it and then some jolt or tug of my equipment would make it hurt again. Before we got to the top of the ridge there was a little dip in the ground, and here we saw first-hand what we had previously seen from a distance.

The shambles was so complete and such a stinking hideous mess that it was hard to notice anything in particular, although the one man crucified on a wagon axle stood out above the rest. As we passed it by a few men fell out from the line of march and began to vomit, or retching as none of us had anything in our stomachs, bright yellow spills of stomach bile that looked toxic and disgusting in the snow. Some because they were overwhelmed by disgust and others simply because they could not help themselves but otherwise might not have given a damn. Because many of us had seen it all before, at one place or another, at one time or another. Though perhaps our cousins were becoming a little more creative as the years went on. I saw Feuersanger doubled over and as the roar of engines had suddenly grown much louder from beyond the ridge I walked over to straighten him up, grabbing him by the hood of his parka. He cursed me for an ass and as I persisted in trying to get him going he cursed me all the more, interrupted by another fit of retching which flecked my boot and trouser leg.

"If you'll just let me finish, Hake. Get away from me. Just get away from me. Ah, Jesus Christ."

He stumbled off as if he could not stand the sight of me, finishing in the snow a little further away. I felt rightly told off and let him be. He struggled to his feet, spitting and wiping his mouth, glaring about, looking one more time at the upright wagon axle with what now looked like hatred more than nausea. The man's arms were spread out and crucified with barbed wire to the metal leaf springs and barbed wire was wrapped in a mock crown of thorns around his head in the little joke so often favored by our cousins. With their typical enthusiasm they had elaborated upon this scheme by wrapping barbed wire all around his face and throat and shoving the end of it into his mouth. His open eyes peered out through this tangle as if still seeking some means to extricate himself. His parka had been removed by our friends the better for them to carve a huge cavity in his belly which now gaped emptily at us in a kind of silent depravity; this out of the other little features of the scene was probably the most revolting and I had to hold still to keep my own guts from starting to rise up. I felt the folds of something inside my belly begin to ripple back and forth and I had to breathe very carefully. In the snow at the base of the axle lay the man's guts in a large and strangely tidy heap, frosted over and blubbery looking in the look of something not quite frozen solid yet. Obscene, bulbous, and whatever. Rising at the apex of this remarkable sculpture was the wagon wheel itself at the end of its axle, hanging like a large wooden halo or circle of fuck or something above the man's head and looking quite distinct from everything else up there in the sky.

Und so weiter.

It was true I had to admit that we had treated our cousins rather shabbily over these years. At times we had treated them rather shabbily. Of course not everyone liked to say as much and though I might admit it to myself I still had long held firm to the belief that if I ever saw another Russian within arm's reach of myself I would either strangle him with my bare hands or else puke my guts out just to look at him. No matter how many times you had seen the work of these animals nothing could ever numb you to it completely.

Nonetheless—and regardless that some few of us were still bent over with long strings of slobber hanging from their mouths—you would still have grown numb to it to quite some degree and as the roar of engines was growing far louder it was hard to be distracted for more than a few moments unless it took perhaps a minute longer to loose the last strings of bile from your stomach out into the snow. There were also other distractions which must blur everything into the force of a dream though that is only a poor way of saying something; they would be upon us at any moment and yet still we had to struggle with the wagons loaded down with our wounded brothers. Rather than rush past this scene of nightmare we were weighed down and maddened by the final insult of having to struggle on slowly through it. All around the upright wagon axle was the smashed-up litter of equipment and horses crushed in half and dead men embedded on the wooden splinters of wagons all crushed flat into the snow, blood everywhere, burst-out innards everywhere, everything everywhere, a stinking hideous mess so complete that as I mentioned it was difficult to notice any one thing in particular. Pieces of paper scattered all over the snow with everything else, identity papers, men from the Wikings; that was who they had been. Finally some of our men started to run off, unshouldering their weapons and carrying them up to the top of the ridge as if to form a defensive perimeter but I thought really it was the first sign of panic. They would keep on running and just disappear beyond the other side.

I will no longer attempt to describe it except by saying it however I can. The feeling that trying to describe it at all would be no more than some sickening crime or insult is augmented by the explosions of filth that burst through my mind whenever I think of trying to describe it; for otherwise the job would not be that difficult. It would not be so difficult to do except for these waves of obscenities that seem to burst my mind; almost as if I were under some kind of obligation to spew them out and let any clear picture of what happened from that point on founder under a million tons of shit.

For I could describe it easily enough; it just takes a certain amount of will, a certain amount of will and steadiness of the nerves, not so much to describe it . . . but rather to keep that immense wave of filth at bay long enough to say anything at all. . . .

You have perhaps heard that men will either not say anything at all, because they are unable or unwilling to do so; or else that they will speak with a kind of calm dead-clear matter-of-factness that is not necessarily a true indicator of their emotional state, but serves only to indicate that there is no other way to proceed.

As often as this is true, it still means nothing and is therefore a lie. Men will keep silent if they are unable or unwilling to speak; or if not, then they will say anything, say anything at all. The Russians stormed up the hill wearing women's underwear and breathing great clouds of shit which they set afire as it spewed from their mouths. There. If I give in just a little to this compulsion, then it is easier to go on. I must still work to keep the rest of it at bay, from overwhelming me, but so be it.

Enough. You can see that I survived, that I have still lived.

To continue.

At last the wounded began to give voice to the fears which up to now must have stifled them for the better part of sixteen hours. They cried out, screaming as they saw they would be left behind, cursing with an insane invective. It was frightful to behold and even those of us who had not started to run away stepped back from the wagons. I saw Ord screaming at men to keep on and it was true that most of us just kept on, stepping back up to the wagons and ignoring the cries of the wounded and throwing our shoulders into it again, or else driving the panje horses with whips or clubs till they were driven to their knees into the snow. They struggled up again. The beasts pulled the column to the top of the rise. We were too exhausted and perhaps already afraid to fear anything more we might see from up there. We just looked, looking out everywhere. Great patches of sunlight swirled with the fog across the distance, mingling with the fog or breaking away from it. Some of the men indeed had just kept on running. We could seem them running down the opposite slope, some almost to the base of the ridge by now. Some of the Cossacks milling around down there turned and began galloping towards these men, leaning down from their saddles as if to grab their victims by the neck and yank them from their feet. Instead they used their sabres to hack at anything they could reach, leaning almost out of their saddles in a frenzy, blood gouting up here and there the only thing as bright as the sword-metal itself. Some of our men had the wherewithal to start firing, blowing a number of them out of their saddles. Others simply kept on running and either escaped or were run down, hacked to pieces.

Yet all of this was only one small scene within the entirety of what was visible before us. T-34s roamed everywhere down in the valley, rumbling in so many different directions that at a glance they seemed almost harmless, as if they were so addled by the number of victims they had to choose from that a man might feel he had a chance to escape in all the confusion. This was the very first thought to enter my mind. Escape. Escape. Chaos equals escape. But I did nothing and just stood there watching along with everyone else. Indeed you might have felt, if only for a moment or two, that you were separate and removed from everything going on down there. Explosions blew clouds of white powder up from the snow but in fact there was not too much of this. The tanks mostly used their machine guns, and even more than that they mostly just overran the wagon convoys and ground them with their tracks into the snow. Long swaths of blood and debris were visible from as far as a mile away. The place was not really a valley but only a confusion of little dips and gullies with each housing some separate scene of madness, T-34s rising out of nowhere as if surging up from someplace underground; columns of men likewise disappearing into nowhere as they fled into some small ravine not clearly visible from where we stood. Tanks following them in, roaring on out again a few seconds later. Reversing their tracks, turning around and roaring back or else heading off in some other direction. A few spinning their tracks in circles and throwing up great sprays of snow until they caught sight of something else to run down. Between each such scene there were other gullies that were still empty; and there were some still where we saw other columns like our own that for the moment continued to march on unseen and unharmed, threading a maze of horror beneath the morning sky just as we ourselves had done during the night; and if they too were overrun we didn't see it. Some simply disappeared from view, heading God only knew where.

Groups of men marched, or fled, in one direction or another direction, some heading in entirely opposite directions, others heading directly towards each other. I saw two columns intersecting in a flat place in the distance, a small jam-up of wagons and horses where they met, yet each continuing on its own course as if oblivious to the other.

I felt as weak as at any time during the night before. The only idea to hold onto was that it seemed possible some were going to escape. I didn't know. Orders were being shouted around. We wanted to obey, to do something, but it was hard to obey because every officer and NCO seemed to be shouting something different. Weist came along and ordered us to get back behind the ridge. He shouted he was going to take us on a different way out of here; "BACK TO DOGOLYE!" someone screamed crazily at him; Weist ignored the man, shouting orders at everyone within hearing range. It seemed as good an idea to obey him as anyone else. With all we could see below I doubted anyone would march on straight ahead whether ordered to or not. I turned around to see what there was to see behind us, the way we'd just come from. The crucified fellow and the rest of the Wiking Schweinerei sprawled down in that little hollow a short ways back; they all looked untidy and rather inconsequential and I looked beyond them for other possible escape avenues across the landscape. Men began taking Weist's instructions to heart perhaps more than he would have wished and fleeing in the other direction now, running away back down this damned slope we had worked so hard to get to the top of; and the wounded began crying out all over again, screaming, some of them flopping out of the wagons and reaching around to grab hold of the legs of any of these cowards or just anyone. There came a tremendous roar much louder and closer by than any of that business down in the valley; it froze me where I stood. The bastards. . . . I knew the bastards had been lurking right under our noses all along. I found myself thinking this. I twitched my head and saw off to one side along the top of the ridge something rising up out of what must have been another of those little gullies in the terrain; at first nothing but a long straight black arm sticking up like the great arm of a kraken rising up through sea billows, rising up very long, very large. They were right next to us. The long cannon was followed by the dirty white turret and then the rest of it, tracks spinning up snow into the air; there were two of them, the second tank following immediately behind the first. The distance could have been no more than a hundred feet. The first fired and the shell roared overhead; the second fired at a lower angle and delivered high explosive into the wagons at point blank range. I was blown off my feet. I felt a great rushing inside me. I felt like I had been knocked loose from my body. Terror pulled me back together and I started to run but tripped over something and sprawled in the snow and found that I could not bear to move. I crawled a little further and then again could not make myself move. The two T-34s were in amongst everything in seconds, grinding directly through the middle of the column, smashing wagons and everything else. I watched one of them churning at high speed back out into the snow, veering around at high speed in a long turn, bucking about like a speedboat; then running up towards the very head of the column and turning around again so it could make a good long run the entire length of everything. This it did. It ground everything beneath its treads in an unbelievable stinking mess, bursting out the guts of horses which shot up into the air on either side; men too, men too, except that they were too small and seemed to just disappear underneath. Screaming and the roar of engines merged into some kind of single sound. The tank churned the length of the column, wheels and treads spraying things out; then it stopped and backed up a little; then it stopped again, rocking on its springs only a few yards from where I lay. Long various shreds hung from its sides, from the wheels, track links, from springs and tow hooks and any metal protrusion that flesh or splintered wood could get hung up on. It reversed treads and spun around where it stood, howling louder in this gear. The treads in reverse of each other spun around and around in the snow while the tank remained stationary apart from turning slowly in its own circle. As it turned I saw the treads on the other side clanking in a long chain over the wheels and bearing along a human hand jammed in the tracks and then a head perhaps belonging to the same body dangling by its scalp, by its hair, caught in the track-links and going around and around the same as the hand, around and around. The gears screamed again. The treads stopped spinning; the tank rocked on its springs; the hand jerked to a halt, waved slightly back and forth, the head also nodding back and forth, eyes rocking around over everything and giving me a glance, *guten Morgen, mein junger Kerl.*

Dein Arsch auch, I replied. So it seemed. I started to get up again and walk, for what reason I could not imagine. There were only a few other shapes staggering around, everyone else appeared to be dead, ripped to atoms. There were some ground into the snow who were still hideously screaming but somehow I thought of them as dead also. It occurred to me that I was dead also and felt startled to know this must be true. Rather than run away I walked slowly along beside all of this. I saw another T-34 drive by with a long string of something trailing from its axles. It went away somewhere. I looked down and was curious to recognize different people, many of them strangely recognizable in spite of what had just been done to them. There was Weist, there was Heidemann. There was Lahl, there was Riedl. There was Feuersanger. There was Barkhorn, with his purple underscarf trailing away among smashed-up things. I thought I saw

Bollinger sitting by a wagon tongue but I looked away. I was aware that the Cossacks were here again, riding around, swinging at things. I understood that I was dead and felt no alarm; only that this must be what it is like. I seemed to continue along not quite connected to the ground. I looked over to the other side of the main column of shambles and saw Heidemann, whom I thought I had just seen lying crushed on the ground, walking along over there, walking at the same pace as myself. A Cossack came past and sliced deep into his shoulder and rode off. Heidemann flinched and his arm seemed to sag away a little and he began to bleed there. I saw him curling his lips back into his gums and he shut his eyes. Then he opened them again and kept walking. After a few more moments he seemed to notice me. We stared across at each other but said nothing. We had not stopped and we continued walking along the same as before. After a while I realized I was not looking at him anymore and I looked over again to see if he was still there, which he was. Other men perhaps like ourselves not quite realizing we had all been killed were also wandering around here and there. Some of them moved more quickly than others. It occurred to me that those ones must still be alive. I felt frightened suddenly and did not know why. This feeling of not being connected to the ground. . . . I felt too buoyant suddenly and this scared me, I felt like I was about to rise away from all this but rather than please me the sensation filled me with terror. I looked up at the sky in alarm and as quickly looked back at the ground again. I found that I had approached a small cluster of the more quickly moving men. There were only a few I recognized. The only name that would come to me was Bollinger's name; he turned to face me. I spoke to him.

"I'm dead. They killed me, Gustav. Can you help me? Do something to help me, for the love of Christ."

He looked at me and then looked away and shouted something, then looked back at me again.

"Snap out of it, Hake! There's no time for any shit. Snap out of it. No one can help you now."

"You can help me, you bastard. You're the only ones left that can do anything. Help me, you idiot! You stinking sack of shit! Can't you hear me?"

"Sit down and get out of the way, George. We're getting out. No one's going to take you by the hand. You can come with us or not."

"All right, all right," I said. Something like a soap bubble went off inside my head. Instantly noises all around were very much louder, and the spaces of silence between things were there as well. I checked to see if I still had my weapon. I saw that I did not. I tried to see if I was hurt, to feel if I was hurt, but I couldn't feel anything and was too addled to check more carefully. I looked around and took an assault rifle from a dead man, checked the magazine. I looked around but still could not make any sense of what was going on around us; I could only make sense out of people nearby, it was like near-sightedness. I looked around for Bollinger again, not wanting to lose sight of him. I began to recognize a few others. Grote. Marcks. Lindemann. Bollinger came back, crouched down in the snow. I did likewise.

"That's better. I can hardly lead the rest of these children out of here by myself."

"All right. Where to? Where can we go?"

He looked around, squinting, eyes sunk deep in their sockets, shaking his head.

"Are you all right, Hake? Tell me if you're not."

"Ja," I said.

"All right then. We can only go wherever they're not. I don't know where that will take us. Just keep heading west. You've got a better sense of direction than I do."

I looked into his eyes and realized there was a kind of pleading sitting in there. He was still in a state of near-panic. We were crouched here talking as if in a kind of lull, as if the T-34s and the sabre-swingers had momentarily ridden off to continue their business elsewhere. I looked over his shoulder and was shocked to see that they were all still out there only a hundred feet away. Milling around, laying into other little groups of men; I didn't even know, I was too shocked to really make out what they were doing. He must be mad, I thought. Instantly I realized that no one was getting out of here alive except alone and by his own self and maybe with the help of the love of Christ.

"Jesus shit," I said, turning away from Bollinger and blinking back tears which came over me for no more than an instant. I saw another corpse nearby and began pulling cartridge cases out of his belt and stuffing them into the pockets of my parka. I stayed down close to the ground and looked around to see if there was anyplace I could possibly go. I saw Bollinger again and a T-34 looming just behind him like a mirage. It looked a hundred feet taller than he was. An explosion knocked him off his feet, and then the thing had him across the legs. He was screaming and flopping in the snow. The thing came to a halt, rocking slightly on top of him. I rolled on my back, determined not to move, not to breathe. I looked up into the sky which had grown quite clear and rather gentle looking over these morning hours. I shifted my eyes by a fraction, and I saw something to one side up there. I turned my head a little, barely able to move, and saw a familiar fellow hanging up there in the sky.

I've seen you somewhere before, old boy, I thought.

Yet it was not the Wikinger shithead that we'd seen hung up at dawn. I saw that it was not. It was the old boy himself, nailed high on a wooden cross that was no axle tree. I saw him hung up high on a wooden cross quite close by, and I saw nothing else. I was amazed to see the living face of this man but that is not really right for I was past all that. His naked chest, his breast bone, hung out into the air and his belly was sucked in like a cave. His forehead was bloody and his hair was matted with blood, he looked out horizontally somewhere across the sky. His eyelids were flared back and his eyes bulged as if they were being slowly pushed out of his head. Just from looking at his eyes I could see that his breath was almost gone and that he would no longer be able to speak. His mouth hung open in a dead gape and his lips were curled tightly back into his gums, curled back so tightly that they almost disappeared. He was naked except for rags hung around his hips and his legs hiked up against himself like a naked man trying to cover his balls, his feet curled up under him and nailed there. His eyes began to move a little bit, his head sagged out a little bit, his eyes now looked down at the ground though they seemed maybe not quite capable of seeing anything. I saw the veins in his neck begin to flex and then he flexed one arm a little bit trying to pull it away. He grunted and his lips curled back even more tightly into his face and he wrenched his left hand out from the nail and his whole body swung down and over like a gate as the arm came free. The blood and gristle remained on the nailhead. I followed the hand down, down, reaching down through the air. The fingers brushed past the T-34 and reached down for Bollinger's hand which was clutching about insanely. He—Jesus Christ—stretched out his fingertips and Bollinger's fingertips knocked against them but could not close or hold still and with a final lurch the Christ reached further and grabbed him by the wrist and with an unearthly shriek of effort and pain straightened back up on his cross while pulling Bollinger free into the air. Bollinger screaming horribly was ripped away across his legs and the rest of his legs remained pinned beneath the T-34. The Christ rose up with him into space into the morning air. I saw them rise away. They were gone.

I stayed still for some hours and when at last I dared raise my head a few inches I saw with disgust that I was still not alone. They were all a little further away now but I still had no nerve to move and so laid low for a while longer. They seemed to be rounding up groups of men down in the valley and shooting them. But the rest was all confusion as before and I dared not raise my head to study it more carefully. After a while I convinced myself to move, though I knew I could still be seen if anyone looked this way. I felt that I could wait till dark but I didn't care any longer and felt for some reason that my chances now were as good as any. The sun was still high in the sky. I had no desire to wait for dark. My patience was at an end. I wondered if I was still mad after all but it seemed to me that I wasn't; I felt clearly enough that I wasn't, and as that was all I had to go on I accepted it and put it out of my mind. I hadn't felt at all mad since the first time I'd run into Bollinger and I put everything I had seen since then out of my mind. I began to crawl away through the wreckage and the various stupid and disgusting remnants of the whole nightmare, assuring myself that there were a thousand things to hide behind around here. I could only hope that I wouldn't run into some blasted Russian poking around in the mess. But there seemed to be no one in the immediate vicinity. I made my way back behind the ridge. Once I got away from all this shambles I would be out in the open and would have to move still more carefully. I was not really in a careful mood and accepted that this might work to my disadvantage. I looked down where the Wikinger ass was still hung up on the wagon axle and for some reason the sight of him filled me with an unspeakable contempt. I had no idea why. I left.

The sun was still high and in fact it might not have passed noon yet. So what. I worked my way through one little gully after another and saw our colleagues out there on a dozen different occasions and burrowed myself in the snow. It seemed that it was now time for a party. That was not unusual with them. Drinking, shouting, shooting, whatever went along with that. There began to be a few wooded areas and I ran into some of our men. I recognized no one and if any were from my own division I didn't know it. A few were Wikings which you could tell by the collar tabs under their parkas, if not simply by the way they carried themselves. When they began arguing about how to get to Lysyanka I laughed in their faces. Those who laughed along with me came with me, or I went with them; the rest went off in some other direction. I figured there would be no one but Russians in Lysyanka who could all kiss my ass, except that I wasn't going there. Of course I didn't really know where I was going, but I didn't have it in my mind to look for that place any longer. A sizeable contingent agreed with this view. The highest-ranking officer there did not, but there was no mutiny nor any crazy railing about what to do. Those people went one way and we went another way. Those too terrified to leave the shelter of the woods stayed in the woods. There began to be other patches of woods and we slipped among these as carefully as we could. The Russians would surely be combing them but it was better than wandering in the open. The day passed by. We saw more groups of Ivans and occasionally some of them murdering little groups of our own people down in some ravine or other. We had nine men in our group. There was talk of some river called the Gniloy Tikich, which I dimly remembered Weist saying something about, ages ago. Apparently it was beyond Lysyanka. Strangely it did not take us all that long to get there.

As we had wandered all day long without getting nabbed by the Russians, we were somewhat disappointed to reach this river and find a scene every bit as horrible as the one we had left in the morning. We marched on down there regardless, not having much comment about things anymore. No one said anything about trying to find another way around this time. The woods sheltered us almost to the river's edge and then we crossed a few reedy snow-covered dunes and then we were there.

The Russians at least seemed to be keeping their distance this time. There were only a few T-34s and they stayed up on the dunes to one side shelling and machine-gunning everything in sight. Apparently they did not wish to come any closer. As if the dementia down below might infect them somehow, as if even a thousand stark naked men might somehow be dangerous, the way a swarm of ants could be dangerous if you waded into the middle of them. Anyway they remained up where they were, firing their cannon and blowing great holes in the water where the swimmers were. The water was ice cold and a number of men were trying to make it across still fully clothed. All were drowned. This tiny pigshit river, which I now dimly remembered having crossed a few months ago, was now a roaring torrent several hundred feet across. The frost had not been severe enough to hard it up again. All the meltwater from the thaw roared down it still. When I came to the bank I saw a human chain that had made it more than halfway to the other side, naked men linked hand to hand out there and others still in their parkas linked hand to hand, buckling in the current. I watched for a few minutes and then they were all swept away by the current. The ones still near to us made it back to this side; almost all the others went under; a few almost to the other side actually made it out and crawled up over there, standing stark naked in the cold. The Russians sent a few bursts over there but concentrated mainly on the ones on this side. I found a little hollow where I could sit down and give the situation some study.

The river steamed like a cauldron, all this steam rising up like a white wall while sunlight fell bright and clear everywhere else. Yet you could still see through it easily enough, all the men drowning, horses drowning, sleds and wagons pushed in there and then swept away just as easily. Tree limbs swept past, chunks of ice, a truck axle, blobs of melting snow. From time to time a few men somehow struggled out to the other side. Strong swimmers, I supposed. The gunfire on the bank was getting more and more dangerous and I was beginning to get fed up with being surrounded by so many murdered helpless people once again. There didn't seem any longer to be much panic, though everything was still chaos; I supposed everyone was past all that by now. I pulled back my hood and opened up my parka. I pulled all the cartridge cases out of the pockets and tossed them aside. I gave the matter some further thought and took my parka off and lay that aside. Then I cursed with a feeling of sickness. I'd forgotten about my shoulder. It hurt when I pulled my arm out of the parka but otherwise it seemed only to hurt when I moved it in certain ways. This did me in for several moments and I had to shake my head to keep from sinking into depression. I moved my arm around this way and that, testing it. I didn't know. I wasn't a strong swimmer but I could swim. Still I wasn't in any hurry to get into that water. I stripped off my boots and the heavy elephant's leg coveralls. Then the rest of my uniform and my underclothes. I was naked. Good, I thought. I hadn't pulled any of that shit off my body in weeks. I was fairly heated up from marching all day and the sun did not feel too bad. There'd been a lot of colder days than this one. I watched some other men go in, all of them naked now. An explosion blew spray over me and gave me a taste of what was to come. The shock helped a little. I got to my feet, peering back up the dunes to make sure I wouldn't be killed at the last instant before I got into the water. The tanks were firing at some place a little further upstream.

The shock from the spray did help a little when I first waded in. All the same the cold was almost too much to bear. I started swimming and made it a ways out before the current started to get really bad. I saw my arm was going to give me trouble and in a moment of terror I thought of heading back. Steam tore by all around. I kept on.

EPILOG

Narrative of Hans Scheidies, Scharfuhrer, SS Wiking Division, 19 February, 1944

I was out. After being in the water for so long the air did not feel cold. It felt warm. I had not expected this. I groaned, grunted, sobbing, some kind of noise. The air blew against my naked skin with a kind of soft friction that felt almost unbearably good. I wouldn't have expected it. Feeling began to return to the outer layers of my body, or maybe I was imagining it, but it seemed so.

I lay my forehead against a tree limb.

My innards still felt frozen. I had the distinct sensation that my heart had stopped and tried not to think about it as I knew it could not be true. It was hard not to think about it. Then I felt it beating within me, beating so violently that I did not know how I could have missed it. I was no longer concerned. The air still felt warm on the surface of my skin. I looked back the way I had come. Back across the river.

I saw others out in the current carried away before my eyes, swept further downstream to life, to death. I looked to see if there was anyone near enough to the bank that I might assist them. There was no one, and I felt relief. The ones struggling out in mid-stream disappeared down the river, to be followed by others like-wise passing before my eyes. The steam rose up all around them.

The far bank was not empty, as I had somehow expected it to be. I had somehow imagined that I had been swept miles away and washed up in the middle of nowhere. But the far bank was just as crowded with men as the place where I had first waded in, wherever that was now. Steam blew up everywhere but you could still more or less see through it. The Russians were over there. More tanks, more Cossacks. Some of them remained stationary as before up on top of the dunes but others were coming down now, roaring in, riding in, murdering naked men where they stood or else driving all of them out into the water.

I had seen quite a number of whorehouses over these last few years but what was going on over there was the most unbeliev-able stinking whorehouse I had yet seen and I hoped never to wit-ness its like again. I looked over my shoulder to see where I was. I started climbing up the bank through the snow and little bushes growing there. From the top of the bank I could see a little better and I could see other men around a bend struggling to climb out of the water. I had to look inland for a moment, if only to see what was there, and I saw other groups of naked men straggling out across a snowy plain, many of them screaming, barking like dogs. Then a sense of duty prevailed upon me. I climbed back down to the edge of the water to help anyone I could.

I helped pull as many men out of the water as I could and only stopped when I realized I was starting to freeze to death. The sun was bright and I had not felt cold at all for I didn't know how long. There had begun to be other men on the river bank, armed men wearing heavy parkas who I understood must be from the reception committee, Bake's people, all of them pulling men out of the water and assisted by other naked men including myself. Most were removing their parkas to give to the swimmers while the rest were perhaps too busy to think of doing so. When I real-ized I was going to freeze I had to ask one of them to give me his parka. He pulled it off without a word and wrapped it over my shoulders. It did not make me feel any warmer and I began to tremble uncontrollably.

"Go on! Go on!" he shouted. "There's a village back there! Hurry up and you'll make it."

He turned back to the water.

When I reached the top again I saw no village but only the same snowy plain as before. A few shellbursts blew up snow at one place or another. There were men out there and there was nothing to do but follow them. Other people from the reception committee were heading towards the river bank and I tried to see where they were coming from. Tiger tanks were up on a high place shelling the other side. Out on the plain medical people with red crosses on their arms were scattered about helping whoever they could and perhaps hoping to attract other survivors by their armbands which they did not normally wear. I was given an injection of something and pointed towards the village which I at last began to make out in the distance. The situation over here was as chaotic as on the other side of the river. There were too many refugees to help all at once and many were still naked as they struggled towards the village. Or simply collapsed before they could get there. I gave my parka to a man who looked almost finished, trying to help him to his feet and get his arm up around my shoulder. I could only struggle with him for a short distance and then I didn't know what to do. Some other people came up and took him from me. I was almost there. I staggered into the first isba I came to and collapsed naked into the straw.

•　　•　　•

Later in the day I saw Bake step through the door. His head looked still more skull-like than usual. He wore the same black field cap as always. After a moment he recognized me and came over to shake my hand. He said it was all nothing but a great pile of shit and if everybody weren't got out of here quickly the Russians would have us surrounded all over again.

"Scheidies, yes?"

I nodded.

"I met you at Akhtyrka."

I nodded again. I clutched at the blanket that was my only garment.

"I'm rounding up any officers who can take charge of people. Are you fit to go?"

"No, not so much." I tried to laugh a little. I said, "I'm ready whenever you give the word."

"All right, good. You needn't step out the door just yet. The medical people have to see that everyone is fit to travel. How many men do you have in here?"

I gaped at him. I looked around in the dimness. I said,

"My apologies, Herr Oberst."

He interrupted me as I spoke.

"Never mind. Just count whoever is here and find anyone that needs special attention. Whoever is in here belongs to you now. The medical people will be coming by again."

"When do we leave?"

"As soon as possible. You'll receive orders as soon as possible. If everything goes to shit before then then just take your people and start heading west."

"The Russians are here again."

It was a question and a statement.

"No, not quite yet. Goodbye, Scheidies."

He left.

It was Schanderowka all over again. I was too spent to be upset by this. At least with Bake you could feel a bit of confidence.

I'd been talking to him wearing nothing but a blanket. I sat down in the straw again next to the stove, huddled amongst all the others in here. Probably most of them had overheard our conversation. If anything I felt more tired now than when I'd first stumbled in. I knew no one here and had not spoken to a soul in all these hours. I rested for a few more minutes and then got up again to see who was was here. I only wished Bake hadn't spoken so loudly. But doubtless he'd been in a hurry.

"All right now, men," I said. "Everything will be all right now."

When the medical people came they informed us the situation was not as critical as was thought at first. From the looks on their faces I accepted that perhaps this was true. I asked for no explanation, only that they tell all the men, who had begun to get restless. For me the prospect of not having to keep everyone's morale up was as much of a relief as anything else. I collapsed in the straw and slept for a while.

Time passed. Other people came in and then left. The most seriously frostbitten or injured started to be evacuated, which included a dozen people from this hut. Others lay dead in the straw, in the dark. I started to argue that Bake had given me responsibility for these people. A panzer major informed me that all previous orders were countermanded. All those who had become separated from their own units while crossing the river would be placed under command of officers from the relief force.

All right then, I thought. Thank God for that.

I slept again. I began to feel sick, feverish, but tried to sleep it through. I would be roused from time to time by my own teeth chattering. I put a piece of straw in my mouth and chewed on it. Men groaned around me in the darkness. At some point I became aware of a peculiar conversation going on nearby.

Two men were arguing. Similar conversations had drifted in and out of my ears throughout the day. They would be arguing about how soon we would be evacuated. Or else they would be reliving it all all over again. Or else they would be asking if anyone had seen so-and-so still alive. Or else they would be talking some horrible incomprehensible gibberish to their neighbors or themselves. After a while I began to realize that this conversation I was listening to was more of the latter type.

"Stop it. Stop it, Barkhorn. Father. Excuse me. I don't know how to address you."

"Surely you must know, junge. Never mind. Father will do. Or Barkhorn will do. But you weren't alone back there. I saw it too."

"Don't talk nonsense. And don't try my patience, Barkhorn. There might be one skinny bone of civility left inside me. Don't test it."

"I understand. Feel free to speak however you like. It's all right, son. But I saw it too. My God, boy, I saw it too. You weren't alone. Does that mean nothing to you?"

"Listen, you bastard. Now listen here, Father. Ah, shit, for the love of Christ."

The voice trailed off, gasping, I couldn't tell.

"It's all right, son. I'm sorry. Forgive me. I haven't said a word to anyone all day long. But when I saw you lying in here I had to say something. Perhaps you're right. Perhaps now is not the time."

"Yes, yes, all right. Some other time. Please leave me, father. I can't. Not now. Just leave me alone."

"All right. I just couldn't keep silent any longer when I saw you here. I had to say something. Son. Look at me. Let me touch you. Just let me touch your hand for a moment."

The voice—the chaplain's—was trembling now too. The other man made some kind of strange noise, began cursing quietly. He said,

"No, don't do that. Don't do that. Just leave me be. Some other time. If we ever get out of here alive we can talk about it. I don't give a shit. Just not now."

"And suppose one of us does not live to speak to the other? Do you want that ? Are you willing to carry it alone inside you? Listen to me, boy. Perhaps you're stronger than I am. I don't want to carry it alone. Forgive me for thinking of myself. I can see you're upset. Forgive my selfishness."

"I forgive it, you crack-brained sack of fuck, but if you don't leave me I'm going to thrash you. I'll forgive you all you like. I mean no disrespect, Father, but I'll thrash you and you know that I will. I saw you dead out there too, priest. I saw your blasted skull ground flat into the snow. Eh? What about that? Are you going to tell me you saw that too?"

"You must have been mistaken. You can see that I'm here. It must have been someone else."

"Yes, yes, it must have been someone else. That's right. I saw it as plain as I see you now. But it must have been someone else. So what? Who cares? Are you finished now, Father? I won't warn you again. I'll strike you if you say one more word to me."

"All right. I'm going. Good luck to you, son. Just tell me your name. I've seen you before, but I don't know who you are. I want to know that I'll be able to look for you again. By God, I saw it, I saw it too. Do you hear me? I saw it too, junge. Don't forget. Swear to yourself that you won't forget. Do you hear me, son?"

I saw a shape standing up in the firelight. A squat man, an older man. Clear beads of sweat were on his cheeks. I didn't recognize him from earlier, he must have wandered in from somewhere. Another shape shot up who had his back to me, and he would have been on the chaplain if not for several other men who rose up and dragged him back to the floor. No doubt they must have become upset by his filthy talk. I waited for the struggle to continue, which meant I would have to interfere. I was already starting to get up. But that was it, it was already over; the other man was simply lying back in the straw staring at nowhere.

I said, "All right, get out of here, Father. You said you were leaving. Be so kind as to do so."

It would have tried my patience too, listening to this padre or whatever he was. He sounded about as cracked as the other man had accused him of being. He was a fool; all those types were. I waited till he was out the door. I thought about just letting the whole thing pass. But I couldn't let that kind of talk come out of a soldier's mouth. It would have meant trouble somewhere down the line, if not for me then for someone else.

The two who had dragged him back to the floor stepped aside. They waited to see what I would say. The other one lay at my feet, a smallish, dirty-haired man. The man was staring maniacally at nothing, but he didn't look crazy; or at least not as crazy as the priest. It was only the look of a man who simply couldn't stand the sight of things anymore. It was not so unusual.

Heat rushed to my head and my whole body was flushed with sweat. I felt like I might be sick and pushed my hands against my temples. I said,

"Listen here, soldier. I hope none of us ever sees the likes of this day again. I'm in no mood to tell anybody off and I'm not going to threaten you with anything. Just make sure I don't hear another word of that talk so long as you're in here."

The man blinked, exhaled slowly. As if he found this agreeable enough. He looked up at me calmly and said,

"SS puke. How many chaplains you got in your own outfit? Heh?"

He laughed a little bit. It was all I could do not to shoot him where he lay. Suddenly he rose past me, shrieking curses out the door where the chaplain had disappeared. During the night I was lying in a wagon bed headed west. I was burning with fever but even more afraid I was going to freeze to death. We were all heaped up with every kind of blanket and overcoat, but every time the wind blew I felt it cut right through my guts. The clothing I had salvaged was soaked through and freezing and I thought it would surely kill me. I hardly felt strength enough to sit up; I grabbed another soldier by the collar and told him to say something to the driver. My teeth were chattering so badly I could hardly get any words out. I knew I wasn't the only one. I said we had to halt and make a fire or a lot of us were going to die. The soldier looked at me and climbed up to the driver's seat. I'd seen Bake one more time before we left and he'd said it was over twenty miles to the new main line. We were all lying in another panje wagon and I knew half of us would never make it that far. I heard the soldier talking to the driver and the bastard said he wasn't stopping for anything and we'd all be happier freezing to death than have another T-34 grind over our skulls. The soldier started arguing with him and the driver let loose with such a deluge of curses that I thought it was that same bastard all over again, that crazed fool back in the isba. I'd had half a dozen men hurl him headfirst out the door into the snow back in wherever that place had been. Already during this night I'd awakened from half a dozen dreams of delirium and for a moment I couldn't be sure if this weren't another one. The soldier was making no headway with the driver and I tried to shout but it only came out as some kind of croak. Other men now took up the cry, shouting at the driver to halt. I sank back into the wagon bed. Some other man moaned in his sleep and rolled over on top of me. I was determined to do something if it took the last bit of my strength, but somehow I found myself drifting into sleep and crazy dreams again. Terrible, terrible dreams. The next time I woke up I felt a little warmer and the sweat was cool instead of burning on my face. I pushed a man's boot off my neck and stared up at the sky. Black sky. White stars. The wind had dropped to a little breeze. After a while I heard someone else arguing about something with the driver. The driver responded with another explosion of cursing. No, it wasn't him, I thought. It sounded very much like the same man. But it must be someone else. For the time being I didn't care any longer. It was nothing. It was all nothing. I figured we would get there before long now. I lay there and stared straight up overhead. Light began to come slowly across the sky.

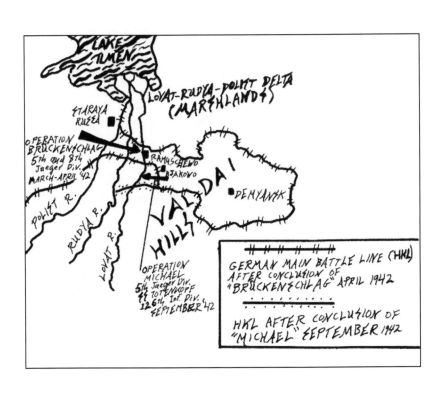

LAKE ILMEN

LOVAT-RUDYA-POLIST DELTA (MARSHLANDS)

STARAYA RUSSA

OPERATION BRÜCKENSCHLAG 5th and 8th Jaeger Div. MARCH-APRIL '42

RAMUSCHEWO

BJAKOWO

VALDAI HILLS

DEMYANSK

POLIST R.

RUDYA R.

LOVAT R.

OPERATION MICHAEL 5th Jaeger Div. SS TOTENKOPF 126th Inf. Div. SEPTEMBER '42

╫╫╫╫╫ GERMAN MAIN BATTLE LINE (HKL) AFTER CONCLUSION OF "BRÜCKENSCHLAG" APRIL 1942

‒‒ · · ‒‒ · · ‒‒ HKL AFTER CONCLUSION OF "MICHAEL" SEPTEMBER 1942

Supply Flights into Demyansk Cauldron, April 1942

DEMYANSK

Demyansk was a small town in a remote area. So was Cholm. So was Velikiye Luki. So was Velizh. So was Tikhvin.

All of these towns were the sites of terrible struggles, all of them taking place more or less simultaneously, yet separated by many hundreds of miles. This was the character of the Russian war. Most of these names have faded into obscurity. They were obscure to begin with.

At Demyansk a large German force, including the SS Totenkopf Division, was cut off and surrounded by the Russians for nearly four months. The besieged men were supplied entirely by air; it was their only lifeline. This happened early in '42, during the same winter that saw the near destruction of the German army before Moscow, bringing some of the lowest temperatures ever recorded in northern and central Russia.

The battle for the Demyansk cauldron lasted throughout that winter and went on nonstop for over a year. A German relief force managed to break through to the cauldron in April of '42, yet this land corridor was never more than a few miles wide and was in constant danger of being overrun by the Russians. German units were bled white trying to keep Demyansk from being surrounded yet again. A thousand miles to the south, a similar situation began to develop in the autumn of '42, around the Volga city of Stalingrad. Stalingrad finally fell, and the German Sixth Army was annihilated. Demyansk held.

DEMYANSK

A Year in the Cauldron, January 1942 to February 1943

PART ONE—*Jaegers*

In October there was almost an air of celebration. The men of the 5th Infantry Division were to be pulled out of the line. They were to be pulled out of Russia.

They were to be sent back to France, to be re-outfitted as a Light or Jaeger Division.

The Landsers, most of them anyway, had no idea what a Jaeger Division was. This, of course, made not the slightest difference to anyone. It was like tripping over a log one day. All of a sudden they were leaving. Leaving Russia.

The two month lull in the activities of the Army Group Center had allowed time for large amounts of supplies to be brought forward over the terrible Russian roads, over the railroad tracks that were perversely of a different gauge than all the rest of Europe. All this was part of Stalin's plan, just as it had been part of the plan of every Russian leader going back for hundreds of years— keep any potential invaders at bay by making the most basic conditions of transport as difficult as possible. As abjectly miserable as possible. . . . Perhaps only the Germans with their obsessive industriousness could have advanced as far as they did, sending out whole legions of pioneer battalions and Todt Organization laborers to rebuild the roads, to rebuild the bridges, to rebuild the railway lines to the standard gauge. It was an overwhelming task, comparable to rebuilding the infrastructure of an entire country. And not just any country, but a country whose surface area covered more than half of the Earth's largest landmass.

In 1812 Napoleon's Grande Armee had invaded on only a narrow front, aimed like a spear at Moscow and the heart of Russia. In 1941 the Germans invaded along a front that was fifteen hundred miles wide, stretching from the Black Sea to the Baltic. This was the area that they had first to destroy and then rebuild, according to their own designs.

Despite their great energy and organizational skills, the Germans were not up to the task. Basic conditions in Russia remained a filthy mess, from the first day to the last. But they did their best, and this was no small accomplishment. The front of Army Group Center had remained stable since the end of July— that is to say stagnant—while Hitler pursued other goals in the north and the south. It was perhaps one of the most disastrous misjudgments in the history of war. The 5th Infantry Division, almost alone out of all the million and a half men facing Moscow, were to be spared from the nightmare that was to follow. Spared. They were to be pulled out of Russia. . . .

Of course they had no real sense of what lay ahead for their comrades still in the line. But all the same, this feeling of getting a reprieve at the last minute ran very high among the Landsers of the 5th. Even by October they had already seen enough. By October, after only four months of fighting, the division had already lost a third of its strength, killed, wounded, or missing. Many killed, far more wounded; and all those who were missing were almost certainly dead.

They had participated in the last great push to take the capital, Operation Typhoon, which had commenced on the second of October 1941. After two months of German inactivity in this area the Russians were taken by surprise, encircled, and subsequently annihilated in the usual inconceivable numbers. Thus went the great encirclement battles of Vyazma and Bryansk, the culmination of a half year of fighting which had seen the world's largest army nearly eviscerated.

By mid-October the men of the 5th had finished cleaning up the remnants of the Vyazma pocket, a task which included a great deal of killing. Killing, killing, killing. When a disorganized and panic-stricken mob of Russians, desperate to break free of the encirclement, tried to overwhelm your line there was nothing to do but bring up every available weapon and kill, kill, kill. Otherwise you would die. You or them. No Banzai charge on a remote Pacific island against a thin line of American Marines would ever equal the unbelievable—and absolutely hopeless—onslaughts of the Russian army in that first year of the war. On every occasion they would be encircled by a fast-moving yet relatively thin line of German troops. The fire-control tactics and close cooperation between units of the German army was at that time unsurpassed by any army in the world, and it was only this ability of small groups of men to concentrate tremendous fire-power in a small area that allowed the Germans to hold their line. The result of this was killing, killing, killing. Perhaps in Russia more than elsewhere was the exact nature of war reduced to its most fundamental element. Kill, kill. . . . The Landsers became dazed, exhausted, enraged, and frightened by all this killing. It did something to your senses. Already overburdened supply routes became further burdened by requests for great quantities of lime. Lime. But there wasn't enough. The rotting, reeking bodies in their hundreds of thousands were piled up and burned, or else simply bypassed and left to stink. Bypassed indeed. . . . Moscow was still over a hundred miles away, and no one wished to linger around these ghastly open-air cemeteries at Vyazma. Even the vultures could not bear them.

For all that many German soldiers had seen things which would disturb them for the rest of their lives, the offensive, Typhoon, had begun quite promisingly. A rainy September had given way to a few weeks of fine weather at the beginning of October. During this short time nearly a million men had been erased from the lists of the Red Army. But then the mud season, the Rasputitsa, set in. The great offensive was stopped dead in its tracks. Only a few German spearheads managed to struggle onward, with a stubbornness that angered and appalled the Russians. (Just as the Russians with their own peculiar brand of stubbornness would anger and appal the Germans.) The phrase "sea of mud" is just that—only a phrase. Yet if it were anywhere to take on the form of literal truth, this truth would be found in Russia. The autumn rains did not sink into the ground, to be spirited away underground; rather they spread out across the surface of it, transforming ditches into canals, transforming ponds into wide-spreading lakes that resembled areas flooded artificially by means of dams, thus to create the man-made lakes and reservoirs which always have that curiously dead and unnatural look about them, wherever such projects are undertaken in the world. In Russia there was nothing artificial about these lakes, though they did bear somewhat that same aspect of blighted and unnatural ground, whole forests of trees, of telegraph poles, of anything at all, rising strangely out of several feet of water. The villages became islands on high ground, or else swamps on low ground. The railroad embankments became causeways passing through a kind of Netherlands area (Niederlandischegebiet) that stretched for a thousand miles.

Anyplace that was not actually underwater became mud. That sea of mud. It was not unlike quicksand. In fact in most respects it very much resembled quicksand. Occasionally men drowned in it, and horses did so far more often. This was because by and large the German army was not motorized, and the horses formed the backbone—indeed almost the entire structure—of its transport system. The motorized units and armored spearheads ranged far ahead, but the great bulk of the army consisted of thousands and thousands of men and horse-drawn wagons following slowly behind, walking, walking. To bring supplies forward through the mud was a terrible ordeal, and horses by the thousands were soon driven to exhaustion, collapsing in the mud and then disappearing beneath it. To pull free a man who was sunk up to his knees in mud often required the assistance of half a dozen of his comrades; to pull free a horse often required the assistance of motor vehicles, tracked vehicles, even prime movers. And as often as not they could not be pulled free. The mud—the earth itself—had a greater tenacity than most mechanized countermeasures. The graves of horses in Russia would be comparable to the graves of buffalo on the American plains of the 1870s and 80s.

If this was a tragedy, it would be overshadowed by other mass-graves, all in human form. Vyazma and Bryansk were mass-graves. The plains east of Kiev were a mass grave. The hills and copses of Uman were a mass grave. All of these places were battlefields, filled with dead Russians who might have formed the entire population of some smaller country. And then there were other mass graves, other kinds of mass graves, which were not battlefields at all. . . .

The latter have been the subject of much subsequent study, conducted by men of various nations over the second half of the century. These studies will continue.

• • •

The muddy season had reached its high point—or its abyss—when the men of the 5th received orders to be transported back to France. Their jubilation was therefore understandable. The purpose of this move was anybody's guess. Why Hitler suddenly felt the need to outfit a new Jaeger division was—like so many of his decisions—not terribly clear. Every conceivable unit was needed then and there for the final push on Moscow. But orders were orders, and for the men of the 5th these were good orders.

Now, if only they could be implemented.

There is a certain irony in reading over this chapter of the division's history. The struggle with the mud is described in some detail. The curiosity is that the men were no longer struggling forward, but struggling backward. And this was no retreat. It was no more than a plain and simple attempt to reach the nearest railhead, so that their new assignment could be put into effect. Orders to pull the 5th Division out of the line were received on the 13th of October. It took until the beginning of November for the last units to make their way back to the railheads at Smolensk and Rudnya, wading through the seas of mud. The divisional history reports: "The march was an agony, and only the thought of returning to the homeland enabled us to keep going."

The transport trains were waiting steam-up at the railheads. Goodbye to Russia. At least for now.

The first snow had already fallen at the beginning of October. Only a light snow, that dissolved instantly beneath the muddy rains that followed. But as the 5th Division was struggling to get out of Russia the snows were already beginning to fall again.

The two dozen or so trains required to transport an entire division steamed back towards Germany. Back through Smolensk, back through Vitebsk, back through Minsk, back through Brest-Litovsk. Each of these towns contained new cemeteries, marked by birch-bark crosses in their many thousands. The German dead. The mass graves where the Russians had been buried would contain, by and large, ten times as many human remains.

Yet for all the dead, there were also all the living. Streams of prisoners in almost unimaginable numbers marched back from the front, the living remnants of the great encirclement battles. They walked along the bad roads beside the railroad embankments, plainly visible to the men of the 5th passing above in the railroad cars. The Landsers had seen these great masses of prisoners at the front, yet even now they could scarcely believe the numbers of them; hadn't they just killed all these people, by the thousands and tens of thousands, at Vyazma only a few weeks ago? And so they had—but the living still outnumbered the dead. Perhaps they were only corpses exhumed from the battlefield, reanimated somehow and set to marching God only knew where. For they still looked dead enough. Skeletal, eyes like saucers. . . .

Most of the Russian prisoners began their ordeal of starvation at the very moment of capture. They were sent off marching to the rear, in immense columns that were barely guarded or even unguarded. Starvation beckoned almost immediately and many escaped that fate by fleeing into the woods to join the partisans; or to become themselves the nucliei of the partisan bands that were now cropping up everywhere. Yet the great mass of the prisoners did not try to escape. The reason for this might seem another mystery of the war, but perhaps it was not so hard to understand.

Conditions in the Red Army were appalling, marked by that peculiar combination of bureaucratic inefficiency, chaos, and brutality that would endure the length of the war and would somehow carry the Red Army to the gates of Berlin at the very end. The 24 hour a day efforts of every man, woman, and child in the world's largest country would eventually make this happen. But especially in 1941 the army was a horrible mess—especially after the Germans got through with it—and many Russian soldiers were probably not displeased to be taken prisoner. To live in Stalin's armed forces in time of war was to live in a nightmare; and to live in his country in time of peace was not much better.

Voyna ny'chorowo.

They surrendered.

As soon as they gave themselves up they began to starve. The supply organizations of the German armed forces were already stretched to the limit—or past it—trying to maintain their own men. No German general staff planner, nor any other planner, had ever conceived of the unbelievable numbers of prisoners they would now be required to feed.

But Hitler, with the daring simplicity which marked both his greatest and his worst ideas, had already taken care of this problem before the invasion began. The Russian prisoners would not be fed. That was all there was to it. Even Hitler—who never saw things in human terms anyway—could not have dreamed of having almost three million prisoners in the bag during the summer and fall of 41. But his earlier refusal to have any kind of contingency plan drawn up for prisoners—in large numbers or small—took care of the problem in the simplest possible fashion. They would not be fed.

German apologists, even some who were not supporters of the regime, have tried to dress up this situation by re-emphasizing how badly overtaxed the German supply lines were. This was certainly true. Just as it was certainly true that even in an ideal situation, huge numbers of Russian prisoners would have starved. Most of them were already critically underfed, due to the innate wretchedness of the Russian army's own food distribution systems. This was, after all, part of the reason why so many Russians were just as happy to surrender to the Germans. And so there they were. Millions of them. The Germans could not even guard all these men, let alone feed them. Newsreel clips—especially those filmed from small planes a few hundred feet above the ground—showed Russian prisoners packed in masses that filled an entire movie screen from top to bottom, men wriggling amongst each other like maggots swarming on a corpse. This is not some grotesquely poetic way of saying something; on the contrary, the camera hovering some few hundred feet overhead gave exactly this impression, and the skill of the German film editors would suggest that this is exactly the impression they wished to convey.

So. It was just another massive fuck-up, as people using the vernacular of a certain country might be prone to say. Yet another tragedy on a long list of incomprehensible tragedies. German apologists who take this view are not few in number.

Yet for all the truth to be found in these excuses, these excuses are all, basically, lies. Or to be more precise—they are a number of truthful excuses all founded upon a single lie.

For the Germans could have fed these prisoners. Or they could have fed some of them. Or they could have at least tried to feed them. If a great nation tries to do something, then something will be done, even if it is not entirely successful. This was, of course, the single lie—that nothing could be done.

The truth was that nothing *was* done. Nor was anything even attempted. The prisoners would simply not be fed. Nor would the local Russian population be allowed to feed them, nor even help to feed them, nor even throw them a few scraps over the barbed wire of the miserable bare encampments where they were corralled.

The prisoners soon adjusted to a regimen of dug-up grass, dug-up roots, dug-up earth, and cannibalism. The token amount of food the Germans gave them—a few beets thrown in tubs of water—evaporated like water in a desert. It was a holocaust, comparable to other holocausts of the time. The episodes played out in these camps (they could hardly be called prisons, as there was nothing there but the bare earth and the prisoners) would be a fit subject for many highly engrossing tales of horror.

But there were already too many such tales from that era. The three or four millions Russian POWs who were thus starved to death have more or less disappeared from the pages of history. The bare facts are known—even if they are ignored or rationalized. But the details, perhaps fit to stand alongside all the highly engrossing details from such places as Auschwitz and Birkenau, have vanished. At least for the time being.

The 5th Infantry Division steamed homeward across a landscape of nightmare. The thing about a nightmare is—and anyone who has lived through certain kinds of nightmares will perhaps agree with this—that if it goes on for too long, that if it becomes overly crowded with too many horrors and ordeals, becomes overly complicated, as it were, then some things start cancelling each other out. They vanish. The human soul—either as witness or participant—begins to be unable to absorb things anymore.

The trains carried them with infinite slowness back across Russia, perhaps averaging ten miles an hour from one day to the next. The Landsers were scarcely able to absorb all the ordeals they themselves had undergone, let alone what was happening to the Russians. The trains moving at such a slow pace would have given them opportunity to study the countless numbers of Russians starving and walking alongside the tracks. A disturbing sight. Where to place it amongst all the other disturbing things they had seen since last June? Besides, they were tired, they were as exhausted as death; they could scarcely begin to think of anything anymore.

Nightmares also have a tendency to vanish, into the night, or into the past. They are not gone by any means. They simply disappear for a while. A man looks forward to the day ahead. By the end of November the last men of the 5th had crossed back over the German border.

Behind them the snow had begun to fall heavily. It fell upon the Russian dead and upon the million and a half Landsers still waiting to make the last drive into Moscow. The temperature began to fall. It would not stop falling.

•   •   •

A Jaeger Division was an anomaly of the German army. One perhaps associates it with the Mountain Divisions. The names are similar—Jaeger, Gerbirgsjaeger. And indeed the 97th and 101st Jaeger Divisions gained fame for their exploits in the Caucasus Mountains and later in the Kuban Hills. They fought in the densely wooded lower heights of the Caucasus while their more purposefully equipped neighbors of the true mountain divisions fought on the highest ridges of the chain, conducting operations on otherworldly glacial plateaus at heights up to 15,000 feet. These Jaegers who had been in the Caucasus also bore other similarities to the mountain divisions. They tended to wear the distinctive cap favored by the mountaineers, which by 1944 would become almost as common as the steel helmet throughout the entire German army.

The men of the 97th Jaegers also had a kind of divisional display set up in their home town of Ulm, featuring mountaineering gear and other trophies from the peaks and hills of southernmost Russia.

Yet they were not true mountain troops, and the men of the 5th Jaeger Division were not mountain troops at all. The nature of this kind of unit can perhaps be more accurately ascertained from the original, somewhat more mundane designation of "Light Division." The divisional structure would be pared down, essentially meaning there would only be two infantry regiments instead of three. They would be allotted a slightly higher number of motor vehicles, PAKs (antitank guns), small portable field pieces, and heavy machine guns. The idea was that they would be able to move more quickly, be more easily supplied through remote terrain, and when the time came be able to strike more incisively in any of the various crisis spots that were becoming the rule more than the exception in Russia.

Yet as many of the veterans of German units were to find out later in the war, these refurbishments were often more in name than in reality. While there was an upgrading in equipment, it was rarely enough to be really meaningful. Especially when compared with the endless trainloads of armaments of all kinds being sent out by the Russian factories beyond the Urals. Experience in Russia tended to deprive men of illusions. A Jaeger Division, when you got right down to it, was little more than an infantry division under a different name. Hitler was fond of bestowing different names upon things; it suited his seeming ability to change things out in the world with only a nod of his head.

The lack of a third regiment was, in a way, the most disturbing thing. In theory, it would allow the division to be sent more quickly across the overburdened rail networks; it would also allow the division to be switched around more quickly on the battlefield. In practice, it meant that the division would be stretched out more thinly over any given sector of front. (To Hitler a division was a division and should hold division-sized sector of the front, whether it consisted of two regiments or three. Once again, the name was the essence.) In practice, it also meant that the exhaustion factor would be neglected. There would be that many fewer men to rotate between the front lines and the rear areas, the pitiful bunker-dwellings that were not that much different from the front lines.

All in all, the Jaeger Division was not one of the more successful innovations of the war. But, perhaps not surprisingly, the new designation was not altogether meaningless. Men tend to fight better under a jaunty name that stands them apart from their fellows. Perhaps such a suggestion is inevitably tainted with a certain amount of cynicism; nonetheless, it is often true. A division of the US Army would probably have carried itself with a certain swagger if Roosevelt had changed it overnight into a Marine division. And they probably would have fought harder. At least American veterans of these branches of the service might spend a few evenings debating the truth or falsehood of this idea.

But to return to the third regiment. Its lack was also disturbing to the men of the 5th for more personal reasons. What it really meant was that one of their regiments would be left behind. Left behind in Russia.

The jubilation during those filthy October days was confined to the Landsers of the 75th and 56th Infantry Regiments. The men of the 14th were to be left behind, absorbed into the ranks of the 78th Infantry (later "Storm") Division. On a filthy October day, on what passed for a parade ground in the middle of some Russian village, General Allmendinger bade farewell to these men. As was the custom, he thanked them all for their long service in the 5th.

Orders were orders. And in any case, the Landsers were far more used to receiving rotten orders than good ones. So the mood in this abandoned regiment might be difficult to pinpoint exactly. To say that they felt let down would probably be an understatement. To say that they felt fucked over once again by the rarefied higher headquarters swine would probably also be an understatement. But to say that they felt betrayed, "written off," might not be true. These bitter phrases did not enter the soldiers' vernacular until later in the war. So far the war was still going well. Currently, it was being conducted in a stinking hideous quagmire; that was true. But the soldiers were used to victory, and as yet victory was still the only thing they knew. Doubtless there would have been a number of them—whether a large or small number probably no one will ever know—who were glad to remain to take part in the final drive on Moscow, the culmination of everything. The end of everything. Surely that would mean the end of the war.

The mud of that season was like a certain dreary version of hell. The men remaining behind did not look forward to other versions. Rather, they looked forward to the first frost, when the ground would hard up again, when operations would continue, when the whole ordeal of the Russian campaign would be brought to its conclusion in Red Square.

DEMYANSK

•   •   •

By the last week of November, the other two regiments had come to the end of their long train journey and were now set up in the Upper Loire Valley in France. They knew this area from the West campaign in 1940. God lived in France. Every German citizen had heard this for over a hundred years. Whenever German armies invaded France they would find that this adage was more or less true. And so the adage had endured as part of modern German folklore. France was a ripe and wealthy place, and people lived fairly well there even during the occupation. Particularly the German soldiers lived well there. Better than in Germany anyway. The food, wine, and women were all good, very good. The resistance movement, compared with the partisan uprisings in Russia, was almost non-existent. It was not even a joke, as a joke must have some substance to it. Later this would change. In 1944 SS units who were used to having a good time in France would become enraged by the sudden change in mood of the French citizens, by the mass uprisings that took place almost overnight at the time of the Normandy invasion. Sleepy places like Oradour-sur-Glane would be erased from the map and burned into history.

But all of this would happen later. By that time the 5th Jaeger Division would be back in Russia. It would have already been back there for a long, long time.

The men liked France, but it was still not home, and that was where they wanted to go more than anywhere else. The first leave trains, die Urlauber-Zuge, were arranged almost as soon as the men arrived in the garrison towns along the Loire, and everyone in the division was rotated back to his home town during December.

By this time they would have begun to hear rumors of the fate of the Army Group Center. Moscow had not yet fallen, and with each passing day civilians and soldiers alike would listen for news of this event. In its peculiar way the German propaganda machine was not entirely untruthful. Goebbels considered his propaganda organization to be part of the modern news media; and no matter how highly sugared it might have been by the

National Socialist commentary, a great deal of real news was made available to the German public throughout the war. The weekly newsreels were as explicit as anything to be seen in the Western nations; they showed maps, dates, place-names, troop movements, all in great detail. They neglected to mention that much of what was occurring in Russia was a terrible ordeal. They neglected to mention that almost the whole of the Army Group Center was on the verge of being wiped out less than thirty miles from Moscow. Yet for all that, the newsreels did reveal a great deal. Given a little practice, even a dullard could begin to read between the lines. Goebbels did not make this nearly as difficult as he might have. And the news to be read—read and seen in movie theaters throughout Germany—was not good.

For the Landsers who had been in Russia the news was more ominous still. They knew what it was like out there. They knew the real meaning of these sudden massive fund-drives set up by Goebbels, calling on every German citizen to donate furs, wool stockings, scarves and other warm clothing for the soldiers at the front. The citizens would have themselves guessed that something was amiss in this situation. But to guess that something was amiss was not the same as having any real idea what conditions were like out there. They heeded Goebbels' call with a certain community elan, glad to be called on to help the war effort in some meaningful way, especially since it did not inconvenience them to any great degree. The drive to collect warm clothing was a tremendous success.

Unfortunately, almost none of this clothing ever made its way to the front. It lay heaped up in endless strings of boxcars at depots in Poland or in the Russian rear areas. The onset of the worst Russian winter in over a hundred years had come near to paralyzing the transportation networks. The preceding mud season had already brought horse-drawn and motor vehicle transport to the point of collapse. Now in December the railroads were also brought to a near standstill, blocked by snowdrifts so deep that even the Russians would claim they had never seen the like of them before.

Many trains did get through—they had to get through— assisted by the superhuman efforts of the Todt laborers in clearing the tracks, to say nothing of the armies of Russian citizens likewise "enlisted" to do this job. But the results were not good enough, at least not good enough to bring those boxcars of clothing forward to the men who had now begun to die of the cold. The trains that did make it through carried almost exclusively ammunition and fuel; or else more men, men called up from all corners of occupied Europe to stem the disaster looming before Moscow.

And even these men, after the appalling weather conditions at the front had finally been understood, were not equipped with winter clothing. The men of the 205th, the 83rd, the 330th Infantry Divisions, to mention a few, had all been doing occupation duty in France; they had only vague, ominously vague, ideas of what lay in store for them. They were entrained and shipped with great urgency out of France and across Germany. And not a single one of them carried any more article of winter clothing than any of the divisions that had been sent into Russia back in June.

Rarely has a modern army become embroiled in such a logistical travesty.

The men of the 5th Jaegers, on the other hand, had a much clearer idea of what to expect. And they too were called upon by the High Command, called upon to return to Russia in the dead of winter. They might have hoped for some new assignment. No soldier ever knows where he is going to go until the orders finally come. Their training and re-equipping as a Jaeger Division had barely had a chance to get started. Their minds were on the home leave that most of them had just been granted. They had only just returned from their homes in Germany to the barracks and drill grounds in the Upper Loire Valley when the word arrived.

All things considered, they could not have been much surprised.

They too boarded the trains, the trains that had carried them all out of Russia only two months before.

Even they had not experienced the worst of the Russian winter. They had gotten only a taste of it, on that agonizing march back to the railheads in October and November. Even then a great many Landsers had come down with frostbite or other associated illnesses—rotting feet, pneumonia, raging fevers brought on by the exhaustion of the body.

It is hard to say what they would have thought when they saw they were being sent back to Russia without a scrap of winter clothing. What could their mood have been? There had already been some grumbling, especially among the officers and veteran

NCOs who had been with the 5th since back in the early 30s, about the callous amputation of their sister regiment from the division. Such things were not done lightly—or more precisely, they were not taken lightly. But that was war. Units were separated, reshuffled, reorganized, and sent off to one place or another. The circumstances of this separation had been more trying than the actual fact of it. Most men, especially the Landsers, barely knew the people in their own regiment, let alone some other one. By the time they got back to France, most of them had probably forgotten that the 14th Infantry Regiment had ever existed.

But Russia itself . . . they could not have forgotten that. The reality of Russia could barely have left their minds in two short months. The nightmare might have left them momentarily, beneath a Christmas tree in a warm home somewhere in Germany, with their family beside them there. But only momentarily. . . .

Who knows what strange conversations might have taken place on those troop trains steaming slowly back towards the Russian frontier. No winter clothing? Betrayal? The ineptitude of the rarefied higher headquarters swine once again? Perhaps something like that, but perhaps resignation and a kind of strange inertia would have been stronger forces than any complaints. The enormity of the events of the past few years would have caught all of them up, from the most cynical to the most blindly faithful. And the events of the past six months had been more enormous still. The German armies were at the gates of Moscow; at night they could see the searchlight beams from the towers of the Kremlin.

The cold grew more and more bitter as the trains passed through Poland and East Prussia. Most of the Landsers were in empty boxcars piled with straw, with a single pot-bellied stove at one end providing the only warmth. Perhaps more than anything else there would have been that age-old military tradition of nervous expectancy, of waiting to see what it would be this time.

Narrative of Gunter Nierholz, Oberleutnant, 5th Jaeger Division, February 1942

Back in October there were many who thought we had reached the limits of our endurance. But there is always more. Always more.

And perhaps I should say there is always worse. But after a certain point you can't compare things anymore.

For one thing, after a certain point of exhaustion is reached, you can't even think. It is difficult to remember things that happened more than a few days ago. There is only the present moment, the exhaustion, the cold, the exhaustion, the cold.

Often upon first awakening, or in that grey state just before awakening, I will have the idea that I am still at home in Tubingen, where I was only a month ago. Or in the barracks in Nevers by the Loire, where I was only a month or so ago. But as soon as I wake up these feelings vanish. They disappear so quickly that they have no reality and it is scarcely a let-down when I feel the cold upon my face and piercing deep into the core of my body. For it was like that only yesterday, after all. And the day before that, and the day before that. Just as it will be today, and tomorrow.

No. I am deceiving myself, I think. There is always at least a moment of deep disappointment, fear, all the rest. It's just that some days are less difficult than others.

We finally detrained in the ruined city of Staraya Russa, under shellfire even as we unloaded our gear from the cars. After almost two weeks in the boxcars it was a relief to be moving about in the open air, even though it was so cold you had to fight back momentary surges of dread. But in the middle of a city the cold was not as frightening; there were buildings around you, shelter, and fires going inside those buildings, only a few meters away. If we had been ordered to detrain out in the open steppe the shock would have been worse.

During the long train ride we had heard rumors of our assignment, but nothing was very clear. Nor was there any time for orientation in Staraya Russa; we were thrown into the line immediately, as the Russians had already penetrated right into the city. Then after a few days things settled down a bit. General Allmendinger gathered the officers in one of the municipal buildings that was still standing, to lay out our plan of operation in more detail.

I can recall the stone buildings of Staraya Russa in some detail. It was an ancient city, more solid looking than other places I had seen in Russia. You might not associate warmth with stone, but somehow within the massiveness of those buildings you felt that the weather could be kept at bay, that relief from it was always not far away. You passed through a huge iron-bound door that might have stood for a thousand years, and once inside there was the warmth from the fires kept going twenty-four hours a day.

Allmendinger informed us of our task. We were to break through to the forces encircled at Demyansk, some fifty miles away. Within that pocket there were some 100,000 men, more or less, all of whom had been ordered to hold out by Hitler. No retreat. Not one step back. They probably would have had the strength to fight their way back to Staraya Russa, if this had been allowed. But it was not.

We listened to all this in that strange condition of half-alertness, putting on that mask of paying strict attention to the commanding general while inside most of us were already nodding off, struggling to absorb the various details of the operation while fatigue sucked at us. The room where he spoke to us was large and drafty, wind and cold sunlight piercing this way and that through the boarded-up windows. Probably that was just as well. If it had been any warmer in there I might have fallen dead asleep.

The enormity of our task was something we could not grasp right away. Still, as soon as he mentioned what we were supposed to do, I was weighed down by a dim fear, a leaden feeling inside my body that was different from fatigue. We were supposed to attack? Yes, that was it, an attack to free the people at Demyansk, that was what he had said. . . .

But how could this be. . . .

The wind blew outside, it blew and blew, driving before it frozen particles that had been carried for thousands of miles.

Allmendinger only introduced the idea into our minds, so to speak. Then he sat down and gave way to General Seydlitz.

Seydlitz was what you might call a charismatic figure. You received this impression in a glance—a curious sensation that I would recall when meeting a few other such men from that war. Model, for example, though he was also somewhat of an ass; still, he had that quality about him, and the ability to get his men to do the things that had to be done. As for Seydlitz, the calm that he exuded was almost like a physical presence, some larger entity that was suddenly there in the room with us. Yet he looked around at the men who were there and there was no aloofness in his eyes.

You would have grown used to not always trusting your first impression of the various personalities that would crop up in the great war machine. Many bore only the facade of command. And if that was so, it did not usually take very long for the first cracks in that facade to appear. But in fact this was only normal, the day-to-day face of men conducting operations under terrible strain. Men did their jobs, or attempted to do them, as best they could. The true charismatic personalities were few and far between; it was in the nature of things to be that way.

Seydlitz introduced himself. We knew who he was, though only a few of us might have spoken to him personally before. He informed us that a week previously OKH (which since December meant Hitler himself) had placed him in command of Operation Bridgestrike, the operation to force a relief corridor through to the Demyansk area. The force at his disposal was only a single corps—that is to say we in the 5th Division, along with the men of the 8th Division. They too had just returned from France; they too had just been re-outfitted as a so-called Jaeger division, just like ourselves. And they too had made that terrible march back from Vyazma, only a few months ago. Their general was Hohne, who sat at the spindly table next to our own General Allmendinger.

Seydlitz said,

"Gentlemen, this is not a large force. I will lay out the situation and try neither to mislead you nor discourage you. It is a task that calls above all for fresh troops. I trust that your short layover in France has invigorated you somewhat. I apologize to the men of the 5th who were thrown into the defense of the city immediately upon their arrival here. I will see to it that they are set up in quieter positions for the few days remaining before the attack. If our cousins from the east allow us that luxury, then we may proceed with the operation.

"It will not be easy. That is why you are here, men of the 5th, men of the 8th. You have been rested, but your previous experience in Russia is of critical importance. This is no task for garrison divisions just called up from France. The unfortunate weather conditions since your arrival have no doubt made an impression on you. No doubt you have been wondering about the arrival of winter clothing. Allow me to be blunt. Do not count on it. I was granted an interview with Herr Hitler only a short time ago. He informed me that the operation to relieve Demyansk has the highest priority, and that the two divisions of the strike force will be the first to be issued winter clothing, when it does arrive.

"You might guess that when this will happen is not yet known. The operation cannot wait for that. Therefore you will be given free rein to collect all possible clothing that can still be found in Staraya Russa. I have asked the other divisions in this sector to cooperate as much as possible, even though they also are critically short of this equipment. Your quartermasters must set themselves singlemindedly to this task. Any disputes that arise between units will be settled by me personally. Over the course of the winter a certain amount of clothing has been collected from Russian civilians and from every other source that can be found. You will be given access to every depot in the city. Nonetheless you will find the cupboards somewhat bare. I again remind your supply people to use all their ingenuity.

"Let us move on to your dispositions for the attack."

He continued. The somewhat peculiar tone he had adopted when mentioning Hitler would have been noticed by even the most fatigue-dulled among us. In these kinds of staff meetings and operational meetings Hitler was almost never referred to as Hitler, much less as "Herr Hitler." He was the Fuhrer. But there was no time to dwell on this now, and during the remainder of the meeting Seydlitz did not refer to Hitler again.

While Demyansk itself was over fifty miles away, the nearest units in the pocket (or the "cauldron," and it was here that I heard this word used for the first time) were only half that distance away. Their positions were just beyond the Lovat River, which flowed into Lake Ilmen a short distance north of Staraya Russa.

When the divisions of the strike force had fought their way to the Lovat, orders would be issued to the troops inside the pocket to strike across the river and link up with us. The relief corridor would then be established.

So the distance was not that far. If we could cope with the weather and the enemy, then the distance could be covered.

●   ●   ●

The attack began on the 9th of February. As mandated not by the High Command, but by the personal order of the Fuhrer himself.

DEMYANSK

At his behest, neither army groups nor armies, but only a single corps of two understrength divisions, attacked eastward into the wilderness. So our calvary at Demyansk began.

•　　•　　•

My impressions of that first attack remain dim, highlighted by incidents of one kind or another. We were not prepared. Perhaps mentally we were prepared for the worst, but if so then we were not really helped by it. Mental toughness can only go so far before the lack of basic materials for survival erases every other consideration.

I remember the wounded receiving emergency aid from the medical people. Their first consideration was not to bandage the wounds received from Russian fire. That was hardly necessary, as the cold was so bitter that the blood hardly flowed. Blood gouted only from wounds that were mortal anyway, where men would be dead within minutes if not seconds. In all other cases the medics' first consideration was to give immediate injections to keep the wounded from falling into shock. Even only slightly injured men were subject to this—the cold would cause them to lapse into shock within a few minutes. If they were not brought out of it by the injection of powerful stimulants, then they would settle down in the snow somewhere, to be found dead not long afterward.

I was attached to regimental staff but soon found myself assigned to one of the aid stations, where every available man was needed. I had no training for this kind of thing, but you discovered quickly enough that the simplest kind of assistance could sometimes bring a man around, helping him hold on to the lifeline of consciousness by talking to him, shaking him, slapping him or gently ministering to the slightest need, heaping straw upon him, offering him a smoke, offering him something to drink or anything to nibble on, reassuring him as best you could, trying to get him to look you in the eye, to maintain a few words of conversation so he might feel his mind beginning to rise away from a coma.

But yes, this could only go so far. When one was dead I would go to the next, and then to the next. Some of them regained consciousness, and I would try to keep my mind on them and not on the ones who just went away while my hands were still on their faces. They needed the drugs; they needed the attention of the medics. I myself delivered any number of these injections. We were somewhat better equipped with emergency medical supplies than we had been back in the autumn. Equipment designed for men stranded on mountain plateaus beyond the reach of any help. It was no less necessary in the snow wastes beyond Staraya Russa. Perhaps for a number of them it meant the difference between life and death. The rest died anyway.

I remember exhaustion overcoming me, that and the feeling that I was going to die of the cold myself. I remember thinking of finding some excuse to return to the regimental command post, where my normal duties were. These thoughts would prey on me while I automatically went outside to help bring in another load of wounded, thinking that just to make one more journey of a few meters outside the door would drain the last of my strength. Those who arrived, of course, had already made journeys of several miles or more. I kept on no different from anyone else. There were any number of other staff or supply people there to help the medics. The divisional chaplain took command of a sled-train to go out towards the attack, where it was reported that fifty wounded men were stranded on the other side of a minefield. He returned several hours later and those who had survived the journey were hurriedly carried off the sleds and borne inside. The rest were simply pushed off the sleds into the snow, with eyes still wide open, many of them. I remember the chaplain wandering around outside the door in a daze; for a number of minutes he kept looking among the dead to make sure any were not still breathing out there. This went on for a while, and he must have reached some point of confusion; I remember someone going outside to speak to him.

The attack, such as it was, was a failure almost from the start. If I remember correctly, our first goal was not even to strike out towards Demyansk. Events had overtaken us; our first goal at that point was to break through to help some other unit that had been surrounded right on the outskirts of Staraya Russa. I do not know what happened to them, nor who they were. The survivors amongst our own men returned to the start lines at the edge of the city.

For the next month we remained there, or else we fought our way to a few outlying villages. The attack continued, but only in a manner of speaking. These villages changed hands on numerous occasions, and we were on the defensive as often as not. Demyansk, the Lovat River—those places might as well have been on the moon; for weeks on end the entire focus of our existence centered around ruined clusters of isbas, places like Pripjetino, Utschna, nondescript piles of ruins whose names we only remembered because they provided the only shelter from the cold.

The snow grew deeper and deeper as one snowstorm followed another. At length even the Russians could not struggle through the snow any longer. It was like trying to walk through the ocean. We were subject to constant air raids, which caused us more casualties than we'd suffered in the first attack. The black, half-devastated villages stood out like beacons in the snow-fields, bombed one day after another. Yet there was no place else to hide. To disperse our men out in the wilderness was not possible. Towards the end of February the temperature had fallen farther still, until readings of fifty below zero became commonplace. The wind blew from the east.

How we kept going is hard to understand. We will say as much to ourselves, these many years later, on those rare occasions when the few or us who are left get together in some town in Germany. But for us at least it is not really necessary to say anything, as we were there. Whether one mutters something intelligible or not, it doesn't really matter. But to describe it all to a stranger, that is difficult. Because even the facts do not suffice. The facts, after all, even if possibly containing the truth, are not the same as experiencing something. This is an essential difference, perhaps even an obvious difference. Yet I must say that this idea never really occurred to me until this very moment, as these words came down on this page. It gives me a strange feeling of relief, all of a sudden. I must sit and think it over for a few moments.

All of that first winter was beyond, somehow. Beyond. There were more than a few survivors who were kept in mental hospitals till the end of the war, and even long afterwards. Men who had been wounded might recover from their wounds, sometimes anyway. Men who had been broken by the cold seemed sometimes to be a different kind of case; though even for someone like myself, who was there, it is hard to know just how to say this.

The second phase of the attack, which began in late March, seems a little easier to describe. The words do not seem quite so distressing.

The second phase was better organized. Our divisional artillery, which did not arrive by railroad until several weeks after that first horrible failure, was well established by that time and gave us essential support. Also, the first winter clothing had finally begun to arrive. We were perhaps overcome by revulsion, or even stranger feelings, that it should arrive now when the winter was almost over. But we were grateful in any case. The cold was still very bad, and the snow was if anything deeper than it had been in January. Up to this point we had mostly been wearing white camouflage capes, which at a glance resembled winter gear, but in fact provided us with no more warmth than a bedsheet. The new gear was heavily padded and included quilted trousers that reached up over our bellies.

The disgusted remarks which greeted the late arrival of these things gave way in a matter of moments to sheer relief, the relief of having anything at all.

We should have been removed from the line, sent staggering back somewhere to homes for exhausted men. But one day gives way to another. You begin to understand the meaning of that. General Seydlitz gathered the staff officers together to lay out the plans for the second attack. We had seen little of him since that first meeting in Staraya Russa. But from this point on he stayed close to us, and he was to be seen at many places in the weeks to come.

Demyansk was still surrounded. The situation had not changed. Nothing had changed. But when the second phase of the attack began on March 21 we had, at least initially, better success. On the first day we broke through the Russian positions and reached the snow roads that led back towards their rear areas. Aerial reconnaissance had revealed to us the presence of these roads, which were the only means by which any kind of motor transport, often including tanks, could go anywhere. They were deep channels that wound like canals through the snowfields. We could have followed them all the way into our men trapped in the cauldron, and indeed we attempted to do so. But the Russians counterattacked savagely to block them from our use. Once again we spent days on the defensive for every day that we managed to move forward. It was slow and terrible. We now had a few tanks and assault guns at our disposal. At times they were unable to fire at nearby targets because the banks of the snow roads were higher than the traverse of their cannon. Yet we could not have advanced without them. We also made use of the small portable field pieces designed for the mountaineers, which could be dismantled and carried on sleds or on horseback. Other kinds of heavy weapons could not be brought forward except with great difficulty.

The snows began to melt in April. It was yet another ordeal. In Russia it was in the nature of things for one ordeal to be followed by another one. The only variation came from long intervals of boredom and other kinds of mundane distress or mental anguish. The first thaws did not melt all the snow. Even the notorious thaws of that land could not have melted all this snow at once. It would have flooded creation. But what did I know of it? Perhaps in other years it did exactly that. Nothing could surprise you in that country.

In any case the operation proceeded a little better for a week or so. The tanks and assault guns were able to get around a little better. The Russians also stepped up their counterattacks. More fighting . . . a few occasions of mutual exhaustion . . . more fighting. The meltwater spread out in wide lakes across the snowfields. The melt-ponds reflected the sky, reflected the shapes of men and vehicles at the edges of them. Clouds drifted deep within the meltwater even as they drifted slowly overhead. Perhaps in dreams near the ends of our lives we will be able to take pleasure in remembering these beautiful sights. A few brief periods of frost would hard up the ground again. The fighting took on a more desperate character, as it was deemed essential to break through to the cauldron before the real thaw began. The Russian attacks also grew more desperate, as they no doubt had the same thing in mind.

By mid-April the thaw had come for good. The attack was not called off. We advanced in a state of near-paralysis through knee-deep water. Men struggled to do anything, to march from one place to another, to eat, to relieve themselves, to find dry ground at night; even firefights would seem to take place with a kind of unreal lethargy. The wounded would be borne out with infinite slowness, many of them looking like men who had given up hope—or not even that, but like men who had given up any idea about anything. That was it, the look I can still remember. The warmer days brought the torment of nights that were still below freezing, when your soaking clothes would freeze on your skin like death itself. Frostbite gave way to pneumonia and everyone was sick whether they fell out or not. Fires were lit at night with a kind of methodical, almost sacramental desperation, and on occasion you could see other fires quite nearby through the woods, where the Russians were. One side could easily have ambushed the other. Whether from unspoken mutual agreement, or whether from an exhaustion that superseded the need for it, there was not too much of that; the nights were mostly quiet, dead. Yet still there remained enough natural treachery and cunning on either side that you could not lose your fear of ambush, except when fatigue drained out everything.

The heavy padded suits that had given us a week or two of comfort became soaked through with freezing water and you wore them like iron. They were heavy like that. I began to dream of shooting myself, or of being shot by the Russians in some skirmish. These were only thoughts. I did not wish to die, even during periods of the worst exhaustion. But to keep your mind focussed on survival, on continuing, was a depressing task and this depression would bring strange thoughts to your mind. It was my responsibility to encourage other men who were tormented by the same kinds of thoughts. At that time I was in command of a company in the forward areas. The drain of officers had been severe and so I was detached from regimental staff to lead a combat unit.

Seydlitz also appeared frequently, even in the forward areas. I had some idea of what all these visits to different places must have demanded of his strength. When there was still snow on the ground he would sometimes show up on skis. Later, if a road was passable through the thaw he would show up by car; other times he would arrive on horseback, and a few times I saw him just wading up as if out of nowhere, not accompanied by anyone.

He never gave orders to any of the company commanders, or at least I never saw him do so. The daily tasks would come down from regiment or division, often no doubt instigated by Seydlitz himself, but he did not meddle with the chain of command at our level. He simply showed up there. By that time the fighting strength of companies was often down to thirty or forty men. Sometimes less. It was curious to see the commanding officer of a corps visiting with such small groups of men. Usually officers from any command level higher than battalion would not appear so far forward. This is not a slur on them. With certain kinds of officers these visits would only be meddlesome anyway; the junior officers would feel themselves under the eye, so to speak, under a certain pressure to perform well, and this anxiety would inevitably be conveyed to the Landsers. When the performance of certain kinds of tasks means the difference between life and death, the pressure of these watchful eyes can be stressful indeed.

Then there are those kinds of senior officers who show up at these moments, who have a better understanding of this problem. Seydlitz was one of these. If an attack was ordered he would stay only briefly, speaking to a few people, letting the rest of us see him there; but he would not remain to make sure that the thing was carried through. He would trust that we would do our best, and if the thing were not carried through on that day then it would be carried through on the next day, or the next, until the end. He had some idea of what men were capable of, of what can be accomplished by little speeches and what cannot be. He had some idea of when men were giving their best and when they were not.

Above all, we had to endure. His presence was helpful in this respect, I believe.

By the end of April the attack had again come almost to a standstill. Our fighting strength was too low. Supplies could barely reach us, and as for reinforcements, there were almost none. The lack of our third regiment led to difficulty. Since the end of March we had been attacking two regiments abreast, and obviously there could be no rotation without the third. Finally some kind of rotation became necessary, or the men would simply have been unable to continue. But then to attack with a single regiment brought poor results; the Russians were too strong to make any headway.

In the end the regiments became almost meaningless entities. It was up to the individual battalions to keep going, switched around wherever there was a new focal point for an assault or some crisis developed from a Russian counterattack.

Our lack of strength . . . and then the weather. The melt-season was not so muddy as what I remembered from Vyazma. It was mostly just water, water everywhere. The entire area around the Lovat became a swamp extending for many miles. Perhaps it did not destroy you and humiliate you in quite the way the mud had done. And it was not like what we had undergone back in the winter, which perhaps I have spoken of too briefly. But by this time we were too tired to care. Your mind would simply be emptied out, incapable of comparing one thing to another thing. There was only the exhaustion and the cold, the knee-deep wading, the preoccupation with finding some place to build a fire at night. Ambushes, death, apathy. We had entered into a large belt of forest and for weeks had been unable to reach the end of it. This forest became for us the only world in the world, just as the villages of Utschna and Pripjetino had been in February.

We knew, or at least we were told, that the Lovat—and thus the edge of the pocket—lay just at the other side of this forest. So perhaps our goal seemed closer, somewhat more real. I hesitate to say. In the dense woods you always had the impression that you might pass through some last barrier of trees and find yourself at the end, standing on the bank of that river. But the end would not come, and so the forest seemed to go on forever. We lived in it. There were no front lines or trenches or anything of that sort. Battlegroups large or small waded through the trees, falling upon one another, killing, vanishing back into the thickets. A few assaults focused around filthy villages isolated in the forest. On sunny days the upper limbs and branches of the bare trees would dry out and bear on their surfaces the strange warm look of dry, sunlit wood; which, I must say, gave a certain feeling of repose to your suffering, even while you waded onward through freezing water, beneath all those tangled limbs.

By this time, also, the great fleets of transport planes were always passing overhead, bringing supplies to the men at Demyansk. They flew over us at very low altitude and their numbers seemed endless, though perhaps this was due to the same planes making the same journey over and over again. They would fly towards the Lovat and seemingly within minutes they would be flying back on the return leg, and this also contributed to the feeling of our goal being near. They were a strange and impressive sight, those fleets of planes coming over at treetop level at all hours of the day, and I would see them again in dreams long after the war. We were dropped supplies on only a few occasions; almost all of it was meant for the men holding out in the pocket. It was their lifeline.

Demyansk thus began to seem both nearby and yet still very far away, someplace that we could never see and perhaps never would see. It was about this time that I began to think of Demyansk as being some kind of island in the sky. I don't know what I mean by this exactly, as no clear picture of such a thing ever appeared in my mind. It was just that those words would often come to my mind, in the evenings in the forest. Demyansk. The thought of that place took on its own kind of reality, which had nothing to do with what we saw there when we finally made it through. I would remember the island in the sky, which existed only in some exhausted, bleary imagination deep inside the forest; I would remember it every bit as clearly as our long stay inside the pocket itself.

It would have been around the 20th of April. My company had been sent to a flanking position, there to defend against the Russian counterattacks that consumed so many of our days. The woods in this area had been torn up by artillery fire and offered a better field of fire than the deeper thickets around. Also a number of trees—or the dead, twenty foot stems that were the remains of trees—had been cut down for the making of corduroy roads through the swamps. This clearing-out also gave us a better view of things. We were able to set up good defensive positions behind the various piles of logs that had not been used for the roads. Many of the pioneers were being used as infantry; so that construction work on the corduroy roads had dwindled to a crawl, just as everything else had done. But we were glad for the protection offered by all this material left lying around.

There were a few stretches of firmer ground around here. The water was scattered across it in puddles and long thin sloughs, whose reflections traced the sky in various strange and fragmented patterns. But all in all the ground was drier. It was another sunlit day. In Germany the buds would have begun to come out almost a month earlier. Here there was nothing but the grey sunlit nakedness of the tree limbs and the dried-out mud everywhere. But that was not too bad. Nature stripped down to its essentials . . . and for the first time in many months it seemed these essentials did not appear in the form of some overriding torment, but were only quiet in their places around us.

We waited for the attack, while also hoping that maybe we would be left alone today. The Russians like ourselves seemed to have used up most of their available strength. After long tours of duty at the front, you could begin to tell the difference between these periods of quiet—the quiet that was only the buildup for another massive attack, and the quiet that was more like exhaustion, emptiness, death. It was hard to picture a major assault ever being launched through these flooded woods. None of our actions up to now had been that kind of thing. You had a sense of things dwindling, the Russian resistance dwindling, your own ability to move on also dwindling, petering out.

They came in the late afternoon in about battalion strength. They were accompanied by three armored cars which indicated they too must have built a log road near to our positions. We could not see this track but only the cars bouncing and jolting over the surface of it, moving laboriously through the trees. They did not inspire the same fear in us as tanks. We could see the infantry spread out on either side.

We waited till they approached the more cleared-out area where we were. We let go first with machine gun fire at the infantry, driving them back to the edge of the woods. The cars commenced to blanket us with fire and the infantry moved forward again into the cleared, stump-ridden area, and we let them approach quite near before we fired again with all weapons available.

The cars then advanced to better support these men, who were now pinned down behind the stumps and in the watery sloughs. They were not tracked vehicles and navigated uncertainly over the patches of dry ground. We had seen large numbers of these vehicles the previous year and knew they were thinly armored; with even the light infantry PAKs we could have disposed of them in a few minutes. But as yet we had not been able to drag any of these guns over to this position. Instead we found we must rely on the Russians to lurch on stubbornly to their own destruction. This they did.

The first car turned broadside to avoid a watery patch and got hung up on two stumps. We blew out the tires and blistered the viewing slits with small arms fire. The turret in the rear carried a medium caliber weapon whose fire was mostly inaccurate. Our log breastworks protected us. The other two lagged behind. The infantry assault had lost cohesion and the survivors began to fall back. We gave them no opportunity to reorganize and cut most of them down before they had reached the end of the clearing. The first car continued to fire from almost point blank range until it must have used up its ammunition. Doors opened on the far side and the crew tumbled out. They did not get far.

The other two cars now attempted to pull back but both became stranded in the maze of fallen logs and waterholes. Without infantry support they were helpless and they were abandoned by their crews, a few of whom managed to escape into the woods in the distance. Those vehicles were entirely unsuited to this kind of terrain. In fact under most circumstances they were pretty useless. This was the first time I had seen them in combat since Vyazma.

Sergeant Heit led a small group of men out into the killing ground. They kept to the lee of the first armored car to avoid fire from any stragglers still back in the woods. They moved cautiously and fired upon any wounded Russians who remained in the sloughs. This was necessary in order to avoid taking a bullet in the back. With like caution they approached the car itself. I saw him pull open the lee door and peer down the length of his weapon as he pointed it inside. It would have been a surer thing to give a long burst into the interior but there was the danger of ricochets. Apparently no one remained alive inside. He climbed into the cab and pulled shut the other door on the far side, then peered through the armored slit at the terrain beyond.

I sent another group out with Sergeant Meijer, who moved up to the car and then both groups advanced slowly beyond it in the direction of the other two. The rest of us stood ready to fire. Again they used the two cars in the distance as shields between them and the further woods. They fired on other wounded and they fired at the slits on the cars in case anyone still remained in there. A long burst came from somewhere back in the woods and they went to ground. Those of us at the logworks fired with every weapon, light mortar included. We could see no targets. Three bursts from the mortar sent limbs and sticks cartwheeling above the trees. We waited. Heit's and Meijer's people moved forward again. After they had investigated the two cars they placed charges inside. One blew out with a quick bang, the other burned for quite some time until the panels were blistered white from the heat. The things had the potential to be a nuisance. Even burnt out there would be little to prevent snipers from moving back in there during the night. I studied the terrain to see if it might be suitable to move our positions out that way, then waited for Heit to make his way back to talk it over with him.

They were accompanied by a single Ivan whom they had not shot. Heit brought this man to me and the rest collapsed behind the logworks, their nerves played out by the firefight and the short walk following it.

The Russian had the Asiatic features of an Uzbeki or some other Siberian. It was mostly these kinds of troops we had been fighting over these past months. They were better clothed than we were but otherwise looked nearly done-in; there had been reports of starvation or near-starvation in the Russian units. None of us here spoke Russian and we could not communicate with this man. Often these Asiatics spoke only a few words of Russian to begin with. I radioed a request to the rear to have some people brought up to take charge of him, as I did not wish to spare anyone from our position to escort him back to battalion.

We searched him for concealed weapons, stripping him down till he was almost naked, then letting him put his clothes on again, except for his felt boots which were more or less raffled off to Private Thayer. He kept putting his hand up to his mouth and we gave him a little to eat and a smoke. If we could have fed these Russians I think most of them might have come over to us. It might have ended everything in a more timely fashion.

The escort showed up in the evening. I saw that Seydlitz was with them. Our own unfinished log road came to an end several hundred yards to the rear. They were in a Kubelwagen which stopped at the end of the corduroy. I started wading back there to greet the general. He did not wait on me but came forward with the three men accompanying him. They struggled through the tangled brush at the edge of the roadway but then took to my example and stepped down into the water and waded along the sunken track until we met.

"How do you find duty with the infantry, Nierholz?"

These were his first words. I had never spoken to him previously and did not realize he knew me.

"It is a filthy struggle, Herr General. The Landsers are good men."

He looked at me. I felt a little startled to hear these words coming from my mouth and quickly saluted him again, an odd looking gesture no doubt. He seemed to pay this no heed.

"Are your positions underwater?"

"No, sir."

"Let's go on then."

We waded in silence back up to the logworks. My men stepped back a little to give him room, an instinctive gesture.

He studied the prisoner for a minute but said nothing to the man. The interpreter was back at battalion where a few others had been brought in during the day. Seydlitz said something to his escort and they took the prisoner back towards the Kubelwagen.

"That is your name, isn't it?"

"Yes, Nierholz, sir."

"I thought so. How many casualties did you take today?"

"No casualties, Herr General."

He had been looking out over the stump-field. He looked at me again.

"None. That is correct?"

I had taken a head-count an hour before. Yet I found myself turning around to look at my own men, staring at them. They looked back at me, or looked at Seydlitz.

"Yes sir, that is correct."

A curious look came over his face. I didn't know what he thought. He put his hands on his hips, glancing back along the watery alley where the prisoner was wading with his other men. He moved forward into our positions, addressing a few of the Landsers, saying, "How are you, men?" and things of that kind. In a way they seemed more at ease in his presence than the officers would have been. I gave a look to Sergeant Heit and he quickly ushered the general to a sheltered place. I followed him there.

"Very good, Nierholz. I will mention your action to General Allmendinger. Perhaps you are suited to this line of work."

"Yes, sir."

"Your radio message mentioned those cars out there. They did not bring up any tanks then?"

I answered in the negative. He asked about Russian artillery fire and I also answered in the negative.

"Maybe they're reaching the dregs of things. One does not get overly optimistic, eh? In any case this was well done."

"They did not carry on with their usual persistence, sir. Sergeant Heit is of the opinion they were not experienced troops."

"There are containers from the field kitchen in my car. Send a few of your men back there. I would have brought them up right away, but my aides feel more comfortable if they have their hands free for their weapons."

He smiled faintly. I motioned to Sergeant Meijer. I said, "Yes, sir. It is not an unwarranted concern. The general is no doubt aware there are problems with infiltrators."

"Yes, of course there are, Nierholz. All right then. Did Captain Strecker inform you of your assignment for tomorrow?"

"No, not yet, sir."

Strecker was the battalion commander. He had taken over that duty after relinquishing command of this company to me.

"Your radioman should receive orders before long. Strecker wished to ascertain that your report of no casualties was correct. Some of the field officers have acquired the habit of not reporting minor injuries."

"We had a few men cut by flying splinters. We were lucky today, sir. The men appreciate your concern."

"Good. Tell them I appreciate their efforts. Their reward will be to reach the Lovat tomorrow."

He stood up and began to tell them this personally, proceeding along the logworks again. He had a good enough eye for cover and Heit did not need to nurse him too closely. He informed them of tomorrow's operation and offered a few words of encouragement, but did not say much on the whole. The lack of enthusiasm visible on the men's faces brought no comment from him. Yet I saw that he looked all of them over very carefully. There were those who still wore the winter uniforms, emaciated heads rising disproportionately like sticks out of the thick padding. Most had discarded those things by now. A few were in their shirtsleeves even as night drew near. One man stumbled as he rose to attention and had to sit down. He did not try to rise again. Seydlitz studied them all with a strange intentness. He said a few words to Sergeant Heit and then returned to me. Meijer and a few others had brought up the soup containers and the men fell to eating, looking relieved to have something to occupy themselves. Relieved to be eating, above all.

I had said nothing when he mentioned the Lovat. I did not know what to think. Conflicting feelings swirled amongst fatigue, the dull acceptance of the daily assignments whatever they might be. Seydlitz told me that we and another company would be pulled out tomorrow and sent over that way. He made no suggestion as to whether this would be an easy or difficult task. He said a battalion from our sister regiment, the 56th, would strike for a place called Ramuschewo, a village on the banks of the river, somewhat to the north of where we were.

He said goodbye and turned to give a last study to the scene of today's action. A look of unmitigated disgust seemed to pass over his features. I was startled and looked away. I glanced at him out of the corner of my eye. He was staring at a puddle that lay at his feet. It was like a hole of the evening sky above. He did not leave for a few moments and I found myself waiting for him to go.

He started wading back along the sunken roadway. I should have sent two men to go with him but by the time I thought of this he was almost back to the corduroy. I was annoyed with myself but then put it out of my mind. It was sunset. The general stepped up onto the log-road like a stump reaching out of the water. The Kubelwagen disappeared, bumping slowly back through the trees.

• • •

The radio instructions were brief and the upshot was that I had to go back during the night to talk things over with Strecker in more detail.

By the afternoon of the following day we had crossed over several tributaries, only creeks to judge from their banks, but the water spread far beyond in either direction. We were making for the Lovat while Kurzich's company flanked us on the north side. Who stood to the south of us I did not know. The woods were very dense again. Endless willowy thickets, hardly trees. Three men were killed by a burst of fire that could have lasted no more than a few seconds. It must have come from very close range but we saw no one. We kept up a steady fire for at least ten minutes, using up a great deal of ammunition. After I gave the cease-fire we laid low for a while longer, reckoning with the terror of the close woods. Despair sucked at you like the uglier ally of exhaustion. We made radio contact with Kurzich's company but where they were in relation to us we could no longer ascertain. There was nothing for it but to keep going. Our head count then was twenty two men.

We had to leave the dead. We would have laid them out on dry ground but there was none nearby. We left them propped up in the little trees which bowed beneath their weight with a strange elasticity. It was an unpleasant sight. In one sense the woods appeared nearly impenetrable, but if you knew where to look you could spot things quite some distance away through the thin boles. So the dead men were visible for a while behind us. Only a few minutes maybe. We marched on. We kept on by compass heading. We had left the start lines before noon, informed that the river was only a few miles distant. That this final effort should be made by less than thirty men was somehow beyond my grasp. Day-to-day events had long taken on that kind of unreality; inwardly I would be shaking my head, but I hardly paid attention to myself anymore. We were no more than a well-armed patrol. I supposed that was not so far outside the normal scheme of operations. But Strecker had not made any mention of reconnoitering. We were to get to the Lovat and then stay there. What follow-up forces would come later had not been made clear. Probably the strike against Ramuschewo would be more of a concerted effort, but I didn't know any of the particulars of that.

We were there in the evening. The forest gave way to a wide plain dotted with only a few copses. It was actually less flooded than the woods. A low rise as even as the edge of a ruler stood up a short distance away, at the edge of the plain. Even before we got there, I knew.

It was a kind of alluvial aggregate where already the grass had begun to show. In other words, the bank of the river. The evening light was very clear. The river was a few hundred yards across.

The far bank was similar to this one but a little lower. You could see into the land beyond. A long edge of forest stood almost at the horizon. Before it lay a wide dull plain whose colors appeared more forceful in the twilight. Trees and what looked like a few items of junked equipment stood up here and there, spaced generously from each other so that the place had a kind of wide park-like aspect. There were a few dark isbas also rising solitary from each other. A few more isbas stood closer together on the bank of the river.

The radio operator was busy for a while. In the meantime we could see the fleets of transport planes continuing to sweep in some distance to the north of us. They flew at such low altitude that they seemed almost like a long train travelling along some invisible railroad embankment. Their reflections passed quickly over the water and then disappeared into the land beyond. The men stared at the planes as they always would do.

We could see people in the distance on our side. Through field glasses I saw they were ours, Kurzich's men no doubt. I sent a runner over there.

We received further instructions over the radio. I sent a flare up into the twilight. A green flare rose in response from the opposite bank. We followed its arc in the immensity of the sky. We sat down to wait. A boat appeared on the river, an open craft with oars pulling slowly over to us. It took them a little while. I looked around at my men. They looked out there, or sat staring at the ground. A man nearby sat with his head in his hands, his palms covering his eyes, weeping in silence.

I became aware of the smell of cigarette smoke. The air was clear. Low flocks of birds followed the passage of the transport planes. We sat around a clump of four or five trees. The bank was otherwise bare except for the grass, and a few men drying themselves in the sun out there.

No one got up until the boat was close to the shore. Then Heit and myself and a few others went down to the water's edge. We waited among dead reeds. The oars were raised and three of my men waded out, while several from the boat also jumped down into the water. They pulled it in among the reeds.

There were seven of them in all. I could see no insignia and did not know if their officer was junior or senior to me. Words were bandied about but they made a greater silence among us more noticeable. I remembered a strange thing suddenly, that when I was very young my father had often seemed like a stranger to me, even though he was friendly and I saw him every day. When he returned home from work at the end of the day, or especially when he returned from a journey of a week or so, I would feel a little embarrassed or unsettled by his presence. This was from when I was very young, and I had given no thought to this for many years. It was only that I was not as used to him as to my mother.

I remembered this for a moment, in the curious silence just before we started to speak to these men. Cigarettes were useful amenities in these situations. We offered each other smokes as if this were more heartfelt than conversation. More people began to speak, and the rest of my men came down from the top of the bank. The strangers were from an SS division. The rest of their people had established a corridor on the opposite bank leading back to the cauldron. Their commander identified himself by last name without giving any rank.

"Nierholz," I replied. "5th Jaeger Division."

We shook hands.

"Who are you?" I said.

"Totenkopf," he said.

"Totenkopf."

"It's good to see you," he said, smiling now.

We walked back up to the top of the riverbank. He stared here and there, absorbing new surroundings. He was blond and filthy. My people resembled his like the same group of men approaching themselves in a mirror. As for them being SS, I gave it a few moments' thought, as I had not come across any of these units in Russia before. We stood around talking lightly for a little while, then we returned to the business at hand. The radio operator was still kneeling by the receiver. I gave him the message and he sent it out. Someone laughed loudly nearby. I fell to talking again with Madrich, his name was. Other men began talking more loudly nearby, warming to each other, grinning a little.

"The hell with it, it looks about the same as over there," he said. He laughed quietly.

I agreed. Then I lowered myself slowly to the ground, resting my back against a tree, staring dully out at the still evening waters of the river. I stayed by the receiver waiting for the reply. Soon the transport planes were flying back across the river at the same low altitude as before, a long train of them drowning out all other noise for a minute, their shapes passing quickly along the surface of the water only a hundred feet beneath their bellies. There and then gone.

DEMYANSK

PART TWO—*Totenkopf*

Only in strange and deluded dreams did the lonely cauldron at Demyansk have anything to do with Moscow. Dreams are private. Thus, it is difficult to know by how many people they are shared. Yet it was almost certain that these dreams passed through the mind of only a single man.

Demyansk lay in the middle of an area called the Valdai Hills. Only in the endless sweep of the Russian steppe and forest would the small contrast of this region suggest the name of hills. The tallest of them might have stood a hundred feet high. The low wooded ridges were cut through by numerous small tributaries leading to the Lovat, each such tributary scarcely wider than a man-made ditch; yet they wound with a strange charm through these miniature valleys, giving a certain intimacy and smallness to the landscape. In other words it was different from the more typical Russian immensity and on occasion might have brought a certain peace of mind to the Landsers stationed there. Narrow, grassy meadows followed beside these tributaries, with the low hills rising on either side, and the divisional chaplains of the men trapped in the pocket often held open-air services in these places. These were held in the rear areas. The pocket at its widest was forty miles across.

It was indeed like an island in some respects. Many men were stationed here for over a year; and so it became a peculiar kind of place, almost like a small country geographically not far from its neighbors and yet completely isolated from them, with clearly established frontiers that changed little or not at all. There were more than a few who thought of the island in the sky. The transport planes roared in over their heads day and night, a daily drama in the sky that became both ordinary and never-ending and brought a strange yet not quite describable force of events to the backs of their minds, the curious and steady pumping of adrenalin that is charged by the constant close-by droning of piston-powered airplane engines, which pilots and other ground personnel throughout the world in the era before jet planes had long recognized as being not only a mere sound but one of the singular and underlying forces of their lives.

It had the loud yet almost soothing steadiness of a drama that went on in its single rhythm, rarely punctuated by any changes or disturbances. The Soviet air forces almost never attacked these long silver strings of JU-52s. Why this was so no one knew for sure. The presence of even a few German fighter planes would usually be enough to send any Soviet squadron scattering in flight, unwilling to engage in combat. Yet the Luftwaffe had spread itself thinly across Russia just like every other branch of the armed forces, and it was a rare spectacle to see two or three ME-109s in the skies over the cauldron. The JU-52s were almost defenseless, and surely the Russians could have wrought havoc among the air-trains if they had set their minds to do so. But this did not happen.

The relief flights into Demyansk between January of 42 and January of 43 were in fact the first great airbridge in history. The success of this airlift was, unfortunately, to have terrible consequences for the men trapped within another city later in that same year, far far to the south of the Valdai Hills, along the banks of the River Volga.

Immediately to the west of the pocket the hills diminished into the swampy woods and floodplains of the Lovat. There were in fact three major rivers in this area, all flowing parallel within a few a miles of each other, each emptying into Lake Ilmen a short distance north of Staraya Russa. The delta was a maze of waterways that was nearly incomprehensible, both on the map and on the ground. Even further upstream, away from the delta, the courses of the rivers often became entangled with each other; at some points it was nearly impossible to tell which was the Lovat, which was the Rudya, which was the Polist, or if they were not in fact different courses of a single river, or if in fact the whole idea of river or rivers might only apply a misleading terminology to this terrain.

These were the areas traversed by the 5th and 8th Jaegers under Seydlitz in the months of January, February, March, and April. As the Lovat was the stream that bordered the cauldron, it was this name they heard most often.

The first boats began the ferry service across the Lovat on the 21st of April. The first telephone cables were laid across the river.

Contact with the world beyond. The cauldron had now been officially relieved. The siege of Demyansk was lifted. The bridges which had been destroyed by the Russians back in January were hurriedly rebuilt, those fine wooden structures which were the pride and also the curse of the German pioneer battalions. (So many bridges in Russia, engineered with such fine workmanship; destroyed, rebuilt, destroyed, rebuilt, destroyed again. . . .)

Though the cauldron had been relieved, the soldiers still remained within it; there was no relief for them. The men of Seydlitz's corps, the survivors of it, were obliged to advance into the pocket itself. Beyond the floodplain the ground rose very gradually across bare country towards the wooded hills. It was like a long ramp raised only a few degrees above the level, a long bare ramp for the slow ascent of the living and the dead. The men of SS Totenkopf, along with the Landsers of the 290th Infantry Division, had established this corridor out from the pocket to the river. Its focal axis was a single road leading from Demyansk to the destroyed Lovat bridge.

The survivors among the Jaegers might have been interested or perturbed to recognize that this single road was in fact the corridor itself. At no place during those late April days was the corridor more than a mile wide, and in many places it was only a few hundred yards wide, and in many places the blasted remains of the Russian KV-Is and T-34s were parked right on the road itself. The lifeline on the ground was still little more than a thread, and it would remain thus for almost the entire year to come. The aerial lifeline continued to pass in those great fleets just overhead, no different now than back in the winter.

In effect, Demyansk was still very much a cauldron, and it would remain so. This catchword would remain on everyone's lips until the very end.

But a lifeline on the ground, no matter how tenuous, must bring some stirrings to men's spirits. This was inevitable. The jaegers advanced into the pocket through the forward areas that were junked, blasted, denuded of all vegetable life; and these sights caused some of the older men to think back upon the craters and dead ground at Verdun and the Somme, memories now thirty years old.

For the moment the scene was also peaceful, dead and peaceful. The first birds sang in the wrecked evening trees, they perched on the twisted metal remains of one vehicle or another. The Russians had also bled themselves to exhaustion. Such a state of affairs would not last long. It never did.

Many of the jaegers never reached the distant peace of the hills. Almost immediately they were set up along the corridor itself, right at the edges of the very road upon which they walked. To establish a strong defensive perimeter on either side of the relief corridor was of the utmost urgency. They set up next to the Totenkopf men, next to the 290th Division men, next to a few other units that were quickly sent out from the pocket.

•   •   •

As mentioned a little while ago, the lonely island at Demyansk had nothing to do with Moscow. Only a few people would ever think otherwise. In particular only one man would every really think otherwise.

Moscow . . . where the greatest battle in the history of the world had been underway since the beginning of October, and whose last exhausted pathetic frozen and anguished dregs were only now dying out in April of 1942.

It was in the nature of things in Russia that one ordeal would be followed by another. In some closely connected scheme, it was also in the nature of things that one ordeal would be overshadowed by another. Finally, it was in the nature of things for many ordeals to be overshadowed by many other ordeals. It was a great patchwork of lost and murdered souls.

It was perhaps only in Hitler's mind that the cauldron at Demyansk had any bearing upon events in front of Moscow, which lay over two hundred miles away to the southeast. The commanders in the field might properly have guessed that this epic trial of endurance at Demyansk would never have any effect on anything except Demyansk itself, and on the men trapped in there. To Hitler, however, the Valdai Hills must be held; this salient deep in Russian territory was to serve as a springboard for further operations against the capital.

General Seydlitz might have suggested to him, in whatever diplomatic language he could muster, that this whole idea was absurd. He had in fact visited personally with Hitler just a few days after the first link-up with the pocket had been made. He had flown back to Berlin and met with the Fuhrer in the Reichskanzellerei.

It was a short visit, whose main purpose had been the awarding of the Oak Leaves from Hitler's own hands, a follow-up decoration to the Knight's Cross that Hitler had bestowed upon Seydlitz back in December. Only a few days later Seydlitz was headed back to the pocket. He flew there, he and his aides aboard one of the old tri-motor JU-52s.

Thus he passed over the southern shores of Lake Ilmen, a body of water comparable in size to one of the smaller American great lakes. Up to this point he had never seen it before, though he had lived for almost half a year less than twenty miles from its shores. It was a storied place, like all the other large bodies of water in Russia. Within thousands of square miles of steppe and forest, the few large lakes would have that effect on men's imaginations. All the Landsers around Staraya Russa, Demyansk, the Lovat, anywhere in the Valdai Hills, would remember Lake Ilmen, though only a very small percentage of them would ever see it.

So he looked down there on the water that stretched on northward to only a dark blue horizon of water. He looked down on the ruined town of Staraya Russa. He looked down on the Lovat-Rudya-Polist delta and silently shook his head. It was a waterland. Wide belts of forest stood up in the water like scatterings of dead rushes. That was the world that had so recently been the world, the place of months where men grew older by years. Enough. He was a military man and if not for the futility of the whole business he would have kept his mind focus ed on the matters that still lay ahead. He did not see the breakthrough to the Demyansk pocket as yet another triumph of German arms and German endurance. Endurance . . . that above all, by God. But he did not see it that way, even though he perhaps better than anyone else knew that that was exactly what it had been. But he could no longer accept this face of things.

By this time there were a great many officers who had developed a strong distrust of their leader Adolph Hitler. This was so particularly among the highest ranking officers in the field, those in charge of armies and army groups. This situation had been in place since before the outbreak of war, and had its basis mostly in differences in social class and soldierly tradition. The most basic precepts of military common sense had also played their role, yet Hitler's amazing success in the Polish campaign, in Denmark and Norway, and above all in France had subdued many of his critics among the senior field commanders. They might even have felt themselves finally coming under his sway, imagining—as much of the German populace had already done for years—that they were being led by a man whose vision of things transcended the ordinary bounds of accountability, of reasonable chances for success or failure.

And success was everything. Or at least it had been up to now.

The first winter in Russia had begun to change all that. Feelings of distrust had changed into deeper and more terrible judgments. While the generals did not have to endure the daily ordeals of the common soldier, they had a much stronger understanding of a problem that was perhaps still more fundamental— which was that Hitler's grasp of the feasibility of military operations had entered into the realm of unreality. Such judgments began to cloud the minds of many of these officers. Some still held their criticism in abeyance, thinking that Hitler's past miracles might still lead to future miracles in ways that remained beyond their understanding. But the hope of this—if it was a hope—was dwindling for many.

General Seydlitz belonged to a smaller group of men who were linked by an even stronger bond. They not only distrusted Hitler, but actively loathed him.

As of yet there was no conspiracy. Many of these men were not acquainted with each other, or perhaps had become superficially acquainted during different assignments over the long course of their military careers. Many spoke to each other only in private, and even then might not have given vent to their deepest feelings. But if this bond was as yet unspoken, it still existed.

Seydlitz had always disliked Hitler. This in itself was of no importance, and did not distinguish him from hundreds of his fellow officers. This dislike took the form that can be seen at all levels of human existence, when two men meet each other and one or both finds that through sheer differences of personality he cannot stand the other. Seydlitz had felt this way since the early 30s.

His experiences over the last few months in the wilderness between Staraya Russa and the Lovat River had exacerbated this attitude. His recent meeting with Hitler had finally crystallized it into a permanent and almost tangible shape within his thoughts. He loathed the man.

The agonizing passage of months in the snowfields and in the Lovat swamps was now played out beneath him in a matter of minutes. The quaking galvanized steel frame of the old tri-motor crossed above the flooded woods, crossed over the river, and continued the additional twenty miles to the airstrip outside Demyansk, touching down on the bumpy Valdai plateau.

He had not been to this place before. Upon receiving Hitler's summons, he had flown directly out to Berlin from Staraya Russa. It was left to Generals Allmendinger and Hohne to make that first meeting with the overall commander of the pocket, who was General Graf von Brockdorff-Ahlefeldt. The two commanders of the 5th and 8th Jaegers deserved that honor.

Now it was Seydlitz who rode in a staff car from the Demyansk airfield to meet with Brockdorff-Ahlefeldt. The Graf was, in the English language, a count. The cauldron had thus acquired another nickname. Seydlitz found himself being chauffeured through the County of Demyansk. It was the Landsers who called it that.

•   •   •

Brockdorff-Ahlefeldt was an older man whose time in the cauldron had aged him still further. The normal wrinkles of age now hung in emaciated folds on his face. His eyes were sunken and distracted like the eyes of an old man who has not much further to go. On occasion his cheeks still bore a peculiar ruddiness. When combined with his overall look of failing health, this ruddiness leant him the aspect of a corpse recently pumped through with embalming fluid. Keeping him on display among the living, as it were, for a little while longer.

Of course he was not quite that far gone yet. The decay, while accelerated, would still take place gradually over the course of hours, days, weeks, and months. Nonetheless when Seydlitz first met him he was shocked by his appearance. They were in a command bunker that had been constructed within the ruined foundations of a school building in Demyansk.

Seydlitz was the "Savior of Demyansk." Brockdorff-Ahlefeldt was the "Hero of Demyansk." Thus were they identified in the popular press. The bunker had electricity from a generator but was still dimly lit. They sat at a small corner table in a kind of antechamber, removed from the larger map tables in the main room.

At the moment Brockdorff-Ahlefeldt had other things on his mind than the arrival of his colleague. He was not pleased by this. He had been looking forward to his meeting with Seydlitz. In fact he had been anticipating this meeting with feelings he could not quite articulate even to himself.

Yet he found himself overwrought by another meeting that had taken place only a few hours previously. He had relented under the badgerings of Theodor Eicke and granted him another interview to discuss the condition of the SS Totenkopf Division. He could have and no doubt should have refused this request. To prepare for his meeting with Seydlitz was reason enough; more than that, he did not need to give Eicke a reason.

But his will was eroding. Even more than the stress of being surrounded for months on end, of being responsible for the fate of 100,000 men, of coordinating a hundred shoe-string defensive actions to keep the Russians from over-running the pocket—even more than these things, the stress of these sickening conflicts of personality was eating away at him. Sickening. . . . Even just a few months ago he might not have used this word. But now he could think of no other. It was more than just his own poor health. It was an anger which was beginning to eat at him more piercingly than all the other more pressing daily crises. Anger at Eicke, anger as well at his own draining strength, his growing inability to cope with the unheard-of conduct of this bastard.

Words like this were also foreign to Brockdorff-Ahlefeldt. He was not of a fiery disposition. His family had been part of the German nobility for hundreds of years. He was basically a man who relied on his own calm inner resources, who took advice from his staff and did things as they had traditionally been done in the army. He was a gentleman, although this word was already too archaic to convey whatever it might have conveyed in the past. For that would suggest that Brockdorff-Ahlefeldt was a mere relic, which would not have done him justice. All in all, he was simply another man in Russia doing a terribly difficult job which had brought him up to and then beyond the limits of his own human resources. He shared this in common with thousands of other men. One day led to another and so he continued, as did they.

Unfortunately his personality was not well-suited to dealing with a man like Theodor Eicke. Under normal circumstances, he would not have had to deal with him. The chain of command would have obviated the need for this. Eicke was his subordinate, whose rank as a divisional commander entitled him to no more say in the conduct of operations than any of the other divisional commanders. Earlier in the campaign Brockdorff had felt a certain grudging—and sometimes quite sincere—admiration for Eicke, whose sometimes irritating drive and tenacity had often produced results. Brockdorff did not tend to feel jealousy or antagonism for anyone who produced results, especially in a campaign like this one. Sadly, all this had changed over the course of time. Eicke was a one-time Nazi party functionary who, unlike some of his colleagues, had turned himself into a courageous front-line soldier; he was a whining, meddlesome, hot-headed, personally courageous bastard who would have been shown the door months ago under almost any other circumstances.

That this had not happened caused Brockdorff-Ahlefeldt a gnawing distress. Rage was foreign to him and thus he was eaten up from the inside out. Rage was foreign to him and thus the rage that had nearly paralyzed him after seeing Eicke several hours earlier had left him feeling still more used up and worn away, no longer certain of anything, least of all himself. He had requested a few tablets from one of his aides. He spent the next few hours before Seydlitz's arrival sitting quietly in the bunker at that same corner table. He rested his head against the wall, staring calmly through half-lidded eyes at all the dim paraphernalia of command set up in their normal places around the dimly lit rooms of his headquarters.

• • •

Seydlitz said,

"You have heard of the incident with Sponeck?"

Brockdorff-Ahlefeldt regarded him. In only a few hours a kind of intimacy had developed between him and the other general, an intimacy which was in fact somewhat disquieting; yet which had also returned a few pulses of life to his sense of well-being.

"Yes. Back in December. Only rumors of course. We were a bit far removed from things even before the encirclement."

"It was a disgrace," said Seydlitz.

Brockdorff-Ahlefeldt nodded non-commitally. Inwardly he whole-heartedly agreed. Seydlitz had been speaking bluntly almost from the moment of his arrival. It would take the older general a while longer to work himself up to the conversational tenor of the other.

Seydlitz said,

"They were in immediate danger of encirclement. Sponeck had only a single division to defend a hundred miles of coastline. Then the Russians were at his back. A man who can take such prompt action in a crisis should have been promoted."

Brockdorff looked to one side to conceal a twitch in his left eye. He had more or less managed to put the morning's encounter with Eicke out of his mind. But inevitably certain things would still strike a nerve, which would in turn strike other nerves. He said,

"I hear he has been sentenced to death."

"Hitler had already drawn up orders for the firing squad. I would be reluctant to give myself credit for intervening. I simply happened to be there at the time. There were others in the high command who objected strenuously, and I do not use that word lightly. In any case the order was rescinded. Sponeck's sentence was commuted to life imprisonment. He is in Spandau now."

"I see," said Brockdorff. He considered for a moment. "Evil tidings give way to news only slightly better. The last I heard he was still sentenced to die."

"The order may be reinstated at the Fuhrer's pleasure. Leeb and Hoeppner were merely cashiered. I understand that

Guderian has been reassigned to a desk somewhere. Sponeck is the only one who is actually in prison. He was only a divisional commander, of course."

The two generals were speaking in private. The other members of Brockdorff's staff had been dismissed for the day. Telephone operators, messengers, and an officer-on-duty were still present elsewhere in the bunker, as well as various and sundry others whose presence was required around the clock in the nerve-center of the pocket. Brockdorff had intended to invite Seydlitz to his private quarters, yet somehow their conversation had swept along for hours and they remained in the small antechamber, the curtain drawn only partially closed. Brockdorff had left his personal aide-de-camp, Major Bruner, stationed just outside in the larger maproom.

The fate of General Sponeck had become a rubbing point, a very sore point, for half the senior commanders in the East. The other half either had said nothing or perhaps, in the onrush of terrible emergencies, had even commended the swiftness of the judgment.

Sponeck's division had been engaged, at least in a relative sense, in a sideshow. (Sponeck was actually a corps commander, but his only other division had been transferred to another battlefront.) While the Army Group Center was being torn into fragments in front of Moscow, the 11th Army far to the south was operating to clear out the last Russian resistance in the Crimea. With the exception of the great fortress of Sevastapol, which still lay in enemy hands, the operation had succeeded. By early December of 1941 the Crimean peninsula was German-held territory.

At the far eastern end of the Crimea stretched a narrow fifty-mile long finger of land. In effect it was another peninsula at the very end of the larger peninsula, where the important ports of Kerch and Feodosiya were located. Sponeck's 46th Infantry Division defended this area, which reasonably should have been occupied by at least a corps, and indeed had been just a few weeks previously.

By this time, however, every unit commander in Russia was fully aware that he must make do with whatever forces he had.

The Russians first made a sea landing at Kerch, the defense of which required almost all of Sponeck's manpower. They then made a second landing fifty miles to his rear at the base of the peninsula. There were almost no German forces here. The finger was only about ten miles wide and could have been blocked-off by the enemy in a matter of hours.

Sponeck foresaw the imminent destruction of his division. He acted on his own without permission of 11th Army headquarters or any other higher command. The lines of communication had been broken, and he acted without hesitation. The 46th Division fought its way back out of the so-called Kerch Peninsula, narrowly escaping encirclement, and established a new defensive line just within the Crimea proper. Not only had he saved his own men, but he had effectively bottled-up the Russian landing forces within the long finger.

Within a few days Sponeck had been relieved of his command, flown back to Germany, and sentenced to death.

The bliss of hindsight did not bode well for Sponeck's defense. It turned out that the Russian landing force at his rear was not as strong as first reports had indicated. Furthermore, the Russians had lived up to their typically inept standards of organization, which in essence meant that even an initially successful operation was rarely followed through to its conclusion. The Russian tactical command at critical junctures on the battlefield was frequently nonexistent, due to the field commanders' fear of reprisals for any kind of failure, for the slightest deviation from the orders rigidly sent down from above. Above all in any kind of land-sea operation, the quick initiative and flexibility of commanders in the field is of critical importance. Such practices did not exist in the Soviet armed forces. The result was that most of their landings from the sea were brilliantly conceived; immediately upon establishing a beachhead, they became exercises in chaos and inertia.

All of these facts would be starkly outlined under the normal glare of hindsight. As the war went on the Germans would learn to rely on these shortcomings of their enemy; it was perhaps the main circumstance which allowed an exhausted and completely outmanned German army to hold on in Russia for as long as it did.

But this was still 1941. Russian incompetence had already been witnessed in any number of places, but on the whole it was not yet part of the basic operational body of knowledge which every German commander would begin to utilize instinctively during the terrible shoe-string defensive actions of 1943 and 1944.

Thus Sponeck's retreat and prompt establishment of a more-easily defended line was viewed as an act of unnecessary rashness. In some quarters the word "panic" was deemed more appropriate.

Hitler himself almost immediately found a word that suited him still better. This word was "treason."

He had issued the "no-retreat" order early in December. The "not-one-step-back" order. The motive for this order had had nothing to do with the Crimea. Its driving force was the collapse looming before Moscow. In the face of disaster Army Group Center was not to retreat. Army Group Center was not to move one inch backwards.

Whether field commanders in other parts of Russia, even in a place as far removed as the Crimea, considered themselves also bound by this order is open to debate. Certainly every single one of them knew of its existence. General Sponeck could never have pleaded otherwise.

In other circumstances, in other armies, in other nations, Sponeck's action would inevitably have led to a certain division of opinion. Perhaps he did act rashly, was overhasty in his assessment of events. Or perhaps he acted with the cold decisiveness which is as rare among military men as among people in general. In the Soviet army, he most likely would have been shot out of hand. In the German army this was an unheard-of practice. Sponeck was the first of Hitler's field commanders to be sentenced to die.

As Seydlitz had mentioned to his fellow general a few moments earlier, other commanders had met with different fates. Faced with encirclement and annihilation before Moscow, Hoeppner had pulled back elements of his Fourth Army to form a cohesive defensive front. For this he was cashiered. Guderian had done the same thing with his Second Panzer Army on the southern wing of the Moscow front. He had even gone so far as to hide this fact by issuing misleading, if not downright false, reports of his movements to the High Command. Guderian was also cashiered. Guderian was perhaps the brightest star in the entire German armed forces. Thus his come-uppance might have pleased some people; jealousy is a part of the human condition. In any case he was gone too, at least for the time being.

Von Bock, in overall command of Army Group Center, had been allowed to resign for reasons of ill health. These were legitimate reasons, as he had been close to having a nervous breakdown. He had relayed Hitler's orders only to find commanders like Hoeppner and Guderian refusing them point-blank. They were stronger men than he was, and they expected a fellow senior officer to stand up to Hitler as they had done. Instead Von Bock did nothing, and he found that his nerves had reduced him to a state of near-paralysis. He found himself the object of criticism both from Hitler and from his subordinates. He was an unpopular commander, perhaps deservedly so. By the end of December he too was gone.

Von Leeb was also cashiered. His offense did not lie in the direct refusal of an order, but rather in his loud and persistent objections to the conduct of operations. As commander of the Army Group North he had responsibility for the Demyansk area of operations. In blunt language that someone like Seydlitz would have understood only too well, he had informed Hitler that to maintain the deep salient at Demyansk was to invite disaster. Furthermore, all the troops stationed around Demyansk would have been put to better use if sent to reinforce the decimated armies around Moscow. Leeb argued, indeed he demanded, that Demyansk be abandoned in favor of a much shorter defensive line in front of Staraya Russa. Hitler's idea that the Valdai Hills could be used as a springboard for further offensives was belied by certain facts, which Hitler chose to ignore. On the map these facts did not exist, and from beginning to end Hitler conducted the campaign in Russia almost solely by looking at the map. Thus he saw distances but not geography. Actual terrain did not exist. The extensive swamps and river deltas that separated Demyansk from all other German forces did not exist. The supply lines that were already stretched to their limit just to maintain the salient did not exist. On the map the already conquered areas were a fact, upon which the extreme tenuousness of supply arteries had no bearing whatsoever. To not only maintain Demyansk but to advance further into the wilderness beyond Demyansk was no more than a map-bound flight of fantasy.

Von Leeb had perhaps the most traditionally Prussian, old-style bearing of all the field marshals in Russia. Or at least he looked the part. There was not a trace of hair on his skull, which would gleam brightly under the intense ceiling lights of Hitler's map rooms. The monocle which he wore in his right eye seemed a natural part of his demeanor. His gaze would appear more direct than arrogant. The consternation visible on his face when Hitler discussed operations with him also had a strange directness to it, in contrast to the more well-concealed feelings of certain other generals. Von Leeb's demeanor was so unguarded that an onlooker might have thought it indicated shock or even disbelief.

He was not as volatile as Guderian, who had a peculiar talent for matching Hitler's violent tantrums with equally violent outbursts of his own. Guderian remained either in the wings or in active command until the end of the war. Von Leeb was merely blunt; it was the steady and unyielding directness of a basically level-headed man. This Demyansk business was far from his first disagreement with Hitler. It was to be his last. At the end of December he too was cashiered.

Thus he was gone even before Demyansk became surrounded in January.

General Seydlitz's orders to relieve the Demyansk cauldron had come not from the new commander of Army Group North, Von Kuchler, but from Hitler himself.

All of these cashiered or otherwise shelved officers had come from the highest levels of command—the leaders of armies or army groups. They did not face a death sentence. Sponeck was the exception. As a corps commander, he did not move in those circles. The boldness of his action was quite poorly received.

It also happened that his action stood out like a sore thumb. The Crimean Peninsula, and by extension the Kerch Peninsula, jutted not unlike a sore thumb into the Black Sea; the territory Sponeck had lost there stood out with an unnerving clarity on the map, not obscured by the vastness of the land across mainland Russia. Hitler was in the habit of gazing at the map for hours on end. The distinct outlines of this one blight would not fail to catch his attention. And so Sponeck remained in prison, to wait and ponder on his fate.

•　　•　　•

Word will get around. The remotest command posts in Russia, down even to battalion or company level, would have heard at least some rumor of this Sponeck business.

Seydlitz would have been outraged in any case for purely professional reasons; but his sense of the incident was augmented by his having watched the proceedings from close at hand. He had not actually seen Sponeck, nor on this occasion had he been granted an audience with Hitler. His objections were no less vocal for all that, even if they had to be conveyed through Hitler's staff generals and other assorted go-betweens. In fact it was only coincidence that he had been in Berlin at all, called there to receive the Knight's Cross, the prelude to the Oak Leaves he would receive during his second visit in April. Hitler had been present during both these awards ceremonies, had in fact laid the black ribbon around Seydlitz's neck in both instances. But the first time was a week before he heard any word about Sponeck's troubles. During the second visit, from which he had just flown back to Demyansk, he had other matters on his mind.

These other matters were of more immediate concern not only to him but to Brockdorff-Ahlefeldt. It was by now past midnight in the schoolhouse bunker. Brockdorff was fatigued, drained as he always was by late evening. Out of necessity he had stayed awake through many late night meetings, dealing with one emergency or another in the pocket. But this conversation with Seydlitz was another matter. Seydlitz seemed able to read the exhaustion in the older man's face, but perhaps against his better judgment Brockdorff gave no signal that he wished to retire.

Seydlitz said,

"Even when I saw him just a few days ago, I still wanted to say something about Sponeck. But it is difficult enough to bring a single matter to that man's attention, let alone two. I had promised Hohne and Allmendinger that I would speak to Hitler on behalf of their troops. When my corps finally broke through to the Lovat we had a total remaining strength of perhaps two battalions. By now you've no doubt seen some of these men yourself. They deserve a rest. To say as much is an understatement. More than that they absolutely require a rest if their fighting strength is not to evaporate completely. Hear me out a moment longer, General. I believe I can read your thoughts."

Brockdorff's eyes had turned brighter, narrower, as if pricked out of some deeply meditative state. His lips parted, but then he merely nodded silently at Seydlitz.

Seydlitz said,

"Men, men. It's all nothing but men, by God. Forgive me. We are as guilty as he is, in some ways. I have been bedeviled by many strange thoughts of late, Brockdorff."

"Go on," said Brockdorff.

"I tried to describe to him the condition of the soldiers. I am not a foolish optimist. But I thought in light of all they had just accomplished, he might at least turn a sympathetic ear. The bastard was a Landser once himself, by God. Yet to talk to the man you might think he had walled himself up inside a monastery for the last hundred years. He gave out not a single word of human understanding. He didn't even make a pretense of it. You can't be sure if he is even listening to you.

"I suppose I shouldn't have been surprised. In fact I wasn't. But I keep thinking about it now, Brockdorff. Strange thoughts, I tell you. As I said."

Indeed, pictures of Hitler formed and grew clear in Seydlitz's mind even as he spoke. These pictures were from only three days earlier. He saw again the single massive desk at the corner of the over-sized yet sparsely furnished reception room. . . . The light of a late April evening falling in semi-opaqueness through the tall curtains to one side, as tall as three men. . . . The quiet polish of the floor into which Hitler would stare abstractedly. The awards ceremony had been concluded, and it was only the two of them in the room then like two small visitors who had remained after-hours in a wing of some vast and silent museum. It was the first and last time Seydlitz would ever be alone with Hitler.

Hitler was polite, as he generally was. His terrible outbursts of temper demanded a good deal of his strength, and he reserved these almost exclusively for the more obdurate generals in the high command, and for the even more obdurate senior field commanders like Guderian and Von Leeb. Seydlitz was merely the commander of a corps who had been summoned to receive a medal. Hitler was, in fact, entirely unaware of Seydlitz's highly vocal opinions about Sponeck from several months before, for the simple reason that his staff had not seen fit to convey them.

Now he listened to Seydlitz's entreaties with that peculiar abstracted look, that look of deep, unknown preoccupations hiding behind a mask of civility and even vacantness. At first, Seydlitz had taken the fact that he had even consented to speak to him at all as a good sign. When he was dismissed a few minutes later he was not sure if the man had even been aware of his presence. No, he didn't know what to think. Being with Hitler, at least in one of his quieter moods, was like entering into a trance, into a kind of murky seance that linked both the ordinary and the inscrutable. For some people, the effect of this was charismatic. For others, it was bewildering. For others, it was merely numbing.

Seydlitz had left the Reichskanzellerei in such a numbed state, feeling almost that Hitler had imparted some of that same vacantness to him. The feeling did not last long. Almost immediately upon stepping out into the open air he felt as if he had been struck, so violent was the feeling of disgust that welled up in him. He thought of the scarecrows wandering through the swamps of the Lovat, disembodied souls, all of it.

Seydlitz said,

"Forgive me for all this. I'm sure we could both use some rest. But you were about to say something."

"Yes," said Brockdorff.

He remained silent for a moment, staring into Seydlitz's eyes, then looking past the partially drawn curtain into the large dim maproom where Major Bruner sat asleep in a chair. Brockdorff thought of just letting it pass. He was very tired. There would be a lot of business to take care of in the morning, what with the disposition of new troops in the pocket, what with the inevitable Russian counterattack that would come soon.

Seydlitz's entreaties on behalf of his men, on behalf of Hohne's and Allmendinger's dead-eyed and exhausted men, had struck a spark in Brockdorff. At first it was a mean and ugly spark. His sudden start forward beside the little table had been an involuntary sign of antipathy as much as interest. Yet he knew instantly that this antipathy was misguided, and the strange and somewhat unsettling bond that was developing between him and Seydlitz remained unbroken.

Brockdorff said,

"I can understand your concern. General Allmendinger in particular is very disturbed about the condition of his men. You are right, Seydlitz. They deserve rest. And they deserve congratulations for what they have achieved. But rest above all. Yes."

This expression of sympathy was belied by another shard-like gleam of bitterness in Brockdorff's eyes. He said,

"My troops in the pocket also need rest. How we managed to hold out for this long is sometimes beyond my understanding. Particularly back in the winter there seemed very little hope. Whole units were wiped out to the last man. Why you and I are sitting here now instead of the Russians . . . I don't know. Perhaps only the Russians can answer that.

"Of course it appears to be the same everywhere. No relief for anyone, no rest for anyone. The whole German army is no more than a few grains of sand scattered on a beach, waiting for the tide to come in. One moment, Seydlitz."

Brockdorff called gently into the other room. Major Bruner opened his eyes, stared blankly at the opposite wall, then looked through the curtain at the general. Bruner disappeared and then came back a few minutes later with a small decanter of brandy and two tumblers.

"I do not make a habit of this," said Brockdorff. "I already live in luxury, compared with the men out there. So be it. I must tell you that I had a particularly unpleasant conversation this morning, shortly before you arrived. The things you are saying have had the unfortunate effect of bringing it back to my mind. Prosit."

Seydlitz raised his glass and sipped quietly. Brockdorff took a short gulp, then quickly set the tumbler down, as his hand had commenced to tremble. He consumed this spasm of energy by raising his fingers to his lips to wipe away a few beads of alcohol there.

He said,

"I saw Eicke this morning. He is a very persistent fellow. Have you met him?"

Seydlitz started to reply but Brockdorff waved his hand.

"Yes, yes, of course you have. His men were attached to your command back in December. It slipped my mind. So you have an idea of the kind of man he is. He too has shown a very persistent concern for the state of his troops. In fact he wants the Totenkopf Division to be relieved immediately. There is nothing left of them but scarecrows . . . all of that . . . the usual thing."

Seydlitz's eyes narrowed. On a personal level, he had about as much use for Eicke as for Hitler. But Eicke at least knew what conditions were like in Russia. And his men fought well.

"Yes, that's the thing," said Brockdorff. "All of my other divisional commanders have expressed similar concerns, especially now that the pocket has been relieved."

"The relief corridor is no more than an illusion," Seydlitz broke in stonily.

Brockdorff stared at him. The lingering ruddiness in his cheeks flushed brighter.

"Yes. Yes, Seydlitz, that is so. I can do nothing but refuse their pleas for relief. The decision is not in my hands anyway. The divisional commanders are forced to accept this, as they have accepted it for many months. Now your men—Allmendinger's men especially—arrive in the pocket and he too wants relief."

"Allmendinger is a good man," said Seydlitz.

"Yes, he is. That is my impression too. You know it is only normal for field commanders to lodge these kinds of protests from time to time. They see the condition of their men and wonder what is to become of them, what is to become of all of us.

"But the situation is still very tenuous here. If not desperate. They accept what I tell them and carry on. It is the only thing we can do. Eicke, however. . . ."

Brockdorff lifted his fist in some inscrutable gesture. He stared at the wall and placed his fingers on a candleholder in a niche there. As if to straighten something. He lowered his hand to the table, brushing the half-full brandy tumbler to one side.

"Eicke will not take no for an answer. It is more than just his persistence. His manners border on. . . . I don't know what. It is more than just unmilitary."

Seydlitz said, "He is in the habit of requesting special favors. I remember that from last year. The SS people seem to have a problem with that kind of thing."

"It depends," muttered Brockdorff, as if suddenly trying to view things more positively, if only to restrain himself. "Some of them are quite reliable. Even Eicke could be counted on in an emergency. He is nothing but a boor, but you get used to dealing with all types under your command. In the winter his men fought as hard as anyone in the cauldron. In fact we might not have made it through without them. Even I had to admit this.

"But the bastard is always full of himself, and now he is full of all they have accomplished and all they have suffered. As if the other units in the pocket were merely sleeping in their beds all winter long. That's the kind of insult he can fling about. Yes, now you catch my drift. It seems he has been harboring this resentment for quite some time. This morning he brought me a list of battalions, companies, even platoons, that were wiped out to the last man—in strict obedience to my orders, as he said—trying to hold onto some village or other during the winter."

"I see," said Seydlitz. "A pity. And so now he is demanding that Totenkopf be withdrawn. My deepest sympathies for him and his men."

His remark was as dry as the atmosphere on a deserted planet. The irony of the situation lingered in his thoughts for no more than a few seconds. Less than three days earlier he had been making the same pleas on behalf of his own men in Hitler's very presence. Yet, as Brockdorff had just said, he was beginning to catch the drift of this business with Eicke.

Brockdorff continued, and as he filled in the details Seydlitz found himself thinking he could have foreseen every one of them; yet he listened no less intently for all that.

During his recent trip to Berlin he had seen the headlines praising the valor of Theodor Eicke and SS Totenkopf, their last-ditch resistance month after month along the frozen perimeters of Demyansk. The same kind of talk could be heard in the corridors of the high command, it could be heard among Hitler's coterie, it could be heard from any number of mouths.

The relief efforts of his own corps, of the 5th and 8th Jaegers, had merited a few paragraphs in the news and a brief mention in the Wehrmacht communique. Seydlitz was beyond this kind of jealousy anyway, at least so far as it appeared in the news media.

But Brockdorff was describing a situation that was more real and more immediate. He was describing what amounted to a series of savage insults. Eicke had accused him of bleeding his men to death, of assigning his men the most difficult and senseless tasks while neighboring army units had cowered in their bunkers in varying fits of weakness and incompetence.

In Brockdorff's view every unit in the cauldron had narrowly managed to survive the most terrible of ordeals. The casualties of the Totenkopf men would only compare with the casualties of every other division. Some of the army units had in fact suffered even worse.

SS general or not, Eicke was still subordinate to him, though often enough Eicke conducted himself as if he had not the slightest inkling of this. It was one thing for a subordinate to lose his temper during the long stress of difficult, even nearly impossible, operations. Like almost any field commander, Brockdorff had dealt with such situations in the past. Sometimes a stern dressing-down would resolve the issue. Sometimes even a sympathetic ear. It depended. It depended on the situation, it depended on the man.

His run-ins with Eicke had been regular occurrences over these past months. Perhaps Eicke had been mollified, at least on the surface, by Brockdorff's praise for the tenacity of his men, which he had stated quite calmly and sincerely. But the argument of this morning—less an argument than a kind of depraved tirade—had gone far beyond the bounds of all that. With any other subordinate, Brockdorff would have relieved him of his command at that moment.

A normal chain of command could not function under such an ongoing barrage of intolerable and unjustified insults. Yet Brockdorff had suddenly felt powerless, a sensation which only aggravated the daily ebbing of his personal strength. He was not in a position where he could relieve Theodor Eicke of his command.

"The man is a blowhard," said Seydlitz. "He has a capacity for wasting a lot of talk. He must understand that the decision to withdraw Totenkopf is not in your hands anyway."

Brockdorff had been talking for quite some time; now as the other general replied he found himself staring into space, as if through the underground walls of the command bunker, as if through the rubble of the ruined schoolhouse, as if through the distant clouds that might pass through the night sky beyond the limits of the cauldron. The distant droning of a plane penetrated his thoughts. He blinked, found himself staring into Seydlitz's eyes.

He said, "Yes, he knows that very well. He is a beef-cheeked National Socialist revolutionary swine who has a great deal of energy. I am only one channel for his complaints. From what I understand, he has also sent personal messages directly to Himmler demanding that Totenkopf be relieved."

"Remarkable," said Seydlitz. "May I ask how you found out about such goings-on?"

Brockdorff shook his head dully. The cycle of fatigue had returned with finality, at least for one evening. He looked like a near-ruined man; it was the same look that Seydlitz had been so struck by many hours before.

"Local politics. The County of Demyansk. The Landsers call it that, you know. My little fiefdom. Hm. We must rest, Seydlitz. There is more, a great deal more. We will be very busy here quite soon. The Russians will see to that. But perhaps we will have the opportunity to speak again. I welcome your arrival here."

Brockdorff meant this with all sincerity, yet as soon as the words had left his mouth a feeling of anxiety opened in his stomach. This conversation with Seydlitz was very strange, and what it might lead to he did not know. To hell with it. He was dead tired, almost too tired to stand.

In spite of this he forced himself to rise now, pressing his palms down flat on the little table. Seydlitz rose also. There were small private sleeping areas in the bunker, but more and more Brockdorff found that he could not get any rest here. The house that was his actual residence stood only a few hundred feet away across the street. He thought a few moments in the night air might help a little. Like many people tormented by stress and fatigue, he found that fatigue did not lead to a decent sleep but rather to the lack of it.

The two generals left Major Bruner in the maproom, passing through the nerve center and leaving via a heavily sandbagged and timbered corridor that resembled the entrance to a mine. Generator-powered bulbs fluttered dimly. The corridor was short and almost level, a ramp ascending at only a slight angle before it came to a flight of stone steps that had been part of the original cellar foundation of the schoolhouse. The two men stepped up into the night air. A sentry saluted stiffly and Brockdorff placed his hand on his shoulder without speaking.

The street was empty. A very few lantern lights shone dimly behind curtained windows in a few buildings. The smallness of these illuminations seemed little more than moonlight caught in the windows. The immense Russian night lay overhead. The stars still hung there with the relentless intensity of the winter sky, but the temperature had grown milder and it was possible to study the heavens without being distracted by the bitterness of the cold. The two men did this for the few seconds it took to reach Brockdorff's residence.

Von Brockdorff-Ahlefeldt was a Graf, a count of centuries' lineage. Seydlitz's full name was the Graf Von Seydlitz-Kurzbach, though for reasons lost even to himself he was generally referred to only by his first name. He also was a German count. Two men might be as different as night and day, yet the noble houses of the past would still link them in ways that barely required comment or even reflection. For it was all a matter of something that was lost in the past. Almost all the noblemen serving in the German army accepted this, and indeed had accepted it for so long that it scarcely, if ever, entered their thoughts any more. The meaning of all Europe's noble houses had been wiped out in the first great war; whatever this second and still more terrible war was about, it had nothing to do with that. That . . . whatever that was. For something of that unspoken bond still existed, no matter how vague, archaic, unremarked-upon; even at times, if you will, faintly embarrassing. There were noblemen at high levels of command and also those who served in battalions and companies. (Though nearly all of them were commissioned officers.) There were a few overbearing exceptions, arrogant and superficial types who still seemed too aware of their older status; yet almost all of those who bore noble titles conducted themselves no differently from any other grain of sand scattered across the endless ocean of Russia. The past was the past; and the present was beyond all of them, just as it was beyond any Landser freezing in a trench or buried in the earth.

What of it then. . . .

Except that there was still something, even if it was beneath them to remark upon it to each other in the most private of conversations. What of it then? They could no longer say. Sponeck's title was the Graf von Sponeck; he who lay sentenced, helpless, and ordinary in a military prison outside of Berlin. Perhaps it was all lost to him at this moment, if he lay deep in sleep in his cell; or perhaps he too was disturbed by sleepless nights, no different from Brockdorff-Ahlefeldt in the town of Demyansk a thousand miles to the east.

Brockdorff's orderly arose from sleep as the generals entered the small house. Brockdorff told the man to see to any of Seydlitz's needs. The house was dark, lacking electricity, lit only by a few candles. A few minutes later the older general lay in a bed in a small room with boarded windows, staring into the darkness above his face.

DEMYANSK

●　　●　　●

The operational meeting took place back in the schoolhouse bunker at eleven o'clock next morning. SS General Eicke was not there, even though this meeting was more important than usual. Clearly his absence had to do with the ugly squabble of the day before. Eicke was the kind of man who could engage in a screaming argument one day and act the next day as if nothing whatsoever had occurred. This was not so much because he had the decency to restrain himself—though he could do this too, if he felt like it. But the main reason for these abrupt and surprisingly fluid changes in his temperament was that loud and occasionally screaming tirades were second nature to him; thus he did not lose much sleep over them, and as often as not on the following day he would look if anything somewhat invigorated, or at least momentarily relaxed. He was not nearly as unnerved by his own behavior as were the others who had to deal with him. Perhaps this is stating the obvious.

So one might have expected him to put in an appearance at this meeting, looking, as he often did, more in command of himself than anyone else present. But he wasn't there.

This could have been taken as another sign that it was high time for him to be relieved of his command. The normal military terminology of "gross insubordination" would have been suitable here. Especially in light of the other incidents already related by Brockdorff-Ahlefeldt. Seydlitz found himself thinking about this during the minutes before the meeting began. The atmosphere in the bunker could hardly be called awkward, as no one had seen fit to say anything about Eicke's absence. In his place stood one of his regimental commanders, Max Simon, who also doubled as Eicke's executive officer. Simon had presented himself as if nothing out of the ordinary was in the air.

Seydlitz found himself wondering what he would have done in Brockdorff's place. For an army officer to relieve an SS general of his command would no doubt have far-reaching political ramifications; though it would be hard to say just what these would be, as nothing of the kind had ever happened before. Nor was it very likely to happen in the future. Nor, for that matter, was it very likely to happen at this very moment. Not very likely, no. . . .

Perhaps the army officer would find himself relieved of his own command. It was a situation that was more complicated than the mere refusal of one of Hitler's orders. One could now see very clearly through something like that, one could see the prison cell or the blood-stained wall that lay at the end of it. No, this was more complicated, and in its way more intriguing.

Seydlitz possessed a sharp mind, a mind that did not tend to get lost in the tangled corridors of its own thinking. And so he found that his mind had suddenly gone blank.

Intriguing, maybe. But to relieve the commander in the field of one of the SS divisions. . . . It was complicated only in a sense, while in another sense it was clear as glass, as clear as the blankness that was suddenly in his own head. Because there was no point in even considering it.

Seydlitz felt disturbed, disturbed to be wondering what he would have done in Brockdorff's place. To be wondering what a man with better nerves and a stronger will would have done in Brockdorff's place. Because there was still no answer for it.

He felt a dull heat rising in his armpits that was perhaps a momentary fit of shame. Brockdorff was by now hardly more than a shell, a good and hollowed man; yet, rather than this being the key to the problem, Seydlitz saw that it really had no bearing on it whatsoever.

So he gave no more thought to what he would have done in the other general's place. The blankness in his mind was a clear blankness and when the brief prickle of shame ebbed away he set his attention on the details visible on the large map spread out before them all. The map of Demyansk and its environs. The map of the cauldron. Beside him stood Max Simon, who continued to appear oblivious to any unpleasantness in the situation. Seydlitz glanced at him as he might glance at a lizard. Yet he made no move to step away from the Totenkopf executive officer, nor did he feel any impulse to do so. The meeting began.

Along with Simon and Seydlitz were the commanders of the other divisions in the cauldron, some of them accompanied by their operations officers, others alone. The jaeger generals Hohne and Allmendinger were there. Seydlitz had already greeted them

and told them of his conversation with Hitler. They had responded with disappointment and a calm bitter lack of any surprise. Of
his long conversation with Brockdorff the previous night, he had
said nothing.

The large table map around which they stood showed that
Demyansk was no longer an island surrounded by enemy
strength. It was now a peninsula with a large head and a very narrow neck. This neck might more aptly have been called a thread,
from which the head could be easily severed; from which, to
judge from the map, the head might just topple off of its own
accord.

The thread. The neck. The relief corridor. In position to defend
this passage were the 5th and 8th Jaegers, the 290th Infantry
Division, and the SS Totenkopf Division. Brockdorff-Ahlefeldt
was of the opinion that still more units were needed to defend this
area, which must be transferred in from other areas around the
cauldron perimeter, or else brought in through the relief corridor
from outside. There was no demurral among those present. It was
clear to everyone that the Russians would soon counterattack
along the corridor with all their strength.

Seydlitz had no criticism of these troop dispositions. Under
the circumstances it was the only thing to be done. Except, of
course, for the one obvious thing, which was to abandon the cauldron altogether. The futility of it all weighed down upon him, no
less than it had done in the JU-52 crossing over Lake Ilmen and
the Lovat swamps.

To bleed men to the bone over some worthwhile objective . . .
that was bad enough. But at least the objective could achieve solid
form in a commander's mind, shutting off other considerations.
That was the way it had to be. Yet this idea of objectives, of the
goal, of the task, suddenly became loathesome to him in a way
which he had not felt before in his career. To consider whether an
objective was worthwhile or clearly useless . . . the whole notion
suddenly filled him with disgust.

Nothing could be more useless than holding on to Demyansk.
The cauldron, the salient, whatever you wanted to call it, was
pointed at nothing except the uttermost ends of Siberia. By correlation, nothing could be more useless than to bring in still more
troops to reinforce the cauldron. By correlation, nothing could
have been more useless than the nightmarish months of struggle

by his own corps to relieve the cauldron in the first place. Relieve the cauldron. It was a joke. If not for the endless fleets of supply planes still landing at the airfield at this very moment, Demyansk might as well be written off, a lost cause no different than it had been back in January.

If all these opinions were the specific focus of Seydlitz's disgust, it had suddenly assumed a much larger and more incoherent form. He shut his eyes and a red wall suddenly slid up behind them at the forefront of his skull. He stepped backward a step, then stepped up to the table again. It was too much. The worthlessness of it all was too much. The self-righteousness and self-importance of his own criticism was too much. It was all too much. Dutifully he listened to the dispositions set out for the 5th and 8th Jaegers, whose commander he still remained; offering suggestions to Brockdorff-Ahlefeldt, calmly eliciting the opinions of Hohne and Allmendinger and anyone else who had anything to say.

Max Simon also maintained a calm demeanor, which perhaps was not feigned. He conveyed no instructions, demands, requests or other messages from his chief Eicke. He voiced no criticism of Toptenkopf's assignment to continue holding on in the most dangerous sector of the line. When Brockdorff-Ahlefeldt declared that a further widening of the relief corridor would be necessary to prevent it from collapsing—in other words, a further series of desperate attacks—Simon said nothing. His few comments suggested assent rather than stone-faced acceptance of these orders. This might have surprised some of those present, who knew that Simon could at times be as vocal as Eicke himself.

The men around the map table might have presented the same faces they always did—their customary demeanors, their selves—or they might have presented expressions that were somewhat different from their usual appearance. To describe any such subtle changes as being out of character would be too strong. For the moment, the map dictated everything, and the map brought a certain consensus to those within the bunker. How long this consensus would last, no one or anyone might judge. For the moment, it was clear that the energies and personal feelings of everyone must be subordinate to the task of keeping the Russians from severing the relief corridor. Aerial reconnaissance had already revealed the massive enemy buildup on either side of it. And for once, aerial reconnaissance might have been considered almost superfluous. The map showed the relief corridor stretched out like the neck of a chicken waiting for the ax.

This image was grimly apparent to everyone in the room. Brockdorff-Ahlefeldt was also struck by its resemblance to something else.

It was he who had opened the meeting, bringing the larger matters to everyone's attention; at a certain point he had then allowed his chief of staff, Colonel Felsner, to take over the arrangement of more specific problems. This was fairly routine not only in Brockdorff's command but in the army as a whole. He then presided quietly, answering only questions that he alone could be responsible for.

That this arrangement also provided him with a few minutes to rest his mind might have been apparent to more than a few men there. Brockdorff had stood up to his burdens as well as he could for a long time, but his physical—and no doubt his mental—condition could no longer easily be disguised. So be it, he thought. He did not fret over any judgments or reservations in the minds of the men around him, almost all of whom had conducted themselves up to now with direct and simple loyalty; with the exception of Eicke and Simon, he had not doubt that this would continue to be so. Even the latter two men, despite the bickering they tended to carry around with them, were basically trustworthy. While Colonel Felsner was outlining the logistical, tactical, and other problems inherent in shuffling the defending units around the cauldron, Brockdorff stepped back for a moment, accepting a cigarette from his aide Major Bruner. He turned and glanced at the large wall map hanging behind him. It was the map of the entire Soviet Union. The town of Demyansk did not exist on this map; it had been written in with grease pencil, some fifty miles east of such better known places as Staraya Russa and Lake Ilmen. Almost halfway between such better known places as Leningrad and Moscow. In the mind of a grand strategist this might have given Demyansk the aspect of a hinge or linchpin—a place of critical importance. But the folly of this notion has been discussed elsewhere.

Not for the first time, Brockdorff was struck by the immensity of Russia. The German line stretched for three thousand miles, from the Arctic Ocean to the Crimea. The Crimea, where palm trees grew in the old czarist spas of Yalta and Feodosiya. It was the longest continuously fought-over line of battle in the history of the world, dwarfing the trench networks across France and Belgium where Brockdorff had fought in the first war. The terrible grandeur of this situation was by now also familiar and banal, if not rather depressing. The more striking fact was that the great sweep of the German armies across Russia still covered no more than a fraction of the landmass as a whole, an area that on the wall map appeared no more than a sliver. A beach . . . a few scatterings of sand. To those stationed there, Demyansk often seemed like some remote outpost in Siberia. Yet Siberia still lay beyond the Ural Mountains, and Siberia itself stretched for four thousand miles to the edge of the Pacific. All of it. . . . Russia. Russia. Russia.

In 1941 Hitler had declared that the Soviet Union was a house of cards that would topple at the first blow. Even while still flushed with the great victory in France, few generals had placed much faith in this prognosis, though they all might have hoped that they were wrong and Hitler was right. He was the Fuhrer and he had been right before; he had been right so many times that it was unnerving to the generals, no less so than to the other nations of the world.

But now it was a year later, and Russia still remained. Not only the great goals of Leningrad and Moscow, but the trackless wilderness of ninety percent of the rest of the country still remained.

To see this situation so clearly visible on the map would give Brockdorff pause for thought every time he studied it, even though this too was now shrouded with the banality of long-familiar facts. An onlooker at the moment might have guessed him to be studying that three thousand mile battle-line, perhaps pondering the place of Demyansk in the overall scheme of things.

In fact he was looking at something else, checking something that had struck him while looking at the large situational map of the cauldron spread out on the table. Yes, he thought, the comparison was quite apt. Poor Sponeck, he thought.

Brockdorff was a hero in the newsreels only because he was the commander of the men trapped in the cauldron. The decorations he wore were symbolic of his command and the performance of his men; they had not been awarded for personal bravery of the highest order, as had been the case with Sponeck, who had been awarded the Knight's Cross for courage under fire in the French campaign.

But Brockdorff wasn't really thinking about decorations either. He was not thinking about medals, but rather about the shape of Sponeck's terrain—the lost terrain that had cost him his command.

Yes, he thought, an interesting similarity. Demyansk was no longer an island but a peninsula, albeit a peninsula surrounded by a sea of land, by a sea of countless thousands of Russian infantrymen, tanks, and artillery.

The Kerch Peninsula at the end of the Crimea was surrounded by water, by the Black Sea and the Sea of Azov. Yet the shapes of these two far-removed peninsulas were now quite similar. Especially since the relief corridor had been established across the Lovat. A corridor no more than a mile or two wide at its widest point, a chicken neck even scrawnier than the narrow neck of land where Sponeck had made his valiant or impulsive, clear-headed or foolish retreat back in December.

Given these comparisons, Brockdorff might have come to some conclusions, ominous or otherwise, about certain possibilities regarding his own eventual fate. But in fact he did not conclude anything. The shapes of two small patches of terrain—one circumscribed by the sea, the other by the grease-penciled lines of the siege-perimeter—caught his attention only for a moment. He did not wish to pursue these thoughts further, not now in the middle of the operational meeting, nor later in his own privacy. For one thing, he was not terribly concerned about his personal fate any longer. To glance at the distinct outlines of Kerch and Demyansk on the wall map had consumed only a few seconds.

An apt comparison.

What of it?

Nothing.

He extinguished his cigarette, from which he had taken only two puffs, and stepped back to the cauldron map on the table. When Colonel Felsner finished talking the other generals said what they had to say, and then Brockdorff spoke again for a while. He tried to keep his concentration from wandering and was perhaps successful. The Russians were useful insofar as they tended to keep everyone's concentration from wandering very far, no matter how worn out a man might be by countless situational meetings not so very different from this one.

In the back of his mind Brockdorff was waiting for all of them to leave, to drive back to their various divisional headquarters at their various perimeter points around the wasteland. Presently they did so. Seydlitz and Simon, Hohne and Allmendinger, the rest of them. Brockdorff remained alone in the bunker except for his command staff. In effect, alone.

Brockdorff retired to the curtained antechamber where he had stayed late with Seydlitz the night before. He told Major Bruner that he required nothing, and then he sat there with his head resting against the wall and thought of nothing for a while. Thoughts of nothing included Eicke and Max Simon, they included Seydlitz and Sponeck, they included Hitler and Himmler, they included the present moment and the unbearable winter just barely past. They included the different shapes of land and they included the shapes of dead men lying in mud and snow and they included the shapes of the faces of the men who were with him day by day and the shapes of intimate facts that he had come to know about their lives. He saw all of this fleeting and undisturbing within the wider shapelessness of nothing at all, the blank space of the half hour's rest he now allowed himself here.

● ● ●

Theodor Eicke might not have been overly perturbed to hear himself characterized as a beef-cheeked National Socialist revolutionary swine. No doubt the tone of such a remark would have provoked him a bit. But the gist of it would have brought no argument from him.

He was a revolutionary and would have excused all his actions as the actions of a revolutionary, except as the years went on he no longer found it necessary to excuse anything, neither to himself nor to anyone else. It might well have been so from the very beginning.

He had always wanted to be a policeman. This might have seemed an odd career choice for a revolutionary, but the Nazi party was full of odd characters with different bents.

He had been a party member from the earliest days, a Jew-hater, Bolshevik-hater, faggot-hater, and sometime murderer. For a while he became quite an unstable person, and was almost banished from the party by Himmler for threatening to place a homemade bomb in the office of one of his fellow Nazis, a rival in a local power struggle. Faced with a jail sentence, Eicke acceded to Himmler's suggestion that he spend a few months in a "sanatorium," that is to say a hospital where doctors could observe him closely at all times.

Perhaps this stay did Eicke some good. For the remainder of his life, he generally managed to keep his choleric temperament on a leash, sometimes a short leash, other times a longer one. Perhaps he had begun to realize that he made people nervous, and that while this might be a useful quality in some situations, he did not want it to hinder his prospects for an important career in the party.

Over time his career began to take shape. It was said that he had used his own sidearm to dispatch a number of the parties involved in the Night of the Long Knives in June of 1934. Or, it was said, he had merely offered certain of these parties the use of his pistol, so they could do the job themselves. Nonetheless, quite a few of the faggots involved in that disgusting incident had been reluctant to commit suicide in the honorable manner; and it had been necessary for someone else to blow out the brains of a substantial number of them. That this someone else would have been Eicke has never been proven, though several witnesses later identified him. In any case he would not have acted alone. A lot of people had to be murdered that night; this necessitated a lot of murderers. Eicke was involved with and probably in command of one of these squads of killers.

That the Night of the Long Knives had to do with homosexuality as much as with an alleged struggle for power has been discussed in various places; the true importance of the one facet as opposed to the other is still open to debate. Large numbers of homosexuals had been attracted to the National Socialist movement from its early days, due to various reasons which are also still open to debate. By 1934 the presence of all these fine young men was becoming an embarrassment to Hitler. Still more embarrassing was the fact that it was becoming harder and harder to conceal the sexual preferences of so many of the party's core members from the public. They did, after all, have the disturbing tendency to enlist more and more younger men to their cause.

And at this time, as indeed he was for many years, Hitler was quite engrossed by the opinions of the German public. He needed them, and they needed him. No one needed homosexuals. Some things never change.

Ernst Rohm was a homosexual. He was Hitler's oldest deputy, possibly his most faithful disciple, and as a disgusting and embarrassing faggot he was also the principal target of murder on that night in June of 34. Hundreds, perhaps thousands, of other men were murdered on that same night. As head of the SA, Rohm was a powerful man, and perhaps Hitler viewed him and many of his cronies as threats to his power. This, in any case, was the alleged motivation for the slaughter. Rohm's last words before receiving a bullet in the back of the head might have belied this scenario. He was reported to have said, "I do not understand. If I give my life here, I give it to Adolph Hitler."

The shock and confusion on his face was undisguised and duly noted by his murderers. Eicke was said to have been one of them, though this too has not been proven. He might have been elsewhere at that moment, if only in the next room, murdering some other batch of faggots from Rohm's coterie.

Many of these murders took place in the bedrooms of the Hotel Constanz, a resort on the shores of the Bodensee in southern Bavaria. Thus many of these men were murdered in pairs, for the simple reason that they were found in bed together, in one bedroom after another.

The Constanz Hotel on the Bodensee was the primary setting for the Night of the Long Knives. Many other victims were murdered simultaneously at other sites throughout Germany. Still others were thrown into jail cells or bare cellar rooms and murdered a few days later. In some versions of the events, Rohm was taken from the hotel and shot by Eicke in one of these empty cellar rooms.

This was blitzkrieg, "lightning war"—though in a civil rather than a military sense.

The reader will excuse this somewhat lurid digression into events that have little or no bearing upon the men trapped in the Valdai Hills nearly a decade later.

For Eicke though, it was a beginning. From this time forward he was an important man. He was not prominent in the public eye, though in the labyrinth of Nazi organizations and sub-organizations this was not unusual. His manners in public were a bit crass even by Nazi standards, and Heinrich Himmler still had recurring doubts about his mental stability. Eicke had a face like a cement slab and a voice shaped by ardor and brutality—brutality either casual or enraged. A very thin line for someone like him.

He became commander of the large body of SS troops held in reserve for duty at the various concentration camps. For a while he was also the commandant of one such camp, which was Dachau. For many years Dachau was the administrative center for all the other camps. These were still the pre-war days, the days before the camps became industrial death-factories. Death was still a regular occurrence in these places. It was merely dealt out a little more at random.

Not all the inmates at this time were Jews. Those who were Jews were despised by Eicke, those who were there for other reasons were also despised by him. He was a revolutionary and he despised without exception all or any opponents to the revolutionary government. The Jews, of course, he had always despised.

No one really liked doing duty at these concentration camps. They were unpleasant places. They brought out the worst in a man. Even someone like Eicke, who had dreamed of becoming a policeman and now wielded a great deal of police authority, would not have looked forward to doing permanent duty in one of these places. Most camp commandants were in fact assigned on a continually shifting, temporary basis; S S Reichsfuhrer Himmler might have preferred a more permanent and stable situation, but realistically he was forced to deal with the problem of morale, and realistically assignment at the camps was among the least coveted duties in the SS.

Eicke did not complain about this duty. He merely wanted something better for himself, and for his men. If Jews, homosexuals, political subversives, and other reptiles had to be murdered, he would take his turn at it; though he had his own way of going about such things. He wanted to run a tight ship, and he took steps to remove the most sadistic guards from Dachau, replacing the random acts of grotesque sadism which had been common under the previous commandant with a more organized, more"disciplined" system of repression and torment for the prisoners. Beatings, executions, and other measures were meted out according to a highly detailed code of regulations, which he drew up according to his own ideas about punishment and revenge against the enemies of National Socialism. He was a good police-man, but all the same he desired more. Ultimately what he desired was to lead his men in battle.

His wish was granted, though only indirectly at first. Several regiments from his command participated in the invasion of Poland in 1939. Eicke himself remained behind in Germany, at the main Totenkopf training center at Dachau. His men were, techni-cally speaking, not soldiers (certainly no one in the army would call them that) and if they were to perform well in combat they would require a great deal more basic military training.

The few units that had been detached and sent to Poland would justify this view. The campaign was over quickly and they saw little combat action. What actions they were involved in tend-ed more towards the murder of Jews and Polish civilians. Right from the very start they conducted themselves almost entirely independently from any army command. Orders regarding mili-tary situations from the army units were routinely ignored by the Totenkopf men; such orders merely interfered with the specific business of killing Jews and the larger business of terrorizing the Polish population in general.

The Totenkopf men were small in number and, compared with what was to come later, their acts of murder and mayhem were small in scope; merely local nightmares, so to speak, depending on which town they happened to be stationed in. Nearby army field commanders were nevertheless shocked and disgusted and protested vehemently to whatever higher govern-mental or military authority they thought might lend an ear. The war was still very young and feelings of shock and disgust still perhaps had a certain freshness to them—as if they might some-how be meaningful, have an effect on something.

The army commanders still had a good deal to learn. Their protests were ignored.

The army for the most part withdrew from Poland in order to prepare itself for the next campaign, wherever that might be. The Totenkopf regiments also withdrew, returning to the base at Dachau for more intensive combat training. Yet more Totenkopf units were now sent out to Poland to do occupation duty there, which meant further exercises in enslavement, extortion, terror, and murder. They were soon joined by other branches of the SS, all of them detached from the bizarre crazy-quilt of organizations that constituted the SS as a whole. The byzantine structure of all the SS agencies has confounded historians to this very day; yet at least it might be said that they found a common purpose in Poland. The acts of depravity that soon became commonplace could only be compared with the countless similar acts that would be seen in Russia two years later.

Theodor Eicke, meanwhile, had yet to see action on the battlefield. At Dachau training exercises were stepped up, discipline was tightened down, National Socialist exhortations of every kind became part of the daily regimen. One reward for Eicke's efforts was that Hitler now gave the go-ahead for Totenkopf to be organized as a fully equipped combat division.

They were the third SS unit to be thus recognized. The first was SS Leibstandarte, a unit which had originally been Hitler's personal bodyguard. Due to their elite status and exacting requirements, Leibstandarte remained a somewhat smaller force until later in the war. The second unit was formed from various other SS agencies—not so closely connected to the camps as were Eicke's men—and this force eventually became the SS Division Das Reich.

All three of these units—Leibstandarte, Das Reich, and Totenkopf—took part in the invasion of France in May of 1940. They formed only a small percentage of the German military force. In fact Leibstandarte was still only a regimental unit at this time. Their conduct was, for the most part, little different from that of the regular army. France was not Poland, for one thing. There were far fewer filthy Jews in France, and of course there were no filthy Poles. During the six week campaign there was one incident involving SS Leibstandarte in Ourtheville, where a group of British soldiers who may or may not have surrendered were slaughtered in a barn.

One might understand that such incidents will happen in war, even among allegedly more civilized countries.

Or one might decline to understand this, given the disturbing frequency of such incidents as the war went on, so often involving units of the SS.

There was also an incident involving SS Totenkopf at Le Paradis. This incident was more clear-cut than the one at Ourtheville. A group of about two hundred British soldiers who had surrendered were lined up in front of a stone wall and machine-gunned. Two of them feigned death among the heaps of their comrades. They later escaped and brought news of this event to other British units.

One might emphasize that this was an unusual action, at least in France in 1940. The commander of the Totenkopf unit was reported to have been upset by the savage resistance of the British immediately before they surrendered. (The British unit was surrounded and only gave up when they ran out of ammunition.) They had been holed up in a stone farmhouse, an easily defended position, and had inflicted enormous casualties upon the attacking Totenkopf men. The casualties were in fact shockingly high, more comparable to loss rates in Russia a year later. The Totenkopf commander also insisted that the British had been using explosive dum-dum bullets, which for some reason were considered illegal at that time. The truth or falsehood of this allegation has never been proven. Even the commanders of other Totenkopf units were somewhat dubious about this. There were those who felt that Knochlein, the officer involved, had simply lost his head and needed some excuse that would justify, not only his murder of the British defenders, but the awful holes torn in the ranks of his own men.

Army officers who witnessed Totenkopf in action elsewhere in France had their own views. The Totenkopf men fought with a savage elan, attacking heavily defended positions with the enthusiasm and single-mindedness that Eicke had instilled in them over the preceding years. Unfortunately, as combat soldiers they were still rather incompetent. One army general (this was Hoeppner, later cashiered by Hitler in front of Moscow) referred to Eicke's brand of leadership as no more than a kind of butchery. And it was the spilling of German blood he was referring to, not the massacre of British prisoners.

In any case the French campaign ended almost as quickly as the Polish campaign of the year before. The German occupation, at least initially, was conducted in a reasonably civil manner. Once again the great majority of the German armed forces were withdrawn in order to begin preparing for the next campaign, wherever that might be.

Even certain SS commanders felt their men needed still more training before they could effectively compete with their brethren in the army. Though they might not have said as much in public. Eicke was certainly not pleased to hear himself referred to as a butcher. Nor was he pleased that Totenkopf had been singled out as a special case, receiving far harsher criticism than either Leibstandarte or Das Reich.

Eicke's view all along was that the army men simply did not understand what real National Socialist ardor was all about. Blood was meant to be spilled.

But he wasn't stupid. Even other SS men might have called him pig-headed, but he wasn't stupid. Blood was meant to be spilled, but that didn't mean he wanted his soldiers to look second-rate. After the fall of France the Totenkopf training exercises at Dachau were stepped up even further. Eicke drove his men and punished any that did not measure up to his standards. Unlike certain other SS commanders, he could not threaten his men with tours of duty at one of the concentration camps—for the simple reason that that was where so many of them had come from in the first place. Eicke took the next logical step, which was to suggest that if they did not perform better they would find themselves doing tours of duty at the camps not as guards, but as inmates. This seemed to catch everyone's attention.

Not only was combat training stepped up. Eicke, perhaps more than any other Waffen-SS commander, was noted for the intensity of his National Socialist instructional programs. Lectures on such well-known topics as Jew-hating, Jew-killing, Slav-hating, Slav-killing, Bolshevik-hating, and Bolshevik-killing were daily affairs. There were any number of lecturers, including Eicke himself, and inevitably these lecturers would present the same overall themes with various personal differences in tone and speaking style. A rabid speaker on one day might be followed by a more methodical, even dull, speaker on the next day. This was of course only natural. Men will vary in certain ways.

It is interesting to note how these lectures were recalled by many SS veterans after the war. It is a recurring theme that the ordinary SS soldier, even the ordinary SS officer-candidate, did not always pay a whole lot of attention to these lectures. They were frequently boring, interminable affairs, full of a lot of hot air and tedious ramblings. At least this is how they are often recalled in the minds of a lot of these men. An objective listener might imagine what it would be like to attend one—or several hundred—of these lectures, and think that the SS veterans are not being entirely dishonest.

Soldiers throughout history have been known to possess a certain impatience when it comes to being forced to sit through the long-winded speeches and other exhortations of their commanders. But this is not to say these exhortations never have any effect on them. Doubtless quite a few of the Totenkopf men would have found Eicke's speeches quite agreeable, if only they didn't have to listen to so many of them.

●　　●　　●

It is hard to say just when the Waffen-SS soldiers became transformed. Transformed, that is, from members of a more or less paramilitary, political body, to members of a fighting organization that would rival any military force in the world.

Certainly this transformation took place in Russia. But it would be hard to say just when this happened—or if there was ever any particular "just when."

The Russian campaign was an abyss that was both very gradual and very steep. It was a terrible journey that was both very slow and overwhelmingly swift. It was like nothing that had been before.

The few SS divisions in Russia were scattered more or less at random among several hundred army divisions. Cooperation between the SS and the army was much better than it had been previously. It had to be. The nature of the Russian campaign forced men to fight together, to respond quickly to each other's needs, or die.

The combat performance of the Waffen-SS improved dramatically. Army officers soon became impressed by the urgency and force with which these men could respond to almost any situation. Such responses were called for in Russia, time and time again, on and on, on and on, from the very beginning to the very end.

Therein lay the seeds of much bitter fruit. Casualties among the SS still ran higher than in the army. Army officers tended to view this as the ongoing result of SS fighting tactics, which, while more refined than they had been in France or Poland, were still savage and direct—often very effective, almost always very bloody.

In theory, even in practice, the SS men might have agreed with this assessment, but there was another side to it—a side that slowly grew more and more aggravating, like an infected sore. Over time many of the SS men came to think that their losses were due to the army's giving them the dirtiest jobs to do, demanding the impossible of them time and again. Over the short haul they might have taken a perverse pride in this notion, as elite fighting units will tend to do. But that was the problem. In Russia there was no short haul. Russia was more than just a campaign. It was a kind of eternity.

For the first few days of the campaign Totenkopf was held in reserve, their combat effectiveness still being somewhat suspect. This did not last long. At the end of June 1941 they entered Russia, after assisting in the defeat of the Soviet forces in the Baltic states. Almost all the inhabitants of the Baltic nations greeted the Germans as liberators, and the erstwhile Soviet occupiers did not contest these areas too heavily. But upon entering Russia proper, Totenkopf found a different story.

They were part of the Army Group North, whose operational range was eventually to extend from Leningrad in the north to the Valdai Hills in the south. In mid-July of 1941 Totenkopf captured the town of Opotschka, just inside the old Russian border.

Casualties again were appalling. During this single, relatively obscure action Totenkopf lost almost as many men as did the US Second Marine Division during the notorious assault on Tarawa in the central Pacific, two years later, half a world away.

Army commanders once again made a few deprecatory comments about SS fighting tactics, but soon army commanders would have enough to worry about regarding casualties in the army. Over time the blood shed by the Totenkopf men caused less of a stir. There was too much blood being shed everywhere.

Eventually the only men concerned about Totenkopf casualties were the Totenkopf men themselves. Eicke, in personal command as he had been in France, began to take a different view about leading his men into battle. It was not a question of his own personal courage, which was never lacking. It was rather a question of seeing the fighting force which he had built up over the years being nearly destroyed within a matter of months. Other battles followed after Opotschka. Endless battles, interminable battles. Battles that today are almost lost to history; but which perhaps will someday be resurrected by history, as people and nations develop deeper perspectives about the Russo-German War. This remains to be seen.

Long before the ordeal in the Demyansk cauldron, Totenkopf had been nearly bled white. As early as August of 1941, Eicke was complaining via all channels available to him about the near destruction of his division. Eicke was severely wounded by a mine and transported back to Germany; he continued his protests from there. His place was taken by his chief deputy, Max Simon, whose complaints became if anything now more bitter than Eicke's.

Army commanders who for a while had been pleased by the tenacity of the Totenkopf soldiers now became warier whenever they had to deal with either of these two men. Eicke recovered from his wounds and returned to Russia, taking over from Simon once again. He was distressed to see that the state of his men had deteriorated still further in his absence. Eicke now saw fit to channel most of his complaints directly to Himmler or even to Hitler himself, leapfrogging over the normal chain of command in a way that was rare even among other Waffen-SS units.

These communications were secret, private; they were "SS business"; but there was already enough tension between Eicke and the army field commanders to whom he was supposedly subordinate. They could read it in his bearing, they could see it in his face, they could hear it in his voice. Some, like von Manstein, thought quite highly of Eicke and his men, but it seems a fair likelihood that others were beginning to regard him as a very prickly character. They might have called him worse things, if any of them ever had opportunity to read any of the private messages he was sending to Himmler, in which he reviled the army units in numerous ways.

The soldiers of SS Totenkopf, on the other hand, remained invaluable. By now they had proved their combat worth time and again. For this reason neither Himmler nor Hitler had any intention of taking them out of the line. Himmler informed Eicke that every unit in Russia, army or SS, would have to take its losses. By this time the Totenkopf Division was stationed along the Lovat River between Lake Ilmen and Demyansk, where they would remain for over a year. They would remain in the line longer than SS Leibstandarte, longer than SS Das Reich, their losses mounting, their replacements reduced to a trickle.

When Demyansk was cut off and surrounded by the Russians in January of 1942, Eicke found himself under the command of the Graf von Brockdorff-Ahlefeldt, who had been placed in overall command of the situation—the cauldron.

So for a short operational history of SS Totenkopf up to early 1942. A bit of speculation might be apt at this moment. The personal reactions of Hitler and Himmler to Eicke's protests are not known. Hitler had a capacity for being entirely unmoved by any number of things. Generally speaking, the suffering of the SS soldiers did not seem to perturb him any more than the suffering of the Landsers in the regular army. As for SS Reichsfuhrer Himmler, his official communications in response to Eicke carried a certain note of petulance, perhaps even irritation. It is possible that the two most powerful men in Germany were becoming as weary of Eicke as Eicke's commanders in the field.

If so, it would have made for a peculiar, though tenuous, bond; between the Fuhrer and the head of the SS, on the one hand, and the men who had come to despise them, on the other hand; men like Seydlitz and Brockdorff-Ahlefeldt.

Narrative of Lt. Erich Nierholz, 5th Jaeger Division, June 1942

Every day there is another barrage. They vary in length and intensity. Often they are followed by Russian attacks, but not always. The barrages cause the most casualties.

The months in the Lovat swamps now seem a blur, recent though they were. Artillery barrages were nothing then compared to what we are receiving now. Men from other units, people who were trapped all winter in the cauldron, say these barrages have been commonplace all along. Some disagree though. They say they are getting worse.

There is no place to escape them, no rear areas. The corridor where we are stationed is only a mile or two wide. Supposedly the only place where one can move about safely is within the larger pocket around Demyansk. I have still not seen that town.

Heit is dead. Meijer is dead. Artillery fire both times. Others have been killed in close combat during the Russian attacks. We were few in number when we first arrived here. The replacements we've received have not been enough to bring us up to strength. Occasionally the older men ask if there is any hope for relief. They seem to ask this out of some compulsion, without really expecting anything. I have no answer for them.

We seem to function through the hours of a day like men who have given up hope; though in a way this seems to make things less hard on our nerves. At least, for the time being, we are no longer wading in water up to our waists. I try to remember that. During a few quiet hours it seems something to be thankful for. But sometimes not.

The terrain is battered everywhere. At first there was spring greenness but mostly that has been blasted away. The weather has been rainy and a few green sprouts continue to push up, but it is a losing struggle; mostly it is a brown wasteland everywhere. At times the ground seems less like the earth than like a razed city. Shattered trees look like rubble; the hulks of Russian tanks stand between the lines like abandoned trolley cars; shellholes resemble blasted cellar excavations, bunkers that have been destroyed by shellfire, other bunkers still intact but not looking much different. We have much to do, digging more bunkers and fortifications at all hours, except when we are under attack.

My father was in the Ypres salient in 1917. I shake my head. Things escape my understanding. The transport planes continue to fly in low overhead, day after day, yet they seem to have nothing to do with us anymore. I don't know why. I pay less attention to them. They are part of the landscape yet have nothing to do with it. I can't explain it. My head is growing feeble. I feel I cannot lead these men anymore. I have received a commendation for my tour with a front-line company, but find myself wishing to return to regiment. It is only a little safer there; that is not the point. I am tired of being in command, I am tired of having men look to me all the time. Months ago I accepted this responsibility willingly, and was gratified when I found I could do the job; but now there is something about it that keeps wearing at me. Every time I take charge of another action I feel a disturbance which is more than just fear. Maybe fear will grow stronger and blot it out eventually. I concern myself less with the little doings of the men than I did months ago. This seems not to disturb them, if they are aware of it. I think of what is happening to me and imagine it is the same with them.

June 14

The rain continues. Even the small privilege of being on dry ground is now disappearing. It has rained almost every day this month and the trenches are beginning to look like the swamps where we were before, back in April. The bunkers provide the only shelter from the barrages, but that is where the water is the deepest. To crouch down there in the dark, staring at the faces of other men in the light of a candle, the flame trembling with each shellburst, sending shadows like splinters across the walls . . . that is daily life now.

You are in water up to your knees, like a sailor down in the bilge of a ship. Men get out of the water by sitting crosslegged on the few bits of furniture we have installed down here, or else they just dangle their legs apathetically in the water. There is never enough room for people to sit down on these dry spots, or to lie down. I had determined I would not arrange special favors for myself, in other words I would not insist on having a dry place to sit whenever I came in. Now I think I was foolish to behave this way. Most of the men will automatically surrender some place for me, but the ones that do not instantly get on my nerves. They seem to realize this but do not care, taking advantage of my generosity in sharing the conditions on an equal basis. Pettiness. . . . I can see it in myself also.

I realize now that it was Sergeant Heit, before he was killed, who kept the ill-mannered ones from taking advantage of my goodwill. Merkel, the new company sergeant, is not the same kind of man. After all we have been through, I can hardly believe the irritation this situation causes me. I will simply have to do something to change it, though the idea of taking charge of such a petty business only makes me tired. In any case, from now on I will have my own place; any reprobates who can't adjust to this will be told to leave the bunker. If they are insolent enough to ask for an explanation they will receive none.

I am disappointed in myself. But it doesn't matter. At least I have made the decision.

June 15

Rain.

It is either rain or clouds bearing rain. You watch them drift in slowly above the horizon. There are almost twenty hours of daylight, but not sunlight. Endless hours of murk, opaque walls in the sky, forming and unforming. Cloudbanks like bodies being torn slowly apart, like the corpses around the trenches that pull slowly apart from the weight of their own waterlogged rot. During twenty hours of daylight there will be the occasional shaft of sun breaking through, sometimes a large wall of sunlight roaming like a kind of creature out across the battlefield. The wrecked tanks become lit up, become something other than themselves for a moment or two, then fade back into the murk again, senseless pieces of junk.

Just this little bit of activity in the sky is like a kind of show; men emerge from their torpor to stare for a few minutes. The landscape is naked and blasted and there is nothing to watch but the sky. The sky is enormous around here. But still, it isn't much.

The Russian attacks will come slowly through the mud, through the mud and the rain. You see their infantry advancing out there, wading laboriously through the bad places, advancing slowly like sewage workers trying to find the source of some break in the system. We beat them off day after day; it is rare that they actually get into our trenches. Then the close-up hell that lasts for ten or fifteen minutes before we rout them out, where you have no time to think of anything. How anyone survives these incidents no one knows. And it does not bear thinking about, because, as I said, it is the artillery fire that gets far more of us. If the Russian infantry assaults ever match the power of their artillery, then I think the war will be over in a few days. It is a frightening but not unpleasant thought.

DEMYANSK

Their tanks too are not as frightening as they were a year ago. I find myself thinking I must be an idiot to say such a thing, but I believe it is so. They mostly seem to not know what they are doing, and if they reach the trenches ahead of their infantry we can knock them out rather easily. You just have to get used to it, get used to the idea that they can see hardly anything and in some ways are more helpless than a naked man, if that man happens to be carrying a satchel charge. Acts of courage that might have made you wet your pants a year ago have become commonplace. A T-34 becomes stranded in the trench lines, and a Landser climbs on board to exterminate it like a worker performing some task at a construction site. Daily business, a routine job, wage-earning. It is not that much different from performing a routine but dangerous job, like working in a coal mine or on a high bridge, where ordinary workers are also killed from time to time.

No, it is not like that. I say it is, because sometimes it seems that way. But it isn't. You just feel that if you have been through something like this, day after day, then you have the liberty to describe it however you please. There is no one who will ever be able to defy you.

The tanks are more dangerous when they simply keep their distance, grinding to a halt some hundreds of yards in front of our positions, then blasting everything with cannon fire from that range. With anti-tank guns we could dispose of this problem too, but we have too few and most have been put out of action by now. So things become tight. We have to wait; wait for him to come closer, so we can finish him off, or wait until the strain of being alone out there gets to be too much for him, and he retreats back to his own lines.

It is only another form of heavy artillery. The only German tanks I've seen are the few wrecks that were already here when we first arrived. Once in a while if things get really tight a few assault guns will be sent up to help us.

Demyansk. The Valdai Hills. We must have gotten lost somewhere along the way. I don't know where these hills are. From most any observation point you can see for miles, and there are no hills here. It would be like calling the floodplains of Holland the Dutch Hills. Rain. Sometimes I think back to a year ago. For it has been exactly a year now, June of '41 to now. A year ago we marched in a burning sun through clouds of dust that choked us and made us pray for water. Now in June of '42 there is rain. Rain. Rain. So. A different year.

June 24

Orders from above. Situational meetings. Strecker, myself, the other battalion and company commanders. I catch sight of General Allmendinger in a car on his way to the regimental command post.

We are informed that there will be another operation to widen the relief corridor. We conducted several such attacks in May. They were successful to a limited extent.

No one wants to try it again, not now in this rainy weather. I understand that Allmendinger, or Seydlitz, or somebody, has already postponed further attacks on several occasions. These delays have only allowed more time for the mud to deepen. After one of these meetings Strecker says to me,

"Just remember last year. All we need is one or two good days of sunlight. The mud will dry up like bricks."

Yes. Last summer that was true. And it is summer again now, little though it resembles it. I have no idea if this rain is unusual, or if last year's stifling heat was unusual. In any case the rain shows little inclination to stop. When it does stop there are only more clouds rolling overhead, bearing more rain to some other place.

I suppose what he means is that there is still a chance the attack will be conducted in dry weather. But it will be left to chance; the word is that there will be no more postponements. It will go forward now regardless. The operation is set for June 28. There is a rumor that it is to coincide with an attack along the entire front down in the south of Russia. But this is only news such as you would read in a newspaper; it has no bearing on us here along the Lovat.

In the afternoon Strecker calls me back to the battalion command post.

"I'm sending you on an outing, Nierholz. You've been up in the forward posts too long. We have a group of replacements coming over the Lovat bridge. Your company has the lowest strength so you'll get the best share. If you go back to regiment they'll have a car or cycle there that you can use. I just need someone to make sure the new people don't get lost trying to find their place in the line."

"Where do I meet them?"

"Meet them at the bridge. Guide them in from there. Make sure they don't wander into any of the bad places. You know what I mean. All right?"

I nod. "Thank you, Strecker," I say.

"You've done pretty well, you know, Nierholz. The hell with it, you're one of us now. I expect you back here before nightfall."

The divisional vehicle park has been moved somewhere closer to Demyansk. Less harassing fire there. When I get back to the regimental command post I find only a few cars parked here and there. I would prefer to go alone but the supply officer says I'd better take a driver.

"You do want to get there in one piece, after all," he says matter of factly.

He calls to a corporal who leads me over to a Kubelwagen. We drive off in the direction of the river.

I am not in the mood for conversation and the corporal gives this up after a few minutes. He is a decent fellow, with that relaxed, hell-for-leather look that drivers often have. I consider that this is the job to have, if you have to be doing something in this place. Not that it isn't dangerous. Movement within the corridor attracts fire. I don't need to be told that, though he says so anyway. But it seems that driving about to different places would help relieve some of the tension. I might ask him about that but I want to be alone with myself for a while.

I am beginning to notice this about the burden of command, if that is not too foolish a way to be saying it, especially for a mere lieutenant. But I've begun to see that what's been troubling me more than anything else of late is simply the desire to get away from people. Even amongst a group of other men a Landser is more by himself, I think, because he is not responsible for anything. This is a way of saying he is left alone, even if he is surrounded by people all the time. He is responsible for doing his job, that is true, but it is not the same kind of thing.

I don't know if this is true, but it seems true. At least the foul mood I have been suffering from of late starts to make more sense.

To be detailed out of the line for a few hours; you could hardly call it a favor, though Strecker seemed to look at it that way.

And I am looking at it that way myself. A little outing. That's about right. I feel good.

We drive back along the single main road towards the river. This is the route we marched in on back in April. In the mud the road is hard to distinguish from the surrounding terrain. Its course is marked by the wrecks of tanks and other vehicles, like channel markers in a harbor. We pass through a particularly heavy stretch of wrecks.

The corporal says,

"A month ago we had to detour around this stretch, or else drive like crazy if we were in a hurry. The Russians had it sited very nicely. But it's a little safer now."

"Good," I say.

I look around to see if there is anything I recognize from when we first marched in. But I can't tell. It is a junkpile. The ground and the mud are junk. Everything is. We make slow going through mud and around shellholes, pulling over one time to let a column of vehicles pass by going in the other direction. If it were up to me, I would be satisfied to drive on all day, into the night, into the next day, just to keep on driving. But I know the distance to the Lovat is not far.

Before the other column has passed us by the corporal starts to drive off again, detouring out through the mudfields.

"Hold your horses," I say. "There's no use getting stuck."

"I'm sorry, sir. One doesn't like to sit parked by the road around here. It's all right. I do this routinely."

I say nothing. For an instant I feel a surge of the irritation that has been wearing at me these past weeks. Mud flies into the driving compartment but I am already muddy. God damn all of this, I think. We are heading straight for a ditch but before I can say anything we are across it, bumping over a wagon bed that was lodged down there. The driver looks at me and grins, then quickly turns his head away when I look back at him.

Good, I think.

We bounce back onto the road and head down to the bridge. We reach the river a few minutes later.

There are quite a few men in this area. Men, horses, vehicles, wagons. My driver keeps to his instincts and parks some distance away from the larger congregations, though who knows where the shells will fall? All right. It will give me a few minutes to collect my thoughts before I have to meet everybody. I tell him he doesn't need to wait. I won't be going back with him. Then I get out of the car and walk over to the edge of the river.

So. Here it is again. The Lovat. My mind is empty. I see what there is to see and that is all there is. It is enough for now.

I walk along the top of the riverbank, back towards the bridge. I have not seen it before, this famous bridge. It seems that when we first crossed the river we were to the north of here, but I can no longer remember for sure.

The water is lower now than in the meltseason, in spite of all the rain. Dark stains on the bridge pilings mark the descent of the water. It is not an impressive bridge. The workmanship is good as always; otherwise it is not an imposing structure. Vehicles are crossing it slowly. Meanwhile barge-ferries which look like flat, detached sections of some other bridge are also crossing the river, bearing other vehicles. Evidently the bridge will only support so much traffic.

So there it is then. The crossing to the world beyond. I begin looking for the people I am to meet.

A group of Totenkopf replacements has just come over, assembling on this side and waiting under a stretch of riverside trees, waiting maybe for someone like me. I approach a traffic control officer standing at the end of the bridge. The traffic control officer tells me the 126th Infantry Division is scheduled to cross over next. An entire division . . . it will take all day for them to come over. The traffic officer says that if my people arrive he will squeeze them in somehow. I tell him we have to be back in the line before nightfall, but in fact I feel no urgency and hope the lack of it in my voice is not too evident.

In fact a strange elation suddenly rises right up through me and I have to look away, staring into the distance.

For a moment I feel odd and conspicuous. I pull a more severe expression over my face and ask the traffic man a few questions. Where have they come from, the 126th Division? France?

"France?" He laughs quietly. "There's no one left in France except stomach battalions and Hitler Jugend. They're all defending the coast, you know. Waiting for the English invasion. A nice wait. If we'd only left the Russkies alone we could all be waiting over there. Fighting the champagne war. I wouldn't have minded fighting that kind of war for the next twenty years."

He sounds as if he was there, not too long ago. I ask him this, and he says yes, he was stationed in France only a month before.

"Hitler Jugend on a nice long holiday. Christ, a long holiday. After a while I got to liking it so much there that I didn't care when my next home leave was."

I tell him I was there myself, not so long ago, though it doesn't seem that way; it seems outside of any time. But I talk with him about France for a few minutes anyway, though my time there was so short I hardly know what to say about it. A few weeks in the Loire Valley in November. I smile agreeably and absorb the fondness of his own reminiscences, as if I might share them with him. Then I say,

"So how do you like Russia?"

He gives me a look.

"What kind of question is that? Is there more than one answer? Ha. How do I like Russia? Very good, fellow."

I laugh a little. He is a tyro here but his words are apt all the same.

"So where have these people come from?" I ask again, just marking time by this point. He consults something that looks like a railroad schedule.

"They've just been shipped down from Novgorod. Probably that means somewhere along the Volkhov River. There was a big mess to clean up up there, from what I understand."

A big mess. I wonder how he would describe the place where we are now. He was a French garrison tyro and now he is a traffic control tyro who has been out here less than a month. Apart from that, I might find him perfectly agreeable, someone to share a few Pernods with in a cafe back in Nevers. I remember that the French women looked good and not particularly unfriendly either, the young ones especially, though I didn't have much time to talk to any. Christ.

It has begun to rain again. A fine drizzle rolls across the river-banks, settles on the surface of the river. In some other land it might be almost pleasant, a misty day in June.

Novgorod, as I remember from the maps, is on the northern side of Lake Ilmen, not so very far from here. Like a kind of sister city to Staraya Russa on the southern side. Or at least a glance at the map might put that picture in your mind. The Volkhov too I have heard of, from reading the armed forces newspapers which we always use to wipe our asses with, but which beforehand we tend to read quite thoroughly, as they are one of our few diversions down in the filthy bunkers. For months we have been reading about a great battle taking place on the Volkhov River, under conditions that beggar description, or at least that is how the newspaper describes them. And up there I suppose they are reading about a great battle taking place between Demyansk and the Lovat, if such things are of interest to them. The army newspapers are, as I mentioned, more useful for personal hygiene.

For some reason I find myself visualizing these places for a few moments. I imagine the Volkhov as being some kind of mirror-image to the Lovat, incestuous sister rivers in the remotest and most forgotten forests of hell. It looks like I will be waiting here by the bridge for some time, and perhaps I will find myself speaking to these men of the 126th, comparing experiences and so on. Yes, maybe so. But not just yet.

I make one more attempt to be business-like by asking if any companies from the 5th Jaegers are listed on his schedule or whatever it is.

"Yes, yes, I thought I already showed it to you. They might be there already for all I know. I can telephone to the other side if you wish. I'll squeeze them in for you."

"Ja, gut," I say.

He busies himself for a few more minutes, shouting directions to different groups of people, a brusque hurry-it-along manner; then I see him walk off to a bunker nearby, from which telephone cables are laid down to the river.

I sit down on a sawed-off stump on the bank. The water passes slowly about twenty feet below. Some distance to the south another bridge is under construction. It looks like a railroad bridge. The pilings are higher, so that the track can be laid without gradient from the height of one bank to the other. As yet it is only a framework, a skeleton standing quietly in the rain.

I look across the water. Strange emotions cloud my mind and I shut my eyes for a while. When I open them again the opposite bank is there, a few hundred yards away. It is a little higher than this side, high enough so that I can not see into the country beyond. I make some effort to remember a few things. Pictures of the dense April swamps and the other months come back to me. My head is full of these things, yet my mind is blank. It is not so bad somehow. I feel tears welling at the backs of my eyes but they do not seem so bad either; instead of running down my cheek they sink back into my eyes. I find myself staring at a small boat parked in the reeds on the far side of the river. It is some kind of non-descript local craft, hardly bigger than a canoe, hulled with black canvas or something. A greyish drift of sunlight lights it up for a moment, lights up the green reeds around it.

A great hole widens in my brain for a moment, a hole filled with beautiful sunlight from a fine day in Germany many years ago.

I look over towards the communications bunker. The traffic man has not reappeared. I look at the trucks and the horse-drawn wagons of the 126th crossing the bridge, moving slowly, vehicles at a walk, men at a walk.

There is a Kubelwagen down in that column, an officer sitting in the passenger seat. I think I recognize him. Yes, who is that. . . . I can't place him. There are SS markings on the car door. No doubt some more of the Totenkopf people crossing along with the other division. That must be it then, but where have I seen him exactly. . . .

Feurbitscher. Feurbitscher, that's his name. Oberfuhrer. Standartenfuhrer. Their ranks are confusing. Where? Not in the trenches. No, it was longer ago than that. It must have been back in April, the morning after we made the first crossing. I can't remember who all I spoke to, but not him; I must have seen him from a distance. Madrich, that was the name of the first one I met, in charge of that little rowboat crossing to our side in the last light of the evening. During the night more boats came, and then I crossed the Lovat with my men. Entering the cauldron. Feurbitscher, he was in command of the Totenkopf battlegroup waiting on the other side. One of them must have said his name.

He has an appearance that you might remember. The goatee, maybe that's all it is. A goatee like a U-boat man. Thin face, deep eyes. I look at the man in the Kubelwagen passing below, him, the same man. Traffic is backed up for a few minutes. The car idles on the bridge, in the rain. I look again at the bunker where the traffic-controller disappeared. He is back over by the bridge now, arguing about something with the driver of a truck.

Planes sweep in at low altitude at that moment. More JU-52s, a wide and roaring umbrella of them. My adrenalin shoots up, seeming to hoist me by the armpits. I get to my feet as the planes pass overhead. They fly very low and seem to issue from some source just beyond the opposite bank of the river. Their shapes are distinct beneath the clouds, giving a strange depth to everything, the sky. I wait for them to pass by but then more of them come over. The noise spreads out over everything. I walk through it towards the end of the bridge, towards the bunker there.

June 28

I slip in the mud and press my hand down on the belly of a man lying there. The skin gives way like scum coated on a pond. My hand plunges through into the guts.

I fight back the gagging in my throat, rocking my head back and forth. I thrust my hand into the nearest puddle I can find. The slimy feel of the guts will not wash off. I thrust my hand deep into the mud at the bottom of the puddle, pulling up a fistful of it. I squeeze the mud between both my hands, scouring with it, scouring madly. Water will not clean that slime away; only dirt will do the job, thick heavy mud, as thick as possible.

I keep digging my one hand into the mud like a man possessed, clutching at the mud, wiping it against my palm until the slimy feel begins to scour away. I fight back the urge to gag again. I can't do it; I retch, a convulsion in my belly. I crawl off to get further away from the corpse. I get most of the slickness off my hand but some kind of stickiness remains that I cannot get rid of. I rub my hand on my trousers, clenching my teeth, then parting them a little.

We would go fishing for eels on the Weser River. They would have that same slime on their skins that would get all over your fingers when you handled them, that nothing but dirt and river mud could scour away. I grunt again, clenching my eyes shut like the clenching of my jaws, rocking back and forth on my heels.

I sink down a little, kneeling in the mud. I open my eyes. A Landser is hunkered down in front of me. He eyes me in silence, his face tight-lipped. I try to speak but I can not make myself part my lips. He tosses me a rag but I do not pick it up. I stare down into the dirt, concentrating on the dull mud, until the feeling passes through me.

"Water. That's what I need," I say finally. "How about it?"

He glances at the water bottle at my belt but offers me his without comment. I could not stand to drink from my own just now.

I drink, just taking a sip at first. Not knowing if maybe it will make it worse. I drink a little more. I hand the water bottle back to him.

"Who are you with?" I say, wiping my mouth, still glaring into the mud, not looking at him.

"Sergeant Merkel."

"Where is he?"

I am aware of him pointing at something, and I lift my eyes to see him pointing at the bunker nearby. He passes his hand over his lips as if now he too is uncertain about opening his mouth. He is one of the new men.

"All right, boy. Take a rest for a few minutes. We'll see how things look."

I slop over to the bunker in a half-crouch. We have worked our way up this far in small groups. Merkel's group reached the bunker first and took it out in good fashion. He has a flame-thrower section with him, and from a distance I see the black oily smoke and hear the screams from within. I come across the man with the tanks on his back, standing down in a trench at the entrance to the bunker. His knees are buckled, and he leans his tanks against the wall of the trench, loosening the straps a little, like some bearer trying to get a rest from his load. I ask for Merkel and he shifts his forehead slightly to one side. A small trail of vapor still shimmers from the nozzle of the flame gun.

"Shut that thing off, for Christ's sake."

"It is shut off, Herr Leutnant."

He stares at the other wall of the trench, not looking at me. I see flashlight beams in the darkness beyond the entrance to the bunker.

"Merkel," I say.

"One moment, Herr Leutnant." A moment passes. "Shit," he says in there.

The smell is bad enough just standing outside. But the cooked smell is cleaner to my nostrils than the other horror from a few moments earlier. The flashlight beam passes over seared faces, what looks like faces. Burned black heaps of things. Merkel comes out.

He is grimacing but looks more composed than some of the other men. I start to speak to him but he shakes his head, spitting frantically for a few moments. I offer him my canteen, closing my own eyes to shut off the gag reflex again. He is not one of the new ones; he was transferred over from another battalion after Heit was killed. He's been out here since Staraya Russa in January.

He is coarse, loud-mouthed, and not particularly respectful. I do not care for him, perhaps because I sense he feels the same way about me. His men do not seem too fond of him either. His redeeming asset is that he takes care of business well enough.

For the moment that is enough for me. Personalities matter no more. There is only business. Business and shit. They go hand in glove.

He says he has had two killed. It is the same with my group. Two killed.The wounded are already on the way back to the rear, the bearers bearing them away through the mud.

For a moment the roast-smell singed some of the revolting gut-odor out of my mouth. But now I can't stand it here either. No one else can. The inside of the bunker is a black ooze, like a stinking meal forgotten by someone in an oven. Wordlessly we back down the trench to get away from it, the flamethrower man shuffling along. Other men are strung out along the trench, some peering further into the Russian lines. Russian dead lie sprawled in standing water at their feet.

I look for a spot where I can raise my head without a sniper putting a bullet through it. I exhale, nostrils flaring with the tension. I come to a heap of timber where there are a few cracks I can peer through. Two other men are already studying the landscape from there. I raise the binoculars to my eyes.

The Russian positions are deeply echeloned. We have made it through their first line and come I'm not sure how much farther by now. I only hope that this will be far enough. I am too frightened to lead the men any farther now, unless I am to make a great effort of will. I try not to think about it. I wipe a film of rain off the lenses and look out there.

I am surprised to see greenery in the distance. As if we have come to the end of something. Lush grasses stand up a few hundred feet away, tall and slightly bending. Mist drifts over them.

A few small trees are out there, dark leaves rising and falling.

With the exception of the short trip over to the bridge, it is the most green I have seen in several months. A small feeling of relief passes through me. The end of shell-fire terrain, maybe, the end of trench-mortar terrain, the end of the local shitworks. And maybe also, the end of the Russian positions. But that is impossible to say. They can camouflage anything and do it better than anyone. It is a pleasant sight but a bad feeling begins to twist in my belly again. I was intending to stay where we are until further orders come from Strecker or regiment. And I am not about to change those plans. Except. . . .

The green in the distance pulls on me. I feel it in my groin.

Still farther in the distance stands a high black line of trees, of deeper forest. Like the forests around the Lovat. I curse, setting the binoculars down.

"So. The slum-boys pay a little visit to the country."

It is Raubach saying this, one of the two standing behind the timber heap with me. A sly-mouthed but otherwise cooperative enough fellow.

"Did you see anything of interest, Herr Leutnant?"

"I wish I did. There's bound to be something interesting out there, whether you see it or not."

A few other men have come over to the vantage point.

"River maidens," says Raubach to no one in particular.

I tell the others to disperse before the shell fire finds us again. It has been quiet for about five minutes, which is about as long as quiet ever lasts. They move grumbling along the trench, looking for other lookout points, a few risking their heads in the open air to peer out there for a second.

Either shellfire or the Russian counterattack. I don't know which worries me most.

A few strikes come in over the next few minutes, but it is too scattered to be called a barrage. I know by now that we are nowhere near to breaking through their lines. We have come across no artillery parks or vehicle parks or any other sign of a rearward area. I am waiting to hear from Strecker over the radio.

A sense of initiative which I might have felt back in the Lovat swamps has gone dead inside me. With Heit I might have talked it over—our next move, I mean—but I do not wish to do the same with Merkel. I study the lush clumps of grass at the end of the barren ground. There is a sudden movement within the mist-blown grass. Like a large animal wending its way somewhere, invisible in the reeds.

I sense the instinctive reactions all around me and shout instantly with my own instincts.

"Stop! Don't fire! Don't fire!"

The machine gunners have their bolts drawn back.

I see the pennants through the field glasses. Jolting and swaying above the grass like some stiffer species of grass. A command car appears first. It is followed a moment later by an armored personnel carrier. They emerge from the tall grass.

"They're ours," I say.

Totenkopf vehicles. They have been operating on our flank. They must have broken through somewhere ahead.

Good, I think.

The green forest in the distance suddenly looks more appealing.

"Let's give them a few bursts anyway," says someone. "What do you say, children?"

"Shut up," I say. "Send up a flare. Let them see we're here."

Today's friendly signal is red. Merkel loads the cartridge. The dull sizzling thing goes up and bursts like a small powder of blood against the overcast. Red, answered by white. Within seconds a white flare shoots up from the Kubelwagen out there.

Men on foot emerge from the grass, the tall reeds. They wear the SS camo blouses. From a distance they look like greenish mudshirts. I suppose that is the idea.

Then other men come out, twenty or thirty of them. Bareheaded, unarmed. Prisoners. The SS men motion the prisoners to climb into the armored carrier. Five or six of them climb in through the rear hatch and then the doors are pulled shut. The armored carrier moves off again, following behind the Kubelwagen.

The remaining prisoners are herded against the reeds. Tall grass like a backdrop there. A man with a light machine gun steadies the barrel on the shoulder of a comrade and begins firing. The Russians drop like marionettes with their strings cut. A few start to run off. They are cut down by the other SS standing around. Two others with pistols are already walking among the bodies. A few dry cracks are carried off in the breeze. My men stand in the trench and observe all this without comment.

The Kubelwagen drives on back towards the rear, drives slowly through the mud. Rocking from side to side, wheels spinning. I wonder what fool would bring a vehicle like that so far out into these shit-fields. One of the higher-ups wanting to make an impression, no doubt. I have already seen the Totenkopf pennant on the fender but doubt that Eicke himself would be out here. It is him though. I recognize him from where I am standing. I raise the binoculars to be sure, though I know I am not mistaken. I have seen pictures of him and I have also seen him in person. He sits in the passenger seat wearing a leather overcoat, mud-goggles pushed up on his forehead. His expression bears the dull fatherly patience and impatience of a schoolteacher, a very large man, sure of himself. He must be crazy, I think. I recall that Seydlitz used to take these same risks back in the winter, but this does not incline me to change my opinion about Eicke.

A few moments later the Kubel becomes stuck in a bog-hole. We are treated to the spectacle of Eicke's aides climbing out and doing various useless things to free the vehicle. Eicke steps out and walks off a bit to get away from the mud flying up from the wheels. He has a bulldog face and he shouts wildly a few times. Then he turns aside, staring back towards the green area in the distance, not looking all that perturbed.

My men are enjoying all this to no small degree. A few of them glance at me, probably wondering if I am going to tell them to get out and help.

"Stay where you are," I say.

Eicke looks over this way. I cannot tell if he can see exactly where we are. He lights a cigarette and waits for the tracked armored carrier which is coming up from behind. An SS man jumps over the side and speaks to Eicke, while the carrier moves around to get in front of the Kubelwagen. The rear doors open and one of the prisoners falls out the back. He glances about in bewilderment, then lowers his head and stares at the ground as if not desiring to witness his fate. But there is no pistol pointed at his neck. He is merely kicked in the back by two other SS men who jump down, then hustle him back inside the vehicle. They drag a towing cable over to the bumper of the Kubelwagen.

Two shells explode simultaneously a few hundred yards away. Eicke barely looks over there. He glances up at the sky as if looking for a change in the weather. He tosses his cigarette away and climbs back into the Kubel. The towing cable jerks once and then the two vehicles move off again, still coupled to one another.

By this time the SS man who first jumped down and spoke to Eicke is approaching our trench.

He looks familiar. That is the thing with them though. They all look familiar. Alike.

In the newsreels the SS men all look alike, on the drill grounds, at the cadet schools, at the great party rallies. But you figure that is just the way they do things for the newsreels, just for show, thin blond athletic types with long foreheads.

But it isn't just that either. Even in the filth of Russia there is something about them. If you pretend otherwise, then you will only be pretending. Whenever my men chance to run into a group of them, they will generally stand about, talking nonchalantly with each other, smoking, assuming strangely relaxed attitudes, as if the idea of sizing each other up is the remotest thing from their minds. Maybe this is not just a pose, some of the time.

The thing is, I'm thinking he looks like the first one I shook hands with on the banks of the Lovat, in the twilight of that April evening. Madrich. I still remember the name, because it is the only one I heard besides the name of their commander.

The Totenkopf man now climbs down into the trench, nodding at a few of my men. As he comes closer I see that it not only looks like him but it is him, after all. He looks a little less skeletal than that other time. The men direct him to me.

"Guten abend," he says. "Gruppenfuhrer Eicke has asked me to convey a message. He says you all have the breeding of field rats."

He looks at me and looks around at my men.

"Is that so?" I say finally.

"Yes, his exact words."

His face is a mask. Yet I realize that he is a little bit amused. I am not sure if this lessens my desire to put a bullet through him. Next he is offering me a cigarette. I take it slowly, automatically, realizing that he still has not recognized me.

A moment later he does though. He extends his finger partway towards my chest. I nod. He shakes his head, smiling a little.

"Nierholz?"

I nod again.

"That was a fine evening, that day. I don't think we could say how glad we were to see you. Ja. How far is the Lovat from here, do you think?"

I blink. I say,

"I was over there a week or so ago. To tell you the truth, I have no idea."

"Not far," he says.

I shrug. It is starting to rain again. He starts to speak again but I interrupt him. I shout down to Merkel to bring up the radioman. The radioman comes over and starts to say he has still not been able to make contact with battalion. I cut him off.

"Never mind battalion. Try division. A message for General Allmendinger."

"That band is not for company use, Herr Leutnant."

"Do as I tell you."

The operator waits. I repeat the brief compliment from Gruppenfuhrer Eicke. Madrich looks a little taken aback, then shrugs his shoulders and busies himself peering through the cracks in the timber heap.

"All right, just a minute," I say.

The operator continues to fiddle with the knobs but keeps his eyes on me. I say,

"Contact made with Totenkopf on right flank of third battalion."

I ask Madrich if Eicke wished to convey any more specific information about the situation up ahead. He takes on a more business-like look.

"Not from the Gruppenfuhrer personally, no. I can tell you that we have advanced about half a kilometer beyond those reeds. It's nothing but a little oasis. Beyond there is more shit, and then further beyond is that forest which you can just see from here. We are established at the edge of it. How long we can stay there I can't say. We heard a lot of tank engines rumbling back in the woods. Counterattack, whenever the cousins set their minds to it. Eicke went back to find the assault guns, he's a little put out they haven't come up yet."

"Assault guns. What a treat," mutters one of my men. Madrich looks at him. He goes on,

"If we can't hold there we'll have to come back this way. So tell your fellows not to get too trigger-happy. It's all right, Nierholz. Most of us are used to him by now. You'd enjoy hearing the things he calls us sometimes. Forget about it. It doesn't mean a damn thing."

I am not appeased. Nor do I particularly care any longer. I say, "I hear he was blown up on a mine last year. He doesn't seem to learn, does he?"

Madrich nods soberly.

"Learn? Christ no. It's only the real die-hards that enjoy riding around in his car. In fact they don't enjoy it much either. But what can you do?"

I have no idea. Waves of disgust pour through me whose meaning I do not even know; they dissolve into the fatigue that overrides everything. He gives me a funny look for a second, maybe wondering why I don't relax a bit. But I don't really know what he thinks.

He says that if we want to see better what is coming, I could send a few men beyond the reeds, where there is a better view of the forest in the distance. I consider that this would be a good idea. Already we can hear gunfire starting up again. Already I have been listening for the sound of tanks, everyone has been; the men, who at first looked pleased to hear that Totenkopf was established out in front of them, now look anxious again.

Madrich says there are no sheltered positions beyond the reeds, so I send out only five men under Merkel to watch from there. Madrich goes with them, heading forward to find his own unit again. Casually he says goodbye to me. Before he has turned entirely away I can see the tension etched on his face again.

He climbs out of the trench and moves off towards the mist-blowing reeds with Merkel and the others. Two of them start firing into the dead Russians heaped in front of the reeds. Maybe they've seen movement. Maybe it's only their nerves. It makes the rest of us jump though, some of us start cursing at them. Merkel curses at them out there as well. The rain begins to fall harder. The barrage comes out of nowhere. They're trapped out there, all seven of them. With the first cracks tearing through the rain they start to run, slopping through the mud, but there is nowhere to go. They are too far away to get back to the trench. The rest of us crouch deep, burying our faces in the muck. After the first strikes I look out through the timbers to see if any of them have survived but the next pattern follows instantly, falling halfway closer to the trench, blowing mud and debris over everyone in here. Some of the timbers collapse. A few of the men in the trench are fleeing down into the bunker where the burned Russians are. The rest remain crouched down, foreheads pressed against the trench wall, eyes shut tight, or some with eyes wide open.

PART THREE—*Brockdorff-Ahlefeldt*

It was October now. It was raining. The mud season had begun. It had been raining nearly all summer and now in the autumn it was raining once again. The yearly ordeal of mud, the rasputitsa, had set in.

The entire area of the Valdai Hills and the Lovat delta had been waterlogged throughout June, July, and August. The gloomy skies of autumn had swept overhead even by mid-July.

So one might expect the onset of the mud season to not be particularly noticeable. But it was. It was no different from the year before. The sun, on the few days when it appeared, was no longer strong enough to dry the land. Operations came to a halt.

In a sense it was more of a relief for the Germans. They were holed up in heavily fortified positions now; it was not like last year, when they had stubbornly labored on through the quagmire, labored on like grim fools towards Moscow, ignorant then of what the Russian weather was and would always be.

It was a misery, of course, the trenches often thigh-deep or waist-deep with cloudy water; but if one could measure things in small increments, one could say that the misery of stationary warfare was better than the agony of advancing, or trying to advance, in these conditions.

The Russians, on the other hand, had known better all along, and for the time being their attacks along the perimeter subsided. In particular the relief corridor was no longer in such imminent and nerve-wracking peril. The corridor. The neck. The Landsers called in "der Schlauch"—the tube. A word with a certain vulgar suggestiveness.

In September Brockdorff-Ahlefeldt had managed to carry out an operation which he had been planning for some time. It was a question of when the heavy skies would dry up long enough for mobile operations to proceed. For a while it looked as if this would never happen. Finally there were a few weeks of sunnier weather towards the end of September. It would be the last window in time before the rasputitsa brought everything to a standstill.

The attack was code-named Operation Michael, in honor of the great offensive that had smashed through the Allied lines in the spring of 1918, breaking nearly four years of stalemate on the Western Front.

The current affair was nothing so grandiose as that, and Brockdorff-Ahlefeldt must have looked on the code-name with a certain wry appreciation. Only Hitler seemed to take much interest in code names for assaults, personally decreeing titles which might have been more properly decided upon by subordinates or intelligence officers or whomever; often changing names which did not suit him, which did not fit in with his peculiar grasp of how things were destined to be.

Brockdorff-Ahlefeldt had no idea whether "Michael" was another of Hitler's code names. It did not interest him. His staff people and divisional commanders in the cauldron thought it an encouraging enough label, as far as such things went.

Michael had finally begun on the 27th of September and succeeded fairly well, though at the usual high cost in battle casualties. Rather than attacking outward from one side of the relief corridor, the attack had originated along the larger body of the cauldron, catching the Russians in the flank, so to speak. In effect another corridor had been driven out from the cauldron and then westward towards the Lovat, some miles south of the original corridor, thus trapping the Russians between these two landbridges. Once mopping-up operations had been completed, there remained a single broad landbridge to the cauldron that was now four or five times wider than the original corridor.

One could breathe a little easier. This meant everyone in the cauldron, more than 100,000 men.

Fresh troops had been brought into the cauldron throughout the course of the summer, yet the attack had been carried out in large part by veteran units of the whole ordeal, that is to say SS Totenkopf and the 5th Jaegers. This was the reward for the so-called elite striking troops; whether such appellations were unfair to the rest of the troops no longer really mattered. Only survival, relief, food, sleep, and hope mattered anymore; and the progress of one day to another without the cauldron being overrun by the Russians.

The Jaegers and Totenkopf had been reinforced by the regiments of the 126th Infantry Division, who were fresh troops only in that they were recent arrivals at Demyansk. Before then they had been embroiled in the savage fighting along the Volkhov River, the area known colloquially throughout the Eastern Front as "The End of the World." The veterans from that exceptionally dismal region more often referred to it as "The Asshole of the World." The swamps along the Volkhov were even more extensive, densely-wooded, flood-prone, mosquito-ravaged, and trackless than those along the Lovat. But after a while, to veterans of either place, such comparisons might seem as no more than academic exercises. It was what it was. All of it was what it was. The Volkhov, the Lovat, Demyansk, Staraya Russa; the Ssinyavino Hills, Lake Ladoga, the Neva; Rzhev, the Lutchessa Valley, Velizh, Velikiye Luki, Demidov; Voronezh, Charkow, Izyum, Sevastapol, Rostov, Stalingrad.

Stalingrad. That long narrow city on the banks of the Volga, which lay nearly a thousand miles to the southeast of Demyansk, the ugly village in the Valdai Hills. Stalingrad . . . the source of so many of the Wehrmacht communiques over the last few months.

Stalingrad and then still beyond Stalingrad, to the Kalmuck Steppe and the Caucasus Mountains and the ultimate south. The Manytsch River, the Kuban River, Novorossiisk, Tuapse, the Malgobek Heights. At this time the true mountain divisions were holding out along the glacial passes of Mount Elbrus in the far south of Russia, thousands of feet above the treeline. Their supplies were carried on the backs of mules across ice-plateaus several miles in diameter, ringed by peaks on all horizons each higher than the highest of the Alps.

All of it was what it was.

Operation Michael was no more than a local affair. The newsreels in Germany, somewhat less explicit than they had been earlier in the war, mentioned only a limited attack to straighten the defensive lines in the region south of Lake Ilmen. The 126th, the Jaegers, and Totenkopf had gone in abreast beneath sunny skies, slopping through muddy fens and fields covered with standing water that for the moment was only ankle-deep, supported by a few tanks and new-model assault guns, by artillery batteries that had been husbanded along that neighborhood of the cauldron, by one of the few squadrons of Stukas that had not been sent off to southern Russia. The Russians had been caught off guard and initial progress was good, but the enemy positions were deeply echeloned and there was no quick breakthrough to the Lovat. The Russians had turned small villages into small fortresses, now fought over tooth and nail in the floodplain along the east bank of the river, just as other tiny villages had been fought over on the west bank back in the winter and early spring.

On and on. On and on.

The Lovat was in fact reached only on a narrow front, the attack thus achieving a kind of funnel-shape growing narrower from east to west. A few Totenkopf battalions that had advanced the farthest were cut off by Russian counterattacks. They barely escaped annihilation, pulling back and re-establishing contact with elements of the other two divisions.

Casualties ran high among all units of the attacking force. The Jaegers and Totenkopf, barely more than skeleton forces earlier in the summer, had received a certain number of replacements. Totenkopf had in fact received fewer than the army. Many of these men now lay dead in the watery thickets, along with the corpses of the old veterans.

So the operation could not be called a complete success. But the corridor was wider now; the Demyansk cauldron no longer so much resembled the head of an animal with its neck stretched out on the block. And the onset of the rasputitsa would provide a further defensive barrier, at least until the frosts came in November.

This was the last offensive operation of any consequence in northern Russia, even though it was hardly more than a temporary reshaping of the trenches. Fighting would continue along a static front until 1944, a filthy, shell-torn, and grisly business that much resembled the French and Belgian landscape of WWI; the only difference being, perhaps, that these trenches and isolated strong points were strung out through vast areas of abject wilderness. Now the second winter was approaching.

Meanwhile the war of movement and great campaigns continued far to the south, driving on Stalingrad, driving into the empty lands that bordered the Caucasus Mountains, where the Landsers found Asian camels watering at remote desert wells.

•   •   •

Eicke was gone. For reasons which Brockdorff could not clearly ascertain, he had been transferred back to Germany at the end of June. Brockdorff would not dupe himself into believing this had anything to do with the increasingly ugly disputes between Eicke and himself. He suspected Eicke had grown frustrated with airing his complaints from a thousand miles out on the battlefield, and had somehow pulled strings that would bring him closer to the ear of Hitler and SS Reichsfuhrer Himmler. But if this had been his intention, then his pleas had continued to fall on deaf ears, for the Totenkopf Division still remained in the trenches around Demyansk.

Brockdorff could not repress a certain feeling of contentment. How little he had felt of that over these long months. . . .

It was more than the fact of Eicke's departure. That had brought him not contentment but simple relief, of a burden being lifted from his shoulders. Now he only rarely awoke in the middle of the night feeling that a red switch of anger had been thrown in the back of his head.

No, this contentment, this smug feeling almost of revenge, had to do with a picture of Eicke now getting in Hitler's and Himmler's hair, harassing them endlessly, interfering with their daily business, doing all the busy and fulminating little things that Eicke was prone to do.

Brockdorff had no way of knowing whether or not this picture corresponded to reality. But on occasion he would think it so, on the few occasions when he bothered to think about it at all any longer. Even such demi-gods as Hitler and Himmler would have a difficult time ignoring the commander of one of their own SS divisions.

The pettiness of the whole situation, of his own thought processes, still ate at him; but with Eicke gone the whole situation had become a little easier to deal with, or not deal with.

Yet it seemed that this Demyansk business might go on forever, and with Totenkopf still stationed in the Valdai Hills it was always possible that Eicke would return. Brockdorff refused to think of this. It was with a certain serenity that he realized he was capable of blocking this from his thoughts.

In any case almost four months had passed by, and still Theodor Eicke had not returned.

Eicke was gone. And Seydlitz. Seydlitz also was gone. Like participants in a drama that might have reached some strange and wrenching climax . . . yet without warning they were removed from the stage; and the ordinary events of days had simply gone on, gone on. The corps of the Graf von Seydlitz-Kurzbach had been absorbed into Brockdorff's command. Seydlitz had been reassigned, transferred to southern Russia, where he had taken command of another corps stationed in the obliterated factories of Stalingrad.

Stalingrad. Despite the danger which continued to threaten the Demyansk salient up to this very moment, the name of this far-distant city was on everyone's lips, from the Landsers to the headquarters people, from the supply echelons to the JU-52 pilots who still touched down daily at the airfield.

The name itself, Stalingrad. Stalin. Stalin's city. No one needed to make a point of this. The name spoke its own meaning.

There was also something of that same feeling from the year before, when they had all been waiting, waiting to hear that Moscow had fallen. Another year had passed and now it was Stalingrad. Moscow was no longer the target in 1942; the great operational goal was now far to the south—Stalingrad, and the oil fields of the Caucasus. The Wehrmacht communiques had first mentioned Stalingrad at the beginning of August; the first little maps of the Volga had appeared in the front-line newspapers handed out to the troops. The 6th Army had penetrated into the barren steppe country of southern Russia even more quickly than the advances of the year before; they had crossed the Donets; they had crossed the Don; they had reached the Volga, and the fall of Stalingrad seemed only a matter of days.

Yet months had gone by, and still there was no word. Stalingrad had not yet fallen.

Brockdorff often found himself thinking of Seydlitz, trying to picture what it was like down there. A thousand miles deeper into the hinterland. Perhaps not so very far, in the Russian scale of things. But still, far enough.

Of course there was another aspect to this preoccupation with Stalingrad. This took the form of an abiding resentment and muttering among the troops, among the Landsers and also among the line officers and staff officers, which Brockdorff could not fail to catch wind of. They felt abandoned at Demyansk, relegated to some forgotten corner of the war which still might see the death of them all. Stalingrad was often mentioned with a certain tone of sardonic irritation, of soldierly humor and resignation; the way soldiers will often talk when the main sweep of events has left them behind, out of the limelight, away from the attention of the nation, yet still never very far from the grasp of destruction, of daily casualties that continued to come in the most hideous or ordinary forms.

Brockdorff could sympathize with these undercurrents, as he felt exactly these things himself. But he was a soldier, and that was war. There would always be a main event at some place or other, and there would always be lesser affairs everywhere else.

But if that was one idea of war, it was still hard to accept that Demyansk was now a sideshow. All summer long the Russian attacks had continued even more ferociously than in the winter, massive waves of infantry and tanks slogging through the mud. The relief corridor had nearly been severed on four or five different occasions; the state of emergency in the German lines was so continuous that the feeling of crisis had grown almost dull, dulled into a kind of dull redundant tension, day after day. On and on. The weeks, the months; the rain, the mud; the barrages, the Russian human-waves.

The Landsers were also soldiers, no matter how reluctantly, and they were forced to accept the situation as it stood. The day-to-day life in the cauldron was their life; life in the mud, in the dugouts, in the little forts beneath the hulls of wrecked tanks, in the Russian barrages, in the great attacks, in the daily local raids and infiltration parties, in the sometimes strange and peaceful little stream valleys in the rear areas, in the supply depots, and in the field hospitals. In this life the news of Stalingrad was only a kind of distraction, source of rumor or gossip, the venting of bitterness, anger, or exhaustion, something which all the same they thought of less often than their own homes back in Germany.

For the first time in more than a year some of them were being sent home on furlough. After the partial success of Operation Michael and the beginning of the rasputitsa, leave was granted to a few of the Demyansk veterans. But these rotations took place only gradually. A Landser might wait for months to take his scheduled turn. He might awaken at night in the pitch-dark of a bunker wondering if he would be killed the week before his turn arrived. How could he not wonder about this? Or perhaps he would worry even more that all furloughs would be cancelled indefinitely, at the first sign of another Russian attack.

More troops were arriving all the time. Few were sent out. The dead were buried in the cemeteries in the Valdai Hills, in the narrow meadowed valleys along the streams.

•   •   •

It was October and Brockdorff was beginning to fade now, to sink more quickly into himself. The endless string of emergencies had come, at least temporarily, to a halt; and Brockdorff, whether consciously or not, now allowed himself to settle into the deep nervous exhaustion that in a few more months would lead to his death.

He was in Demyansk. He would be in Demyansk forever. He would not be buried there, but he would remain there even so.

He spent less time in the command bunker. He could still be reached within seconds, in the little house across the street. He slept later, went to bed earlier, in the small candle-lit bedroom. He took pills that helped him sleep; he took other pills that helped him stay awake. All year he had resisted these small medical attentions. Now he relented.

Outside, the town was in ruins. Upon his first arrival in September of 41, Demyansk had seemed a miserable enough place, too large to be a village, too small to really be anything else. The poor wooden houses were built along mud streets, lined with rickety picket fences, overgrown with a kind of weedy, mosquito-plagued lushness in the summer, dreary in the autumn and spring, and snow-buried in the winter. The few larger municipal buildings of the Communist era resembled warehouses, cracked and untended even before the barrages and air attacks had destroyed most of them. The ruined schoolhouse, site of the command bunker, was one of these anonymous, almost unfinished-looking edifices of the new workers' paradise. In October of '42 two of its walls were still standing and the other two were heaps of rubble. Across the street lived Brockdorff in one of the ancient sagging log houses that were as much a part of Russia as any other thing.

There were a few old churches inside Demyansk. Others stood in monastic isolation out in the landscape of small hills, or at the edges of tiny villages. The churches were almost the only things in Russia that could be called fine things. Many of them had been turned into storehouses and granaries by the Reds. For a while, after the arrival of the Germans, the local people had begun to visit them again. But it was not long before most of them were destroyed by bombs and shellfire; destroyed during the terrible winter battles, or else somehow surviving intact, only to be destroyed during the terrible summer battles. In any case, there were few locals to visit them anymore. Most of the civilians had been evacuated long before, sent away even before Demyansk was first surrounded. They had been shipped off to other parts of occupied Russia, hundreds of miles to the rear, to work as slaves or to starve to death in areas where there was little food, or to be randomly murdered in various antipartisan operations, or to be executed as hostages in light of the continued failure of such antipartisan operations. Some out of desperation had simply joined the partisan bands, though it was a terrible enough life. Others had made for themselves a tolerable enough living working for the German supply organizations, finding that their lives were often better under these conditions than under the rule of the Communists. Others still had been deported to do slave labor in farms and factories in Germany, where they were frequently treated like animals.

It was all madness. The collision of Nazism and Stalinism had brought about a madness worse than anything that had gone before. Yet it was all familiar, in a certain way. Madness in Russia was a kind of ancient tradition, achieving a certain dull stability over the centuries, a kind of soul that was at times more ghastly, at times more resigned. In barren Nazi camps the Red Army POWs continued to die of starvation and to cannibalize the flesh and intestines of their dead comrades, guarded by German sentries or even by their own countrymen. Countless thousands of Russians—Russians, Ukrainians, Balts, Tatars, Cossacks, Caucasian mountain tribes—so dreaded the return of the Communists that they continued to help the Germans with a deep sense of mission and loyalty. Meanwhile countless thousands of other Russians continued to be murdered by their erstwhile "liberators." The kinfolk of the murdered ones loathed the Germans as much as any people on earth.

Countless thousands of other Russians simply did not know what to do anymore, where to turn, whom to hate, whom to obey. They survived or they were killed, one way or another.

•　•　•

But Von Brockdorff-Ahlefeldt was not thinking of civilians. They were gone from the cauldron, all except for a few. There were no partisan bands east of the Lovat anymore; there was not enough room for them to hide in the cauldron.

The ruined town was quieter now than it had been for some time. Grey autumn sunlight filtered quietly through boarded windows. The rumble of artillery from around the perimeter of the cauldron had subsided. Within Demyansk itself only a few shells ever landed. The town in the middle of the small hills was beyond the range of all but the most powerful Russian cannon. The air raids had subsided. And the persistent roar of transport planes from the nearby Demyansk airfield had also subsided. This noise above all was noticeable by its absence—a kind of bell-like quiet on a few sunny days, causing some German soldiers to glance into the distance, listening intently at nothing.

The few squadrons of fighters and Stukas had all been sent to southern Russia. Most of the JU-52 transports had been sent there as well, and it was their absence that made the clearest space of quiet in the autumn. The transport squadrons were needed to supply the remote spearheads in the Caucasus and along the Volga. The Demyansk cauldron was now supplied across the Lovat bridge, or across the small-gauge railroad bridge that had been constructed nearby. Only occasionally did the droning of a single plane taking off or landing penetrate Brockdorff's thoughts in the wooden house.

He was suffering from ongoing bouts of ague and fever. It was probably the same ailment that the Landsers referred to as swamp-fever, which made so many of them resemble stick-figures in the battle lines. Bouts of anger, sometimes brought about by recent memories, other times by nothing at all, would cause Brockdorff's condition to worsen. At other times a strange dreaminess, almost otherworldliness, seemed to possess him.

He was seated at the edge of his bed in the small room with boarded windows. He was trying to gather the energy to stand, to leave the house and put in an appearance at the command bunker across the street. Instead he found himself staring into the cob-webbed mirror that rested atop a bureau by the wall.

His orderly should clean that off, he thought. Dust. Cobwebs. He had lived for months in this room without noticing them.

Candlelight flickered.

An observer in the room might have looked into the mirror along with Brockdorff and seen a certain kind of man. Even in decay there remained a certain kind of boyishness in his expression, in his eyes, which is sometimes associated with the decadence and easy-living of the upper classes, an expression which will appear on the faces of the aged alongside the faces of the young. A decent, orderly, somewhat indecisive face. But what exactly can be read in a face? No learned man has ever been able to establish this to the satisfaction of the world. Brockdorff was slightly cross-eyed; this and his tall, careworn head gave him the appearance of a large aging bird of some kind, blinking about with faculties worn down by the erosive forces of nature, by age, by the endless struggles with everything.

But he was not a grim-looking man. Regardless of what went on inside his head, there remained almost permanently the faint suggestion of a smile on his lips. On his lips, or perhaps in his eyes; the look was subtle enough that it would be hard to say which of his features caused this effect.

Perhaps this smile meant nothing in particular, perhaps it was only another manifestation of that peculiar upper-class bearing, that almost vacuous-looking air, which some noblemen possessed in lieu of the more usual arrogance.

Like most people, Brockdorff would be least able to judge his own appearance. A man is more often a better judge of his own soul than of his outward appearance to the world.

He stared into the mirror and found himself thinking of his wife. He thought that his own face reminded him of her. Why this was so he did not know. He glanced at the small photograph of her beside his bed, and saw that the resemblance was not quite so striking there. No. The picture was almost thirty years old, for one thing. Yet when he glanced in the mirror again he saw her again. The feeling did not strike him as odd or uncanny. Sensations and wordless emotions passed within him. This past night he had slept well for once, assisted no doubt by the powders of the surgeon attached to the corps headquarters, by the brandy which he had begun to drink more regularly. Yet in the gloom of another morning he felt once again like a man who had not slept for days. He picked up the wristwatch that lay on the bedside table next to the picture of his wife.

An airplane droned somewhere in the distance. Fifteen more minutes then, he thought.

But he did not want to think about it. He called through the partially open door, telling his orderly to awaken him when the time came. Just a little more rest.

He did not wish to lie down again, and he sat dully with his back resting against the bedboard, the back of his head resting against the vermin-infested wall of the room. The lice and other small life lived inside the wall; if it were built solidly enough they would generally remain in there. A general's quarters were kept somewhat cleaner than a Landser's bunker out on the perimeter.

Thoughts came to him which were sometimes less angry, less overwrought, than they had been in previous months. He recalled a visit to one of the Totenkopf battlegroups back in the winter, that unspeakable winter. It was a normal inspection visit. It also had to do, no matter how tenuously, with the morale of the troops, with the obligation of a commander to put in an appearance among men who by that time had passed beyond the limits of everything. The temperature was forty five degrees below zero. On a day without wind this was almost bearable. Snow was falling heavily. At such extreme low temperatures heavy snowfall was unusual, but the snow had continued to fall throughout the winter in great quantities.

He had almost been unable to reach the regimental command bunkers behind the lines. His car could not negotiate the drifts in the roads. Over the radio Eicke had warned him not to come; Brockdorff had put that down to Eicke and his inclination to stay removed from interference from above. But the SS commander's advice had not been ill-founded. Brockdorff and his aide Major Bruner had been obliged to leave the car stranded in a drift; they finally arrived at the Totenkopf positions in a panje-wagon driven by an SS man, this driver bundled up so heavily that he seemed to be sitting beneath a mound of furs piled up on the front seat.

Drivers, couriers, the men in the supply columns, needed heavier protection against the cold than anyone else, if they were to be able to move about at all in the open. Their frostbite casualties were worse than those of the infantry in the forward dugouts. Brockdorff had been distressed to learn of a few incidents of men in the supply columns shooting themselves in despair, committing suicide after days out in terrible blizzards, carrying out their normal duties into the depths of whatever those last minutes were. Most of the men adapted somehow, survived somehow, God only knew how—and then there were those who did not. It was hardly even distressing, because in truth there was no word for it. The winter in the cauldron went on. Brockdorff found himself admiring the huge bundle of clothing worn by this Totenkopf driver.

His admiration became subdued when he reached the command bunker of the SS regiment and found other men clothed equally as warmly, staff officers, front-line officers, ordinary soldiers, all of them.

They all looked scarcely less brutalized by the weather than the men of neighboring army units. Yet their clothing was better, much better. Some of it had been taken from Russian civilians or dead or captured Russian soldiers; they all did this, everyone in the Germany army did it to survive. Yet much of what he saw in the SS bunker clearly came from some other source. More than just subdued, Brockdorff was startled, taken aback. He noticed Major Bruner also staring at the SS men, all the while trying not to stare. Brockdorff opened his mouth to say something, then pressed his lips together, thinking he would go through with the inspection first of all.

This was Max Simon's regiment, and it was he who led Brockdorff around. Eicke's battlegroup, kampfgruppe, was stationed in some other part of the cauldron. The various divisions along the line had been broken up into these different battlegroups, divisions in less threatened sectors detaching companies or battalions to reinforce units in the more endangered areas. In no small part because of the tenacious reputation earned by the Totenkopf men, the two most prominent battlegroups were commanded by Eicke and by his chief subordinate Max Simon. A regiment of the 290th Infantry Division was also under Simon's overall command in this sector.

Brockdorff's reason for visiting Simon rather than Eicke was simple. While Simon's positions had been difficult to get to, reaching Eicke would have been nearly impossible. The amount of snow was unbelievable. Men said this matter-of-factly from day to day—the snow is unbelievable. While the cold, the greater killer, was so bad that it could hardly be spoken of. Men spoke of this through the expressions in their eyes.

Simon met with Brockdorff wearing a quilted fur overcoat that would have done justice to a czar. Brockdorff could no longer restrain himself. He asked matter-of-factly how the Totenkopf people had come by such sturdy clothing.

Simon baldly replied that most of it had been flown in from an SS depot in Riga. A certain Gruppenfuhrer Jeckeln, an old crony of Eicke's, had heard of the plight of the Totenkopf men and done everything possible to assist them. Simon did not mention that much of this clothing had been liberated from Jews murdered by the Einsatzgruppen at various places in the Baltic states. Simon may not have been aware of these exact particulars, though he had himself participated in the murder of Jews and other civilians in other parts of Russia; not to mention at Dachau, already years ago.

Many of the army commanders such as Brockdorff remained more or less unaware of this. Which is to say, they were also more or less aware of this.

Brockdorff still hardly knew what to say. His first thoughts—
if one were to exclude inchoate feelings of rage and bafflement—
were of the army regiment currently under Simon's command.

Simon shared with Eicke that peculiar insensitivity to what
should have been highly sensitive subjects—a trait not so uncom-
mon among the ranks of the SS. Yet at this moment he seemed to
guess that Brockdorff was thinking about something. He hastened
to say that the clothing had been distributed without regard to
rank among all his men. The Landsers detached from the 290th
Infantry Division had also received their share.

"Very good then," said Brockdorff.

It was all he could think of for the moment.

They were still in the regimental command bunker. The place
was dimly lit like every dwelling in Russia in the wintertime. It
was warm though, solidly constructed, insulated by great drifts of
snow, heated by stoves and by the bodily warmth of the men
inside. If one could find shelter one could stay warm. But that was
the problem with war. Men simply would not remain quietly in
their rooms, as a certain philosopher once complained.

Brockdorff was struck by something which he had noticed in
the past, which was Max Simon's strange resemblance to SS
Reichsfuhrer Himmler. The two men did not look identical exactly, but there was something peculiar about it all the same. Both
were balding, gnome-like, bespectacled creatures. Simon was
slightly larger, his features toughened by fighting, by the stress of
command, by various other ordeals. He was a brave, resourceful,
and highly decorated officer. Experience in Russia had given a
leathering to his skin and to his very presence, as it had done to
almost everyone else in the East. Whereas SS Reichsfuhrer
Himmler was quietly derided even among the SS for possessing
all the leadership qualities of an elementary school teacher. Still,
they very much resembled each other. As if Simon were
Himmler's sturdier, yet less conniving, less exalted, older brother.

Brockdorff made these same observations that he had made in
the past, if only to distance himself for a moment from the other
issue. He still did not know what to think. Meanwhile snow continued to fall outside the bunker, creating a deep and heavy layer
of silence that was almost like a sound, muffling the lesser sounds
of shellfire that rumbled dimly through now and again.
Brockdorff and Major Bruner sipped from mugs of tea handed to

them by Simon. After the visitors had warmed themselves for a few minutes they went back out into the weather, towards the forward positions, accompanied by the SS officer.

The communications trenches were dug out better than the roads leading to the rear areas. SS men continued to dig them out even while the officers walked through. The snow drifts added to the height of the trench walls, so at points they seemed almost to be passing through some underground chasm, with only a narrow thread of murky sky above.

•   •   •

The snow stopped falling for a few days. The cold grew worse, but with a break in the blizzard-weather it was possible to move about more easily inside the cauldron. A week after Brockdorff's inspection of Simon's positions he was visited by Eicke at the command center in Demyansk. He had not seen Eicke in over a month; the occasion was thus like receiving a visitor from beyond. In the meantime there had been only radio communication with Eicke's end of the cauldron, like weather stations in the Arctic linked by only the nothingness of electricity.

It was difficult to receive clear situational reports over the radio, to issue proper orders. With traffic passable through the drifts for a few days, Eicke had come in person to Demyansk.

His men were being wiped out, he said. The Russian attacks were killing them; exposure to the weather was killing them. If they could rest peacefully in their bunkers they might manage all right. But almost every day they had to go out, into the blizzards, into the murder of the climate, counterattacking, retaking some shattered village that the Russians had taken the night before.

There was something about Eicke that left Brockdorff unmoved. He was not demanding Totenkopf's relief at this point; they were under siege, cut off from the main German lines by thirty miles of frozen swamp; obviously there could be no relief for anyone. Brockdorff expected Eicke's complaints to be leading up to something, but the SS general simply rattled on, as if not knowing where to turn. Eicke bore that unsettling and ambivalent expression of a mastiff that at one moment might be looking for some sign of approval from its master, while at the next indicating that it might want to tear the master's throat out. He was like that, after all—a murderous, highly ambitious man, yet possessed of a certain nagging insecurity that might cause him to look about for respect or approval from unlikely sources. He had come a long way in his career and was perhaps more sure of himself than he had ever been, yet still this trait never entirely disappeared. After months in the cauldron the frayed edges of a man might occasionally reveal the deeper elements within. He was an unnerving human being.

But it must be said, too, that Eicke and his men had risen to the occasion more than once during this long ordeal.

Eicke left Brockdorff unmoved, but other things still disturbed him. The army commander mentioned his visit to Simon's positions and agreed with Eicke that the SS men were in terrible shape. Simon had led him into dugouts where SS men had saluted them with fingers black from frostbite. Simon had showed him first-aid clearing stations packed with frozen or wounded men who could not be moved to the field hospitals in the rear. The snow was too deep for that kind of traffic. After whole wagon columns of wounded had arrived frozen to death at the field hospitals, Simon had decided to keep them in the forward areas. There was no other choice. The men in these clearing stations beggared description. Brockdorff felt ugly moments of guilt over his choice of a military career, that guilt which someone who has reached the rank of general only rarely, if ever, allows himself to feel. He felt it and pushed it aside. His initial anger over these special shipments of warm clothing to the SS men—which amounted no more and no less to highly preferential treatment—had graduated into thoughts which he could barely describe to himself.

Warm clothing or not, a man still had to remove his mittens in order to squeeze the triggers of his machine gun. In combat a man could not wear them at all for long periods of time; they were too clumsy, interfering with the instant reactions that separated the living from the dead. Warm clothing or not, the SS were still in the most threatened part of the line, had been stationed there by Brockdorff's own orders; the continual raids, counterattacks, and patrols out in the open, the nights spent at listening posts out in the open, had ravaged them to the point of collapse, warm clothing or not. The fact was that every unit in the German army, even those that had somehow procured warmer gear, was still too inexperienced to cope with the day-to-day realities of the Russian winter, especially under combat conditions. All of the little secrets of survival that none of them knew, that only a few of them were barely beginning to learn. . . . It was a tragedy. Even the Russian soldiers in this worst winter of the century, even the Siberians who were outfitted as if for battle in the high Arctic, were freezing to death around the Demyansk cauldron, driven out into the open, on into the open, by the ruthless orders to attack handed down from their own high command.

In the clearing station—another dimly lit bunker—Brockdorff and Simon were surrounded by wounded and horribly frostbitten men, stretched out here and there in the straw like several dozen Christs pulled down from their crosses. Some moaned, many were silent. Some were dead and would be thrown outside into the snow when their condition was discovered.

For the time being Brockdorff had put this issue of warm clothing aside. Now Eicke was face to face with him a week later, and his normal disdain for Eicke almost prompted him to mention it again. But for the moment Eicke's complaints culminated neither in impossible demands nor insulting tirades; he simply looked worn out, at a loss. Brockdorff found himself sympathizing with the man over a glass of brandy. He said,

"You know I am counting on you. Whether any of our men survive this is perhaps up to God's will. But we must put that aside. I'm counting on you, Eicke. Your men are hard."

"God's will," muttered Eicke. The SS men were not in the habit of hearing about God's will. But Eicke seemed to attach no particular significance to this phrase, no more than Brockdorff had done. Perhaps neither of them knew what to say.

"Yes, Herr General," said Eicke. "You may count on us. You will count on us. I'll see to it."

They passed on to the more specific reason for Eicke's visit, which was the beginning of Operation Bruckenschlag, Bridgestrike, from outside the cauldron. Eicke would need to start husbanding some of his units as reserves, so they could strike out to meet the relief force when the proper time came. Eicke said flatly that he had no reserves. Brockdorff said that other elements of the army divisions would be dispatched to his command. They would continue to hold the line in Eicke's sector, while the breakout force would be composed mostly, if not entirely, of Totenkopf men. This last detail was not mentioned by either of them; it was clearly understood. Eicke himself, no matter how exhausted his own men were, would not think of entrusting such a critical operation to any other unit.

Indeed he looked almost pleased, in a dull kind of way, that something was finally going to be done to break the Russian encirclement. To end things one way or another, before the endless winter killed them all.

The SS general left Demyansk that afternoon. Brockdorff was gratified that the meeting had not been as volatile as some of his past exchanges with Eicke. Indeed Eicke's behavior could almost be called out-of-character, except that the constant flux of the man's temperament made this difficult to say. Yet while feeling somewhat relieved, Brockdorff was also irritated to be feeling relief at all. Because it should not have come to that, a commanding general feeling less anxious because one of his subordinates had not made a fuss for once. Even when not behaving loudly and overbearingly, there was something about Eicke's way of carrying himself that was insubordinate, entirely unmilitary. It was not a question of defiance, which was what most cases of insubordination usually amounted to. Eicke's manner was too natural, too crude, too insensitive to the judgments of others, to really be called defiant. Brockdorff really didn't know what to call it.

•   •   •

Eicke reverted to form during the last week of April, when the relief corridor was finally established. Even he could not be so dense as to think that the cauldron was now secure, yet his demands that something be done about his Totenkopf men reached new heights, or lows. As if the SS men had done their part by now. As indeed they had.

But Eicke seemed stubbornly oblivious to the fact that an army could not function in this way. Especially not in an ongoing crisis. That was what it was, Brockdorff finally realized, the thing that made a dull pressure push up against the inside of his scalp whenever he dealt with Eicke. Eicke seemed to be operating in some other military system, a system where brave units performed great deeds and then were rewarded and honored for those deeds, called home for adulation and victory parades.

As if they were still living in an age of Napoleon and his Guards Divisions, or a Roman age where the Praetorians were feted in the colosseum after campaigns in far-flung lands.

Brockdorff's own personal messages of congratulations to the Totenkopf men for their outstanding performance might have encouraged this view, though it was only a normal practice in the German armed forces to praise units that had fought well. Brockdorff had been sincere enough with his praise. He had simply omitted other elements of bitterness and anger from them. In a way these feelings had to do with the SS as a whole, but that was almost too much for him to cope with, and his thoughts tended to focus more on Eicke himself. With Eicke, that was not hard to do.

It did no good when Brockdorff stated, repeatedly, that the army divisions also needed relief—that Totenkopf could not constantly be treated as a special force that was due special consideration. Eicke would counter by saying they had already been given special consideration—the honor of repeatedly being given the most terrible assignments in the most critical areas. That there was some truth to this would both fluster and more deeply anger Brockdorff, until on a few occasions both men were reduced to shouting senseless accusations at each other. Seydlitz's Jaeger divisions, he had said, had also performed critical tasks, and what was their reward for that? A rest? No, they were simply ordered to hold on in the cauldron along with everyone else. Eicke was not interested in the fate of the jaegers. They were not Waffen-SS men. At last Brockdorff brought up the issue which had disturbed him for several months, the issue of the special shipments of winter clothing received by the Totenkopf Division. If they were delivered special equipment while the Landsers of the army received nothing, then they could be expected to carry out more difficult assignments.

Upon hearing this Eicke had appeared on the verge of turning purple. Apoplexy, thought Brockdorff suddenly. Perhaps that would finish this man. If Brockdorff himself did not suffer it first.

But even in these ugly exchanges Brockdorff tried to remain civil. It was what he had always been accustomed to.

Eicke flushed purple but then in a matter of seconds became almost expressionless. He shared with his supreme commander Adolf Hitler a talent for stonily ignoring the most direct and prickly kinds of criticism. He did mumble something about the responsibility of any divisional commander to see to the needs of his men, but his eyes were elsewhere even as he said this, shifting about for some new tack. Brockdorff had had enough by then and dismissed him from his quarters, as he had done before and would do again.

Before leaving Eicke had left a report on his desk.

"You might find this of interest," he had said.

· · ·

When Eicke left, Brockdorff simply pushed the report aside to tend to other matters. But it was difficult to get this situation out of his head. It was not a question of who deserved what, either rewards or further hardships or anything else. It was a question of command. It was a question of a subordinate knowing there were limits to how much he could discuss anything with a commander; of a subordinate knowing his place, shutting up, and removing himself from any discussion when there was nothing further to be said.

Rather than going over and over this in his mind, Brockdorff had finally picked up the report left behind by Eicke.

It was a report from the chief medical officer of Simon's regiment. The gist of it was not very different from reports he had received from medical officers of the army units. The men were suffering from a variety of fevers, pneumonia, other ailments, not to mention sheer exhaustion, which was reducing the combat-readiness of whole units to almost nil. Brockdorff had seen it all before and he was sick of it. He did not blame the doctors or the men. He was sick of the whole situation. He had been in the army a long time and he was used to treading a certain fine line—a line on one side of which lay sympathy and compassion, and on the other side of which lay shutting himself away from these kinds of thoughts, of getting on with the business at hand.

It was a kind of age-old military schizophrenia, a condition which has perhaps become worse or more strange during the 20th century, as citizens of nations have grown less tolerant of the age-old mental habits of military men.

Brockdorff was no different from hundreds or thousands of other generals, who could send congratulatory messages to groups of horribly mutilated men who had just accomplished some important task or other.

How else could it be? That was war. He could not even phrase these thoughts to himself in such a way, or in any way. It was all too large and he did not think in those terms. He had chosen a military career at age sixteen.

But there was a peculiar phrase in this SS medical report which caught his eye. It could not fail to do so, as Eicke, or someone, perhaps the medical officer himself, had seen fit to underline it.

"...the physical condition of the men has deteriorated to the point where some of them resemble inmates I have examined during my tour of duty at the concentration camps...."

My God, thought Brockdorff.

He did not know which struck him most—the fact of such a comparison being made, or the fact that Eicke would see fit to circulate such a document outside the ranks of the SS.

Again, that peculiar stone-headed insensitivity to highly sensitive subjects ... At times the SS men could be as conniving as old foxes, while at other times they could be simply dense, as dense as the dullest pupil sitting forever in the back of a classroom.

Indeed, Brockdorff might have given this matter still further thought, but for the moment he was simply angry. Angry and exhausted. This still had more to do with Eicke than with this curious medical report. It was not news to him that large numbers of the Totenkopf men had served tours of duty in the camps.

He reread the strange-sounding words and felt a pang of some deeper disturbance, but his impatience with everything had suddenly become too great and he wadded up the piece of paper and threw it in the nearest trash bin.

●　　●　　●

On and on.

There had been that last insufferable tirade on the morning of Seydlitz's arrival at Demyansk, when Brockdorff under other circumstances might have relieved Eicke of his command. Or at least given it very serious consideration. His physical and mental frailty had been growing worse. Anyway, the whole issue had passed by, leaving a certain gnawing humiliation in its wake, but then after a while scarcely even that. Eicke had been called back to Germany. There was only Demyansk. There was only the cauldron. The summer battles had been merciless. Brockdorff could not allow himself to be consumed by squabbles with the Waffen-SS. He needed them too badly, for one thing.

Eicke's replacement, as had been the case the year before when Eicke was wounded, was Max Simon. Simon was not as difficult a man to deal with. His SS rank was equivalent to that of colonel, and this difference between intermediate and senior field rank kept his meetings with Brockdorff somewhat more subdued. Even Simon possessed many of Eicke's traits; they were simply not as pronounced, at least not in Brockdorff's presence. He did not possess quite that oafish and brutal charisma that Eicke had, that force of a physically large and persistent man—which gave Eicke a certain prepossessing aura even amongst those who were repelled by him.

This was not to say that Simon was pleasant or amenable. There was still friction between Brockdorff and the new Totenkopf commander. But for Brockdorff, at least in his own mind, it was easier to deal with now. Perhaps this would only be another way of saying that Brockdorff was growing weaker, his will eroding, refusing to involve himself in any more of these disputes now that Eicke was gone.

At a critical point in the summer battles a Totenkopf battalion had again been nearly wiped out to the last man, defending a key village along the relief corridor against overwhelming Russian strength. The corridor—der Schlauch—was in immediate danger of being cut; Demyansk would be surrounded all over again, the terrible ordeal of the winter would be repeated all over again. Brockdorff had ordered Simon by radio to make an immediate counterattack to restore the situation.

Simon had reported that Totenkopf had suffered over a thousand casualties in two days and could not, or would not, make any further attacks.

Brockdorff realized that perhaps he had demanded too much of the Totenkopf men, had thrown them to the dogs once too often. He might have had Simon court-martialed for the direct refusal of an order in a crisis. He no longer had the strength, the will; perhaps he no longer even had the desire. He did not really know, as he refused to dwell on it. He did not even reply to Simon's message. He ordered the counterattack to be undertaken instead by the 8th Jaegers of General Hohne. When Hohne's men failed to recapture the village Brockdorff had then threatened him with court-martial.

Throughout 1942, in newsreels throughout Germany, Brockdorff-Ahlefeldt continued to be proclaimed as the hero of Demyansk. Der Held von Demyansk. Yet perhaps he too might have been better off relieved of his command. Not as punishment for incompetence or failure. Demyansk in a certain way resembled the battle of Verdun during the first great war, in that it went on and on, on and on and on, month after month, season after season. New blood was needed. New bodies, from the lowest private to the senior commanders, bodies that had not been withered by incessant physical and mental anguish. Brockdorff was not an old man, but at times as summer faded into autumn he possessed the oddly sunny look of someone who was almost senile.

New blood was pumped into the cauldron. Yet the old blood was not taken out. There was no one in the armed forces who thought the place worth defending anymore. No one in the army, no one in the Waffen-SS either. As a springboard or assembly point for some future drive on Moscow, Demyansk was clearly useless. There was no railroad through the town nor anywhere nearby in the Valdai Hills, except for the small-gauge train, almost like a toy train, the "Ilmensee Express," that served as a local supply artery. And the supply roads across the floodplain between the Lovat and the Valdai Hills were among the worst in Russia. But Hitler would not let go. He might have done so, abandoned

Demyansk and the Valdai Hills. He had other fish to fry that summer. The drive on Stalingrad, for one thing, where armies five times larger than the force at Demyansk were coming to grips with their eventual fate.

But Hitler ordered that Demyansk be held. Most of his generals had by this time given up trying to argue about it with him. After Operation Michael still more divisions were moved into the cauldron, so that on the map it might even resemble a fortress. Hitler as always remained fond of the map. The idea of fortresses appealed to him as well.

•　　•　　•

Brockdorff began to dream strange things. He was taking pills now, receiving injections. He was sleeping better than he had in several years. But in this sleep, perhaps influenced by these medications, he began to dream—dreams that were strange, vivid, and intensely complicated, that seemed to last for hours through the course of a night.

Yet they occurred in the depths of sleep and they did not leave him feeling unrested upon his awakening. His own ailing condition left him groggy, weak; yet the dreams did not seem to aggravate this. Indeed, he could scarcely remember most of them, and upon attending to his daily affairs they would vanish from his mind.

He would remember, usually for only a few moments upon first awakening, intensely vivid scenes that were yet only fragments from much longer dreams—dreams which were strange and unsettling but not quite nightmarish, dreams which above all seemed to have some immense, epic quality to them. He could grasp that much even though almost all of the details would escape him as soon as he arose from bed, like a sinker attached to a fishing line plummeting within moments out of his consciousness and into nothingness.

By and large he was simply aware of having dreamed many strange things during these autumn nights. Otherwise he did not ponder them too much.

But his waking thoughts were changed somewhat as well. During the mud of the rasputitsa a certain calm had come over the cauldron. Most people recognized that it was only a lull, that the Russians would again start hurling themselves at the perimeter when the ground hardened in November or December. Brockdorff himself knew this very well, yet for him this lull was also like the end of something.

His manner became more detached; some might have called it inattentive. The whole year-long drama at Demyansk began to take on a different shape during these days, or at odd little moments during these days. His feelings about the Totenkopf Division, for example, even about such people as Eicke and Simon, began to appear to him in a different light.

They were simply different components of some terrible drama, each with its proper role to play, a role beyond judgment, anger, or personal disagreements, a role that might have been ordained in the past or even in the future as some unalterable component of a kind of terrible Homeric epic.

Such thoughts would make him abashed, even a little embarrassed. To a Landser in the trenches they might have provoked an overpowering disgust, the typical outlook of one of the rarefied higher headquarters swine. Generals would always be generals. Though perhaps even a Landser, like anyone who has gone through a long ordeal, might begin to think of strange ways of describing it to himself, judging the inadequacy of words but hearing them pass through his mind anyway, along with the compulsive muttering of cursing or filth that provided a kind of terse and ever-present summary of everything.

Brockdorff was not incapable of putting himself in the Landsers' place, yet even so these thoughts would filter into his mind from time to time, as if some unknown force of events were speaking silently to him. He was sick and on more than a few occasions he was becoming a little addled; in most of his waking moments he was aware of this, more or less.

He might glance overhead at one of the JU-52 trimotors that continued to land at the airfield, passing at low altitude beneath the murk of the sky. He would glance up into the sky and see a vague shape of some distant, terrible grandeur, a shape that spoke clearly enough with all its arrogant falsehood, yet which continued to persist up in the sky in its simplest, most indescribable form—a shape, simply a shape. Even the persistent, far-off droning of the airplane engines would become transformed from sound into a kind of shape within him.

Perhaps he had been visited on and off by such sensations throughout the course of the year, but had refused to allow himself to dwell on them. He had been too busy for such things. They were foolish, vacant, unworthy.

Yet they persisted. And for a while he no longer resisted them as much.

He recalled other incidents from back in the awful winter. He recalled the heroism of the Totenkopf battlegroups isolated out on the perimeter, isolated by blizzards, isolated from his own command post at Demyansk, isolated even from Eicke's command post somewhere out there in the wilderness, small groups of men isolated even from each other.

He recalled the defense of a certain village called Bjakowo by a small detachment of Totenkopf men. Now, on one of these dreary October days, he found himself again in the command bunker beneath the ruined schoolhouse, a dull and uneventful day, himself isolated from day or night in the dimly lit underground bunker; he found himself for no particular reason seated in the alcove adjoining the main operations room, that same small curtained annex where he had held a number of strange and disturbing conversations with General Seydlitz back in the spring.

But for the moment his thoughts were not on Seydlitz. He found himself leafing through the battle-log of his corps, the log where the situational reports from around the cauldron were entered daily by Major Bruner or one of his assistants. He sat quietly in the alcove, with the uneventful murmuring of his staff people carrying dimly through the curtain from the operations room a few feet away, the occasional ringing of a telephone, the comings and goings in the bunker marked by the dull tread of muddy boots; he found himself leafing back through the log-book to the entries for late February and early March. He remembered the terrible days when these entries had been made; he remembered them very clearly. He had read through them then; and now, long months later, he read through them again.

3 March 1942—

"Enemy attack repelled at Bjakowo. SS Obersturmfuhrer Meierdress, garrison commander, severely wounded. Kampfgruppe

Eicke requests Fiesler Storch to evacuate Obstrmfhr. Meierdress to Demyansk. Kampfgruppe Eicke will clear small area for landing of skiplane."

4 March 1942—

"Bjakowo. Enemy attack underway since midday, repelled by evening. Further heavy attacks indicated."

5 March 1942—

"Bjakowo. The enemy renews his attack. Grppnfhr. Eicke again requests ambulance Storch to fly severely wounded out of Bjakowo."

6 March 1942—

"Situation continues very grave at Strongpoint Bjakowo."

8 March 1942—

"Radio message from 16 Army Headquarters Staraya Russa (General Busch) to Corps Headquarters Demyansk (Brockdorff-Ahlefeldt). Praise for the defenders of Bjakowo, full confidence that despite grave ordeal the successful defensive battle of Kampfgruppe Eicke will continue."

9 March 1942—

"7:30 Uhr. Radio message from Kampfgruppe Eicke to Demyansk. Enemy attack supported by heavy tanks at Bjakowo. Request immediate Stuka air support.

"9:15 Uhr. Further transmissions from Kampfgruppe Eicke. Bjakowo attacked on three sides, tanks roaming in the town, last surviving officers severely wounded, including liaison officer.

"11:30 Uhr. Further transmission from Kampfgruppe Eicke to Commanding General Demyansk, re untenable situation at Bjakowo. Stuka support unavailable, blizzard conditions at airfield Staraya Russa. Local ground forces unable to reach Bjakowo despite all-out effort. Garrison fighting to last drop of blood. Repeated requests for air support or the defenders of Bjakowo will go under.

"12:15 Uhr. Fighting strength at Bjakowo reduced to 16 men. Approximately 100 wounded men trapped in town. Air support unavailable.

"18:30 Uhr. Repeated enemy attacks in overwhelming strength, supported by tanks. Kampfgruppe Eicke orders last defenders of Bjakowo to break out at nightfall."

10 March 1942—

"Kampfgruppe Eicke has lost all radio contact with defenders of Bjakowo."

11 March 1942—

"Last 13 defenders of Bjakowo break out to the south. 50 surviving wounded men brought to safety, make contact with combat patrols sent out by Kampfgruppe Eicke. The enemy finds only dead Totenkopf soldiers in the ruins of Bjakowo.

"Obstrmfhr. Meierdress brought to safety with other severely wounded. Command assumed by Untrstrmfhr. Wissebach until blinded by shellburst, later killed by enemy fire during breakout attempt. Despite severe wounds Obstrmfhr. Meierdress resumes command of surviving men.

"Casualty report Bjakowo–85 dead. Breakout attempt to Kampfgruppe Eicke–3 men killed. 18 out of 68 rescued wounded, dead upon contact with Kampfgruppe Eicke. 50 surviving wounded taken to clearing station Eicke, pending evacuation to field hospital Demyansk. 13 survivors unwounded. Obstrmfhr. Meierdress relinquishes command to Obstrmfhr. Lammers, III Battalion, SS Totenkopf Division, Kampfgruppe Eicke."

14 March 1942—

"Radio message from 16 Army Headquarters Staraya Russa (Busch) to Corps Headquarters Demyansk (Brockdorff-Ahlefeldt). The heroic defense of Bjakowo has bought time for other elements of Kampfgruppe Eicke to establish a new main battle line south of Bjakowo. Recommendation of Knight's Cross for Obstrmfhr. Meierdress forwarded to Fuhrer Headquarters/Berlin. Defenders of Bjakowo offer finest example of courage and steadfastness of German arms. Bravo Totenkopf. Hail to our Fuhrer."

Brockdorff-Ahlefeldt set the log book down. He set his palms down flat on the little table on either side of the log book. He stared at the frayed and faded curtain in front of him, through the thin material of which he could make out the few men stationed in the operations room beyond. There remained the faint continuous buzz of noise through the command bunker. Within his mind, deep silence reigned.

Gradually thoughts began to take shape, though for a while a kind of formless shape, a shapeless shape. A shape without clear definition, yet bearing the force that only a strong and terrible shape can bear.

Totenkopf. Bjakowo. Totenkopf. Totenkopf. Dead heroes roaming in the murky sky.

DEMYANSK

A general lived to see men such as these live and die. So it had once seemed. So it still seemed even now. The disputes between himself and Theodor Eicke, between himself and Max Simon, meant nothing, nothing at all. Each played out his role in a drama beyond all understanding. The living lived. The dead walked in the sky, dead forever.

●　　●　　●

He was slowly losing the faculty, not only to be critical of himself, but to be critical of things in general. General Seydlitz, during his short time in the cauldron, had spoken to him of the need "to do something"—saying bluntly that the time had come, or would come very soon, when something would have to be done. Otherwise disaster would consume them all—the men, the army, Germany, everything. Seydlitz had been talking about Adolf Hitler. He had been talking about open rebellion.

He reckoned that in the person of Brockdorff-Ahlefeldt he had a man whom he could trust. Obviously a breach of this trust would mean execution by a firing squad, if not a death still worse. But Seydlitz's trust was not misplaced. The two generals understood each other. But that was also in the past. Seydlitz had been gone for months now.

This was not the first time Brockdorff-Ahlefeldt had heard talk of this kind. For a period of time before the war there had actually been more of it, and there had been men ready to act on it. Brockdorff had been one of these men. In 1938 the country had been on the brink of war, a war for which Germany was entirely unprepared. A war which, in any case, many people thought entirely unnecessary. The German economy was recovering; the pride of the nation was also recovering, even without any great military adventures. Even the masses who adored the Fuhrer were not always so keen on the idea of another war.

But to the generals, even more than to the population at large, it was clear that war was coming. Hitler himself carried the shape of the coming war in his every word and gesture—

false words or true words, the war was apparent in everything he said.

In 1938 it had seemed likely that Britain and France would go to war over the Sudetenland, that part of Czechoslavakia which Hitler had so rashly annexed to the Reich. A plot had been formulated, one of many plots, and probably not the first. Brockdorff at that time had been in command of the 23rd Infantry Division outside of Berlin, a division composed largely of Berliners who were less enamored of Hitler than citizens from other regions of the country. They could be relied on to act, and their action would be to enter Berlin and depose the government, to remove Hitler from power. Brockdorff was only waiting to receive the go-ahead orders from the higher leaders of the coup. If war was declared by either side, then the coup would proceed within minutes; it seemed possible that Brockdorff himself would confront Hitler in the capital, usurp him from his office by his own hand.

It had never happened. Instead of war, peace was declared, a lasting peace for all of Europe. This was the message that Neville Chamberlain carried from Hitler back to England in September of 1938, after that last-minute exercise in brinkmanship had been concluded at the Munich Conference. Brockdorff and his men had been ready to arrest Hitler upon his return from Munich to Berlin, ready to install a government that would somehow prevent another catastrophic war. But it had never happened. Peace was declared. The coup was dissolved.

The following year, which saw the invasion of Poland, there was no coup. There was no talk of it, nor was there any talk of it during the string of surprisingly easy victories that followed during the next two years, including the initial overwhelming successes in Russia.

So Brockdorff was not a stranger to the kind of mutinous talk being uttered by Seydlitz, during a few private, vague, yet utterly unmistakable conversations in Demyansk in the spring of 1942.

Yet Seydlitz was gone now. Gone to Stalingrad. Where perhaps he would find occasion to hold these same private conversations with other generals; or where perhaps they would all be too busy now to do so, consumed by the moment-to-moment exigencies of desperate combat in Stalin's city.

Brockdorff did not know, and in truth Seydlitz's words were more distant from his mind now, just as things in general were.

DEMYANSK

Nineteen thirty-eight was not so long ago. Only four years. Especially to an older man, that was not such a long time. But Brockdorff was fading. He was dying, though at a very slow pace even now. Strange thoughts—or shapes in the place of thoughts—visited his mind, in the muddy autumn ruins of Demyansk, in wearisome inspection trips, in the schoolhouse command bunker where he had spent most of his waking hours for over a year. Strange dreams visited him at night, in the sagging house across the street.

He dreamed often of buildings, dreams filled with incidents as numerous as the thousands of rooms contained by these buildings. Some of these incidents were related in some way to daily events in the cauldron, yet the buildings themselves had nothing to do with Demyansk or even Russia. Or so it seemed. Sometimes these buildings were low shapes spread out across enormous compounds, like warehouses that contained unnerving kinds of objects and goings-on. Yet more often they were very tall buildings, taller than the few skyscrapers that existed in Russian cities, taller than anything that existed in Germany. They were not like any buildings Brockdorff had ever been in or seen before—unless they resembled pictures he might have seen of cities in America. Why he would dream of this he did not know, nor was he particularly curious, as dreams were often unanswerable things.

Perhaps such huge buildings were necessary to house all the rooms, the rooms wherein the seemingly endless incidents of these dreams took place. He could only ever remember a small fraction of these incidents; he only knew that they were the most singular feature of these dreams, apart from the buildings themselves. Long, complicated dreams; different, mysterious events taking place in one room after another, often seeming high above the ground.

He was in a large elevator, almost like a freight elevator but not as crudely finished as that, with several people who were strangers to him, though in the dream their faces seemed distinct enough. In his lifetime he had not been in elevators very often, and then only in buildings a few stories in height. To be suspended in a large elevator several thousand feet above the ground filled him with fear, an apprehension which he did his best to master, often simply shutting his eyes and resigning himself to the sinking feeling in his gut as the elevator descended into the abyss of the shaft.

The doors would open at various intermediate levels. Sometimes there would be narrow corridors lined with small office doors. Other times there would be large galleries or halls, filled with throngs of people. He would emerge from the elevator not onto the gallery itself but onto a long balcony that overlooked it, perhaps a hundred feet above the floor. Hitler stood here one time, perhaps Himmler as well. Yet most of the time he would see only a few people that he recognized, even though the faces of many other unknown people would remain strangely distinct, as if he did somehow recognize them from some other life that was not his waking life.

Often these people were engaged in acts of violence, hunting down an unknown quarry in long pursuits that led from one room to another, from the large hallways to countless smaller rooms, from the elevators to strange interminable corridors and balconies. Odd scenes took place before picture windows looking out on vague panoramas that spread thousands of feet below. Sometimes there were different groups engaged in this violence, hunting each other, ambushing each other, sometimes wreaking havoc among large crowds, other times merely passing through faceless crowds who remained oblivious to the hunters.

Brockdorff found himself cowering beneath a massive desk in an office, certain that his end had come, that a pistol bullet would be delivered to the back of his head at any moment. Several people entered the office; one of them knelt to peer beneath the desk. It was Eicke. His head appeared close to the floor and Brockdorff reached out and gripped Eicke's jaw and tore it entirely loose from his face.

He feared he would be punished for this act, he feared terrible acts of vengeance. He fled and the dream went on, passing through other rooms where he attempted to hide, other corridors and hallways where he attempted to escape. The dream went on for so long and in such a complicated fashion that eventually his fear of awful reprisals began to fade away, though it never disappeared entirely. It was merely absorbed into other series of events, a kind of strange ongoingness that overshadowed actual details.

Perhaps it was in another dream on another night that he was with Eicke again. They were seated by a small table inside one of those large elevators. Surfaces of stainless steel, perhaps also of some kind of wood paneling, shone dully beneath muted ceiling lights. They were playing cards, the two of them, occasionally sipping brandy. Playing cards as if to pass the time while waiting for something to happen, something that would happen momentarily or perhaps only at some indefinite time to come. Speaking occasionally to each other, though each more or less lost in his own thoughts, smoking occasionally from time to time beneath the ceiling lights. The elevator neither ascended nor descended. Brockdorff began to lose his fear of being suspended in the deep empty shaft.

He would recall certain things during his waking moments in Demyansk. This incident would be one of them. Yet, perhaps like many people, Brockdorff could ponder over dreams without really attempting to decipher them. He was not really that sort of person. So he merely recalled sitting by the small table with Eicke.

He could not recall when he had first heard the name of Theodor Eicke. It would have been sometime back in the early 30s. Years ago the situation that was looming in Germany had seemed a frightening thing. He knew of Eicke's connection to the camps because it was a well-known fact. Brockdorff had seen Germany awash in an oncoming tide of pollution and shame. Dishonor. Dishonor among nations. These words had had the clear and unambiguous meaning that wholly abstract words would sometimes have for people. What had happened to those words? He no longer knew. Brockdorff, like many Germans, had never visited one of these camps. They were unseemly affairs—one knew this even from a distance—but then so were most prisons, whatever their reasons for being. Unseemly—that was too mild a word, no doubt. . . .

At one time he might have been ashamed to think that a day would come when he would be fighting side by side with Eicke and his men. Perhaps even now, in 1942, he might have felt such a thing, if it were not absorbed into the chaos of so many other things, things which negated each other, buried each other, transcended each other; or simply went on, went on and on.

The force of events in his waking life was far stronger than even the most complicated of dreams. Thus these dreams seemed to take place in some removed and underground place, somewhere in the deep mud of sleep far beneath the daily demands of life in the cauldron. It was curious that he should dream so often of tall buildings, when in fact his waking hours would lend him the sensation of these dreams occurring far below, in the deep meaningless underground of sleep. But if this contradiction were curious, he did not puzzle over it any more intently than over the dreams themselves.

The large buildings were the chiefly recurring things, yet they were not always present. Once he was stranded on an island off the shores of Antarctica, he and many other men. It was a terrible ordeal that would scar many of them forever, mentally and physically. Yet there was not really any pain in the dreams and so his grasp of this agony would be hard to understand. They must attempt to build boats and escape across the ocean—an ocean which was the only clearly terrifying thing in all those dreams. Rolling with immense and freezing waves, spreading to horizons lit with cold and soul-disturbing light. They would surely die out there. Yet it seemed the only alternative, as they would starve to death on the island.

Some escaped, some were left behind. Some escaped in the boats they had built, or perhaps were rescued by ships that arrived offshore one day. This was never clear. It was not clear to Brockdorff whether he had escaped or remained behind. He had a fear of that ocean, and there was never any moment in the dream where he was actually travelling across it.

This dream so little resembled most of the others that he would remember it more clearly, not only in Demyansk but on his deathbed back in Germany, after he had at last been flown out of the cauldron. Bits and pieces of it would enter his mind during feverish moments of consciousness or semi-consciousness, during the last stages of his illness.

Those who had survived the ordeal in the Antarctic were delivered to a city in New Guinea. Brockdorff knew nothing about this island; he was only certain that that was what its name was. Many had to be hospitalized after their nightmarish experiences, lying in quiet beds in a shiny modern hospital, their faces grey with inner torments. Sometimes there was terrible screaming. Yet this dream like all the others went on, it went on and on. It seemed that after a time most of the survivors had resumed some kind of normal life, living in a city that much resembled a typical German city, though it was surrounded by mountainous, tropical rainforests, at the edge of a warm tropical sea.

Yet it was this same sea that would reach across thousands of miles to the shores of that other island, that frozen and terrible island off the coast of Antarctica. Brockdorff kept returning to this island, and it was never clear if this was only a kind of memory, or if he was still there somehow, had been there all along, staring out at the frozen ocean.

He dreamed not only of himself but of other survivors, even though none of them were men that he knew from Demyansk or anywhere else. It seemed that in resuming their normal lives they would be working in buildings somewhere, or driving in cars or riding in trolleys somewhere, often along the shore within view of that warm tropical sea. Memories would disturb them, strange visions would disturb them, which would occur within the deeper silence of life, of some kind of day-to-day existence returning slowly to them, even while eluding them forever. Men, sometimes with their wives, stepping out of a car along a coastal road, walking out onto a white beach, staring at the light in the sky, or simply aware of it out of the corners of their eyes.

•   •   •

The officer in charge of replacements for the Totenkopf Division was a certain Sturmbannfuhrer Harter. He had his headquarters inside another dreary municipal building in Demyansk. Most of his business was still conducted in rooms and offices above ground, with windows boarded over and in some places sandbagged. A reinforced bomb shelter had been constructed in the cellars beneath the building, a precautionary measure that existed beneath most of the sturdier edifices in the town.

The Sturmbannfuhrer's job was a frustrating one. Over the course of the year only a trickle of replacements had arrived for the Totenkopf units in Russia. The SS as always was strapped for manpower. They did not have the same large and clearly established pools of reserves that the army had. SS agencies back in Germany competed with Waffen-SS units at the battlefronts, sometimes in the most devious ways, to keep control over their human resources. They would keep close tabs over their own men and sometimes siphon off manpower from other branches of the

SS organization. Harter's job was complicated by a number of factors. In reality he had almost no control over the situation, and he might have simply resigned himself to this with a certain measure of calm. But such an attitude did not sit well with him.

Replacements for SS Totenkopf came from a number of sources, what was really a confusing muddle of different reserve pools back in Germany. One of the more frequently used pools came from men doing duty at the various concentration camps, men who had been connected to Eicke and the Totenkopf organization for a number of years. Even for someone like Harter, it was difficult to say exactly what this "Totenkopf organization" was anymore. The combat division in Russia was clearly defined; all the other elements back in Germany remained more amorphous, growing larger year by year, linked together in confusing ways, sometimes labeled with mysterious acronyms that might have indicated subordination to Totenkopf or to some other, rival SS agency, or even to both at the same time.

From time to time Harter would imagine an organizational chart that would create a clear picture of all this. If he had known how to do it, he might have drawn up such a chart himself, if only to assist him in his work; though there was also the possibility such a chart might not have met with the approval of his superiors. He sometimes felt that only Himmler knew exactly how all the SS agencies were interconnected; at other times he would think further on the matter, and find himself doubting that even Himmler could sort it all out, or would even be interested in doing so.

Himmler was too remote a personage to occupy much of Harter's thoughts. He dealt with countless intermediate entities in positions similar to his own. Many of them were the commanders of concentration camps, or the administrative heads of agencies that controlled the camps and their reserves of manpower. Frequently groups of replacements for the Totenkopf Division would be transferred from tours of duty at these camps. Places with names that had grown familiar over the course of a decade—Dachau, Buchenwald, Matthausen, Ravensbruck. . . .

Yet as often as not these replacements would never show up in Russia. The camp commandants, resorting to the usual maze of paperwork, would create some excuse to keep control over these men, perhaps promising their eventual release but somehow delaying it indefinitely, or even transferring them to the other camps that were now being built in the occupied territories.

This was a recurring problem that Harter had more or less learned to deal with, especially when his chief Theodor Eicke was present to give matters the necessary shove in the right direction. Replacements would continue to arrive at Demyansk, no matter how grudgingly released. Harter's personal experience was that quite a few of them were glad to be transferred away from camp duty, even if it meant risking their necks in the swamps of Russia.

Recently, however, other complications had entered the picture. Eicke was gone, for one thing, and Oberfuhrer Simon did not have the same pull with the higher authorities. Simon had vented his anger on Harter's head on a few occasions, though sometimes apologizing after the fact; he knew that Harter was not in a position of power. In recent visits Simon's attitude had been not only angry but ambivalent; Harter had been obliged to listen to and help accommodate these perplexing shifts in policy. For almost a year Harter had been preoccupied with wrangling for new men from every source he could think of, doing whatever he could to have them brought in to help fill the depleted battalions around Demyansk. Now, out of the blue, Simon wanted him to change tack. Suddenly Simon was more interested in getting men transferred out of the Demyansk cauldron.

Inevitably Harter was taken aback by this, though at least Simon had taken the trouble to explain his motivations. On one level his reasons were quite clear. During his latest trip to Harter's replacement depot in Demyansk, Simon had delivered a long and violent tirade, the ravings of a man who was reaching the end of something. Simon had declared that the Valdai Hills were the most worthless piece of real estate in all of Russia. He could no longer stand to see the Totenkopf Division bled to death over these filthy swamplands. He berated Himmler, and he berated the army, as if casting a net that would snare all or any culprits behind this shitty mess. He even had a few quiet words for Hitler, though he seemed reluctant to utter Hitler's name with quite the same fury.

He informed Harter that the Totenkopf Division was going to be reestablished back in Germany. Totenkopf officers and NCOs who were due for home leave would have their leave indefinitely extended; Simon would no longer allow his elite cadres to be returned to Russia, to be bled away in the Demyansk meatgrinder. To arrange this "indefinite" leave was a tricky business which would require Harter's assistance. Simon said that these measures had the full approval of Gruppenfuhrer Eicke; nonetheless, there were other parties who would attempt to prevent their being implemented.

"Who would these people be?" Harter had inquired. He understood Simon's motivations and shared his concerns; he needed to know whom to be wary of, what agencies to circumvent.

"The army," muttered Simon tersely. "Brockdorff, above all. The doddering old count. Listen here, Harter. The bastard is trying to block home leave for all Totenkopf personnel. Apparently he wants us all to die in Demyansk together. His shitty little County of Demyansk. It's the same old story, Harter. Without Totenkopf around to wipe the Count's ass the army divisions will all be over-run in 24 hours. Well, enough is enough. The army's been funnel-ing replacements in here all summer, whole new divisions. If they still need Totenkopf to clean up their mess, then . . . ahh. You understand me, Harter. I know there is only so much you can do, but it is important that you realize what is at stake. From now on, you will make no more requests for Totenkopf personnel to be transferred to Russia. You will not inform Brockdorff, or anyone else for that matter, of any further instructions that come either from the Gruppenfuhrer or myself. I will pull my own strings to get our men home on leave. You will do the same at this end."

"Yes, Oberfuhrer," said Harter. "Jawohl."

They were inside Harter's office in Demyansk. The door was shut. They were alone. There was a single desk lamp powered by the generator down in the bomb shelter. This illumination was enhanced by a kerosene lantern hanging from the ceiling. There was also a dim light filtering in through cracks in the window boards. Harter had taken the extra precaution of leaning long wooden planks against the walls of the building, which resem-bled shoddy lean-tos built haphazardly over all the ground-level windows. Their purpose was to provide an initial screen that would absorb shrapnel, if the Russians pushed close enough to start shelling Demyansk again.

Max Simon sat down, mopping his brow with a handkerchief. His balding head resembled a callused thumb. He removed his spectacles, wiping them with the handkerchief, then setting his spectacles on his trouser leg for a moment and staring dimly into space.

Harter was troubled by something. He knew Simon's anger was not directed at him. He felt free to speak his mind. He said,

"What about the rest of us? Neither you nor I can possibly get the whole division transferred home on leave."

Simon glanced at him, then looked away again.

"No, my dear Harter. Of course not."

He was silent for a few moments. Resting his eyes. He went on,

"Those of us who don't get out will probably be buried here. We already have plenty of dead comrades to share the mud with us. I've written to Eicke. If he wants to preside over the last stand of the old guard, then he might wish to return to us here. Then at least all the originals will go down together. If he finds he must stay in Germany to build a new Totenkopf Division, then so be it. I'm at a loss, Harter. But don't let me discourage you. We mustn't give up."

"Idiocy," muttered Harter after a moment. "So those remaining in the cauldron are to be written off? Is that it? Is that what Himmler wants?"

"I no longer know," said Simon. "The Gruppenfuhrer has informed me that both Hitler and Himmler have promised that we will be relieved. That the whole division will be brought home from Russia. What's left of us, that is. But I've been hearing these same damned promises for over six months now. Nothing has happened. I just don't know anymore. Of course if they are going to rebuild the division, it would make sense to start with us, with the few veterans that are left. But I believe, you know, that they are living in a dream world back there. It pains me, Harter, more than I can say."

"The struggle," said Harter vaguely, having only vague thoughts in mind by this point.

Simon nodded vaguely in the semi-darkness. Or perhaps he was shaking his head.

The meeting had concluded with Harter saying he would do everything he could to implement home leave for those who were due it. And even for some who were not due, so far as that could be arranged. He began to receive messages from people on Brockdorff's headquarters staff, as well as a few personal visits

from these gentlemen, visits which were civil though not altogether friendly. Somehow Brockdorff and his aides had gotten
wind of what Eicke and Simon were trying to do; it did not sit
well with them. Another Russian offensive was expected as soon
as the ground hardened. The transfer of essential Totenkopf personnel out of the cauldron at this time was denounced as a typically underhanded display of SS independence and favoritism.

Harter might have responded with some harsh words of his
own. But instead he took the opposite tack and tried to be as
understanding and accommodating as possible, saying he would
speak to Oberfuhrer Simon about the matter, etc., etc. Anything to
keep these weasels off his back. At least he was spared a visit by
Brockdorff himself. He rarely saw the old count even in
Demyansk; the few times when he did, did not leave him with a
favorable impression.

Naturally, Harter remained fully on the side of Max Simon
and Totenkopf in this imbroglio. He knew how undermanned and
exhausted the Totenkopf units were by this point, and it disgusted him to see the army still trying to control these last battered
dregs of manpower. At this point the percentage of SS men still
alive in the cauldron was insignificant, compared with the four or
five new divisions brought in by the army.

On another level he was weary of the whole business, SS conniving included. It was nothing more than the age-old problem of
interservice rivalry, complicated by irritating political innuendos,
by the inner complications within the SS itself. He was tired of it.
He wanted to get out of Demyansk as badly as any soldier in the
battle lines. My God, a whole year gone by in this place. . . . And
now another winter was coming. The prospect filled him with an
apprehension that at times sharpened into a distinct feeling of terror. The leaden autumn days were already like any winter in western Europe, depressing and yet also ominous with all the signs of
the worse ordeals to come. Darkness. Darkness and the cold.
Would another winter be as horrible as the one just past? Harter
did not wish to find out. He shared with many people in the cauldron the feeling that they might be exiled to the Valdai Hills for
the entire length of the war. By now the besieged divisions had
held out for so long that it seemed they would hold out forever,
bleeding forever, remaining forever. Yet men might also sprout
grey hairs to ponder that no matter how many Russian attacks

failed, no matter how many muddy corpses and rusting hulks were heaped up beyond the defensive perimeter, it was still only a question of time—today, next week, next month, my God, even next year. . . .

Only a question of time, before every German unit east of the Lovat River was overrun and annihilated. When would that be? And who would have escaped? And who would still be here by then?

It was becoming clear by now that the Russians would never give up. By now a man would have this feeling in his heart, in his gut, in his bones; he could only try and dismiss such a certainty from his thoughts, hope that he was wrong somehow, that a larger picture of events would somehow prove him wrong.

Harter busied himself day by day with his usual bureaucratic pushing and pulling. Even while he did manage to get a few key officers transferred out of the cauldron, other small contingents of Totenkopf personnel continued to arrive as replacements, men whose return or even initial posting to Russia had been set into motion before Harter could fabricate some excuse to keep them in Germany. A damnable business. . . . He himself had continuously greased so many cogs to keep replacements coming into the cauldron in the first place, and now he must try and reverse the whole process, all the while keeping the whole machinery of personnel movements hidden from inquisitive eyes.

On a day in mid-October he received orders for another posting of SS men into Demyansk. As usual it was only a small group of replacements, combed out from somewhere in the occupied territories, God only knew where; they would be flying into the airfield that afternoon. Harter was more than usually annoyed, or perhaps depressed. He had been hearing rumors from Simon that the long-awaited relief was finally at hand, that Eicke himself would be flying back into the cauldron—and not to preside over Totenkopf's ultimate destruction, but to oversee their transfer back to the Reich. Harter continued to hope, though like Simon he had been hearing these same kinds of promises for months and months. And today it was not Eicke who was arriving, but only another small group of cannon fodder.

He determined to drive out to the airfield to meet these men, rather than wait for them to report at his headquarters. The gloom in his office was getting to him, a tangible cold mustiness in there, in his own bones. He needed some air, even if the air were cold, wet and unpleasant; even if the drive were only a frustrating excursion along muddy lanes and bone-jolting corduroy roads. In any case it was not far to the airfield.

Before leaving he looked over the papers reassigning these men. From long familiarity with certain obscure acronyms, he understood that they had come from one of the camps, though it was not any place he had heard of before. The commandant had even sent a personal note along with the orders, indicating that due to certain unavoidable delays in camp operations, he was graciously releasing these men for combat duty with the mother division in Russia. Unctuous gibberish, thought Harter. Either the man was simply responding to pressure from above, or he was trying to curry favor with someone, Eicke or someone, God only knew who. Apparently this commandant had not yet been informed of Totenkopf's recent about-face in policy regarding posting more men to Demyansk. Another muddle; it was nothing new. At least the skeletal battalions still fighting out on the perimeter would welcome the arrival of a few new bodies.

Harter had gotten wind of the new construction that was going on, most of it taking place in the occupied territories, above all in Poland. Or the Government-General, as Poland was now referred to with the usual mystifying National Socialist terminology. He knew about this because a number of Totenkopf men, whose postings he had been wrestling over all summer, had been assigned to these new construction efforts. Assigned to new camps, in other words. Many of these places had Polish names, a language generally despised by Germans as being even more unpronounceable than Russian. Harter had made lists of these places, though they were still mostly a blur to him. The men arriving today had been transferred from some obscure village called Oswiecim. The commandant had graciously typed in parentheses the new German name for the place, which was Auschwitz. Many Polish towns had been given German names since 1939. Indeed, many of these towns were only reclaiming their original German names from decades earlier, before half of Germany had been handed over to Poland after that disgraceful Versailles Treaty. The treaty, Harter reflected, which had started this whole sorry mess so long ago, the vengeful and inexcusable conniving of the allied powers which had brought them all to this present state of affairs, more than twenty years later on.

He reflected on this with the long-familiar righteousness and indignation of any German. Yet it was all too long-familiar to take any more than a reflexive shape in his thoughts by now, lost in the depths of Russia. Harter referred to the map of the Reich, which included the recently formed Government-General, hanging behind his desk. Many Polish towns had been absorbed back into Germany itself, as was only right and proper, and these towns bore German names on his map, the same names they had borne for hundreds of years. Other towns in the Government-General were identified in German or Polish or in both languages. He suspected the village where this new camp was located would still be written in Polish, Oswiecim or whatever it was. He suspected that the place was too obscure to even be marked on the map, and after a few more moments of fruitless study he concluded that this was correct.

It was of no interest to him anyway. He realized that a drive out to the airfield in this miserable climate was of no interest to him either. Gloom possessed him. He almost sat down again, but then decided to go ahead with this short diversion. He would be spending enough time in this office anyway, later today, and tomorrow.

He told his aide to go fetch a car and driver from the motor pool. He then stepped outside the building into the muddy streets of the town. Rain hung in the air, a cold thin mist. Like a cold gas that induced a sick leadenness in one's brain, an oppressive yearning to be anywhere else but here. One could grow heartsick cooped up in the dark, shabby wooden rooms of these Russian towns, sick with the feeling of being buried in there for months on end. Yet to step outside into the real presence of the climate was more disturbing still. One never knew where to go in this country, because there was no place to go.

Presently the car drove up, wallowing in the mud like a cow swishing its behind. Across the street an unharnessed wagon lay sunk in slime up to the top of its wheels. It had been there all summer. Deep puddles reflected grey swirling shapes from far above. Harter, who along with Max Simon would be sentenced to death at Nuremburg after the war, stepped into the car.

Demyansk

• • •

Major Bruner was already at the airfield. He stood ankle-deep in mud, a mud which anchored him firmly to the earth. His head was light, his chest was light. They seemed to float, or else something invisible floated inside them.

This rising feeling in his chest made him more aware of his boots holding him down. It was amusing, that was all. As if they were tethering him to the mud, preventing him from drifting away in this state of well-being.

He was surprised that he felt so good. But he did.

He wondered how long the feeling would last. He tried to steer away from any thoughts that might disturb him. But it really seemed that he was going to be all right.

He chatted with some of the others who were getting leave, even a few like Bruner who were being transferred out permanently. They were mostly strangers from different units, yet they all talked as if they had been friends for a long time, talking somewhat quietly, reservedly, and yet with amiability, grinning now and again, like old comrades who had not seen each other in so long they hardly knew what to say to each other, yet feeling that it didn't really matter.

They were all officers there. It would be unusual for an enlisted man to fly out of Demyansk. Their leave would normally begin on the train, the small-gauge "Ilmensee Express" that crossed the Lovat to Staraya Russa, only the first stage of a long journey back to the Reich, a journey which would require many trains, many stops, many days.

Even an officer had to be lucky to fly out, or else high enough in rank that he could count on this special status. At first the front-line officers had congregated apart from the rear-echelon men, but this segregation had evaporated after a few minutes; they stood around in the mud talking of one thing or another, smoking cigarettes, even those like Bruner who smoked only rarely. Demyansk was too small a place and they had all been here too long; they mingled freely, the normal barriers between branches of the service no longer present. A Totenkopf officer talked with a colonel from an infantry division. A headquarters surgeon nodded at something. From time to time they all glanced at the JU-52 out in the mud a few hundred feet away. The trimotor rested in liquid that stood almost to the tops of its tires; someone joked about whether the old crate would be able to take off again; someone laughed nervously.

"Good Auntie Ju," someone said. "She'll be all right, boys."

They had better hope so. But most of them did, refusing to think of any other possibility. The borders of the strip were strewn with wrecks that had accumulated over the course of the year, mostly from the long months when the cauldron had been supplied entirely by air. The planes had landed in snowstorms, in rainstorms; they had touched down in glutinous mud and on cracked and bomb-ruptured ground frozen hard as concrete. Many had been damaged so badly they'd never taken off again. Prime movers had dragged or bulldozed them to the edges of the field, where they now formed a kind of fence around the whole area, like the enclosure for a salvage yard.

The passengers who had just flown in were now assembling a short distance away. There were about thirty of them, SS people, a few officers but mostly enlisted men. A delegation consisting of a junior officer and three enlisted men approached the Totenkopf officer who was standing with the furlough-group. He greeted the new arrivals heartily enough; he was in a good mood, like the rest of them waiting for departure.

He pointed at an SS staff car which was just now approaching the airfield, followed by a small truck. The two vehicles approached slowly, wheels churning, grabbing, spinning, grabbing again. The junior officer saluted and began to walk off in that direction. The three enlisted men paused as one, as if to study this Totenkopf veteran of the by now famous, the by now notorious, cauldron of Demyansk.

It was only an instant before they turned to follow their own commander. Yet in this instant they seemed to pause again, again as one, yet each of them staring off at some different point of the compass now. Though every direction across the airfield would only offer an identical view, a scene of mud, wreckage, more mud, and the low, slowly drifting clouds drifting beyond and above it all. So that each of these three men might seem more absorbed in his self than in the bleak terrain all around; the terrain and the slowly rolling clouds forming a background, highlighting them as if they might be the center of attention for a moment.

The one on the right could hardly have been older than seventeen. He bore the shifty and guiltless eyes of a sneak-thief and murderer, restless eyes watching for any small opportunity. The one on the left was older. He bore the coarse and vaguely grinning expression, the pig-eyed expression, of a hard drinker, bully, and murderer. The one in the center was also older. He had a far-off gaze, as if he were still studying his new surroundings, yet the remoteness in his eyes betrayed preoccupation with some intangible thing equally remote from here. He bore the dazed expression of a farmer who has heard or seen some voice or vision in the distant hills or fields, calling upon him in the midst of life, striking upon his mind in the midst of a dull, difficult, and incomprehensible life, transfixing him.

Who was it that observed these three faces with such unmistakable clarity? Who was either deceived by a face, or struck by the truth illuminated in a face? Was it Bruner?

No.

The Totenkopf veteran?

No.

Or any of the others there?

No.

The tableau dissolved and the three men followed their commander and the other Totenkopf replacements over to the staff car, in which stood an SS Sturmbannfuhrer who now began to address them.

The other men on the field took the first steps of their journey home, walking slowly out towards the trimotor. A fuel truck swung out past them, courteously avoiding spraying them all with mud. Bruner was carrying a picture in his mind, now that he found himself leaving this place. He remembered a certain day from back in the winter, almost a year ago now.

He had made frequent trips to the airfield back then, giving first-hand reports to Brockdorff-Ahlefeldt about conditions out here, the number of planes coming in, the number crashlanding, the number still repairable; how many were fully loaded, how many were improperly loaded, how many were carrying non-essential items at the expense of critical and basic needs. The latter especially was the bane of any large airlift operation, and since the Demyansk air-bridge was the first of its kind, the criteria for supplies was being continuously arranged and rearranged. There were supply officers to see to these tasks, but Brockdorff had relied on Major Bruner to give him direct and unbiased accounts of the situation.

Bruner had found these trips to the airfield oddly stimulating, despite the brutal conditions of the winter. He could not deceive himself into thinking he shared the agony of the men out on the perimeter. Nor even the suffering of those who loaded and unloaded the planes, who often wound up frostbitten in the casualty wards after hours out in the winds of the airfield. There were days so terribly cold that Bruner himself had paid the price, coming down with frostbitten fingers and toes on several occasions. But these had only been minor ordeals, leaving no permanent injury. He could not pretend that he was unlucky; he knew quite the opposite was true.

He remembered a certain day when the wind had dropped, when the air was almost still. The temperature would have remained steady at around forty below. The sky had that blue force which stunned men quietly, so that the memory of its light remained with them long afterward, becoming almost like a scene from childhood, or like a scene from a dream or daydream that never quite has its counterpart in the tangible world. Except on a few days only.

The constant droning of airplane engines, both droning far in the distance and roaring only a few feet away, had had its effect on Bruner as it had had on many other men. That quiet, almost unconscious, yet long-term surge that it brought to one's adrenalin, that might in some small way help combat the nightmare of the cold. Perhaps for the men unloading the planes the cold was so bitter that such small psychosomatic comforts would have vanished entirely, themselves reduced to beasts performing an awful and endless chore.

Yet on this day the wind was still and there was perhaps some measure of peace for everyone there. The sun shone blindingly and without warmth. Yet if you turned your back on it there was a stillness in the blue sky that sucked even the glare away, leaving a quiet nothingness and then the presence of the other things below.

Bruner had grown tired of the engines thundering right next to his ears, and he had taken a walk out to the end of the airfield.

It was the western end, normally the downwind end, the end that pointed towards the Lovat and Staraya Russa. The air was still except for a few lifts in the air, brief gusts that would inhabit his body with the cold but not knife at it.

From the end of the airfield the white terrain sloped gradually away. The airfield was in the heart of the Valdai Hills, those small hills that diminished to distant swamps and river deltas, places not visible from where he stood.

He walked slowly to the end of the airfield, the soles of his boots creaking in the snow. The field was laid out on a long plateau, slightly higher than the other hills around. It was not a high elevation, but it was an elevation nonetheless, and something about it took a curious hold on him. He had visited tall mountains in Bavaria, before the war, been impressed by the peaks; but they were too far above the ground somehow, above the real ground. Or so it had seemed to him.

The terrain of the airfield was raised up like a low platform, a pedestal. Something. It was simply there, retaining the proper kinship to the other terrain spreading away here and there, here and there, not far below. The sky was above. Russia. Just like the earth. Russia. In the near distance low ridges and hills met the sky, quiet snow-covered slopes sparsely covered with fir trees. In between were the small valleys with a few winding patches of bare deciduous trees, marking watercourses buried under snow. Where the nearby hills were lower than the plateau of the airfield, Bruner could see for great distances, other hills forested or sparsely forested, seeming to diminish across such a wide and visible expanse.

EPILOG

Theodor Eicke returned to the cauldron in mid-October of 1942. He stayed for only a few days. When he left he took his division with him, which by this time numbered less than five thousand men. Totenkopf had finally been relieved.

They were to be rebuilt in France as an armored division, in the relaxed environment of the French countryside. They were to become one of the most heavily armed striking forces in the German military, along with SS Leibstandarte and SS Das Reich, the other original Waffen SS Divisions which were also rebuilt as armored units in 1942. Leibstandarte and Das Reich had already been recuperating in France for a number of months when Totenkopf was finally transferred out of Demyansk. Unfortunately for Totenkopf, their period of rest and refitting was to be pitifully short.

Like the 5th Jaegers a year earlier, they were to be called back to Russia after only two months, thrown into yet another crisis situation after the German front at Stalingrad had collapsed. Totenkopf, Leibstandarte, and Das Reich were formed into an armored corps; together they finally brought the Russian advance to a temporary halt, winning a major victory at Charkow in March 1943. During these battles Theodor Eicke was killed when his reconnaissance plane was shot down by Russian anti-aircraft fire. He thus was unable to take his place along with the other defendants at Nuremburg after the war.

Max Simon was there, however. After Eicke's death he again took command of Totenkopf. Later in the war he was transferred to head another SS division in Italy, which allegedly conducted wholesale massacres of Italian civilians during antipartisan actions. Initially sentenced to death, Simon was later given a ten-year prison term instead. The horror of various Nazi endeavors during the war caused the Allies to be excessively vengeful in certain instances; it was acknowledged that some reports of atrocities may have been exaggerated or untrue. The exact particulars of Simon's actions remain obscure; in any case, his death sentence was commuted.

The Russians, not present at Nuremburg, had also sentenced Simon to death—in absentia—for alleged massacres he had conducted in Russia. But he served his prison term in West Germany and was released in 1955.

The Totenkopf Division, under Simon and various subsequent commanders, remained on the Eastern Front till the end of the war, engaged without letup in one defensive battle after another, slowing but never halting the inexorable Russian march on Berlin.

Men who had assisted in the extermination of Jews at various concentration camps fought alongside other men who had only killed people on the battlefield. Men who had volunteered for the SS fought alongside other men who, later in the war, were drafted into the SS. The battle history of the Totenkopf Division, written in 1987 by Karl Ullrich, one of the unit's high-ranking and highly-decorated officers, contains almost four hundred pages of detailed combat actions. The "alleged" intimate connection of SS Totenkopf to the death camps is mentioned in only a single sentence; the sentence is one of complete denial. Ullrich relies on the complex and confusing arrangement of SS manpower sources to suggest, basically, that the Totenkopf men might have come from anywhere but the concentration camps. It should be acknowledged that the actual percentage of camp personnel who served with the division may never be known.

•   •   •

The 5th Jaeger Division remained in the Demyansk cauldron. At the same time that the Russians surrounded Stalingrad, in November 1942, they also conducted another major offensive against the Valdai Hills. As with the seemingly endless attacks that had preceded it, this offensive also nearly managed to sever the Demyansk relief corridor—der Schlauch. Once again, it was brought up short by desperate German resistance.

It was only after the disaster at Stalingrad that Hitler finally acknowledged that the same fate would eventually befall the Demyansk defenders. The Germans withdrew from the salient in February 1943, establishing a shorter defensive line in front of Staraya Russa. The Russians moved in and took possession of Demyansk and the Valdai Hills, that "worthless" stretch of ground. The first great cauldron battle in the East had come to an end. It had lasted over a year.

Unfortunately, the resolute and at times miraculous defense of the Demyansk cauldron led in direct fashion to the later annihilation of the Stalingrad cauldron. When Demyansk was surrounded, it was supplied by air; when Stalingrad was surrounded, Hitler decreed that it also would be supplied by air. It made no difference that the 6th Army at Stalingrad contained several hundred thousand more men than Brockdorff-Ahlefeldt's corps in the Valdai Hills. It made no difference that almost all of Hitler's generals declared that Stalingrad could not possibly be supplied in the same manner. What had worked at Demyansk would work at Stalingrad. So Hitler decreed.

But it did not work. At Demyansk the Soviet air force had been curiously absent; the supply planes had been able to fly in almost unmolested. At Stalingrad Soviet fighters were present in large numbers; the JU-52s flying in to supply the 6th Army were shot down in droves. Blizzards and Russian flak belts also took their toll. Transport planes from as far away as France, Norway, and North Africa were brought in to take part in the supply effort; even so, the amount of food and equipment they were able to fly in was pitifully inadequate, as the German generals had clearly foreseen. The men of the 6th Army began to starve. Before the final capitulation, many of them had starved to death. As the end came near, there were reports of cannibalism. There were reports of German soldiers eating pus, blood, and scraps of flesh clinging to filthy bandages that had been tossed into the trash bins at the field hospitals.

Such an episode had a profound effect on the entire German nation. In one of his rare moods of funk, Hitler declared a week of national mourning.

•　　•　　•

The 5th Jaeger Division took part in the last battles to keep the Russians from overrunning the Demyansk relief corridor. After the salient was abandoned they remained in the neighborhood of Staraya Russa until late 1943. When the Russians overran Nevel they were transferred to fight in that sector. They later fought in the Pripyat Marshes; later still they fought in the Narew Bridgehead outside Warsaw, side by side with SS Totenkopf once again. In April 1945 they were transferred to western Germany and surrendered there to the advancing British and Americans.

Prior to this they had fought exclusively on the Eastern Front since the invasion of June, 1941; they were one of the few divisions in the East to escape Russian captivity.

Almost all German soldiers who surrendered to the Russians were imprisoned deep inside the Soviet Union for many years. For the great majority of them this amounted to a death sentence. In general they were not starved as callously as the Germans had starved the Russian POWs. Nonetheless many of them died from malnutrition over time, or from other diseases, or from wounds received in battle, or from exhaustion after years of forced labor, or from sheer despair, or from a combination of all these things.

•   •   •

General von Brockdorff-Ahlefeldt, the Graf von Brockdorff-Ahlefeldt, was relieved of command for reasons of ill-health, just prior to the last Russian offensive against Demyansk in the late autumn of 1942. He died in Germany the following May. The particulars of his illness are hard to come by. It was widely reported that his spirit had been exhausted by the long ordeal of command at Demyansk.

He received a state funeral attended by many of the most important personages in the Reich, as befitted a national hero. The ceremony was filmed and shown in newsreels throughout Germany, accompanied by music from the funeral march of Beethoven's Eroica.

•   •   •

General Graf von Sponeck, he of Crimean ill-fame, was executed by order of Adolf Hitler in July 1944, after spending three years in Spandau prison.

223

DEMYANSK

• • •

General von Seydlitz-Kurzbach, the Graf von Seydlitz-Kurzbach, was destined to become, in a certain sense, the most notorious figure in the German army.

The so-called saviour of Demyansk was taken prisoner at Stalingrad along with the rest of the German 6th Army. Some months later German soldiers began to hear his voice in every sector of Russia, carried via the loudspeakers of the Russian propaganda broadcasts. They began to see his signature affixed to leaflets dropped by Russian planes.

Seydlitz, speaking as head of an organization called the Free Germany Committee, implored them to surrender. He denounced the crimes of Hitler in particular and of the Nazi regime in general. He called upon them either to surrender or to turn in revolt against a criminal government. For the most part, he called upon them to surrender to the Russians.

For the most part, he was ignored, though a number of German soldiers did heed his words and cross over to the Russian lines. But the great majority did not, and with good reason. From escaped prisoners and other sources, it had become common knowledge that any German who gave himself up would face a brutal imprisonment at best, and torture, mutilation, and death at worst.

It is not known for sure if it was really Seydlitz's voice heard over those countless propaganda broadcasts which blared across the German lines. It sounded like him, though these messages were blurred by the primitive recording equipment. At times the voices of other Germans were heard, captured Landsers and officers, a few other captured generals. But it was Seydlitz who spoke to all of them, and it was his name they all remembered.

It seems fairly likely that these appeals from Seydlitz were genuine, at least to begin with. A man who can resist the worst abuses, death-threats, and other persuasions of his captors may nonetheless fall victim to his own conscience. Seydlitz had already been nagged by the dictates of his conscience for a number of years. And so at last he spoke.

It was difficult to look upon Seydlitz as a weakling and a turncoat. His reputation among the soldiers was too widely known for that. Eventually many did look upon him as a mere turncoat, as that was the easiest thing to do. Others who knew his courage were disturbed in deeper ways. But even they did not always admire him, whether he was sincere or not, whether he spoke for justice or not. How could they admire a man who induced German soldiers to surrender, when such surrender would lead to almost certain death in a Russian prison camp?

They were not deluded; they knew that German prisoners were dying by the thousands in Russia, just as Russian prisoners were dying by the thousands in Germany.

If Seydlitz was driven by his conscience, how could he induce men to accept such a fate? No one knew.

It is possible that Seydlitz was deceived by the Russians, that he received fairly good treatment at their hands, that other Germans he came in contact with also received fairly good treatment. But if he was deceived for a time, it seems unlikely that he could have been deceived for good.

There were rumors that Seydlitz was killed by the Russians after they had made use of him, after the war, or even while the war was still going on; that the recorded voice broadcast over the propaganda loudspeakers was the voice of a man who had already been murdered. But it wasn't so. Seydlitz survived the war; he then survived an additional ten years in Russian captivity. During the war, Hitler had him condemned to death in absentia. Ironically, the Soviets later tried him for war crimes. He was not released until 1955.

Seydlitz's voice was heard all across the Eastern Front, throughout 1943, throughout 1944, on into 1945. His voice was heard outside the siege lines at Leningrad, it was heard along the swamps of the Volkhov River, it was heard at Staraya Russa. It was heard during lulls in countless terrible battles in central and southern Russia. As the war went on, cauldron battles like those at Demyansk and Stalingrad became commonplace. Again and again German units were surrounded by vastly superior Russian forces; again and again they either fought their way to freedom, usually with terrible losses, or else were wiped out almost to a man. Seydlitz's voice was heard on the perimeter of all these encirclements, appealing to German soldiers in one hopeless situation after another. He was heard in the Kuban, he was heard at Brody and Kowel, and along the Berezina River, and in the Crimea. He was heard at Cherkassy, before that last desperate breakout attempt, before the frozen survivors emerged stark naked from the ice floes of the Gniloy Tikich.

Soviet Memorial to Victims of the Einsatzgruppen, Salaspils, Latvia

DEMYANSK

The German armies invading Russia in June of 1941, including the six initial Waffen-SS divisions, consisted of more than three million men. These forces were followed by four SS Einsatzgruppen, special battalion-sized units which each contained less than a thousand men. They operated in the rear areas behind the advancing armies. Their task was to kill all the Jews in Russia. They were also assigned to dispose of Soviet commissars, subversives, and other people that needed to be killed. It was an enormous undertaking, and the Einsatzgruppen concentrated on the Jews.

The techniques of gassing and burning had yet to be refined. Victims in Russia in 1941 were killed almost entirely by shooting.

The shootings took place in remote villages and in large cities. The SS attempted to conduct these operations in secrecy, but their efforts were at times rather slipshod. Outside the Baltic city of Riga, 7,000 Jews were shot in a vacant lot in a period of 24 hours. These activities were plainly visible to many of the Latvian population, some of whom were reported watching through binoculars from rooftops nearby. At about this same time a similar operation was carried out inside Kiev, the third largest city in the Soviet Union. . . .

THE ABYSS OF EARTHLY DELIGHTS

An Anti-Semitic Gathering at the Ravine of Babi Yar,
September 1941

Filthy Jews filthy Jews filthy Jews filthy Jews filthy Jews filthy
Jews filthy Jews filthy Jews filthy Jews filthy Jews filthy Jews
filthy Jews filthy Jews filthy Jews filthy Jews filthy Jews.

A certain Hauptsturmfuhrer Mulhmann was assigned to us at
Vinnitsa. He did a good job there, and I have since used his example as a means of helping the men to carry out their difficult
assignment.

From the beginning it was necessary to conduct these operations in as business-like manner as possible. Muhlmann was
untiring and quite calm, and seemed to have the ability to convey
this calmness to his victims. With only a pistol and a single assistant to carry extra ammunition he was able to despatch over three
hundred of them in less than an hour. The targets were lined up
along a ditch that stretched for several hundred yards. I had
thought that to have the bodies dispersed in this way would be
less upsetting to the men; the large numbers of corpses heaped on
top of each other in previous actions had had an unsettling effect

on some of them. I was constantly obliged to resort to different methods by trial-and-error; it was one of the major difficulties in this whole period of time. It was an enormous and exhausting undertaking for such a small group of people to carry out, and at times my ingenuity was stretched to the limit, having to deal not only with the countless logistical details of the physical operation, but also with the mental well-being of my own men.

The Vinnitsa operation, for example, went well enough, with Muhlmann proceeding in a relaxed and professional manner almost as if he were giving a demonstration at a training school. The Jews were faced away from him along the ditch, and they were stretched out in such a long line that each one could not really see what was happening until a few moments before his turn arrived. Clearly they would have known what their fate was to be, but over time it also became clear that the physical arrangement of these executions was equally as important to a smooth operation as trying to hide the facts from them. At Lwow we had dug a large pit that inevitably became piled deep with bodies. The crowds awaiting their turn became unruly having to look down upon this spectacle, sometimes for several hours; and, as I mentioned, my own men would become unnerved by the sight as the operation dragged on. These operations were always very time-consuming; that, to my mind, was the greatest single obstacle, and the various other complications stemmed from this.

Vinnitsa was no less time-consuming but to my satisfaction the whole affair went more smoothly, with less strain on us all. Muhlmann moved down the line toppling them like dominos, and in the ditch they lay like dominos side by side, leaving a less messy and distasteful appearance. The dead appeared calm and the burial-detail was able to finish up matter-of-factly afterwards. There was a kind of dignity to this operation which I think was helpful to us, even allowing the Jews a certain degree of dignity in their final moments, which I think might have been a useful lesson for future actions of this type. From the beginning I had had no illusions about what a strain this would be for the men, but to actually witness the effect of these long and grueling weeks on their morale was still more difficult than I would have guessed, and I was forced to call upon all the resources of my own leadership abilities. I sympathized with them entirely, as these weeks were every bit as trying for me.

Thus Vinnitsa remains in my mind as a kind of oasis of dignity and calm, an ideal which could not always be met in other places and other situations; but at least we had a model to strive for.

I congratulated Muhlmann on his performance and told him that I regretted he could not remain under my command. He had been sent to us as a disciplinary measure for some lapse at the front. In general these "discipline" cases offered us only more complications. On the one hand, the additional manpower was welcome, at times even indispensable; on the other hand, these men served with us somewhat reluctantly, and their attitudes tended to exacerbate the difficulties I had in keeping my own men functioning as a unit. Some of them took out their resentment at being assigned to us by flagrant acts of sadism against the Jews, which not only disrupted operations but also encouraged my own men towards such practices, a situation which I had striven to avoid from the very beginning. As time went by the large scale of these actions began wearing us down, so that even the most vociferously anti-Jewish personnel among us adapted to a kind of routine; in short, they were too tired to engage in ugly and reprehensible acts.

I grasped the certain way that this would work to our advantage. However, when disciplinary cases were sent in from other SS units, especially from combat units, there was the danger of this stability being upset.

But I should not exaggerate the difficulties posed by these men. Sullenness was more common than flagrant breaches of discipline. In any case it was only one difficulty among many inherent in this task. All in all, I should say, things went about as smoothly as could be expected.

Muhlmann was an exception to the usual discipline cases. He conducted himself so impeccably that I did not seek to inquire too closely about the reasons for his being sent to us. It could not have been anything too serious, as he stayed with us only for a short time. He let on that there had been an incident involving the orders regarding the shooting of commissars, something about his refusal to liquidate a certain female commissar who had been rounded up in a partisan action. I found it hard to believe he would have been transferred to us for anything so minor, and found myself wondering if there was some kind of deeper conflict between him and his commanding officer. His manner with me was so professional that this seemed unlikely, but one never knew. I had the feeling that he would have explained himself more if I had pressed him, but I chose not to. There were already enough unpleasant subjects to deal with on a day-to-day basis.

After the action at Vinnitsa we set up for the night in a balka outside the town. These large dry ravines were one of the curiosities of the landscape in the Ukraine. Like many things in Russia, their size seemed to exist on some other scale of things, some of them like small canyons more than a hundred feet deep. One would climb the side of a balka expecting to find a summit of some kind, a view of further such gorges twisting through a rugged and hilly terrain. Instead one would emerge only upon the edge of the steppe, lush grasslands rolling away to infinity. It was an odd sensation, though of course you would become familiar with it soon enough. In any case they were useful as sheltered spots in which to camp. A relief from the monotony of the landscape which the troops would seek out instinctively. Occasionally even Russian villages would be set up down in these balkas, as if the inhabitants also required some reprieve from the endlessness of their country.

I allowed the men a period of rest for the day following. Previously I had thought it better to keep on moving after an operation, but fatigue was beginning to get the better of us; our vehicles also needed servicing. The heat of the land was overpowering at times and the steep slopes of the balka provided some shade in the early morning and evening. Shelter halves were strung up to provide sunscreens during the midday hours. As always there were some men who would luxuriate in the sun, stripping down to their undershorts, while others sought to avoid it.

I invited Muhlmann to eat with me at noon; he would be taking his leave of us on the day following. My Ukrainian helper set up a small table on a rock shelf in the lower part of the balka. Muhlmann and I sat on folding chairs, eating peas and roast chicken, sharing a bottle of wine, smoking cigarettes. It was a relaxing moment, especially given the hardships of our duty. Though I was sorry to see him go, I knew he was not dissatisfied to be returning to the front; I could hardly hold this against him.

I was somewhat irked to see him wearing the same camouflage smock he had worn when first reporting to us. Surely he did not need to don such garb so far from a combat zone? But I let it pass. It was very hot and he did not wear the regulation field-blouse beneath the smock. The smock was loose-fitting and laced up across the chest somewhat in the manner of a medieval forester's garb; it gave him rather a sporting appearance, the bronze chest of a young man visible beneath the laces, and so I complimented him on his appearance.

He smiled faintly.

"Thank you, Standartenfuhrer."

"Eat, boy. Drink. This will be our last meal together. For now anyway. Perhaps we will meet again someday."

"Jawohl, Standartenfuhrer."

"Ja. But don't address me so formally at mealtime. Rank is no more than a military necessity. No doubt you share the same comradeship at the front?"

"That depends," he said. "I mean, yes, generally that is so."

"Well. I trust that you will do well enough for yourself. I will send a good report along with you. These things happen, boy. Just try to make a clean slate of it. I've had more than a few hard cases here. People who really don't want to learn their lesson. No doubt some of them will wind up in a penal unit. But just set yourself straight and you can put all this behind you."

"Thank you, sir. The wine is good."

"It is," I agreed.

I could see that I had touched on an uncomfortable subject, without really intending to. We needed men like him and I could only hope he would rise above the hardships of these days without any further blemishes on his record. I thought he would. I had not been to the front, but from my own standpoint I had already seen how trying this campaign could be, even for the best of men.

"You'll take us into Moscow," I said. "It shouldn't be much longer now. Then we can all take our leave of this country."

"I hope so," he said, staring up the slopes of the ravine into the sky. We drank and smoked in silence for a few moments. Even with my regular officers it was not always so easy to talk congenially; I had come to accept these occasional mealtime silences as part of our daily intercourse. Perhaps Muhlmann appreciated my putting him at ease; after a space of quiet, himself sipping wine and staring up into the hot sky, he seemed to shed some of his diffidence.

"The fighting up there has been very hard," he said. "I can't say that their resistance is weakening either. But perhaps by the time I get back things will be moving along better."

"I'm sure they will," I said. "You can't stamp out a nest of vipers easily as all that. But when it's done it's done. The world will be better off. Let's hope so anyway."

"Ja," said Muhlmann. "Prosit, Standartenfuhrer."

"Prosit," I said.

We raised our glasses. I drank and watched him drink. I suddenly realized that he looked drunk. Dear God, I thought, perhaps that was what it had all been about. That would shed a whole different light on things.

I looked at the bottle on the table, only half-consumed. No, I didn't wish to think that about someone. It was a hot day and the wine was sweet, certainly not the best. Even if it was true, the matter would be out of my hands by tomorrow. He had performed well and I had seen no evidence of anything else. It was curious that a man should look tipsy so suddenly, after only a couple of glasses. But I dismissed it. In a way it was only another sign of our difficulties. I had had to be careful about the rationing of alcohol to the men. I had given some serious thought about banning it altogether, for it would sometimes lead to them pouring out their inner distress in unseemly ways. But after these actions a man simply needed a drink; I knew it because I needed one myself, and I could not in all conscience withhold this privilege from the men.

Endless difficulties. I could only hope that a promotion lay at the end of this. And above all a transfer to some other duty. I shook my head. I motioned for the Ukrainian sitting nearby to come clear the table.

His name was Vladimir but we called him Ivan, which seemed to suit him all right. He could sit a few feet away for hours as silent as a stone, until you were no longer aware of his presence; yet if you said a few words to him he would become the epitome of smiling congeniality, bowing and nodding, talking in Russian mixed with the few German words he had picked up. I was beginning to see how profound was the effect of the arrival of German manners and common dignity upon these people. There was more to their behavior than mere deference to a conqueror, or even welcome to a liberator, which was how we had been greeted in so many places. I began to understand that they looked on us with a kind of awe, which had to do not only with the many victories of our armed forces, but also with the simple fact of being treated courteously by a foreign army. It was something extraordinary to them, after so many generations of brutality and squalor under the Russian heel, a brutality that had worked its way into the most everyday moments of their existence.

Our Ivan swept up the plates and glasses, handling them with care as if even these ordinary utensils were remarkable objects. I told him to help himself to the remains; he understood my gesture if not my words, walking off to the mess detail while sucking on a few bones.

He and others like him had been quite useful in various phases of our operations. Pointing out the Jewish elements in the population, leading us to the places out in the country where they had taken refuge, places we would have had a great deal of difficulty locating by ourselves. And then assisting us afterwards in many of the more unpleasant details of an action.

"It's a pity," I said, watching him descend to the field kitchen at the bottom of the ravine. The mess NCO, Scharfuhrer Curtin, looked up, and I gave him a slight wave to let him know that the meal had met with my approval.

"Pardon me?" said Muhlmann. He seemed to come out of some reverie.

I said,

"A pity. If we could only leave the whole business to people like him. We don't have to pretend with each other, Muhlmann. This is not an easy job. I don't blame you for a moment for looking forward to returning to your division. I too look forward to the day when all this will be over with.

"In any case. . . . In any case, I was just thinking how it would go easier on all of us if we could just let the local people conduct these operations. They certainly have more enthusiasm for it."

"They would be sure to make a mess of it," said Muhlmann.

"You think so?"

"Damn right," he said.

I nodded, smiling faintly.

"Yes, I agree with you completely. That's what I mean. It's a pity. But I suppose you can't expect any great organizational skills from a mass of peasants. At Ternopol I made the mistake of allowing the population a free hand in the initial roundup. I had thought this would move things along more efficiently, but it was a serious error. Before the day was over we had something like a medieval pogrom on our hands. The Jews who survived fled in all directions. It took us three days to finish up there."

"Hm," said Muhlmann. He looked up at a group of my men standing at the top of the balka. They were skylined there beneath a hot, liquid-looking sky. Their features were clearly visible, yet the sun was so bright that they all seemed darkened in silhouette. The intense light conveyed an optical paradox. It was so bright that it seemed to create an invisible barrier between yourself and other things nearby, separating you from them, yet also magnifying the small details of their features, thus seeming to draw them closer to you. The intense light of this country, as powerful as the heat itself. . . .

There was something almost allegorical about this place, I reflected. The large-scale simplicity of it. A deep ravine. The invisible presence of the steppe just beyond. A few men now quietly descending the slope of the ravine. A few other men scattered about the vehicles and field kitchen below. Muhlmann and myself sitting in silence around the little camp table.

A certain peacefulness passed through me. At length Muhlmann said,

"Ja. Nothing but rabble. It's a funny thing though. The further east you go the less helpful they are. I don't know why that is. It just comes down to more fighting for us."

"The Russians haven't learned to hate the Jews," I said. "At least not as much as the Poles and Ukrainians do. It's only history, Muhlmann. The Jews have contaminated Eastern Europe for a thousand years. This is where most of our work will be done. This is where we see the real need for our work, difficult though it is. The seeds of all the Jewish mess in Germany can be found in these lands. At least we can see that now, more clearly than before."

"Ja. Maybe so," said Muhlmann.

To consider the political realities of our work sometimes made it a little easier. To keep in mind the underlying reasons for our mission, and to know that it had to be done. I would remind my men of this sometimes, men who had begun to be plagued by nightmares of their own wives and little children being murdered, men who complained of dreaming that they would one day burn in hell. My God, my God. What times were these. . . . I could only hope that future generations would not have to undergo such things. Of late I had been shocked by how openly some of the men would make these complaints. It was nothing in the order of mutinous rumblings; far from it; they brought these troubles to me almost as if I were a kind of father-confessor, seeking to unburden themselves. In a way it brought us all closer together, but still it was deeply disturbing to me—to hear the men speak so freely about matters which must be kept as closely guarded secrets, and to find that they struck such a deep chord of sympathy in me that I could hardly discourage them, let alone discipline them. I reasoned that if they felt free to unburden themselves to me then they would not feel compelled to unburden themselves to the rest of the world, once they returned home. They understood the need for secrecy.

I had never harbored any personal animosity towards the Jews, though I had long understood that they and their secret wealth were enemies of the state. To rid one's self of one's enemies was a responsibility that had to be borne. Yet now I saw that even in their very extermination the Jews would wreak their revenge, continue to torment us with their vile presence even from beyond the grave, driving nails of guilt into my men that they would carry for the rest of their lives. The awful, almost diabolical machinery of this process would anger me; there were times when the reality of it was so crystal-clear that hatred would indeed burn in me, and I would look forward to getting on with the job, to personally doing away with every last one of them.

Was this a twisted kind of reasoning? Perhaps. I saw that both reason and hatred were opposite sides of the same coin, so to speak—that either one could reduce your mind to a fog. It was best simply to get on with the job, and then to be done with the job. To be as business-like as possible. Any other modus operandi would only invite trouble.

Even something as simple as a noonday meal would inevitably fall under a cloud. There was no help for it. A few moments of peaceful conversation, that was the most you could expect. The silences in between would make you uncomfortable, but there was no help for that either. I felt a twinge of jealousy about Muhlmann, wishing myself in his shoes; yet strangely, to see him getting away from this business lifted my spirits somehow, like some small omen of hope. He still looked a little drunk, but I was no longer interested in this. I wished him well.

He departed the following day, hitching a ride with a supply column headed towards the front.

I led my men south towards Uman. We passed through bad territory. The fighting had passed through here only recently. The Russian dead carpeted the steppe. The smell was unbearable. Plague-fires dotted the landscape, but there were so many corpses that it would have taken months to burn them all. The smell was enough to unman you. The heat of the land was a furnace. Crows and vultures screeched everywhere, setting your nerves on edge like fingernails drawn across a chalkboard. At length I ordered the column to find another route, but our maps were useless and we wound up wandering lost for an entire day. And still we could not find a way to detour around these dead-fields. The corpse-fires were tended mostly by other Russians, but the few Germans in charge of them looked sick to their very souls. The demoralizing effect of all this put them in an evil temper; we witnessed several instances of prisoners or peasants being shot for some trivial offense, then flung onto the same fires they had been tending only moments earlier. A terrible war. The evil of this place infected my men as well; it infected me. Our action at Uman was conducted with a great deal of brutality, which I made little effort to control. After what we had just passed through on the battlefield our own acts seemed of lesser consequence anyway. I was becoming worn down, my ideas about how to best conduct these operations becoming dulled by a haze of senselessness and confusion.

After Uman we were as business-like as could be, though it was somewhat different from before. Brutality became a part of our business, for I had begun to observe that it was easier to dispose of the Jews after they had been cowed into submission by random acts of terror, stripping them naked and herding them like cattle towards the pits, beating them, setting dogs upon them, shooting a few at random before the general shootings began.

A collective despair would settle on them, a numbed and passive horror, like cattle that had been stunned by hammers. Any ideas of doing this with dignity were ephemeral; the tidiness of the Vinnitsa action was ephemeral; the truth was, I had gone past the point of organizing anything in such a painstaking fashion. I forgot about it entirely, dismissed the idea of filing a report of such a model operation with my superiors. All that mattered was to finish everything as quickly as possible, with brutality or guile, or any other means, it no longer mattered. As we moved further east there began to be fewer Jewish settlements, and these less densely populated. At night I began to think privately of a light at the end of the tunnel; yet at other times I would awaken from sleep in a state of fear, convinced that there would never be an end to these Jews, that we would never be freed from this task. And indeed we were obliged to move helter-skelter all over the map, our steady eastward march interrupted by orders to turn back and clean up some Jewish nest or other that we had overlooked in all the vastness of the country.

An officer transferred to us from another of the Einsatzgruppen brought word of a new method, a more efficient method that was currently being tried back in Poland. Poland. I would have thought we'd have taken care of all the Jews there by now. But apparently not. They were like lice in the woodwork. You fumigated once, and then a month later you had to do it all over again. Even after two years Poland was still teeming with Semites. The new officer explained the methods of the mobile gas vans. The men were spared the ordeal of shooting women and children in the head. But these gas vans had their own teething troubles; for my part I could not understand how a small van could possibly dispose of enough people at one time to really be efficient. The officer agreed that this was still a problem.

"Many problems," he muttered, with the dark twist at the corner of his mouth, halfway between a smile and a grimace, that was becoming common to us all.

"Still," he went on. "Anything is better if it makes things easier on the men. One cannot underestimate the importance of this."

"No need to tell me that," I said. "But I would hate to waste any more time waiting for new technology. We need to be finished with this. That above all."

"Unfortunately, it seems there is still a lot of work to be done."

"Yes, yes. You can't leave a job half-finished," I muttered halfheartedly. A nagging irritability was beginning to take hold of me. Of late I had been wondering if we might not be relieved soon.

"This business should be done by rotation," I said. "Just like they do in a combat zone. It's really too much to expect of people to just continue on like this. Mark my words, these men are not

241

going to be fit for useful duty if they have to see much more of this. The Reichsfuhrer really ought to be more understanding about the problem. I have tried to keep the men's spirits up, but it's becoming more and more difficult. We'll just wind up with a lot of discipline cases on our hands."

"Is it really coming to that?" the new officer said.

"I don't know. Each action is a little different. After the first few weeks it seemed that things were starting to run a little more smoothly. But lately. . . . Some of them are starting to behave like mad dogs. It is hard to punish them, as they have begun to look on their duty as the severest form of punishment. And so it is, by God. I cannot dissemble with them."

"The Reichsfuhrer paid us a visit at Minsk," the other interrupted. "He did not dissemble with us either. He spoke about the need for duty and inner strength when faced with these trials. I believe his sympathy was quite sincere. He did not try to steer away from the unpleasantness of it all. He went along with us on one of our actions. Before half a dozen shots were fired he was on his knees, puking in the grass. I saw that with my own eyes."

"Yes, yes, I heard something about that," I snapped, seeming to warm to something now, releasing things which I had tried to keep within myself. "Politicians. I would like to be one myself. And maybe I will be someday. It's much easier to pay a short visit to some place and then go back to Berlin and put the whole thing out of your mind. I wish we could do the same. You know, I understand the need for it, to limit the number of men involved in these operations. But that's all they understand back there, some abstract necessity; they have no idea of the reality of it, month after month of this, the same men having to look each other in the eye every morning. Ah, never mind. Forgive me. I'm tired, that's all. I'm not myself. Tomorrow is another day."

I reminded myself that I would have to be patient. That more than anything else.

He said,

"I understand your concerns for the men. But to be honest with you, from what I've seen so far, I think you've done better in that regard. In Byelorussia . . . I cannot even describe some of the things that went on there. After only a week or so Nebe had lost all control over himself, over everything. From then on it was really our executive officer who was in command, and he could not

run such a tight ship either. Believe me, Ohlendorff, you should-
n't be too harsh on yourself. Your men keep better discipline than
you give them credit for."

I felt somewhat appeased by this compliment—I took it as
such—though my mood still did not lighten appreciably. I stared
away somewhere, not knowing what to think. I had heard that
Nebe had been transferred back to Germany. I asked if this was
true. The man replied that it was.

"He was about fit for a mental asylum, if you ask me. Or a drying-out ward. He was drunk day and night, starting to babble nonsense at every visitor. When he took his leave of us he was trembling so badly he could hardly climb into the car. I believe some
people have too much imagination for these kinds of operations."

"Hm, " I said.

The fact was, I was starting to come to the same conclusion. I
was not given to wild fancies about things. And perhaps what he
said was true—perhaps more of this attitude had rubbed off on
my own men than I realized. And I saw that my reward for this
was to remain stranded out here in the deserts of Russia, while
Nebe was comfortably ensconced back home again. Still, the
whole affair could not have done very much for his career
prospects. One had to keep that in mind.

As always, I knew that I would regret even this momentary
unburdening of my spirits. It left a bad taste somehow. I was not
drunk, but I felt like a drunk who wakes up in the morning and
remembers babbling idiotically the night before. It was better to
keep silent, difficult though this was at times. In the long run it
was better. I believed that I did still have a pretty good grip on
myself, after all.

I knew very well that on several occasions I had come near to
being overcome by the horror of it all, but those moments had
passed. The thought had passed through my mind to order them
to stop, to order my men to stop, and I had observed this thought
passing through my mind. There was nothing to do but go on,
which we had been able to do.

To my surprise, I received orders to be transferred sometime
around the end of September. I was pleased, of course. I regretted
that my men would not also be relieved; indeed, I felt badly about
this. It was an injustice. In many ways, this whole ordeal had
drawn us very close together. Yet perhaps even that tight-knit

feeling was beginning to fade into a kind of numbness, dullness. Something. Words convey little. I could not hide my elation from myself, or perhaps it was simply relief at this point; but I tried not to show too much of it when I bade farewell to the men.

We were in Kirovograd, not far from Kiev, which had fallen only the day before. Kirovograd was a ruin, a town of heavy industry that combined the old and the modern with unvarying ugliness. The weather was still fine and we were camped on the steppe beside the railroad yard, just on the outskirts of the place. Our few attempts to find quarters in Russian houses and buildings had led to us being infested with vermin; so as the weather remained mild we preferred to set up out in the open country, which was cleaner and more pleasant to look at.

I said farewell to the men in September twilight. I handed command over to Sturmbannfuhrer Hirtwig, the officer who had come to us from Nebe's Einsatzgruppe in Byelorussia. Kirovograd had not been combed out yet, and he would have a good deal of work ahead of him in the days to come. The gaunt hulks of the town were lit white by the setting sun, walls with long rows of empty windows, factory chimneys rising. All of this was in the distance beyond the ripped-up tracks of the railroad yard. As was their practice, the Soviets had destroyed everything before their departure, carting off anything valuable on their retreat to the east; this, of course, did not include civilians.

Small shunting engines moved back and forth across the yard, screeching to a halt every few hundred feet, carrying new sections of track to replace the rails demolished by the Russians. An infernal din that added to the noise of the other repairs going on over there. While to the west, in the other direction, low clouds drifted in silence before the sun. Overhead the sky was deep blue and no longer a burden to us; the great heat of the summer had begun to diminish.

Hirtwig had suggested a farewell dinner in my honor. It stirred me, yet I also found that I had no enthusiasm for it. I had presided over too many strange repasts during these past months. I did not quite know how to express this to him, and instead gave some excuse about having to travel through the night; a car from the Wiking Division on its way to Kiev was standing by for me.

The men assembled in a small formation on the steppe, and I bade them goodbye. This suited me better. Parade formations always have a special quality in the evening hours. I spoke with officers and enlisted men, shaking hands, finding that I had little notion of what to say; it seemed that the mantle of leadership which usually inspired me to say the appropriate things had taken leave of me. I paid this no heed. A few moments previously I had given a short speech. It had lasted only a few minutes. Now as I shook the hands of these comrades it seemed that some of them wished to impart some last words to me, though they too seemed uncertain how to express them. Others simply said good-bye.

I walked alone to the Wiking staff car that stood waiting off to one side. Before stepping in I took a final look back at my men, who remained in parade formation with darkness gathering. I felt relief to be on my way, yet also strange sensations of pride, regret, other things; other things beyond naming, which God himself could not name. Yes, it was a relief, a terrible relief; though surely I was only partially able to absorb it at that time.

Along with the driver there were two other passengers in the car, junior officers heading back to the Reich to take part in some kind of training course. They spoke to me with a certain formality which I was no longer accustomed to. I suspected it was more than my seniority in rank. But I was tired and content to travel in silence for the most part. Night fell. We travelled slowly through the darkness over poor roads. The hours passed by tediously; finding that I was unable to sleep, I eventually attempted to make conversation, asking the Wikingers about their experiences at the front, their impressions of Russia, and so on. Their replies were somewhat perfunctory; I suspected they too must be weary from a long journey. They said that Wiking had crossed the Dnepr at the Zaporzhye Dam and were now in the neighborhood of Novo-Georgevsk, a place I had not heard of. Somewhere far to the south of here.

The night began to be scattered through with the kind of plague-fires I had seen outside of Uman. The armed forces communiques had reported the encirclement of Kiev as one of the greatest victories of the war, indeed as one of the great victories in the history of warfare. Nearly a million prisoners had been taken. This figure was so high that it seemed quite incomprehensible. I reckoned that even if it were exaggerated, the country outside of Kiev would present a terrible spectacle; I found myself hoping we would reach the city before first light. I had no great wish to see again the sights I had seen outside Uman. And indeed the plague-fires grew more numerous, as if the steppe were alive with the watchfires of some nomadic horde. Only the smell would instruct you differently. The darkness could not hide that.

I cursed these Russian roads and asked the driver if he had travelled this route before. He said that he had not and I asked him if he was sure he knew where he was going, scarcely bothering to conceal my irritation, though I accepted that he was simply doing his job.

"The road has been easy enough to follow so far, Standartenfuhrer. This is what passes for a major highway in Russia. We should be there before much longer."

Before the night was over we found ourselves following a large convoy into Kiev. Our pace was slowed to a crawl. Diesel fumes and dust added to the foulness of the atmosphere. All the same it was a relief to no longer be travelling alone through the night, which had its own perils. I was reduced to a state of semi-nausea and tried again to sleep, pulling my cap over my eyes.

I had arranged for a room in the Hotel Metropole, having heard there was running water there. We entered Kiev at dawn. The convoy dispersed to other destinations and we sped quietly along a boulevard beside the Dnepr River. The city was built up along the towering banks of the river, as high as large hills. Fine old buildings rose up around forested ravines that plunged towards the river. The river road was lined with trees. This was the first city I had seen in this country that conveyed an aura of civilization, of life as we knew it. We passed quickly through several checkpoints, then to my dismay we were halted as we approached the city center. An army officer informed me that the whole downtown area was sealed off. Jewish saboteurs, he said. One building after another had been blown up within the past 48 hours. Many people had been killed. The downtown boulevards were nothing but heaps of rubble.

The man looked tense as he told me these things; even as he spoke we were interrupted by a tremendous roar from somewhere not far off. Instinctively I leaped from the car, the driver and Wiking officers doing likewise.

"It's a horrible mess," said the army officer. "They've rigged it to perfection. Every few hours another one goes up. There's no telling when it will end."

I stared at a great column of smoke and dust rising only a few blocks away. In the depths of the river valley the city was still in semi-darkness; far overhead the pall of debris swirled up through the first rays of the rising sun. Sirens began to wail.

"Filthy bastards."

I muttered this to myself. I told the watch officer to direct me to the Hotel Metropole.

"It no longer exists," he said. "That was the first thing they blew up."

"Ah, God damn it!" I shouted. I walked around in a circle for a moment, staring at nothing. I was dead tired, ill from fumes and motion sickness. My uniform was worn-out and foul-smelling. I glanced at the barricade flung up across the street, army and SS men standing there armed to the teeth, many restraining dogs on leashes that were yipping nervously after the blast. An armored car was parked on the sidewalk, turrets swivelling aimlessly at an invisible enemy. I said,

"Direct me to SS headquarters then. Unless they've blown that up too."

"They have," the man said. "That was in the Metropole. Consider yourself lucky, sir, that you did not arrive two days ago."

"Never mind that!" I shouted. My patience was finished. "Obviously they will have moved to some other quarters. Where is that?"

He didn't know. He looked harassed and distraught, but no more than I was at that moment. Another great rumbling noise passed through the air; I could not tell if it was a second explosion or only the sound of walls still collapsing from the first one. Dust rose again into the morning light. The dogs nearby began to howl, sirens continued to wail from somewhere further off. I saw an SS officer in the turret of the armored car and ran over to speak to him. He gave me directions to another building outside the cordoned-off area.

The three Wiking men climbed back into the car with me, their faces marked with tension. The driver looked somewhat relieved when I told him to turn around. The other two as well.

"God damned shit, " one of them said.

We drove off through other neighborhoods, ascending the hills away from the river. Other sections of the town appeared to be undamaged. People began to appear in the streets, crowds walking along tree-lined sidewalks in an atmosphere of strange normalcy, the aspect of a large city in western Europe again. A facade, I thought. The evil of it all. Bolsheviks and Jews. My nerves were still shaken and I clenched and unclenched my hands around my knees.

"Look at the bastards," said one of the Wikings. "Doing their morning shopping. How many saboteurs out there, do you think?"

"Depends how many Jews," his comrade replied. "God damned shit."

The first one muttered something else, glancing in my direction for a moment, then staring out the window.

I recalled the shock wave from the explosion that had rolled through my body only minutes earlier, seeming to feel it again now. I pressed my hands against my face, trying to control myself. It was anger as much as anything. I had seen the aftermath of the Soviet policy of scorched earth and sabotage in countless other towns before this one, and suspected what was going on in Kiev was only more of the same. But on a much larger and more insidious scale. Time bombs. Filthy Jews. No doubt the local Semites had had nothing to do with it, or would claim such to be the case, but it made no difference to me, no more than to my three travelling companions. In the end it was all the same. As the driver had no knowledge of the city we were obliged to ask for directions at several more checkpoints, carefully steering away from the sealed-off zone which apparently covered a large area. I had had my fill of riding around, nearly limp with car sickness by this time. I was on the verge of demanding to be let off just to get some air. At last the driver parked in front of a wide edifice with a large coterie of guard-dogs and black-uniformed men posted at the doors.

I got out and collected myself for a few minutes, sitting on a sidewalk bench beneath a small chestnut tree. The Wikingers stood nearby, staring up at the building with a certain apprehension. No doubt they had the same thoughts I did and were reluctant to go inside. Sealed-off zone or not, it seemed clear that no place in the city could be considered entirely safe at this point. They conferred with each other for a few moments, hands on their hips, looking nervously about as if to find some alternate course of action. At length they shook their heads and walked up the steps past the SS guards. At length I did the same. I didn't know what else to do.

I wished only to report my arrival and then find some reasonably safe place to rest for the day, pending my further journey home. Once inside, I was informed that for some reason the train station had not been wrecked; my relief at this news was countered by the worry that the station might go up right while I was waiting on the departure quay. What an evil mess. The clerk at the orientation counter seemed to read my thoughts.

"Bomb disposal squads have been combing the station since the first explosions. That was two days ago, Standartenfuhrer. The trains have been leaving on schedule since then."

He spoke calmly but distractedly, not quite able to look me in the eye. He did not look happy. I had seen no one who did.

"And what about this place?" I said tersely, motioning at the walls around me. It was only a kind of nervous curiosity, as I had no intention of remaining here any longer than necessary.

"The building has been searched and searched again around the clock since we moved over here. The site was chosen entirely at random, so we are confident these are merely precautions."

He did not look confident, though perhaps a certain businesslike resignation had replaced overt fear. He must have repeated these scant words of encouragement many times by now.

"Were you at the Metropole, by any chance?" I asked.

His eyes narrowed and he shook his head faintly, which I took to mean that yes he had been there.

"Yes. Yes, Standartenfuhrer," he said.

"All right. Carry on then."

I fought down the urge to immediately walk back out to the street. A certain dull disgust passed through me which seemed to calm my nerves; I set my mind on getting my travel arrangements in order. He directed me to another office upstairs.

By mid-afternoon of that same day I had resigned myself to the fact that nothing was going to go as planned. The Einsatzgruppe assigned to the Kiev area had not yet arrived on the scene; apparently many of the roads leading into the city had also been booby-trapped, that or some such reason. In any case the SS agencies already present in town had decided to begin the roundups immediately; the effects of the terrible sabotage had left its mark on the face of everyone I spoke to. I could not disguise the nature of the assignments I had just completed at Kirovograd and elsewhere. Before I could utter a word of protest, I found myself retained by the senior SS commander to assist with these same matters inside Kiev.

A rotten deal of the cards, I reflected. But considering the obvious state of emergency I could make no protest, nor did I attempt to. As I walked out of the SS headquarters a nightmarish feeling washed through me momentarily. I pushed it out of my head, determined only to take care of this business as quickly as possible. The morning sunlight was a relief. I was given a new car and driver and chauffeured to the scene of the roundups, which had already been underway since dawn.

There were large numbers of Jews living in the sealed-off downtown area, which I was now obliged to enter. My anxiety had dissipated a little by now, my thoughts focussed on taking care of the business at hand. Nonetheless I was shocked by the extent of the destruction in the center city. An all-out aerial bombardment would not have levelled the place so thoroughly. The wake of devastation left by the retreating Soviets in other places was nothing compared to this. Smoke and fires were still rising everywhere, doused by teams using great hoses and compressors to pump water all the way up from the Dnepr. There was nothing but rubble in all directions, which in a sense put me me more at ease; there were simply no buildings still standing to be blown up. SS and army details accompanied by civilians were still searching for bodies; I recognized the corpses of both Germans and civilians laid in rows at the edges of the rubble.

"The Kreschchatik," my driver informed me. "It was their version of the Champs Elysee. Or the Kurfurstendamm. The stupid bastards just blew it all to kingdom come."

We were ascending a wide soot-blackened boulevard that seemed to rise across the entire city, from the river to the hills above. Straight as an airstrip only two days before, now transformed to a variously widening and narrowing meander between heaps of ruins spilled out every which way. We drove slowly. We soon came upon trucks filled with armed men, upon men with watchdogs and machine-guns lining both sides of the street. I could see the Jews now, a great rabble being herded and driven on further up the street. The pavement was strewn with the bodies of stragglers who had been shot down or savaged by dogs, dogs trailing leashes fighting over fallen Jews, some of whom were still screaming for help as we drove by. Already the operation looked like a complete mess. I clenched my teeth, angered that I had not even had a chance to shave or find fresh clothes. I had been instructed to oversee the business end of the operation, which was taking place at a city park called Babi Yar. Throngs of dazed-looking Semites effectively barred our way. I had no desire to push through the middle of them, nor to continuously shout out my credentials to the SS men who kept approaching the car.

"Find another route, for God's sake," I told the driver. "Use your head, boy."

He turned off at an intersection and within seconds the dismal scene was behind us. We passed through a few deserted neighborhoods, some in smoking ruins, others somehow spared from the swath of destruction. We turned onto another main street, speeding uphill past clusters of pedestrians who again seemed preoccupied with nothing more urgent than their daily affairs. I felt the temptation to instruct the driver to convey me out of the city altogether, to simply report to the next rail depot to the west of here and be gone. But I said nothing. The driver drove with silent assurance. I tried to look on the bright side—that prompt action in such a difficult situation would put another favorable mark on my record. It was small consolation.

We ascended through autumn sunlight and old yet decently kept-up looking buildings. I looked behind to glimpse the river far below. The driver turned onto another sidestreet and headed back towards the Kreschchatik. I noted that the devastation did not extend this far up the hill. At least not yet. The sidestreet was unnervingly peaceful, yet peaceful all the same. The anxiety, almost a funk, of earlier in the day no longer had much hold on me. I was only very tired, having had no more than brief snatches of sleep for going on two days.

We came across another file of dogs and SS men blocking off the Kreschchatik. I could see the Jews still marching uphill just beyond them. Here the situation appeared a little more orderly. The guards parted to let us through and I flexed my lips apprehensively as the driver calmly conducted me right into the middle of these many thousands of Jews.

"It's just there, Standartenfuhrer. Here we are, in fact."

The car was surrounded by the crowds. Yet they passively made way, some of them staring at the car but making no attempt to block our passage. We drove by a few more SS men wielding clubs and truncheons. Suddenly we were in an open area, a wide grassy space. All the Jews were being herded off to one side. The remainder of the grassy space was empty. I stepped out of the car with relief.

•   •   •

I could no longer bear to look around me but I continued to see things all the same. You could not close your eyes or you would stumble over something or someone. Death would follow.

It seemed that the street was becoming narrower but it was not. The Germans were simply lined up closer and closer to us, forming a kind of funnel through which we must squeeze, packed more tightly together. I passed German faces close enough to touch and saw some staring back at me as if staring into space, and saw some with looks that seemed even to bear pity, a cold and horrible pity; and saw some that were more hateful; then I did not dare look at any more of them for fear that I would be clubbed down or attacked by the dogs.

I kept my eyes mostly to the ground, stepping over bodies or other debris. We had left the ruined areas behind us, down below, and now there was less debris in the street; I did not have to step so carefully all the time. From time to time I would glance up at buildings or houses I had known all my life, at particular address- es I had visited, at particular windows where I might have sat looking down on this street. All of it now altered, yet unaltered. The sunlight was the sunlight of any day in early autumn, falling quietly upon the screaming and the shouting, the endless mutter- ing of bewilderment. I looked to one side at a doorway where a woman of about my age, naked from the waist down, was being assaulted by four Germans who were lined up one behind the other. I stared there for too long, or thought I did; when one of them looked up in my direction I panicked and tried to fight my way deeper into the crowd. I thought my struggle would only attract more attention to myself, or else I would be pushed to the ground and trampled; I looked back wildly to see if any of them were coming after me but the doorway was no longer in sight. I went on, the procession carried me on. I looked here and there to catch some view of my parents but knew it was useless, I had lost sight of them hours ago.

A tall youth stood motionless in the streaming crowd, a tall boy I recognized from my own neighborhood, a young musician. He somehow managed to hold his ground without being swept along or swept under. He was weeping and as I came closer I could hear his sobs; his hands were clutching at his long yellow hair, pulling at it. I passed as close to him as I had to the Germans and when he looked into my eyes I thought he must recognize me. It seemed that he did, though the sight of me brought no change to his expression; he turned his head away, tears streaming down his cheeks and onto his clothes like transparent blood.

I stood next to him, thinking that if he could remain anchored here then so could I. We stood somewhat with our backs to each other, somewhat side by side. For a few moments I had the strange sensation that I was invisible and might collect myself here, pull myself together, and think of something. But I found that I could not think of anything. I remained motionless there, pressed against his body, which seemed to part the crowds coming up the hill. They reformed immediately and went on, including people I recognized, all of us unless it were immediate family giving no sign of recognition or anything. I considered that except for my parents all my family was safe and this thought passed through me like a scream and yet it was nothing; I had already repeated it to myself many times over these hours and I really could not think of anything any longer. My children were safe. It was true. But I could no longer grasp it. I saw everything clearly but could not think. The weeping boy whose name I could not bring myself to think though I had known him for many years was giving ground slowly; I realized that he was pushing against me, that I was moving as well, though only little by little. Suddenly I felt we would be shot or attacked for standing still. I was paralyzed and to set myself in motion again seemed a horror. I stepped out with one foot into the crowd, certain I would be shot at that instant. Shots rang out continuously. I was aware of them and then unaware of them. Now I was aware of them. It was unbearable to wait any longer. I stepped further and was again swept along by the crowds.

DEMYANSK

A car was passing through a line of soldiers barring a side-street. It came only slowly but I thought it would run me down. There was no place to get out of the way. It bumped into people yet somehow they gave way and the driver advanced only slowly with an unperturbed expression. He was a soldier and there were pennants on the fenders and in the back seat was another soldier, a general, an officer. He looked at me through the window with an apprehension that was different from the strange calm of the driver. They passed onward and continued to make way without running anyone down. I was knocked to the ground by another car following on the bumper of the first which I had not seen. It looked like a taxicab, filled with passengers who looked down at me with expressions I could not describe. I was not hurt and struggled instantly to my feet, grabbing at human torsos and shoulders; I had been down on the pavement for only a second yet had felt the press of the crowd like a wall collapsing on me. The terror of it seemed to shut off my breathing and I no longer took any real notice of anything except staying on my feet. Then a few minutes later we were there, somewhere.

It was a wide grassy area with a wall of heaped-up earth or maybe sand dunes in the near distance. There was a rattle of gunfire like machine guns but they were not firing into the crowd; the sound came from behind the dunes. There was a small gap or passageway cut through the dunes and I saw groups of people in tens and twenties being led through there. They were naked. Other people up ahead were removing their clothes, piling them on the grass, standing naked at the end of thousands of other people who were still clothed.

More of the unclothed ones were led away through the passageway. It was true then. They were going to murder us all. I had known as much yet had also hoped they had only killed people on the way up here in order to frighten the rest of us, or because they were mad. It seemed they were not mad. They were going to kill us all.

Nearby I saw another one of the old Karaime sect who had been crying out all morning to prepare ourselves for death, for our ascent into heaven. Hours ago I had been angry, thinking these people were only sowing needless panic among us. They were doomsayers who cried out what our fate would be with the chanting monotonous idiocy of monks. So they had been right all

along. But their songs of doom had remained unchanged for generations and perhaps for centuries; and now a day had come to
gird their cries with louder validation. A quiet day in September.
The sunlight conveyed ordinary quietness to the earth or else held
it suspended overhead, yet still quite close by. The Karaime was a
young man who continued to cry out loudly and calmly even
now, unheeded by people who perhaps before had ignored his
message and who now had no more need of it. He watched the
goings-on up by the passageway in the sand and began removing
his clothes; presently he stood stark naked among all the rest of us
still fully clothed, himself still calmly intoning his death chants,
striding among his fellow Jews.

At length I saw more people removing their clothes up ahead
and this tide of nakedness began to surge slowly and strangely
through all the crowd, coming slowly towards me, towards this lone
Karaime who stood as if patiently awaiting the nakedness of his fellows. The dream-logic of this had a strong force. I told myself I must
get away. In my purse I carried papers indicating I was not a Jew.

I saw a cluster of people around some German officials nearby. They were friends and neighbors who had come to see their
Jewish friends and neighbors off at the train station, as that was
the destination we had been notified of in the early morning; non-
Jewish neighbors or else other non-Jews who had helped carry
our luggage and belongings up the long hill, cart drivers, taxi drivers, now waving documents and papers at a small group of
German officials. I went there. I passed taxi drivers who strode off
and climbed back into their cars and drove away, pushing back
through the crowds.

Some people were allowed to leave. Some were not. I did not
understand it. I showed my papers to a German officer. My husband was a Gentile and so I also bore the name of a Gentile.
Beside the German stood a harassed and angry-looking Ukrainian
interpreter, yet when I approached him his expression softened
and he spoke to me not unpleasantly. I found I was able to explain
myself without stumbling over my words in all the noise.

"Please. I am a Gentile. I came to say goodbye to some Jewish
friends. What should I do?"

He took my papers. My last name, my husband's last name,
was Proliskaya. I did not explain that the friends I had come to see
off were my parents.

"It will be seen to," he said. "If you'll just wait over there for a little while. Someone will be along to escort you away from here. Don't worry, miss. Keep your papers with you."

"Where? Where?" I said, struggling to contain my fear before he turned to speak to someone else. Gently he put his hand on my shoulder and pointed somewhere. I saw a car. Then I looked beyond the car and saw a small group of people sitting on a hillock in the sunlight. I went there. I saw other people who were simply being permitted to leave and almost dashed after them but I did not. I went to the hillock and sat down.

Fits of trembling passed through me, which I was not much aware of. They left after a few minutes. The hillock was warm and sandy and momentarily I thought I was going to fall into sleep. But this did not happen.

For a while I did not look at the crowds I had just escaped from. I wondered where I was, where we all were. The area did not resemble any neighborhoods around the Kreschchatik. It seemed we had been hours walking up that street, but perhaps we had turned off it at some point. I saw buildings standing up around the edges of this grassy place, ordinary four or five story buildings whose upper floors I stared at for some time. A few birds were perched on the ledges there, or on the roof, outlined against the sky. Clouds miles away rose up behind those roofs, drifting slowly from one region of the city to another. Sometimes the roofs seemed to move instead of the clouds, lurching abruptly towards me then lapsing into stillness again. Mostly all was still, rendered with quiet force by the sunlight and the blue sky, which now and again seemed both the same thing, and now again seemed separate things. My children were safe. It seemed that I was safe, though I was not certain of it.

I could not help but look down at the ground again from time to time, though the shock of it was not so great anymore. Naked people were being led through the passageway in the sand. Gunfire rattled in a quiet distance not far beyond. There were great crowds of nude men and women and children now, yet more people continued to arrive all the time from the hill below, fully clothed and many of them carrying their belongings, which after a time they set upon the ground in the dull horror of waiting. From time to time people screamed in horror or protest and were shot or clubbed or set upon by dogs; these instances came and went. Taxis and horse-drawn carts continued to arrive and then turn around and drive away, some pushing slowly back through the crowds, others driving across the empty grass before me and leaving through a gap in the line of guards and dogs in the distance.

The passengers discharged from the taxis seemed to be mostly wealthier members of the community; most of whom, I reflected, had fled the city entirely before the arrival of the Germans, leaving the events of this day to befall the less fortunate members of the community, those from poorer Jewish districts like Podol. But a few of the more upstanding citizens had also remained behind. They emerged with their families from the taxis and looked upon their surroundings, the patriarchs distractedly paying their fares or sometimes needing to be reminded to do so by the drivers, while the passengers gave out stunned looks upon their surroundings, which surely by this point could not have taken them entirely by surprise. It was no longer necessary to be surprised to be stunned, as I knew for myself. They were dressed like well-to-do people setting out on a comfortable journey or perhaps to attend an evening's performance somewhere, conveyed in a split-second into the emotional realm of the beyond upon being let off by their driver not at the theater but on the bald summit of one of the remote sunlit mountains of hell. All these things happened, hour after hour.

From time to time other people broke away to confer with the officials and the interpreters and were politely, some of them, pointed over this way, where I sat among Gentiles on the small hillock. I supposed it was possible that some like myself were Jews posing here clandestinely. The thought occurred to me and then went away. Thousands of things passed through my mind over these hours and went away. Some of these people were allowed to depart immediately, for reasons which I still did not understand. I no longer felt the impulse to dash after them, as I had lapsed into utter paralysis; though in my mind I imagined myself doing this. The rest of them came over to sit upon the hillock, waiting as I and many others had done for many hours. Surely they did not mean to still shoot us, or else they would not have bothered to separate us from the crowd. It was puzzling. From time to time I would remember my parents and feel sick, surprised that I had been able to forget them for a little while, though surprise was in fact among many ordinary things that no longer existed within me, except in various dull or hideously mutated sensations. I did see them out there, after a long time had passed.

They were being led into the sandy defile, where it was easier to see people because they were led through in only small groups of ten or a dozen. My parents walked hand in hand though their heads were bowed and they did not look at each other. I felt a nauseous shame and prayed they would not see me over here; I knew they would certainly not be able to see me and the intense heat of shame faded away but the nausea remained. Then it went away a few seconds later. I stared at their nakedness. I saw them and then they entered the passageway in the sand and were gone. If I had been looking elsewhere for these few seconds I would never have seen them.

The passageway was cut through a row of low sand dunes or weedy looking earth-banks, with a few small trees growing along the top. On top of one dune there was a park bench beside a little tree silhouetted against the blue sky, and a man standing there beside the little tree. The sunlight seemed to darken him in silhouette though I could see his features clearly. I recognized him as the German officer I had seen in the back seat of the car some hours before. All this time I had been half-aware that the car parked near to this little hillock was that same car, that the driver sitting in the front seat and smoking a cigarette and seeming to read from something was the same driver; but it had made little impression on me. Suddenly there was an enormous silence like a huge rock. It was not silence, it was the stopping of my breathing; from the crowd there came still the noise of a great crowd but it seemed shut off from me and I found myself listening. Distant clouds rose slowly from behind the sand dunes.

There came the roar of machine-gun fire, the dull blur of machine-gun fire which lasted only a few seconds. It was the same sound I had heard repeated for hours and hours. Now it was very distinct, the most distinct sound of all this passing time. It struck me like a nail yet I found myself trying to picture if it was really my parents I had seen; I knew I was not mad yet perhaps I was not altogether in my right senses and I had only glimpsed them briefly before they had disappeared into the defile in the sand. I shut my eyes and tried to concentrate on what I had seen of them, to picture for sure whether or not it had been them. I knew it had been them but I obsessively looked and re-looked at these pictures in my mind until they dissolved beneath a crushing weight that seemed to bear me down to the ground. I had to lie down in the sand. I no longer saw anything in particular but I had to keep shutting my eyes as the light of day caused me an unbearable distress. I would then open my eyes because there was no escape in darkness but I kept shutting them again. My children were safe, my husband and my children were safe. My parents were dead. All of this seemed outside of human possibility and I found myself obliged to continue rehearsing strange scenes within my mind, not only from a few moments ago but also from earlier in the day, hours and hours before, even so far back as the early morning twilight when we all awoke to discuss the situation in our apartment on Mellinchior Street.

But I was unable to concentrate. I tried to do so but it was without really trying, as I was no longer capable of it; things merely passed through my mind. Pain or anguish began to erase everything, which I might have been grateful for but the feeling of it was too terrible. My breathing was very still and the lead feeling of being sunk into the ground was so great that I thought it might drive me into sleep. I began to think that I too would be shot. They could never let anyone escape from here. Yet I continued to see with my own eyes that some people were being allowed to leave, that in all likelihood I too would be allowed to leave eventually, to walk home, to ride the trolley car home. But in the meantime I felt oppressed by a burden so strong that I feared it would destroy the rest of my life if I did not get relief from it soon. I pictured being shot or being allowed to go home with equal indifference; but this waiting had gone on for too long, I had to get away. The lead feeling that held me to the ground was so strong that I thought it might drive me into sleep, but it did not. I thought of calling for a doctor, of fleeing to a hospital, where I would lie on a table and be given an injection that would put me to sleep, at least for the remainder of these hours. I pictured this as I pictured everything during this passing time, things entering my mind then leaving it. The gunfire continued.

•　　•　　•

Further down the street I had driven by flagrant breaches of discipline which at one time I might have punished severely. The rapes especially. But technically speaking these were not my men, and I wished only to reach the business end of of the operation and get on with things.

I stood beside a park bench and a small tree above the ravine of Babi Yar. The events below were a powerful thing to witness and I almost sat down on the bench, but I felt this would be unseemly and remained standing. In any case I could see that the terminus of the operation was better organized than what I had seen further down the hill. I was relieved that this was so, but also somewhat irritated; for after surveying the situation I had realized that my own presence here was more or less superfluous.

From where I stood I could see down into the ravine on my one side; and then out across the wide grassy expanse on my other side, into one end of which the waiting Jews had been herded. They had largely been cowed into submission by now, subdued by their own nakedness, a powerful tool of which we had learned to make effective use. I studied the entire setup with what might be called professional appreciation, though I still declined to really imagine a profession such as this. To my left was the grassy area, effectively hemmed in by buildings, with an outer ring of guards and dogs all around the edges of it. Then there was an inner ring of guards and dogs to keep the Jews all bottled up at one end of the expanse, which instinctively struck me as a good idea, though I could not say exactly why. The uncrowded area where my car was parked was a relief to the eye, and perhaps this induced a certain calm on the men and the Jews both. In any case things were proceeding about as smoothly as I could have hoped.

Small groups of the naked creatures were separated from the crowd and led in single file to disappear into the narrow sand passageway a few feet from where I stood. I could just see the tops of their heads as they walked through the defile, which was perhaps thirty feet long. I could then look down on the other side and see them emerging upon the upper part of the ravine. The guards pushed them out onto a narrow ledge with their backs to the sand dunes. Below the ledge the ravine fell off as sheer as a cliff wall for quite some distance. At the very bottom were the bodies which had been heaped up in their many thousands since the early morning, and where our Ukrainian helpers shoveled sand and lime even now, appearing from my height to be no more than workers digging out the initial excavation of a building site, or some such thing. The dead Jews were far enough below that I did not feel compelled to study them too closely. Another burst of machine-gun fire rang out and those led out along the ledge toppled off to join their brethren below. The ledge was so narrow that there was no place else for them to fall. I watched the bodies spill slowly down, it seemed slowly.

It was a well-organized affair. The terrain itself was so perfectly suited to a smooth-running operation that it seemed almost to have been shaped here by some higher power. The depth of the ravine would be convenient for the disposal of the bodies. The narrow ledge made a good aiming point for the machine gun crews, who were established on a promontory several hundred feet away on the opposite side of the ravine. They could thus do their work without having to observe it too closely, which would make things go easier for everyone. They were far enough away across the ravine that you would not even notice them at first unless you happened to be looking for them. Between bursts of fire I would hear their voices carrying faintly through the still air; I could see the small movements of feeding in new belts, the occasional changing of a barrel. I saw them smoking cigarettes and staring here and there while waiting for the next file of Jews to be led out onto the ledge.

All of this was being done by men who had no particular training for the task, though I found myself wondering if the officer in command had somehow learned a thing or two about the operations of the Einsatzgruppen. I had been informed that he was with the machine gun crews on the other side of the ravine, leaving the crowd control over here to his subordinates. If he had had been on this side I would have sought him out to say a few positive words to him, as I could not have orchestrated this action any better myself. I looked to see if there was a convenient way to cross the ravine or go around it, but it seemed to extend through almost the entire range of hills coming up from the river. I decided to remain on this side in order to deal with any mishaps that might arise among the crowds still pushing up from the

Kreschchatik, though at the moment the likelihood of this did not seem too great.

My mood was somewhat lighter than it had been earlier. I considered that with any luck the operation would be concluded by this evening, and that I might be able to leave Kiev by sometime tomorrow. From where I stood I had a commanding view of the entire city, and I took a moment to step back from the proceedings and study the other sights far below. Rooftops and chimneys fell away down the long slopes of the hills; interrupted here and there by parks and trees, a vista that was like a fine dream of great cities anywhere in the world. The Dnepr was several miles away, down in the valley of the city, but even from this distance I was impressed by the width of that stream, by the reach of tall bridges that had a certain grace even though their mid-spans had all been blown. A few barges and other traffic passed along the water, sometimes disappearing behind the tall facades of waterfront factories or drydock facilities. On the other side of the river, which was less built up than this side, forested bluffs stood silently.

The ravine where I stood made me think of the balka outside Vinnitsa where I had lunched with Muhlmann, the young Waffen SS officer. As it had been there, so did this place, this deep cleft in the earth, seem to bear the shape of allegorical events, the force of parables that would be told and retold in the centuries to come, that would somehow redeem all the stress and suffering of these days. Or so it seemed. Perhaps there was truth in this, but I realized I could not think about it any longer, at least not now. I stepped back into the small shade of the little tree, steadying myself by placing my palm against the back of the park bench there. I felt weak. I needed rest. The guns from across the ravine barked again. I turned my back on it all and trudged down from the low dunes and walked across the empty area back to my car.

I wondered how much longer this could go on. I had no idea how many Jews there were in Kiev. I should have informed myself of this at the SS headquarters, but I had been in too much of a hurry.

As I returned to the car my driver stepped out to inquire if I needed anything. I shook my head, placing one boot up on the running board, glancing over at the naked masses a short distance away, then looking off in the opposite direction and taking a moment to smoke a cigarette. I felt the familiar reeling sensation swim through my head for a few seconds; I ignored it, smoking and staring at nothing. I was interrupted by a request from another SS officer who had approached the car.

"Excuse me, Standartenfuhrer. There are several people here who have been waiting to be released. They arrived up here this morning with the Jews. Their papers are all in order, but I wanted to get your approval before letting them go."

"Letting them go? Who do you mean?"

He indicated these several people, who were a group of about twenty or thirty men and women sitting on a small rise a few feet away. I recalled having seen them there earlier, though not quite so many of them.

"They are all Russians. Or Ukrainians anyway," said the officer.

"Very well," I said, thinking the matter over though only a moment passed before I spoke automatically:

"No, no, that won't do at all. Get rid of them, for God's sake. And do it now, so I can see it's taken care of. We can't let any word of this get out into the city. There are always a few Jews who don't respond to the initial summons. If they get wind of this we'll be a week tracking them all down. Do you understand? Take care of it right away."

"Yes, sir."

The officer hesitated. He seemed uncertain about something, and then it came out that he had already released a few people some hours previously. I shook my head in disgust and threw my cigarette on the ground. These men were still not experienced enough. I gave him some harsh words. Finally I said,

"All right, never mind, it's too late to do anything about that now. Take care of these people. Get on with it."

I clenched my teeth, trying not to think what sorry complications might ensue from this fiasco. On a practical level, it would have been difficult to keep the operation completely sealed tight anyway. Especially in the middle of a large city. Inevitably there would be a few witnesses, purveyors of gossip; I had learned this in the past. But the fewer the better. All of these people should have been turned away somewhere further down the hill. If I had been in charge of the operation from the start I would have seen to it. I was angry, so much so that I had to remind myself just to hope for the best, that at worst I would still be leaving in a few days. My God, a few days. . . . I had managed to put the sabotage and the time-bombs and the ongoing climate of fear out of my mind, but now I hardly knew what to think. I lit another cigarette and followed the officer over to the small rise. He was speaking to one of our interpreters, who was in turn discussing something with several of our Ukrainian assistants. They were men who could be trusted, but not the rest of them here. Wretched business. They were telling their fellow countrymen to get up and remove their clothing. I lost patience.

"Never mind that! Just do it right away. Take them over there now."

I pointed towards the defile in the sand. The interpreter and the other assistants shrugged their shoulders and began herding the people away. I delivered another short lecture to the SS officer and then dismissed him. I watched him hurry over to speak to the guards standing by the defile. I delivered a few more irritated remarks to my driver and then entered the car to sit down for a while.

• • •

I had no will to resist. I moved towards the passageway with the others. I stopped, but it was because I felt weak, my knees gave way. One of the Ukrainians kicked me and raised his gun, I thought to shoot me. The German officer, the younger one, shouted at the Ukrainian who then dragged me to my feet and shoved me so violently that I stumbled again. I began to cry, but somehow got up again and walked the rest of the way, which was only a short distance. My tears disappeared as soon as they began. I felt them drying on my face. Dimly I felt relieved that we had not been forced to remove our clothes. We walked in between the sand dunes. None of the others with me said a word.

The passageway made me think of how you would walk through high dunes to get to some of the bathing beaches along the Dnepr. The dunes would block your view and then all of a sudden you would emerge upon the wide view of the river. The passageway was narrow and we were through it in a few moments. About halfway through it lay the nude body of a woman who had been shot in the head, and we were obliged to step over her. Then we emerged into air and light. The guards pushed us out along a ledge that grew narrower and narrower till it was not possible to go further. I was afraid of heights but at this moment I noticed the drop beneath our feet without any particular fear. At our backs was a wall of hard sand covered with blood that had soaked into it and looked strange somehow. I stood still and faced out across the ravine. I had not known what to expect. For all these hours I had had no idea what lay on the other side of the little sand banks and the little passageway. The open air and the absence of all the bodies I had expected to see was a kind of relief, a relief which rose through me in a dull agony for a moment or two, before my eyes adjusted to these surroundings. Now I could see clearly enough the great heaps of bodies down there, though they lay at quite some distance beneath us. I saw more of these men who appeared to be from the western parts of the Ukraine, walking among the bodies, shoveling sand over them, shooting a few who were still moving, while others stood leaning on their shovels in small groups, conversing with each other or looking here and there. I could hear their voices clearly enough though not their words.

"Ah, what a delightful spectacle," I thought, hearing these words pass through my mind with a mad dull perversity which I did not pay much attention to. I began to cry again though all of it seemed only one thing or another by this time. I could not see anyone who was going to shoot us and wondered what would happen now. From somewhere within the city I heard the rattle of a bus shifting gears, somewhere on city streets, city boulevards, a strangely familiar sound that caused me to close my eyes and dream for a second or two. When I opened them again I began to make out the group of men on top of the far wall of the ravine. They were quite some distance away and I had to study them for a moment before I could make out what they were doing, realizing that these were our executioners. A few of them were kneeling by a machine gun while others stood or sat nearby in various attitudes, one of them dangling his legs over a ledge similar to the one where I stood, staring across at us. A little further behind them was a row of park benches and then I realized where I was, at the ravine of Babi Yar. I had been here many times before, on picnics with my family or walking with friends; why I had not recognized it right away I could not say. I was about to be murdered. The machine gun began to fire and from the corner of my eye I could clearly see those furthest down the ledge toppling into space, struck backwards into the sand wall and buckling to their knees and then toppling forward into space. The bullets advanced it seemed somewhat slowly across the line of us on the ledge and just before they came to me I allowed my knees to give way and crumpled down into the air.

It took several seconds to fall, long enough that the terror of falling came to me just before I struck the ground. There was no ground but only bodies. I hit with the sensation of being clubbed in the head but felt almost right away that I was not hurt and a strong sense of clarity came over me almost right away, a strange feeling of normal consciousness which I had forgotten about for many hours. I was aware of half a dozen or so other bodies landing beside me for one or two seconds. I looked at the face of the nearest one, a man who was clearly dead. The suit of clothes he was wearing seemed to mark him apart from all the nude limbs and torsos he was lying on, that I was lying on. Then this distinction faded away. Here and there among the tangle of flesh were the heads of other people, many with their mouths open, eyes open or closed; these heads briefly appearing to be separate from everything else like heads of swimmers bobbing in the water; this impression faded also. I did not dare look at anything else. I lay without stirring for hours until evening time. I looked straight above into the sky.

During this time I was aware of other people moving all around me, stirring, making faint continuous noises like rats moving within the walls of a house. I understood that there must be many who were not dead, who had escaped the gunfire or were only wounded. There was moaning and sobbing, but it was mostly a faint noise that was everywhere. Louder cries attracted the attention of the Ukrainians who I could hear walking out upon the bodies and firing shots. For a long time I felt like a rock and had no wish to move even if I dared to. Then later I could hardly bear to remain rigid in such an awkward position and felt I must stir a little bit, if only to shift my arms and legs, which were causing me a peculiar discomfort which was near to driving me mad. I straightened myself out a

little and felt a great relief and lay there for some time further thinking of nothing. Evening was approaching. I heard a few more
bursts of machine gun fire and saw a few more bodies spilling
through the air directly overhead. One landed across my legs,
which a moment later were soaked with blood. Then for an hour or
longer there was for the most part silence, except for the faint
moaning and scrabbling sounds everywhere, and the noise of the
Ukrainians shoveling dirt and occasionally firing shots.

Gradually I heard them shoveling dirt closer and closer to me.
If I shifted my eyes only slightly I could see them. I did not believe
they could bury so many bodies with just a few shovels and somehow convinced myself that I would not be buried alive. It seemed
they were just scattering dirt everywhere and in the twilight I
could see many of them moving slowly or else simply leaning on
their shovels as if exhausted. But in some places they must have
buried people better than others. I heard a terrible noise, screaming and choking, and saw a young girl emerge from a pile of dirt
nearby, clawing at the air and staring about and screaming more
loudly than other noises I had heard. She was naked except for
dirt and blood and one of the Ukrainians clubbed her with a shov-
el. I heard no shots and the girl was still making noises of some
kind and then it seemed that several of them were dragging her
away somewhere, maybe to be raped, I thought. I didn't know.

By the time they returned it was nearly dark. They mostly stood
around talking but then they resumed shoveling again. When the
first heap of dirt struck my face I was startled; I could not see where
it came from. I was aware of a shape standing beside me but then
my face was covered and I could see nothing. At first I could still
breathe and as dirt began to be piled on my legs and stomach I felt
a strange sense of comfort, like a blanket being pulled over me, that
would calm me utterly and let me die in peace. But I did not want
to die and could not accept it. When more dirt was shoveled on my
face I felt a panic that would burst my head and a silent screaming
within me so violent I thought it would burst my head. I could not
breathe. I opened my mouth. Dirt trickled down my throat but a little air came in also. I remained still.

I heard or had some sense of them walking away. Slowly I shifted my head from side to side till more dirt slid away and I could
feel air on my face. More sand trickled down my throat but air came
also. I looked overhead and saw darkness, the night sky. The dirt on

my body had little weight, there was not too much of it.

At some time in the middle of the night I rose slowly and began to crawl away from Babi Yar. I crawled across the bodies. I could hear moaning far beneath me, voices of people crushed beneath all the bodies, trapped down there. It was too dark to see anything except the night sky overhead and the light from a few lanterns here and there by the side of the ravine, around which I could barely see a few men. I could barely see them and thought they could not see me.

I did not move as carefully as I might have. I felt a deep exhaustion and was also so worn out by fear itself that I no longer felt much afraid. So I moved somewhat carelessly at first, stumbling over bodies. But this unconcern seemed to calm my nerves and it seemed unimportant that maybe I would pay for it with my life, though somehow I no longer thought this would happen.

I realized that I needed to get off the pile of bodies so I could walk more easily. I made my way towards a slope of the ravine where there was only darkness. I stumbled again and plunged my hand between naked limbs into excrement. I could smell it. I staggered from revulsion and felt my human spirit retreating to the nethermost reaches of the fingertips on my other hand. But the feeling passed and I saw that I was not too distressed. I breathed quietly for a few moments while keeping my soiled hand utterly still. Then I withdrew it slowly from the bodies and wiped it on the hair of a man whose head rose up beside my knees. I crawled a little more carefully and soon came to the wall of the ravine, where I wiped my hand again against the dirt, scouring it as best I could.

I knew from other days that the floor of the ravine advanced uphill for some distance, and that near the top the walls were low enough that they could be climbed without much difficulty. I kept away from the dead by walking along little outcroppings and narrow level places along the wall. I walked for a short distance and then there were no more bodies and it was as if they had never existed. The floor of the ravine was covered with gravelly debris and low bushes and I heard the sound of running water, which I knew came from a stream that ran along the floor, flowing in the middle of the bushes nearby. I realized that it must have flowed beneath us, beneath all of us, lying there for all those hours. I looked back and in the glow of a few lanterns I saw the bodies again and a few heads somehow distinct in the midst of them, rising just above the uppermost layer or peering up from just underneath it, as if through little gaps in a hedgerow of human limbs and other flesh. I squinted, then closed my eyes and kept on walking in the other direction.

In the uppermost part of the ravine the bushes grew more thickly. A long time had passed. I was moving more carefully now, afraid of making noise in all the underbrush. It was time now to climb up out of this place. As I started up the slope I was accosted by a boy quite nearby. The shock caused my bladder to empty, though there was not much inside me. He came nearer and informed me that he was still alive, as was self-evident. Something compelled me to reach out and grasp his hand, which nearly caused me to begin weeping again, but then the touch of human flesh repelled me and I took my hand away. He told me he had been brought out to the ledge in the early morning and fallen down just as I had done, even while his father had been shot standing next to him. He said he had no one left and took both my hands. I set them on his head.

We crawled up to the top of the ravine but then could go no further, as we could hear Germans talking and walking about everywhere, and dogs muttering beside them. We remained in the bushes till dawn. I fell on and off into sleep which seemed to last only a few minutes at a time. Each time that I awoke I felt a sense of depression unlike anything I had ever felt before, and was seized with despair that I could not sleep longer.

As it began to grow light we saw a few other people darting out from the bushes not far away, running across a road that ran along the top of the ravine. They were chased down and shot by the Germans. A boy about the same age as the one beside me was walking quite unconcernedly along the road next to an old woman; the strangeness of their demeanor hypnotized me. Then for no apparent reason the woman took fright and began to run down an alley across the road; the Germans came to the mouth of the alley and shot her down in there. The child was still standing in the middle of the road, crying for his grandmother; the Germans came over there and shot him also. We remained in the bushes while the morning grew lighter with terrible slowness.

At some time I heard noises down in the ravine and saw two young women being pushed into a little grassy patch beside the stream. One of them was the young girl covered in blood and dirt

I had seen dragged off in the evening, though now it was four Germans who lay her down and began to violate her along with the other woman. After each took his turn he stood up with his hands on his hips and his member growing gradually limp again, joking with his other comrades as they finished. They seemed to be enjoying themselves and I regretted I could not share these simple pleasures. After the last was done they fired several shots into the women.

There were several days of this still to come, during which I shared many strange adventures with the young boy beside me, although he was murdered at some point. Before this we were obliged to remain hidden in the bushes for a long time. He told me his name was Moika, and I told him I had two children whom I believed to be safe at home. I thought this might console him some-how, but he looked at me strangely. Perhaps he did not believe me. Often he would hold onto me. As the sun rose higher it cast light down into the depths of the ravine and I began to see clearly again the pile of bodies down there. They seemed to lie floating in blood, heads continuously rising up, floating up, through a large pond of blood. I thought I must be imagining this but then I realized more people were alive down there even now, clawing up from below. I saw a few stagger off into the bushes like specters while others sim-ply stood or sat down where they were and were shot down by gunfire continuing to come down from above.

I too was covered in blood which I had not been much aware of before now. It was like some thin elasticized substance which had hardened overnight and now cracked whenever I stretched my arm or twitched my fingers. From time to time I picked at it, peeling long strips off my forearms. The little boy did this also, flicking it in the dirt between us until there grew a small pile of rubbery blood shavings there. From the evidence of my own eyes I began to wonder if my mother and father could still possibly be alive somewhere down there, or somewhere in the undergrowth on top of the ravine; but the expectation of this was too much for me and I lapsed into a dreamy state for hours throughout the afternoon. I saw my parents and also sometimes my husband and children dressed in white and floating above the ravine, my par-ents spinning lightly through the air as if they were young and agile again. I saw them as well travelling along the road beyond these bushes, passing nearby a foot or two above the ground as if conveyed by some unknown means of locomotion.

In the night time we left.

At some time the following day we were crossing a field and heading towards a line of woods in the distance. I could not imagine that we had walked entirely out of the city and thought we must be in a park somewhere. But I continued to look all around and the place was surely out in the country. The grass was tall. I could not remember how we had come here. The little boy would remain close to the ground but from time to time I would stand up to look around. Great clouds passed overhead which trailed shadows in a slow journey across the sunlit treeline before us. The line of shadow was very distinct but I could never exactly see it move from one tree to another one, though eventually it passed across the entire forest. I was possessed by the idea that I had entered into some different era of my life, from some years ago maybe. The feeling was very strong, like something I could actually see before me; like a memory which I could see inside my head but which was also clearly visible all around me. The boy kept warning me not to stand up so much and sometimes he tried to drag me down to the ground. I was clothed, but he still wore nothing.

We passed across the field and into the woods in the distance; at the edge of which were benches, and I thought we must still be in the city after all. We travelled cautiously through the woods, and sometimes it was tempting to remain there. But whenever it was possible to move a kind of inertia compelled us to keep on moving; if we stopped for a while anxiety would come over me. When we were moving it sometimes seemed that I too was conveyed along a foot or two above the ground, which was strange because I was exhausted and my limbs felt like lead; nevertheless I had this sensation and from time to time looked about to see if my parents were nearby again, but I did not see them.

At the end of the woods there was another street with houses on the other side. The boy crawled out behind a large tree next to the curb. I thought he might have forgotten he was naked. Even so he tried to hide himself in a low hedge bordering the street. I wanted to tell him to come back but I did not dare. I heard noises out there and then he cried out to me to stay hidden as the Germans had him. I could not see clearly. I heard shots, they must have shot him. No one looked for me. They must not have understood his words.

At the edge of the woods I scooped up some dirt, as if I were going to lay him to rest there. Then I pushed the dirt back into the empty hole and remained sitting beside it. I stayed there a while, under the tree, no longer able to go on. I had thought that in the end, if we escaped, I would adopt him and bring him to live with my other children.

For several days more I wandered through many strange adventures, escaping death only by one way or another. I wandered onto a farm and was discovered inside the barn by a farmer. He told his son to go fetch the Germans, who showed up very quickly and took me away. I was led into a house back inside the city, and after being held in a room for several hours a German soldier came in and motioned that I was to begin cleaning the windows with some rags that he had. I did this without knowing the reason for it. A few minutes later he returned, and by gesticulating and saying a few German words that I knew, he indicated that I should keep on what I was doing until no one was watching me any longer, and then escape. He cursed at me with a strange concern that I took to mean sincerity, though I found myself unable to believe him for a while. Besides, I no longer had the presence of mind to escape. I was sure I would be shot and busied myself cleaning the windows over and over again. Outside in a little yard I could see a group of very old Jews, the old and the sick, perhaps the very last to be rounded up in Kiev. I didn't know. They were guarded by a young German soldier who sometimes had tears in his eyes and shouted at them, yet when they looked up at him or tried to reply he would turn his back. Finally he left.

Another woman was brought into the room where I was. She too commenced cleaning the windows or tidying up other little things, strange tasks. She had been told the same story and it was she who finally convinced me they would not shoot us if we tried to leave. I did not know whether to believe her; I only followed her when she left. She pulled up one of the windows and we climbed out into the yard where the old people still remained. They looked at us. We walked out along a back alley between wooden shacks and little gardens and a rubbish dump. We wandered in the city and at length boarded a bus that was headed down the long hill. She was less bloody and dirty than I was and I crouched in my seat between her and the window. She seemed to understand and positioned herself to make me less noticeable. Probably this fooled no one but no one in the bus seemed about to take action against us. We drove downhill along the boulevards, beneath the trees along the sidewalks. When the bus stopped at one place she stood up calmly and said, "This is my stop." She took my hand and whispered that I could come with her if I was afraid. I shook my head, as I could think of nothing except reaching my family. The woman, whom I never saw again, made her way down the aisle and stepped out into the sunlight. I looked at her among the other people on the street and the bus moved on.

The other passengers studied me more closely and I became more conscious of the filth and blood that still coated me. I began to think what it would be like to see someone raised from the dead, for that must be what I looked like, wondering what it would be like to see myself through their eyes. This idea struck me with terrible force but then left my mind as had so many other things over these several days, entering my mind then leaving it. The bus passed in and out of the sunlight that fell through the gaps in the tall chestnut trees that lined the street. I could not help but remember countless other sunny afternoons when I had dreamily ridden the bus to someplace in the city, and again had the sensation of passing through some different era of my life. When the bus entered my neighborhood I forced myself to stand and walk tiredly down the aisle as the other woman had done. I was struck by the appearance of buildings and houses, residences that I recognized, and without thinking I stepped down from the bus before it had fully stopped. I stumbled against the curb and fell on the sidewalk. I was too weak to get up right away. By the time I did so a crowd of people had gathered around me and I again felt hopelessness and imminent betrayal to the Germans. But some of the faces were friendly looking. A man I knew helped me to stand and I leaned against him. I knew the house of my husband's sister was quite nearby, but I could not picture how to get there. The man knew this address and he and several other people helped to take me there, seeming to carry me sometimes through the air. A half hour later I was seated in the parlor of my sister-in-law while she thanked the visitors and then sat down beside me.

I was able to remain undetected until the end of the war. Kiev was liberated in 1943, in November. That seemed like the end of the war, though it went on for another two years.

Up until that time I was sheltered by my husband's identity. I was maddened by the fear that some neighbors who knew what I was would turn me in to the Germans. I thought if they got a second chance the Germans might extend their revenge to my two children; this fear seemed very real to me and burdened me so much that I sometimes thought of killing myself. With the support of my husband and his family, who did all they could to keep my spirits up, I was able to endure. It seemed clear that their lives were also in great danger but this complication was so horrible that I could never bear to speak of it. Even after the war I was not able to thank them. Gratitude had been devoured.

During the two years of the occupation Ukrainians were also shot in great numbers. The Germans would seal off city blocks and take the inhabitants away to be shot. These incidents would follow various acts of sabotage or other events that were never even explained. Thus I did not live in fear alone.

I heard stories of other Jews, and once visited one, who had no means of concealing their identities. They were obliged to remain hidden in cellars or closets or attics for more than two years, maddened by the secret assistance of neighbors who risked their lives yet who could perhaps never be entirely trusted. Why not? Because fear was inescapable, though you might become resigned to it over time. I understood this. The one I visited, in a cellar on Borodin Street, matter-of-factly expressed his envy of my freedom to move about outdoors. I understood this, though I was still in the grip of such fear that I did not go outside as much as I could have. He said he had gone outside on two occasions, one time strolling about the neighborhood for over an hour in warm weather. The experience eased his torment, but afterward his fear grew stronger and he could not make himself go out again. I agreed somewhat dully that it would not be a good idea.

Several years after the war I lapsed into a depressed state which lasted, on and off, for over thirty years. Perhaps it was not as bad as it might have been, though what moves me to say this I cannot really say. Occasionally I would feel periods of relief that would come over me with a strange dull ecstasy, where everything about me would take on a strange and uneventful ordinariness, but which would also have some further nature which I am not able to describe. There sometimes seemed to be obvious reasons for this, yet the living force of these periods was beyond reason or any clear description. In any case these periods of relief did not last long and would always fade away. Angels sometimes strolled quietly among the city crowds but the day-to-day facts and difficulties of life were much more forceful; thus strange ideas and even visions seemed of little consequence.

The wave of anti-Semitism that came after the war was difficult to bear. It seemed to be too much. But there it was anyway. What little urge I had to speak of my experiences, once the Germans had gone, was repressed and never surfaced again. The Gentiles seemed to blame the Jews for the terrible suffering the Germans had inflicted on the country, as if it were we who had caused the Germans to come here in the first place. Before the war we had heard only that the Germans were our friends, and even decades later no one could much explain what had happened. The Jews had always been disliked by some people. But after the war this attitude worsened. I found myself unable to give it much thought any longer.

I told my story to a journalist in 1982, who had found out about me one way or another. I no longer felt as badly as I had during the preceding decades, but still had no desire to say anything to anyone. He bothered me for some time until at last I relented, just to get it over with. At this time I was living in an apartment on Mellinchior Street, not far from where we had lived in 1941. I spoke to him for several hours on a day in June. The summer days were long and he came in the evening, when the weather would lift away a little bit, leaving a certain amount of space above the crowded and uncomfortable dwellings of the city.

EPILOG

Medical Record of James Allison, US First Cavalry Division veteran, June 22, 1982

Mr Allison admitted himself to the VA Hospital for the second time this year, having previously been admitted for three weeks in February.

The patient follows a pattern of self-admittance for periods usually lasting two or three weeks; over the past five years he has done this, on average, twice a year.

The rest of the time he resides with his mother in a rural community outside Tallahassee. The patient has indicated that he will feel periods of mental distress coming on and so check himself in to the hospital for a while. Conversations with his doctors show that he also needs what he calls a "break" from his mother. He speaks of her fondly and states that they are close to each other; nonetheless, she continues to be his legal guardian and places limits on his daily life which he finds restricting.

For obvious reasons, his daily life in the hospital ward is also restricted, but he seems to require this change of pace for a time, and stresses the opportunity to visit with other veterans in the hospital, many of whom he has become friendly with on previous visits.

The patient suffers from a schizophrenic disorder which vacillates between moderate and acute. Generally speaking, his impairments are not too severe; e.g., he is able to drive a car, make social visits, go to church, etc. In particular he has a certain comprehension or self-awareness of his disorder, usually a hopeful sign for patients suffering from this affliction. He is highly delusional, and during periods of acute distress firmly believes in these delusions; during milder periods he seems able to understand they are not real. In general he is able to converse in a more or less normal fashion, though in extended conversations he will tend to lapse into delusional ramblings; this is particularly so after times of heavy drinking. It has emerged as part of his pattern that his stays in the hospital will sometimes serve as self-imposed drying-out periods. His disorder follows a clearly established pathology, however, and is not rooted in alcoholism.

Mr. Allison served in Vietnam with the 1st Cavalry Division in 1970. His posting to a combat zone was cut short after two weeks, when strong indications of his disorder necessitated his removal to a supply depot in the rearward areas, where he finished the remaining eleven months of his tour. He was assigned to clerical tasks and occasionally did repair work at the divisional vehicle park. He was not diagnosed with schizophrenia at that time. An initial diagnosis of combat trauma was later changed upon his return to the United States. We have been forced to rely on Mr Allison's memory for most of the details of his time in Vietnam;

apart from clearly delusional statements, his personal recollections generally correspond to his official service record.

Mr Allison was kept in the VA Hospital in Savannah, Georgia, for fourteen months during 1971-72; he was then released to his family (mother and one sister) in Hampton Roads, Virginia. He made numerous visits to the Hampton Roads VA, often for periods lasting three or four months at a time, until 1977, when he moved to Florida with his mother. From that time until the present, he has followed his pattern of several stays per year in the Tallahassee VA. Over time his condition has improved considerably, particularly when he abstains from alcohol. In 1971 he was classified as suffering from acute schizophrenia by physicians at the Hampton Roads VA. At the present his disorder is classified as moderate. His veteran's disability benefits are 100% for life.

Mr. Allison suffers from a wide range of delusions that fit many of the classic symptoms of schizophrenic disorders. Many of these delusions are transient fantasies; others are more permanently and deeply rooted. Some of the most frequently recurring examples of the latter are:

—belief that he was recruited by the CIA at age four and has been working for them since that time. He also believes that he has worked as a double-agent for the KGB, though his convictions about this are not as strong. He is sometimes confused as to whether he volunteered for these duties or is being manipulated against his will.

—belief that he has a close personal relationship with the Pope and other high authorities in the Catholic church—cardinals, bishops, etc. He has frequently mentioned being sodomized with a broomstick by the Pope as a small child in Hampton Roads. This is one of the delusions he seems to understand as being false, despite his powerful recollections of this event. (Since his arrival in Florida he has attended the Hawthorne Baptist Church, and calls frequently upon the pastor, Brother William Tanner. See attached note re conversation with William Tanner.)

—belief that he has killed large numbers of people, usually with an M-16 rifle. He reports having killed, to mention a few examples, eighteen Black Panthers in Hampton Roads during the 1960s; 400 Green Berets at Fort Ord, California, in 1969; between two and three thousand Vietnamese ("gooks") in Vietnam in 1970; several hundred Americans, also in Vietnam; numerous VA hospital physicians and other personnel; and John Wayne.

These should serve merely as useful examples of a much wider range of delusions. Each of these examples may also be expanded by many additional details into a kind of delusional "storyline," which is consistent with other case histories of schizophrenic logic and memory association. Ultimately, all of the delusional "themes" present in the above-mentioned examples become interwoven with each other from time to time.

This point may be illustrated by closer examination of Mr Allison's beliefs about working for the CIA, which evolve into an elaborate delusional history, including minor details which are frequently changed or embellished from one therapy session to the next. During his last stay in February, Mr Allison reported the following, which is presented here in condensed form:

He began receiving messages from his television set at age four, and in this fashion was recruited by the CIA. He also received messages directly via radio waves or other kinds of waves, at times simply "out of the blue," at other times via untraceable devices implanted within his head. He believes that sending messages both through the television and through head implants is typical of the kind of "electronic redundancy" employed by such all-encompassing agencies as the CIA. Recently he has stressed that the head implants were not put there by UFOs as part of an alien research program. Apparently he disdains the current vogue that this belief enjoys among various segments of the population. (However, a glance at earlier files from his case history shows that at other times he has taken this possibility more seriously.)

He reports having been a sales representative of the Nike Shoe Company since age four, indicating that this was part of the cover story assigned to him by the CIA.

He also reports hearing the voice of God through the television, as well as the voices of dead comrades from the war, childhood friends he has not seen in many years, and miscellaneous other voices almost too numerous to catalog. He speculates that not all of these voices are deceptive measures transmitted by the CIA (or counter-deceptions transmitted by the KGB), and he concludes that he cannot always account for the exact nature of them all. In certain of the February sessions, as in various other sessions going back over the years, he will admit to the possibility that he is imagining all these things.

He will sometimes recount these delusions with a certain self-deprecating humor, which this observer has noticed over the years, as if he wishes to impart to his interviewer that he does not always take himself too seriously. Recently, when asked if he really did kill John Wayne, and if so by what means, he replied that that had all been a joke, and that he was not above pulling people's legs at times, particularly doctors' legs. The stress of his condition (he said) sometimes necessitated these little outlets of humor. He reports that despite ongoing bouts of depression and threats of eternal damnation by the Devil, by God, by Jesus Christ, by the Death Angel from the planet Viztriz (etc., etc.) he likes to maintain a good sense of humor and is well-liked by his friends and other people in his neighborhood. Recently he lamented that his humor came "too easily" and sometimes prevented people from taking seriously his deepest fears and concerns. He reports that one of his failed careers was as a standup comedian along the lines of Rodney Dangerfield, and that while some of his neighbors at home enjoy his talents as a raconteur of lunatic stories, he gets no real satisfaction from this.

Mr. Allison does maintain a certain humorous outlook, and his occasional self-deprecatory comments about some of his delusions are rarely seen in the most severe forms of schizophrenia; thus this attitude should be taken as a sign of improving health and mental stability. Nonetheless, it is this observer's impression that he still secretly wishes his delusions were taken seriously (i.e., believed) by the medical staff and people in general. Occasionally he will complain about this lack of respect, what he terms "a failure to understand him." He complains that while he does his best to cooperate with doctors and understand that his delusions are not real, he does not feel any reciprocal effort on their part to truly imagine what it is like to have memories that are as real as any memories could possibly be—for example, memories of being sodomized by the Pope in a broom closet, of having the Devil appear to him in the form of a bituminous lump of coal and tell him he was going to burn in hell, of beating Jimmy Connors in the Virginia state tennis championships, of constantly hearing and seeing God's angels ever since childhood, of sitting on the beach at Khe Sanh Bay with a pretty Vietnamese mamasan and watching Gothic space monsters land on the flight deck of the

USS Forrestal; of these and a great many other memories almost too numerous to catalog.

(His manner of expressing the seeming reality of these memories, and his concern that other people simply failed to comprehend the vividness of them, was taken as a breakthrough of sorts and duly noted in his file; it later became the subject of a lengthy discussion at a meeting of several of his consulting physicians. The thin line by which some schizophrenics can comprehend the nature of their disease and attempt to convey this experience to others is the theme of a growing body of medical literature.)

As mentioned previously, this account of Mr Allison's recent sessions must be understood as being highly condensed; to fully do justice to his delusional world, and to the alternating flux of his pre-occupations with it and his attempts to distance himself from it, would require a much longer report, and perhaps volumes. There is no mention here, for example, of his daily actions with his mother, with his other acquaintances, with the members of his church, with his friends in the VA ward, and numerous other people (he does not live an isolated life), all of which take place in varying degrees of what might be called "normal, day-to-day existence." The latter phrase is clearly an imprecise term, and is included here only because Mr Allison employs it from time to time as a means of referring to his daily life. This seems important to him. He reports that his delusions are inescapable, but that he does not prefer to sit in his room and dwell on them continuously.

In sessions he sometimes complains about his weight, which is in the neighborhood of 300 pounds, though in general he seems more resigned to this than to some of his other preoccupations. He is a compulsive eater, smoker, and drinker. A brief attempt to curb his alcoholism by the use of Anabuse in 1980 was unsuccessful. In one of the February sessions he remarked that he would sometimes look in his bathroom mirror and see "a skinny young guy," rather than "a balding, 300-pound guy." He declared that this was not a hallucination but merely something that he wished to see. His service record shows a weight of 165 upon his return from Vietnam; this weight increased dramatically during his initial stay at the VA hospital in Savannah. He is aware that his condition is gradually improving, and sometimes laments that he wasted his youth (by which he means his twenties and thirties) spending so many years locked away in mental wards.

Miscellaneous other points:

Mr Allison's deep preoccupation with religious matters, in particular with visions and aural hallucinations involving religious figures or divine beings, is a common manifestation of almost every form of schizophrenia; there is ample evidence of this throughout the other files of his case history.

The conspiratorial nature of many of his delusions is also one of the hallmarks of the disease. Apart from some such obvious manifestations as the CIA and the KGB, there are other conspiratorial themes involving the accomplishments and career-opportunities that have been stolen from Mr Allison by a wide range of people and agencies. The title of Virginia state tennis champ was wrongly taken from him and awarded to Jimmy Connors. His ideas for new product lines for the Nike Shoe Company were stolen by jealous co-workers who never gave him proper credit. He claims to be the inventor of numerous other products and devices, as well as the original founder of such karate schools as Cuong Nhu and Tae Kwan Do. Many of his personal conflicts and failures in the military stemmed from jealous superiors or fellow soldiers, though some of these people he claims to have forgiven. (He claims one such conflict was the underlying reason for his alleged killing of 400 Green Berets at Fort Ord. Mr Allison claimed that a "weasel-faced" lieutenant who was jealous of his hand-to-hand combat expertise attempted to kill him with an M-16 rifle. Mr Allison deflected the stream of bullets with his belt buckle; the ricochets subsequently killed 400 men in the surrounding area. Mr Allison pleaded justified self-defense, and the case was dismissed without formal arraignment at court martial.)

These conspiratorial themes are also amply recorded in other files of his case history. At this date, it should be noted that while these conspiracies are real to him, he seems to think of them in a somewhat different light than his religious visions. The religious visions have a powerful effect on his thinking, causing him deep fear and concern; whereas the various conspiracies against him more often seem to bring out feelings of disgruntlement or resentment, perhaps stemming from the notion that he might have made something better of his life if not for his condition. In particular, he is able to talk about many of his conspiratorial thoughts in a more humorous vein, which is generally not true of his religious ideas. This observer has the impression, for example, that Mr Allison is aware that he did not beat Jimmy Connors in tennis; while he may have experienced this delusion, it is typical of a lesser category of things that he does not take altogether seriously (such as his killing of John Wayne). Nevertheless, the firmness of his conviction about these delusions does still vary from time to time, depending on whether he has been having "good" or "bad" days, whether or not he has been taking his medication, drinking too much, etc.

Many of these conspiratorial delusions seem to fit what he describes as his "little jokes"; however, the underlying fear of conspiracies against him, in a general sense, seems more real to him than many of the actual details he describes. Again, he does not seem to really expect people to believe that he "founded the Cuong Nhu karate school, without ever receiving proper credit," but he is still secretly tormented by the wish that people would believe him anyway.

Other points:

The record should clearly state that Mr Allison's disorder is of the genetic variety. In other words, it was not caused by experiential traumas such as childhood traumas or combat trauma. Nevertheless, it seems clear that certain events in his life did aggravate his disorder, particularly his service in Vietnam. (He had never been hospitalized previous to this time.) Some events may have had a strong influence on his delusional world. Apart from his military service, there is a recurring theme of childhood molestation (events that both his mother and sister have acknowledged may have had some basis in reality. See attached note from Hampton Roads VA, re childhood experiences with scoutmasters, nuns at Catholic school, etc.) From this theme arise numerous delusions regarding acts of sexual abuse, involving the Pope, various nuns and priests, evangelical figures such as Jimmy Swaggert, military superior officers, etc. Mr Allison bears an ongoing resentment against homosexuals, though he frequently states that he does his best to be "forgiving" about this, and is concerned about doing his best to be a "good Christian." During several of his February sessions he developed one of his more elaborate delusional histories, having to do with a film company he created in order to make a film entitled "The Defaggers." He described this as a kind of Western along the lines of "The Magnificent Seven," in which the title of the movie would appear in bold lettering above a line of horsemen approaching the audience. They would be given the task of "defagging" various homosexual elements of the population. In further details of the plot he described a kind of half-track or armored car with a laser-type weapon in the turret, which would shoot "defagging rays" at homosexuals in various cities. When asked how such a vehicle would properly fit into a Western film, Mr Allison went on to say that he had been given a certain artistic freedom in his production, as well as a special dispensation from the Pope and secret funding from various evangelists such as Jim Bakker, Jimmy Swaggert, Jerry Falwell, etc.

Mr Allison described all this with what might be termed a certain humorous enthusiasm, consistent with some of his other delusions. There seems to be a certain ambivalence in his attitude which may stem from inner conflicts, i.e., resentment of his alleged molestations as opposed to his desire to be a good person and a forgiving Christian.

Ultimately, his delusional world is so complex that it is difficult to know which, if any, of these delusions have a real basis in his life experiences. Working this out has been an ongoing process between Mr Allison and his doctors.

Brief account of Mr Allison's mental state upon his most recent admittance to Tallahassee VA Hospital, June 22, 1982 (two days ago):

Upon meeting with his physicians (this observer included), Mr Allison appeared to be in a severely agitated state and complained that over the last few days he had been receiving terribly disturbing transmissions from the KGB. He described scenes of terrible violence and was highly upset that he had been selected as a so-called "witness" to these horrors for human posterity. He complained vociferously that his mental condition was too delicate to receive transmissions of this kind and that the unfairness of his selection as a receptor by the KGB was causing him great anger and fear. When asked to describe these transmissions he was largely incoherent. He repeated many times that he had not been drinking and insisted on his need to be kept away from alcohol (i.e., confined to the hospital) for fear that he might harm himself if he received such transmissions when he was drunk (that is to say when his delusional visions tend to be greatly magnified.)

He stated that what he had seen was worse than the visitations of the "death angel from the planet Viztriz and other emissaries of the Devil" who were always telling him he was going to burn in hell. In the consulting room Mr Allison's agitation reached the point of requiring physical restraint; he was administered 200 ccs of thorazine and confined to the special ward. Due to his extreme agitation it was not possible to pinpoint the exact source of his distress. A note was made of several rambling statements about "horrible Jews stacked in his backyard," as previous religious-related delusions recorded in his file involved almost exclusively Catholic authority figures and Protestant evangelists.

Subsequent visits with Mr Allison over the last 48 hours were unproductive until this afternoon, by which time he had recovered somewhat from his agitation and the effects of the thorazine. While still deeply disturbed by the "KGB transmission" he seemed to have experienced a certain relief and was able to talk lucidly. He admitted that he had been drinking heavily after all (as his blood/alcohol levels had clearly indicated) saying that he had been "stoned out of his mind." He expressed fear that the KGB might "transmit again" and requested that the ward personnel stay in close touch with him, upon which point he was reassured by the physicians. He also requested to see Linda Steski, a woman who has been renting a room from Mr Allison's mother at their home and who has visited Mr Allison occasionally at the VA. He was granted access to the telephone in order to reach her. He then described several other terrible scenes he had witnessed upon emerging from the effects of the thorazine, stating however that the "intensity of the transmission" had diminished somewhat. He then seemed less inclined to describe these scenes in detail, and showed more concern about his drinking problem, expressing a great deal of remorse that he had behaved so shamefully while his mother had been away visiting relatives for the day. He also requested to see his pastor, Brother William Tanner.

The patient was released from the special ward and given a bed in the general locked ward. Under the conditions of self-admittance he will remain free to stay or to return home, though a possible change in this status will be discussed by his physicians, depending on their observations and the observations of the ward personnel. From a legal standpoint, such changes in status are difficult and unwelcome to institute; hopefully this will not be necessary.

This report is signed and registered at 2:31 p.m., 22 June, 1982. Weather conditions are typical for North Florida at this time of year. High heat and humidity, cumulous cloud fronts building at altitudes up to thirty thousand feet, likelihood of afternoon thunderstorms, glockenspiels, and little freens observed at altitudes between eighteen and twenty thousand feet, asshole braces variable, Gothic space monsters at higher altitudes reaching up to thirty-three thousand feet, likewise the head of Christ; death angels and smoke towards evening.

signed

Rupert Mecklenburg
consulting physician

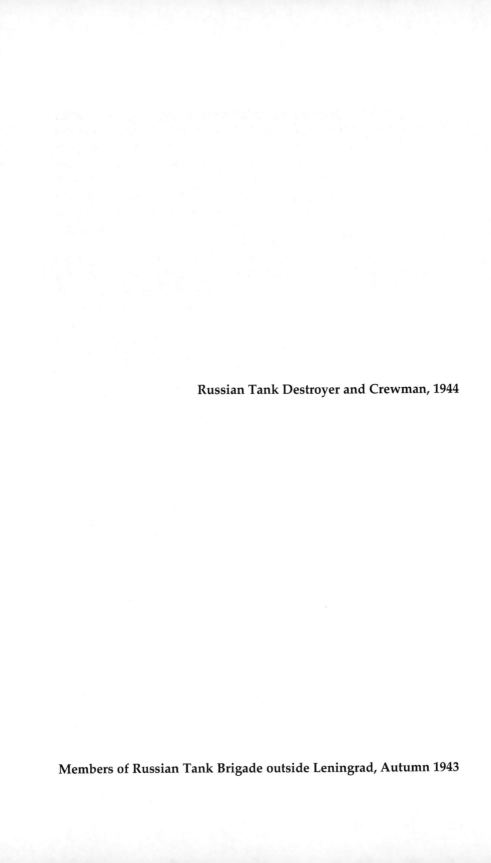

Russian Tank Destroyer and Crewman, 1944

Members of Russian Tank Brigade outside Leningrad, Autumn 1943

DEMYANSK

By the summer of 1944, the Russians had liberated almost all of the occupied territory except for the Baltic States and Byelorussia. In doing so, they killed or imprisoned thousands of their own citizens who had either collaborated with the Germans or were merely suspected of doing so. Non-Russian inhabitants of the Soviet Union, such as Tatars, Chechens, Balts, Cossacks, and others, were punished by measures as harsh as anything meted out by the Germans; these measures had, in fact, been underway even before the war.

One might speculate that the terrible Russian atrocities against German soldiers were in part due to misplaced anger against the brutality of their own government. But if there is some truth to this, it would be hard to say just how much, for German savagery alone was enough to ensure terrible acts of vengeance. Nowhere was this more evident than in Byelorussia, the part of the country that was held longest by the Germans. It was also in this area of swamp and forest that partisan activities were most extensive. The German military, even before the advent of the Nazi regime, had always had a peculiar loathing for partisan warfare. In Byelorussia this resulted in reprisals that laid waste to much of the countryside and widespread executions of civilians. During the great Russian summer offensive of 1944, mass graves and razed villages were discovered in large numbers, the Germans frequently having to flee before being able to erase the evidence of their crimes.

Thus the final curtain was raised on one of the great orgies of vengeance in history. . . .

SUMMERTIME, Or
It Is Good to Find Some Murderers at Last

The Soviet Destruction of Army Group Center, June and July 1944

Weather patterns June through August for Byelorussia.
    1941—Hot. Sunny.
    1942—Cold. Rainy.
    1943—Hot. Sunny.
    1944—Hot. Unbearably hot.

June 28, 1944

We swam in the Berezina. The weather was very fine. After a while we saw bodies floating in the reeds on the far shore. More Germans.

June 29

We approach Bobruysk with the road full of dust. Traffic comes to a halt. The woods are thick and the tank columns cannot get off the road. To stay inside the tank is difficult in the heat. At last we leave the vehicle to rest for a while in the shade of the trees.

DEMYANSK

June 30

Still outside Bobruysk. We are parked in a big field outside the town. The fire from the artillery is deafening. Waves of heat roll across the field from the cannonade, becoming more and more unnerving.

At length we are told we will not be going into the town. It is left to the infantry. The tanks are instructed to remain on the outskirts and take part in the artillery barrage. We have plenty of ammunition, and it is good to have something to do now.

Our driver, Irina Aknyatov, remains outside under the tarpaulin. After the first hour she relieves our loader, Kolparov. We leave all our vents and hatches open. The heat and fumes leave us half-nauseated. The barrage keeps us busy, and finally evening arrives. I am nearly deaf by this time.

To have my ears stopped up makes the heat even worse somehow. We think again of the river, which is still nearby. But we are too close to the Germans at this place. During the night we wait to hear if the town has been taken.

July 1

Orders to move come at two o'clock in the morning. The flames from the burning city of Bobruysk light the sky. We are told to cross the river at a pontoon bridge north of the city and block the Orsha road. The Germans are attempting to escape in that direction.

We drive off with great urgency. To enable us to drive faster we are told to use our headlights, the first time we have done this in a fighting zone. All the same there is an accident near the river and then another traffic jam. The traffic men guide us along a back road, and we do not lose too much time. When we get to the river we have to wait again while the tanks cross one by one. The entire river is lit by the flames from the city. We see more Germans floating in the water, drifting downstream.

At some point we hear a strange sound, the sound of voices singing. It is hard to hear it clearly in all the motor-noise. An infantryman climbs on board, speaking to Irina Aknyatov in the driver's hatch. It is the Germans, he says. They are singing their death-song. We don't know what to make of this, but he assures us it is true. He is an excitable boy, and he wants us to get down and go closer to where we can hear it. Ekhtarin tells him we have no time for that. The infantryman tells us it is something we should hear. He jumps off and disappears, and then we make the crossing. We head for the Orsha road as quickly as possible, though without our headlights now. It is a relief to be travelling in the night-time, despite all the dust being kicked up. It is possible to think clearly, though I am only tense with the thought of what lies ahead. There are only a few hours of darkness. We take up positions on either side of the Orsha road with the first light beginning to hang in the woods.

•　　•　　•

The woods are crowded with our vehicles, tanks and every kind of wheeled carrier. It seems impossible that they could escape through this barrier, and they do not.

In the first light we see two armored vehicles coming up the road from the town, assault guns. They move at a swift pace, slow down for a few moments, then pick up speed again.

At the first fire one of them is disabled, running off one of its tracks and coming to halt. It attracts fire from everywhere. Dozens of strikes raise metallic dust off its armor plate. It starts to burn and we tense up, waiting for the explosion. The other one lets off a few wild shots, then starts to back up. It's unnerving for us, we can only watch. There are too many of us in here, and we did not have time to set up a good firing position; half a dozen tanks from our brigade are spread out in front of our field of fire. We are not equipped with radio and Ekhtarin raises through the turret hatch to watch for any signal to move forward.

Our comrades in front of us are enough to dispose of the Germans. The second one is hit several times while attempting to retreat. The first finally blows up, sending out a wall of heat. Smoke rolls across the road and we can just see the second one driving off, not down the road, but off into the woods. The tanks in front of us advance in pursuit, knocking down trees. We are tight with excitement but Ekhtarin tells us to wait. She too is straining at the leash, straining her head forward. Major Bolkunov drives up in a jeep, waving at all the tank commanders, his assistant also raising the signal flag. We advance, some down the road, some down either side of the road. We are going into Bobruysk.

After only a minute there is another halt. The tanks in front of us are receiving fire from the woods, either from the German that escaped or from some other gun in there. I can see treetops toppling in the woods from other tanks crashing about in there. This is a bad place, in the middle of the road, I shout something at Ekhtarin but she does not reply. Then she tells Aknyatov to turn so we are facing the woods, and back away from the road. We do this. Still we cannot return fire, with so many of our vehicles pushing around through the trees. I begin to curse from nervous energy.

At length the flanking fire begins to diminish, we cannot tell exactly when it stops. The tanks ahead continue to return fire. I want to let off a few rounds but Ekhtarin refuses. She tells Aknyatov to shift position again, backing into the woods another dozen meters. We stay there for another fifteen minutes or so, before Bolkunov drives past again. He is speaking on his radio but also waving everyone forward with his arm, keep moving, keep moving. We advance down the road towards Bobruysk.

We pass German troop carriers standing in the road. It is like a terrible traffic accident. One of them lying on its side. Bodies are scattered across the road. The tanks ahead of us drive over them. I look at Aknyatov in the driver's seat. She peers through the armored viewing glass, shaking her head, cursing. We slow down a little bit. Ekhtarin says nothing. Aknyatov steers to one side a little bit. I look through my own viewing slit but it is hard to see very much. But we can feel the pressure against the treads, like bumping over a few small tree trunks. You would not think anything so small could be felt from inside a tank. I feel a little sick, but no more than that. I just can't help the feeling of it, I wait for it to pass and am glad when it does. Aknyatov looks at me for a second.

• • •

This time instead of entering Bobruysk we are instructed to block off another road leading out of town towards the west. We drive through little woods and farms, then spend an hour or so maneuvering around a swamp. We set up another blocking position among other vehicles that have arrived. We see the first German prisoners herded off to one side of the road. They are a filthy sight and remind me of our own wounded men coming back from the front in the first year of the war. They are not all wounded but they all look terrible, death in their eyes. I will remember that look.

They wear dark green uniforms that are filthy and shrunken-up looking, like clothes that have shrunken up in the wash. They all have long hair like a bunch of artists, which causes a lot of laughter and insults from our people. They stare around blankly like prisoners waiting to be shot, and I wonder if this is what will happen. Sometime during the day they are herded off by infantry-men, though only into a little fenced-in area by a farmhouse a lit-tle further away. I see dead ones remaining where they were before, wounded who have died.

All afternoon we wait, waiting to see more of them trying to escape up this road. Smoke from the burning city rises every-where above the hot woods. We can only be a few kilometers out-side the town. We remain in the tank and from time to time climb outside of it to escape the heat, yet still watching for any signal from Bolkunov or signs of movement ahead of us. We are tense from not doing anything but somehow the time does not pass too slowly with all the noise and activity everywhere, more vehicles arriving through the day, infantry dispersing through the woods, sounds of gunfire and shellfire all the time. And always the oily smoke rising up ahead. A few women from other vehicles come over to talk to us during the day, through frequently these con-versations will peter out because we keep expecting to be told to move forward, unless the Germans come to us first. Most of them are drivers from other tanks or troop carriers.

Finally Bolkunov comes by again in the evening and tells us to be ready to move. When he speaks these words I feel a wave of fear unlike anything I have felt up to this point, yet it passes away almost as quickly as it comes; I only know that it has happened. Scarcely five minutes have passed before he once again comes up and tells us to stand down and wait. This is too much for everyone finally; all at once from every crew in the area comes loud shouting and cursing, a few commanders from other tanks yelling at him and starting to argue. Some of the drivers start their motors, gunning the motors louder and louder.

Bolkunov seems to observe all this matter-of-factly. For a few minutes he is shouting back angrily at one of the tank commanders, yet when the other man walks back to his vehicle Bolkunov appears composed again. He climbs onto the hood of his jeep. The several tanks that started up are switched off again.

He stands up on the jeep and gives us a short speech. It is dark by now but he is lit up a little by the fires in the distance. He commends our eagerness to come to grips with the enemy. He makes a dramatic figure up there. A man beside me mutters that we are not eager to come to grips with the enemy but only tired of waiting. Bolkunov reminds us that we are not trained for night attacks, and the built-up areas of the city will be a trap for many of us. The last of the German garrison is massing on this side of the city to make a break-out tonight. He says it will be much easier to kill them coming up the road towards us like a stream of rats.

"If the bastards are so stubborn as to remain in the town for another night, then we will advance at the first light of dawn. You have my word on that, comrades. But in the meantime you must remain patient and be ready for the first sign of their approach. This morning's action was only the raising of the curtain. That is all for now, comrades."

The man standing next to me, who was speaking under his breath a moment earlier, makes another uncomplimentary remark about Bolkunov. I don't know his name but recognize him as one of Sergeant Illich's crew. He looks at me.

"Nothing but theater. He knows we're just pissed off listening to these changes of orders every ten minutes. It upsets our stomachs."

Just from his manner of speaking I can tell he has been through many actions before. We are mostly new crews and the rougher edges of the veterans are pretty noticeable. I am hesitant to ask him anything but wait to see if he says more. It was the veterans who were gunning their tank-motors, but it was only a way of telling Bolkunov he was getting on their nerves; enthusiasm had nothing to do with it. I don't know what to say but he goes on anyway,

"Don't take it wrong, little sister, but he doesn't want to make a mess of things with so many women in the brigade. He's a little more cautious than usual. He doesn't want anything to happen that will make him look bad."

In the meantime Aknyatov has walked up beside me, and she now curses the man for an ass. He makes some kind of snarling expression and shrugs his shoulders. Aknyatov berates him some more, and he just stands there silently rolling up some majorka. When he has it lit he says,

"That isn't what I mean. He's just thinking of himself, that's all I meant. It's not a reflection on you."

I'm not sure I follow him but he seems reluctant to say more. I can see only that his manner is not insulting. On the whole we have been treated with respect; that is the impression I get. The anxieties we felt upon first being drafted have mostly been dispelled. There is too much else to think about now.

Aknyatov is still staring at him, but her irritation seems to have subsided a bit. She says,

"What do you know about it anyway? He's not the big leader around here. He's only getting his orders from somebody else."

The man shrugs again, busying himself rolling more majorka. He hands one to each of us.

"Maybe you're right. All this fucking around just gets on your nerves, that's all. Just hang around a while, you'll get used to feeling pissed off."

"Stop it, Stepanovich. You don't know how to do anything without getting people upset."

It is Illich saying this, walking over to us. The other man makes some kind of hopeless gesture and walks off back to his vehicle.

"He used to be a commissar," says Illich. "Can you believe it?"

I shrug, supposing it is strange, but what of it. The tension is starting to get to me, probably to everyone. Illich looks unperturbed, but that seems to be his way. I stand there smoking with Aknyatov. The stuff is bad, but that doesn't stop anyone. Illich is staring at Aknyatov, and she hands him her cigarette. He inhales

a few times, then hands it back to her. Even with him, I think. It is
hard to just stand here quietly. But it seems it is becoming difficult
to talk also.

It is about this time that we begin to hear the voices again. The
singing. All our motors are shut off and there is not too much gunfire at this moment and we can hear them pretty well. The night
before I had barely heard it and didn't know what to make of it. It
is still pretty strange, even now.

"Do they always do that?" I say to Illich, after listening for a
minute.

"I've never heard it before," he says. "Not like this anyway."

"They must be near," I say, wondering why people do not
react. I look around expecting everyone to be moving now, climbing into their vehicles, getting ready.

I look down the road. Bobruysk burns in the night. We cannot
see the city but only the flames rising above all the summer trees.
The sound of singing grows louder. Suddenly I feel that my blood
is burning. I turn my head to one side, listening.

"They've had it," says Illich quietly. "They know the game is
over."

Someone says they are playing music through loudspeakers,
the way we do sometimes to irritate the enemy in his sleep or to
muffle the sound of our traffic movements. I ask Illich if that is
what it is and he says no.

"No, it's not loudspeakers. It's people singing. By God, you
can really hear them. They're close by now."

I recall the infantryman from the night before, talking about a
death-song. I open my mouth to say this but then I do not speak.

The singing grows louder but is also still faint and muffled,
and it is only gradually that I realize that I recognize this music.
My blood burns again and suddenly I am maddened by the sensation that I cannot relax, wishing in the name of God that I could
have gotten this first fighting over with by now. I can't concentrate, can't listen. But then in a moment I relax a little more and
can hear it better again. It is not a military marching song, unless
the Germans are in the habit of singing the great Germanic music
when they march into a fight. It is all unreal, it seems that even for
the veteran soldiers this must be unreal. I don't know. We all keep
listening. I find myself remembering visits to the opera house in
Astrakhan. It is exactly the same. Heat within my body keeps flar-

ing up and then subsiding. Sweat runs down my face. I stare up into the leaves of the deep deciduous trees all around, lit by distant fires.

"Long-haired musical faggots."

It is the one from before, Stepanovich. The flames light his face. They light everyone's face.

"Marching band boy's school little choir boys. They've all had their balls cut off. That's the only way they can make a sound like that."

He goes on in this vein with a kind of crazy single-mindedness until at last Illich shouts at him to shut up. I see Illich looking away. I walk off to climb onto our tank. Aknyatov follows me. Ekhtarin is sitting up in the commander's hatch. She is the only one of us who is not new to all this. She shouts something over at Illich, who looks at her and nods and motions for his crew to get in their own vehicle. Others all around us do likewise now. When Bolkunov drives up in his jeep again the tank motors are already starting up again, just like it was an hour ago. I see him climbing on Illich's tank to talk to him and then he runs over to speak to Ekhtarin. Aknyatov is sitting in the driver's hatch looking down the road.

"There they are," she says.

There they are.

• • •

We pass a terrible night killing Germans. As bad as it is, it is still better to be doing it.

We see many terrible sights during the night, at last firing our weapons at sights we can clearly see in all the flames, many tanks switching their headlights on again to spotlight Germans fleeing in all directions. Ekhtarin forbids us to turn our own lights on, a cowardly but perhaps prudent move. She declares that any vehicle that makes a target of itself is manned by fools. We have deferred to her experience all along and place our trust in her. We pass several tanks burning in the night, our own. All the Germans are on foot, darting here and there like schools of fish, shadows fleeing into darkness and then into flames again. I fire the machine gun from the hull, aware that I am doing it now, it is happening. For all that I can see it is mostly chaos and glimpses of things; it is hard to get a good view of anything from down where I'm sitting. I look many times at Aknyatov sitting next to me in the driver's seat; for us it is like being down inside a ship. For the rest of the night we receive no further orders except for what Ekhtarin tells us to do; mostly we just follow the tanks ahead of us, firing at anything we see.

July 2

The firing diminishes towards dawn. Ekhtarin is not sure where to go next, and we park beside a building on the outskirts of the town. She gets down to talk to Illich, who is parked up ahead of us.

The night was hot and the dawn brings not much coolness of the morning. I am filthy with sweat and now that we are not moving I feel suffocated inside the hull. Now that I have time to think I am nervous to get out in the daylight, every window looks like a place for snipers, and we can still hear shots here and there. But Illich's crew is sitting outside their tank, smoking and drinking water. Finally Aknyatov and I climb down and look for a place to relieve ourselves. Olga Kolparov stays behind in the vehicle.

It is a strange feeling to stretch my limbs down on the street, after the night. I look around to see what things look like, but it seems there is too much to look at, even though it is almost all ruins and smoke. Bodies. The ordinary hot quiet of a morning, I am aware of it. We relieve ourselves in the back of a doorway in Bobruysk, the first town I have seen that was held by the Germans. Another tank across the street is parked on top of a German soldier. My stomach lurches like yesterday but it is an automatic feeling that passes into the strangeness and ordinariness of everything around us. We start to feel a little less tense and walk over to Illich and his men. It is good to just talk a little, though there is no news about anything yet. Illich and Ekhtarin have gone on ahead somewhere.

•   •   •

We pass more German prisoners staring out at us from cellar widows. I have seen the first of them being killed at different places, though mostly they are just herded into one building or another. Others stand in the street. We stare at them as we drive by. We are driving towards the main square, where there is room for everyone to reassemble and find out what is to happen next.

As we drive past the first of the big square buildings around the square we see the hanged people hanging from a ledge high up on the tallest building. I sit up on top of the hatch to see better. I try to count but can't do it at first, even though there are not too many. Nine. The length of the ropes is disturbing, each one looks at least thirty feet long. The Germans threw them from the top ledge and they fell almost to the street before they were brought up dangling. One of the bodies is lying in a heap on a lower ledge above the front entrance, a tenth body, the rope bending out slackly from his neck, that rope hanging limply from overhead while the other nine dangle tight as strings.

I begin to look around and see a similar sight at another building across the square. Some officers with cameras are taking pictures, official business.

•   •   •

None of us is entirely unprepared for this. All the same I try to ignore some of the terrible things I see done to prisoners through the rest of the day. Both men and women take part, equal under the eye of God. The heat is like a sickness. Irina Aknyatov has had terrible losses in her family and I see her walking around with a pis-

tol from the tank locker hanging at her belt; she says nothing and
I don't see what, if anything, she does. Most of the afternoon she is
working on our motor, helped by Kolparov and myself and one of
Illich's men. Ekhtarin sees no need to be parked in the square all
day, and she has us drive back into a side street nearby. Other vehicles do the same, though many remain out in the square.

· · ·

As people drive through during the day we hear reports that
the woods outside of town are still full of Germans, still trying to
flee in all directions. We expect to be told to move out again at any
moment. Bolkunov takes Ekhtarin, Illich, and some others in his
jeep back out to the outskirts of town. Later she returns to say that
the roads leading west are jammed with our own vehicles. Other
traffic keeps pouring into town from the east, from across the
Berezina.

"Set up some place for the night," she tells me. "But have
everything ready in case we have to leave in a hurry. Otherwise
we'll leave in the morning."

Her face is grey, more or less composed as I have always seen
it, but grey all the same. The town is full of empty rooms and
buildings, and I see no sense in looking for some place in particular to stay the night. It will take care of itself. There are very few
civilians in the town, and the ones I have seen are in such an emotional state that I hesitate to approach them, having spent much of
the day on the edge of overpowering feelings myself. Some of the
soldiers seem too much in a rage, or some kind of state, even to
assist the townspeople, though others do whatever they can with
a great show of pity. As in a kind of dream I find myself comfort-
ing several later in the day. Jubilation, apathy, horror, pass through
them like waves, and everything else, hunger, incessant talking, or
tight-lipped looks. They are more shocking than the dead and I
cannot absorb it all. There are not too many of them left in the city;
they stand out like specters but then fade back into the crowds of
soldiers, there are far more soldiers, far more bodies.

• • •

We are tired and wrung-out but when Ekhtarin tells us to drive off a little further down the street we do it gladly enough, to get further away from the square. We go only a little ways before we park again. We start to think we will be here for the night after all and start to think about sleep. We rest for a little while in a ruined house but then find that none of us is really able to sleep. It is too hot and it remains the same at all hours of the day and night, even more stifling at night.

I wander about with Aknyatov for a while, relieved when darkness finally comes after an endless summer evening, darkness just to bring darkness over the town after a day like this, even though the heat still hangs everywhere.

I ask her if she used her pistol during the day, not really wanting to ask her but saying it finally so the impulse won't keep passing through my mind. She replies non-commitally with a single filthy expression which angers me because I don't know if she means yes or no. Loathing washes through me, and I put my hand on her shoulder, patting her on the back, staring here and there with my breath stopped for a moment. She points at a crowd of soldiers going into a house with some lights showing up the street and we go there.

• • •

The place looks more or less like a brothel, or what I would expect a brothel to look like. A soldier sits on a table playing a balalaika, with a few others singing. There is a hole in the roof reaching up through several stories to where we can see the night sky. Lantern light reaches into different places up there.

Below, people are sitting on furniture or on the floor, drinking. Little glass vials of vodka are being handed around. More vials and also large bottles are being dumped out into a pot on a table, next to the balalaika player, someone else stirring the contents there. The singing seems strange, but perhaps that is just as well. Aknyatov pours water out of her canteen and walks over to the pot. I tell her to keep a little water in there, just so we don't poison ourselves.

"Hm," she says. Her canteen is already empty, drained on the floor. "Well, it's too late now. Don't worry about it."

She dips her canteen into the pot. A soldier puts his arm around her, bumping her up against the table. She ignores him and somebody else pushes him out of the way. She and I walk over to a place where we can sit with our backs resting against the wall, drinking and looking things over. I haven't brought anything to drink with so she passes her canteen to me.

"So. I don't see anyone I recognize," she says. "Do you?"

"No," I say.

She mutters that it might be good to have friends around in a place like this. I laugh a little. She doesn't look much concerned either. After a few sips I start to tremble, though all in all it's a relief. I shut my eyes and just feel comfortable for a moment. I look up at the night sky through the holes in the floors above. It's good to have a view of the open air, it makes you think of cool air though not much of it reaches down here. We sit there with our shirts partway unbuttoned, like everyone else in here.

Below, I find myself looking at an officer sprawled in a chair, a big chair, with a woman dead asleep lying stretched across his lap. Another woman in uniform sits crosslegged at his feet, staring into space, occasionally stroking the head of a small child that is huddled up against her side. The officer in the chair sits down low with his knees jutting out into the room like a baron. The woman lying across his legs moans, shifts position, lays her head back to stare up through the hole in the roof. She closes her eyes again. He caresses her, her stomach shining with sweat where his fingers run over it. The child, a boy, stands up, walks around the room; he is the object of much attention everywhere, people giving him anything to eat that they have. The woman who was holding him at the foot of the chair continues to sit crosslegged, staring into space. Aknyatov and I continue drinking. I see that apart from the balalaika and a few people singing, there is not much noise, not much noise of people talking. Some other women in uniform come in the door. People shout at them. Two of them look around for a moment and then leave; the others stay. One of them embraces a soldier, talking to him with strange animation.

Another man takes the child and hoists him up onto his shoulder, holding him perched on his right shoulder, walking over to the balalaika player, standing directly in front of him. The music player stares wide-eyed up at the child, still singing, then bends over his instrument again. Beyond the table with the vodka pot the room reaches back into dimness, two people making love in the dimness back there, it looks like. Many of the men are bare-chested and a few of the women are also, or else with their uniform blouses undone, a strange enough sight, especially as the air in this place is somewhat subdued, at least for the time being.

"Gloom. Gloomy," says Aknyatov.

"It's all right," I tell her.

"Just wait a while though."

It seems I am drunk and almost paralyzed after a few sips. I can drink, normally. It must be everything else then. Plus exhaustion. Or else I have been poisoned. But the liquor has no unusual taste about it. It just feels good to sit here and not move, drinking, thinking of nothing, and looking about at all this. Before we came in here I felt tired but also like I might walk around for several days before being able to sleep again, a bad feeling. Now I feel only tired and well-situated in this place, which is better.

"Nice kid there," says Aknyatov. "Nice baby."

We watch the child, who is walking around the room again.

She mumbles something and I see her raising her hand above her head like a student asking something from a teacher. She has her pistol and fires it up through the ceiling. The noise is so loud I fall over on my side.

There are cries and shrieks of alarm. Then silence. A few men start laughing uproariously.

"What's it all about, little sister?" says one from across the room.

She lowers her head and mutters something which sounds like, "Vomit." I ask her if she is sick but she shakes her head and puts the pistol on my leg. Another man seated in the middle of the floor starts saying, "Cuckoo. Cuckoo. Cuckoo," holding a pistol in his own hand in a way that makes me nervous, a revolver with a chamber that he flips in and out for a moment. Some of the other soldiers seem to find this very funny.

"Put it back in your holster, Irina. I don't have any place to put it."

"All right," she says.

She slides it back into the holster. She puts her hands in her hair and stares at the floor. Then she raises her head again. The balalaika player sings more loudly all of a sudden. The man with the child on his shoulder sets him on the table next to the singer and comes over to kneel beside Aknyatov, asking if she is all right. I am aware of people talking more boisterously all at once, shouting different things about anything or nothing.

"Good. Good," says Aknyatov. I don't know what she means. The man kneeling before her says,

"Yes. Everything will be all right. You'll see. What is your name, little sister?"

"Never mind that, comrade. Leave me alone for now."

He puts his fingertips together and stares solemnly at the floor. He looks at me. His face is intense and shining but not unkind. I offer him the canteen. He shakes his head, drinking anyway.

"All right then, sit down if you must," says Aknyatov. "There is room here, after all. What happened to the baby?"

The man looks over his shoulder at the balalaika player. The child is gone. I see a woman carrying him in her arms by the front door, walking out into the street. There is a crash from someone throwing a bottle against a wall, or one of the little vials. The man sits down beside Aknyatov with his back against the wall. Another woman walks over sleepily and lies down on the other side of him.

I nod off now and again, aware of sounds and voices in the room slowly growing louder, more people beginning to sing and sometimes shout crazily. The lantern lights grow dimmer, which helps me to drift off. I use my shirt tail to wipe the sweat off my face, trying to wipe my hair. I open my eyes one time to see that Illich is in here, sitting in a corner with an intense dull-eyed shine on his face. "Illich," I call over to him, not loudly enough to be heard. I open my mouth again but it is too much trouble. Aknyatov is no longer sitting beside me. Only the soldier who was speaking to her before, and the woman sleeping beside him, both of them sleeping now.

I am awakened by a bright light, an electric lantern sitting on the table beside the big vodka pot. The balalaika player is gone ,and I see half a dozen soldiers playing cards there. Young officers, I didn't see them in here before, shouting and looking full of themselves, throwing cards down. I groan, shut my eyes, turn my head to face into some other corner of the room where it is darker. A few kerosene lamps still burning, flames like dim little fingers. I hear someone shouting something about a game of cuckoo, I start to crawl off to get behind a couch where it is darker. Wild laughter comes from the table around the electric light. There is a big crash and suddenly the whole place is in darkness. The darkness makes me feel better for a second. Then I hear people rushing about the room, stumbling over things, loud noises, but everything else is almost silent now. A voice carries through the darkness:

"Cuckoo! Cuckoo!"

Gunfire blasts out from half a dozen places. I am almost behind the couch but am too shocked to move. No, I think. I scramble behind the couch. Someone screams. Then silence, except for more people stumbling around. A voice comes from another corner of the room,

"Cuckoo! Cuckoo!"

Another barrage of gunfire, laughter, furniture crashing. Then strange silence again, this time it seems to last for a minute or so. I hear people whispering in the silence, quiet stupid drunken laughter. I crouch in terror behind the couch, pressed up against somebody else there. I think of shouting something but am terrified of being fired on. The craziness goes on, more gunfire, a woman laughing crazily, cursing in a rage. A few shouts and screams that the shooters ignore.

"Where is he?"

"Cuckoo! Cuckoo!"

"Overhead."

More gunfire. Things fall down to the floor from up in the ceiling, dust and bits of plaster, other things. I look up there, see the night sky over the top of the couch. Stars. Someone crawling around up there, up in the upper stories.

"Cuckoo! Cuckoo!"

The voice comes down from overhead, the gunfire follows. My ears ring. I hear a sickening thud from the middle of the room.

Someone lights a cigarette lighter. A kerosene lamp glows brighter.

"No, you missed me, you bastards. I jumped down."

"Cuckoo! Cuckoo!" comes another voice from somewhere else down below. But there is no more firing. I look around the couch and see them standing around the one who had fallen from the ceiling.

"No, you lose, Morostin. You've been shot through the arm."

"What a bunch of shit. No, by God, you're right. How did that happen? Help me up, you bastards. I've hurt my foot. Never mind that, it's just a graze."

Stupid bastards, that's right. I look over there to see them all looking pleased with themselves, happy fools out of training school. I don't know. Still waving their pistols about. A woman stands up somewhere, when they look over there she hurls a lantern into their midst, striking one of them in the face. One of them shrugs and another one shouts at her, makes a lunge for her. He collapses on the floor. She walks out into the night.

I get up and stumble out towards the back of the building, stepping on people who are still asleep, muttering to themselves, snoring. I walk along a hallway, feel doorways and rooms on either side of me, thinking of sleeping it off again somewhere. But I keep going until I push out into a stinking yard in the back. It is getting light, and I walk carefully so I don't step in anything.

I make my way back towards the street along an alley next to the building, circling around a man and woman making love beside a shed. Their voices are loud. I recognize Aknyatov and smile a little in spite of everything, walking quickly away from them. Out of curiosity I look at the man again, whom I think I recognize, and I do.

I head out into the street. I feel terrible and disgust rolls through me and rolls away, a few spasms of laughter which never quite come through my lips. Unfortunately I start to remember things from the day before and horror rises up in me and causes me to kneel and vomit. I feel a little better but not much, aware that I stink, which does not bother me as much as the feel of my stinking clothes hanging on me in the still air.

The early light is as ugly as death. Everything around me looks like filthy clothes, the air, the ruins, the bodies, the shrunken little trees along the street. I do not know where I am and sometimes see the main square down at the end of one street or other. I realize I will have to go down there if I am to find the tank again. There are people about but I don't want to ask them anything. They probably wouldn't know anyway. I pass four soldiers taking turns pissing on a dead German. They look up at me and I lift my head in acknowledgment. The madness on their faces turns solemn for a moment. One of them smiles at me and I smile back, then walk on. My lips start to twist a little bit, flexing. With anxiety I feel the heat of the day coming.

Once out into the square I am able to find my way again. I walk along the edges of it. There are still too many bad things to see out there, either still going on or else the remains from yesterday. The ropes hanging taut from the high ledges have not been cut yet. Evidence is necessary, maybe. It should be indecent but it is not. I will not be of much use today but console myself by thinking I will not be the only one. I only hope they are not all too drunk to leave, because it will be good to leave.

July 5

We are parked at the edge of a large wood. An empty field rolls to the horizon.

There is an early mist and the sound of doves comes through the woods. Cuckoos, I think, but it is not cuckoos. Drunken bastards. It is doves cooing, lending little souls to small hidden places back in the woods. I always notice the sound of these birds when there is mist hanging in the air, though it is not the only time they make their sounds.

The mist is not really a mist but only a hot ugly haze, as the day goes on and we drive on. Sunlight swimming oppressively up in the haze.

The country is more open here than the deep forests we passed through between Moscow and the Berezina. There is open space like the steppes of home, but it is different from that too. The steppes roll away forever but here the enormous fields alternate with areas of forest that are almost equally as large. We drive along small tracks through these forests that go on for several miles. Yet you get used to the feeling that another enormous field will open at the end of the forest. The forests are like vast low buildings or green tents, because no matter how deep they are you still have the sense of the open country spreading beyond the edges of them. It is a strange sensation. It is in the forests too that we keep flushing the Germans from their hiding places.

We come across a small column of vehicles, firing into it though it seems it was already a wrecked shambles before we arrived. We shoot up the wrecks anyway, wanting to shoot at everything now. Infantry following us in trucks get out to comb the woods. We drive on until we leave the woods and set up a firing line, ready to catch any Germans trying to escape from the trees. We see a vehicle driving at high speed along the forest road, it must have been following close behind us. At first we think it must be one of ours, but as it comes out of the forest it does not slow down and drives right on through our line of tanks, raising a panic-trail of dust. Two of our tanks further back in the field fire on it and it burns instantly, burning men falling out the back of it like things dropping off a mantel.

We wait for a while longer and kill a few Germans on foot coming out of the woods, a few of them trying to surrender. We wait some more and no more appear, and then we are given orders to head on westward to the next town.

Patches of forest stand all around the horizon like strange low monumental things. The haze drifts overhead, full of sun and heat. At the edge of the next woodland along the road there is a village.

We passed one yesterday that was like this. And then the day before that there was Bobruysk, the town of Bobruysk. The place here looks like the ashes from a campfire, still smoking faintly or maybe it is only the heat shimmering now. The timbers of the isbas stand around. Bodies lie scattered around in the ashes like things that have been left to cook and then forgotten. Then there are other people lying in long rows in a garden plot at the edge of the village, between the village and the forest.

It looks little different from the village we passed yesterday, where we did not stop because we were moving in fast pursuit. Aknyatov is driving and here she stops the tank. Some of the others keep on driving into the forest but the others behind us also come to a halt.

Aknyatov walks out into the place. The rest of get out and follow. A few men remain sitting on their vehicles, watching from a distance. The ones lying in the garden plot are not burned. Lying in the black earth fresh as fruit, fresh as cabbage and tomatoes. Soldiers walking through begin to cry out, their wails of anger have become as ordinary as breathing, and so many others just walk through the dead breathing and staring. The people lying on the ground look as if they were all shot down only minutes before. Someone shouts that the Germans must still be nearby and people begin running off into the woods to look for them. Others keep wandering through the village, through the gardens and the ashes of the isbas.

The worst thing to see is not any of the villagers. I walk around the black wall of a house and then stagger back as if I have run into a post. Aknyatov is just behind me and she keeps on walking over there. A German in one of those shrunken-up uniforms is sitting against a water trough. His stomach has been slit open and another German has had his head thrust entirely through the slit, into the first man's belly. Like he is trying to peer into a mousehole. Aknyatov walks up to the sitting man and fires her pistol into his head and then walks off without even looking at what she has done. I am mostly numb at this point and carry little of the feelings from a few days ago. I hear someone talking about partisans, or maybe another group of our soldiers came through here before we arrived. But none of this could have happened very long ago.

We are obliged to wait for a while in this place because half the crews have left their vehicles and run off into the woods to look for Germans. I have no heart for this but am not exactly dispirited either. A strange terrible giddiness washes through me and then passes away and then comes back again. I walk back to the tank and sit on the ground in the shade of the hull next to Ekhtarin. We have nothing to say to each other. A strange heaviness comes over me that is almost like sleep, a welcome feeling but it passes and I am wide awake staring at the hot sunlit dirt beyond the shadow of the tank.

Ekhtarin says, "You know, many of us are not used to reacting to death anymore. It's been going on for too long. But this is really too much. If we see more of this we are really going to wake up and do something terrible."

She talks as if she is reading out loud, reading out loud strange thoughts that are passing through her mind. Over these last few days I have become used to people saying things that are not exactly clear but which must be clear to them. The more sober ones muttering these things as if recounting fragments of a dream that they are still too engrossed in to describe in its entirety. Then the more maddened ones will say or do things which stand out and have no ambiguity.

"We'll all be contaminated," says Ekhtarin. "But maybe if we're lucky we won't regret any of it."

She is not saying much but it is like having teeth pulled, just listening to a few words. I shift my back to her, rest my head against one of the tank wheels.

After a while Bolkunov drives back out of the forest to see why the rest of us have not followed. I hear him yelling angrily when he sees all the tanks and trucks parked here and most of the people still gone on foot into the woods. I hear doves cooing again, cooing back in the trees, sounds carrying through the heat. After a few minutes Bolkunov quiets down and out of the corner of my eye I see him walking in the gardens with his hands on his hips, staring at the people lying in the gardens.

July 6

Another traffic jam. Dust. Heat. Filth.

Another road through a low weedy-looking forest. Traffic controllers drive in jeeps up and down the road to see that everyone stays in column. A few tanks fall out to try and go it across country; they become stuck in marshland.

Much of this country is boggy, even in this burning heat. I think what it would be like in the springtime. If we leave the vehicles to find some shade, we are bothered by mosquitoes everywhere. There is shade beside the tanks but there you are choked with dust. But there is no comfort anywhere so we mostly just wait in the vehicles.

Older soldiers look nervously at the sky. Planes pass overhead sometimes, but they are always ours. I hear people talking of '41, when the terrible retreats passed over these same roads in Byelorussia. The German planes killed everybody in traffic jams like this. But so far we have seen no German planes, and we are too tired and uncomfortable to worry about it much. But then we start to hear the sounds of heavy firing up ahead, and we grow tense again. As usual we look to Ekhtarin to reassure us or at least tell us what is going on, but all she tells us is to be patient. She looks no less tired and irritable than the rest of us, though she tries to see that we do not get on each others' nerves while waiting in this confinement. Aknyatov and Kolparov have taken a dislike to each other, or at least it seems that way, though they say little. They are both moody types, though Kolparov especially keeps it within herself.

Ekhtarin has seen all of this and more for over a year. She tells us about the great battles between Byelgorod and the Dnepr last summer. She tells about the tanks advancing in great waves across the Ukraine steppe, not bottled-up like this. We listen, waiting, smoking, waiting some more. We hear more gunfire up ahead and we just listen.

●　　　●　　　●

At last we get going again. We pass through the wrecks of battle.

We drive past smoking vehicles that have been cleared off the road. They are all ours. There are other wrecks out in the marshland on either side, that tried to get off the road to escape the ambush. Some look bogged-down, but many out there are destroyed as well.

"Just keep going," says Ekhtarin. "Just stay on the road and keep going."

We can only go as fast as the vehicles ahead of us, and if they stop then so must we. But she keeps saying this to Aknyatov. I raise the hatch to look at the wrecks. There are many, the most I have seen. Heat and smoke rising in waves off the dark green metal, mostly heat rising in strange funnels everywhere out to the horizon on either side. The road is raised like a causeway. We move slowly and slowly pass by the wrecks. Many of the turrets are painted with patriotic slogans, crude white paint blistering in agony.

DEMYANSK

ALEKSANDR NEVSKY

MOTHERLAND

VICTORY

ALEKSANDR NEVSKY

MOTHERLAND

STALIN

STALIN

GIFT FOR VICTORY FROM MAGNITOGORSK
FACTORY NO. 3

MOTHERLAND

MOTHERLAND

CRUSH THE FASCIST WHOREMASTERS

VENGEANCE

MERCILESS

DEMYANSK

KATERINA DEMYANSKAYA

POLAR SOVIET

GIFT FROM THE WORKERS OF GORKI

MOTHERLAND

STALIN

STALIN

I see some that I recognize. Many of the slogans are the same and I only recognize the vehicles by some feature or other. It is as well that I see only a few I recognize. Others bear no slogans and no markings and sit in silence in dark factory paint. So it is with our own vehicle. Ekhtarin wanted it that way. Markings attract fire, or maybe it was only some idea she had about luck or vanity. The unmarked tanks are wrecks no different from the others, the ones with patriotic words or numbers. We pass five American tanks, all burnt-out or else burning still. The veterans do not like American tanks because they burn too easily. Seeing is believing. I feel my heart beating.

The unburnt tanks sit in silence and maybe their crews got out to see another day. The dead on the burnt ones are black like the vehicles are black. We drive on. Some people fled burning from their tanks only to drop dead in the reeds twenty or thirty feet away.

Keep going, says Ekhtarin. We pass another one right on the shoulder of the road. Motherland, No. 12. There are only a few all-women crews such as ours. Most of the women are scattered among the men as drivers or signals operators. For us to crew our own tank is a singular honor that we speak little of anymore, though we are not unaware of it. Commissars will come to us and remind us of it, though it is not necessary that they do this. It is difficult, as some of the maintenance jobs tax our strength and more than once we have had to ask for assistance. We do this without humility.

We drive on. My mouth is dry and I look away, then look back again. Motherland No. 12 was another crew such as our own. They might have escaped but we can see that they did not, and we can see them there very close to us as we pass them by. None of them is recognizable anymore, not a single feature is recognizable. We have talked with them a few times but do not know them better than that. Suddenly it seems that I know them better. Ekhtarin stares at them, and she lets out a strange cry. The thing smokes faintly still. Motherland. A flash of light bursts out on the horizon. My mind has gone dull and a feeling of panic catches me by surprise. "Keep going!" shouts Ekhtarin. Another flash bursts out on the marsh, I see the rocket trail moving swiftly and then seeming to accelerate still faster till it strikes something up ahead with a loud clang. An instant's silence contains the entire blank void of sky, then an explosion rolls heat out over us.

Aknyatov accelerates but then we halt behind the other tanks halted in front of us. Ekhtarin rotates the turret. I drop down and lower the hatch. Kolparov loads the charge. Every vehicle in the column is firing out into the marsh. Another rocket trail goes by, I see the flash through the armored slit. It shoots across the road, hitting nothing. We fire with all weapons. Delirium. Ten minutes pass. We drive on. Half a dozen tanks leave the road in panic, now bogged down out in the marsh, except for a few lucky ones that struggle back onto the road. We drive on.

•　　　•　　　•

Minsk has fallen without a fight. The fascists abandoned it. We will be there tomorrow. We drive on, following the long evening into the west. The heat haze is a formless void. Once or twice clouds take shape, rising far above.

July 7

In Minsk we drive into the main square to see over fifty that the Germans have left hanging from the tallest building. New waves of disbelief wash through our own bodies that are still not as solid as we think.

Minsk is liberated. We have come almost to the end of Russia. I don't know if this is fighting, for mostly we are just killing Germans everywhere. Everywhere. Except for yesterday, when many of us died. I have not seen a German tank, except for a few that were wrecked. We see more groups of prisoners waiting to be killed, but maybe they will not all be killed. It is necessary to have some still alive to scream at and spit on, or else just to stare at as we pass them by.

Over fifty of our countrymen hanging from the front of the largest building on the square, I can't count them now. It seems like that many. They all dangle from the ends of those same long ropes, thirty feet long, forty feet long, fifty feet long. Like the strings of a harp, dead music. A hot wind blows through Minsk, many fires burning. The hanged people move only a little in the wind, great long weights.

This city is larger than Bobruysk and hard to be believed. The fields and gardens on the outskirts are a wasteland of thorns and ugly bushes. There is so much ash in the city that it looks like a desert. The emptiest wastelands beyond Astrakhan look something like this, except there are no buildings standing there like there are here. There was ruin in Bobruysk, but here there is more. And they say the city was given up without a fight. It is not all the ash that looks unusual, but the few buildings that remain standing in it, the larger buildings.

We park in the shadows of one that rises from the slope of a little hill. The opera house, a huge square place. It has a strange nobility standing over this wasteland. In its desolation the city seems endless, somehow much larger than the fields and woods we passed through to get here. The sun is hotter, the sky is closer but also bigger. I have a strange unearthly feeling, like some kind of explorer, that is still more quiet and awesome than the terrible things we see everywhere.

A few Germans are lined up and shot at the feet of the hanged. A man in a black uniform screams so piercingly that the air is like a vacuum, carrying only that sound. He is kneeling over a curbstone with his hands tied behind his back. An NKVD man is using a pistol butt to hammer something into the back of his skull, a brass nail or a cartridge case. Finally it ends. The hot wind blows many terrible smells through Minsk as the day goes on, stronger than at Bobruysk, which is also hard to believe.

We set up in a big park in the middle of the city, as if that will be less depressing. There are many wrecked trees but also many that are still standing. But the place is overgrown with thorns and whenever we get snarled up in them we become angrier and angrier. Many people are stunned to silence but it is also necessary to cry out from time to time. It is necessary. There are no civilians anywhere. I hear someone say that many traitors fled with the Germans.

There is something about the park that I cannot abide, though I am reluctant to wander off into the city. There is no water anywhere and people seem possessed by every kind of foulness and depression. Ekhtarin says she has the same feeling about the park so we set up right at the edge of it, next to a wide empty boulevard. The opera house stands on its little hill nearby.

We make a campfire by our tank and sit around it as night comes slowly. The summer evenings are longer than the night;

they are longer than the afternoon, longer than the morning. Hot wind blows smoke above, and then further above evening clouds pass slowly. The shapes of clouds are more distinct in the long evening and bear the spirit of the evening slowly across the land. I cannot help but feel strangely pleased in all this emptiness, I won't deny it to myself. It is a mad kind of thought, but as it makes me more at ease for a little while I do not put it from my mind. There must be something about a great city that is empty. The moon is overhead when the night finally comes.

Olga Kolparov is from the Ukraine and she begins saying things that I have heard a few other people say over these days. She says we have been rightly punished and we can kill all the Germans we like but all of it is still our punishment. We deserve no better, she says, and then she says it over again several times. It is not the first time I have heard such remarks but all the same it is not wise to say them too loudly. Or are we free to speak, here in the graveyard of Minsk? I do not think so. She is struggling with herself, glaring into the fire.

"March off with the traitors then," says Aknyatov. She has taken offense at Kolparov's muttering. Olga presses her hands against her forehead. Ekhtarin and I look around nervously, at Kolparov and Aknyatov, also at other groups of people camped nearby.

"Why must you say anything?" says Irina Aknyatov. "For days I've been waiting to hear it. Let's hear it then."

"Oh," says Kolparov, shaking her head, pulling at her hair. Shadows flicker across her wide face. "My parents are in prison," she says, announcing it to the world at large.

"Good for them," says Aknyatov. "Maybe they're safe there. They didn't have to suffer all this."

"It's a lie," says Kolparov. "They're not in prison. They're dead. I know they're dead by now. They've been dead for years."

"Then why bring it up?" says Aknyatov.

"I don't know. I hear people wailing everywhere in the night. Why must I say nothing?"

"You're not saying nothing," says Aknyatov. "Go ahead. Say what you like. You're right, it's all a big funeral."

"Kolparov," says Ekhtarin.

A moment passes.

"Yes, comrade captain," she replies sullenly.

"Come sit over here," says Ekhtarin.

Kolparov does nothing. Ekhtarin closes her eyes, presses her lips together.

"She is not the only one to say so," I say to Aknyatov. I am stupid to open my mouth but it is done.

She looks fiercely at me. "Don't I know it? Don't I know it? Punishment . . . what shit. What absolute shit. It's all women and children fighting the war now. They can't afford to send any more people to prison till after it's over."

"Aknyatov!" shouts Ekhtarin. "Remember yourselves! Both of you. Both of you."

"Maybe we'll all be dead by then anyway," Aknyatov keeps on. "I forgive you, Olga Vassilyevna. I forgive everyone in the entire world. The Germans came from a place where insects live. Death to all dirty fuckers. Why did you have to start all this, eh? Just so you wouldn't keep me waiting anymore. My uncle was shot before the war. He was a greedy bastard. Wallow in sorrow for your parents. It's time for the mourners to wail."

Ekhtarin rises and kicks Aknyatov hard in the side, driving her foot in, almost stepping on her.

"Ah, " says Aknyatov, staring at nothing. She lies on her back and then looks drunkenly over at me across the fire, though we have drunk nothing.

"You dominate our thoughts as always, Irina Pavlovna," I say.

"You think you know any better?" she says.

"You should be ashamed of yourself," says Ekhtarin, still standing over her.

"Yes. Yes. Yes. At last someone who talks sense. I feel it every day, all the time every day. I am ashamed that the Germans killed everyone I know. I speak sincerely, comrade captain. I am ashamed, ashamed of eternal shit. Where is Kolparov? I've done her wrong."

Out of the corner of my eye I see Kolparov simply get up and walk away. I see her sitting now among a group of soldiers around another fire nearby. Aknyatov remains lying where she is, then she begins howling, grunting, howling at the night. It is like a drunken person cursing at everything, the kind of thing you can hear in any town in Russia, anywhere, at any time. Words mixed up with incoherent noises.

I was very much afraid, for a few moments there. Exhaustion and death make for loose mouths. Ekhtarin saw this too. But it is over now. Aknyatov will calm down when she is ready to. I walk over to sit beside Olga Kolparov at the other fire, hoping the same kind of thing does not start up all over again, not really thinking it will. But I don't know for sure.

July 8

We are told to leave our vehicles and assemble on foot at a place on the other side of the park. We walk down the street to avoid all the thornbrakes that have taken over the park. But this takes too long and finally we just walk through the ugly bushes to get to the other side.

It is about the size of a factory lot, dug up, excavated. Part of it is still within the park, along the far edge of it.

"You must have guessed," says Ekhtarin to me. "Why didn't you say so yesterday?"

"No, I didn't know. It was just a feeling I had. It wasn't anything. You felt the same way."

Even these few words come out in a terrible hurry, as if we feel our breath escaping us. Or else it is that we are holding our breath. But you have to breathe. The smells yesterday seemed to come from everywhere. The same last night, the same this morning. Blown in by the hot breezes and then carried away. Till we might have stopped noticing them, mostly. But now there is no escaping it. People begin to moan, twisting their heads from side to side.

There is a large formation of troops assembled to one side of this place. A commissar, or somebody, I can hardly stand to face in that direction, is standing on a wooden crate speaking through a loudspeaker. No, my God, they aren't going to make us stand here. Up ahead I can see people, standing closest to the pit, already beginning to faint, dropping where they stand. It is already very hot and I am covered with scratches from the thorns and the smell seems to come right into my body. I stumble, I am not about to faint but I think of dropping down where I am, so I won't have to go closer. Ekhtarin puts her hand under my arm. "Courage," she says. I am aware of other people stumbling nearby, still moving forward where the rest of them are.

Next to the pit, between the assembled soldiers and the pit, are many wooden grills or iron grills lying flat on the ground, the wooden parts half-burnt, many half-burnt piles of kindling and planks and debris scattered among these grills, all reeking from the smell of gasoline, of which it can only be said that it is different from the other smell, the more overpowering smell. The black gasoline-burnt bodies are heaped up everywhere on top of these different pyres. Bodies also are sometimes only half-burnt, and children in there, among all the rest.

Again I feel weak and rest my hand on Ekhtarin's shoulder, who is also walking very slowly. I can hear the loudspeaker but not really what is being said, and then even before we quite get there the sound is drowned out by other sounds that start to come out in waves from the soldiers standing there. The commissar standing on the crate lowers the loudspeaker down by his leg, he lowers his head and puts his other hand up against his face, wiping his eyes. He sets the loudspeaker on the ground and sits down on the crate, holding his head in his hands. The cries coming out from the soldiers become like some single indescribable sound.

The Germans must have been interrupted in their work. For there are still more more bodies down inside the pit, sticking up everywhere from the dug-up earth. The smell seems to be everywhere but I know it comes from there and anyway it is too horrible to really even look at. I am aware somehow of the Germans standing down there among the earth and the putrid mess, standing as stiff as posts, like the posts where condemned men will be tied to be shot. But there are no posts, only the Germans standing as stiffly as that. Out of the corner of my eye I see one of them begin to wobble, to sway and then fall to his knees among the bodies. He tries to stand up again but is instantly shot. I don't know who shoots him. Then I see a line of soldiers at the far end of the pit with rifles aimed down at the Germans. They stand over there as still as the Germans with their rifles aimed, though how they can refrain from firing all at once I cannot imagine. Beyond these men are other soldiers, and I see they are standing guard around a large crowd of prisoners standing beyond the far end of the pit. Some of them too begin to faint, just as our people do, and I see and hear them being shot whenever they fall.

DEMYANSK

I look down at all the dead civilians as if through a thick glass plate that is pressed right up against my face, against my eyes. They burned many of them on the grills at the edge of the pit, but there remain far more down in the pit that they did not have time to burn, far more. They wished to erase the evidence of what they had done, to burn it all before we arrived. But we have arrived and the evidence lies dug-up right beneath our eyes. Evidence, guilt, justice, death. A rage burns through me that I think will burn all the revulsion right out of me, that will enable me to bear the stench and stand at attention with all the others here. But it does not last, it fades away and I am exposed to everything again.

"Natasha," I say to Ekhtarin. "I am going to be sick."

"Yes, all right," she whispers. I can barely hear her. I bend my knees to lower myself to the ground, but then I cannot bear to go down at this place. I grab hold of her and I feel her lurching to a stop, standing stiffly there. I support myself against her. I gag but nothing comes out, only a little saliva against the back of her shirt. Another empty convulsion comes up through me. Tears come to my eyes, like sweat, it is all too much to feel anything except for the rising in my stomach. I stare blankly at the ground around my feet, at other pools of vomit here and there. A great roar of noise, of human voices, passes through my ears, it has been there all along.

"I've got to get away from here, " I tell her. "They can't make us stay here."

"Keep moving, Aklaba," she tells me. "Everyone is walking away now. Just keep going."

I look over her shoulder and see the troops beginning to move all at once, but they are not walking away, they are all walking slowly along the edge of the pit. It is a long wide excavation like a factory lot, and it will take time to walk the length of it. For a little way we pass behind the half-burnt grills with the black bodies piled on them, blocking our view of the pit just beyond. The gasoline smell is a relief but it is too strong, and I begin to gag again, my head starting to throb. I narrow my eyes until I can see only a slit of vision and tilt my head up at the sky, following a bird that passes up there, a bird in a slit of sky.

I pull myself together a little bit and let go of Ekhtarin. We walk slowly with all the others, and finally it seems none of this is happening after all, it will be over in a few minutes. I straighten myself up a little bit, feel cold sweat on my face becoming warm again. I feel little thorns clinging to my uniform, inside it. I see Aknyatov just ahead of us, her arm around Olga Kolparov. I see Aknyatov staring down below. I stare down there again. Another German down there begins to sway back and forth a little bit. He is shot before he can fall, if he is about to fall, and then he falls. Among the bodies. They start to look more like all the other things I have seen recently. I keep my shirt up over my mouth and nose, keep walking, look down there or look around at nothing, either way. There are about twenty Germans still standing down in the pit, and they start to look more and more like posts, not even scarecrows but just posts, the heat shimmering up from them like everything smoking. I see the eyes of the living still in their eyes, I do not know what to make of it. As we near the end I see an officer shouting down there, and I hear him telling them to climb out of the pit. He waves his pistol at them and they begin to climb out of the pit, crawling over everything and climbing out. Most of them stumble as they do this. They are not shot now. It is a miracle. My spirits rise and then sink again. I keep walking. The ones climbing out of the pit are herded back among the other prisoners still standing at the end of it. Some of the ones climbing out are clubbed to their knees by the rifle butts of our men who were shooting at them before, breaking bones, but no more shooting.

•   •   •

The rest of the day lasts a long time. We walk on the wide streets all around the edge of the park, not willing to struggle through the thorns again with the smell hanging everywhere. I want to just wander off into the city, to get away from here, sit with my back against one of the chimneys. No doubt I will come across many other bad things out there, but this does not concern me, I just want to get away from the park.

But I do nothing, except to follow dazedly behind the others, who dazedly follow their own footsteps. We wind up back at our tank, where we were parked the night before. I half-expect Ekhtarin to tell us to drive off a little ways, like we did at Bobruysk, but she says nothing, she looks no different from anyone else, I cannot bring myself to make any requests of her.

For hours we hear the sounds of shooting from the other side of the park. Loud regular volleys for hours like a kind of clock. Good for them. We are maddened and grateful only that they did not make us stay any longer in that place.

The rest of the day lasts a long time. It is hard to think about anything so the dull hours do not wear on us exactly, but still the day goes on and on. Bolkunov and other officers come by giving people things to do, servicing the vehicles, assigning them to collect water from tanker trucks, wherever they may be. Some people obey, some people do not obey, some people stand up and walk in circles for a few moments and then sit down again. For once there is no shouting, no cursing or threatening from any officers anywhere, though we remain on edge expecting one of them to lose his temper at any moment. Ekhtarin sits by the tank doing nothing and so the rest of us also do nothing. Olga Kolparov's face is marked by the inability to say what she is thinking, or maybe that was only last night; I do not know what she is thinking now. Aknyatov's face is like a stone but she stays close by Kolparov, patting her on the back sometimes, and sometimes it makes me think of a kindly executioner who is patting his prisoner on the back in the last moments before it is to time to go. But this is a crazy thought, nothing is going to happen to Kolparov, I don't think so anyway.

One time I told Kolparov I had seen the trains of people pulling out of the station at Astrakhan, before the war, the ones who were on their way deeper into Siberia or God only knew where. I told her this only as a way of saying I understood, or that maybe I did. She had told me about her parents already some months ago. She is a shy farm girl who does not know how to say very much, though there are other reasons for not saying things. When I spoke to her then she also said little, nor has she looked to confide in me since then or become close to me in any way. The boxcars in Astrakhan were full of enemies of the state, many enemies, many enemies, who looked very bad, and some who were already dead were pushed out onto the tracks and left behind in Astrakhan. This happened many times, I knew, though I only saw it myself once or twice, and only from a distance. I did not tell her any of this but only that I had seen the trains. Confidences are dangerous but cannot be helped sometimes, we are comrades after all; thousands of other soldiers also mutter things from time to time, they cannot help themselves either. I know that people have been shot for making loose remarks about Stalin, about the party, about anything at all; I know that people have been shot for saying innocent things that had nothing to do with anything; I know that people have been shot who had never even opened their mouths, who were falsely accused, and they were shot anyway. The danger of this is so ever-present that it becomes almost normal, like living with a natural disaster in your country. But that is only a poor way of saying it.

Yet still people talk sometimes, with terrible dark humor, or simply because they cannot help themselves. I know people who were shot for saying far less than what Olga Kolparov said around our little fire last night; yet still I do not think anything will happen to her, of course nothing will happen to her, but in truth I cannot even think about it at all. There are so many murderers among us, among our own people, yet what is the use to dwell on such things?

No one can do anything about such a state of affairs, nor even think about it; not any longer. Instead, there is war. It is a relief for us to be killing Germans, to be killing someone. I know it is true. I know it is true. It is good to find some murderers at last. God forgive me for the vile unworthy thoughts that pass through my mind, and I know He does, for my mind is empty as air for hours at a time.

We are hungry but do not eat. We are thirsty and would drink, but none of us goes to look for any water. We are hot and filthy and during the long days driving in the tank we are half-sick from heat and motion-sickness and fumes and for long periods of time are not much afraid of death. Then suddenly, at random moments of the day or night, you will come to your senses, or feel like you are coming to your senses, and be paralyzed by fear; but the hours just go on anyway. Illich says it has all been too easy these last few weeks and when we come to real fighting then we will see something. We have seen many things and when we come to real fighting we will see that too. A few tanks burning horribly by the side of the road, and it could have been us in there, but Illich says it is nothing yet, and we will see. The infantry comb through the woods after the fleeing Germans, shouting, "Stalin! Stalin! Stalin!" Two years ago there were only a few women in the army, and I was a girl in Astrakhan, visiting my cousin in the hospital. He had lost an arm and he told me not to pity him but to be grateful; he told me that at the front the only hope was to be wounded, even terribly wounded, for otherwise there was no hope for anyone there. He said it was a shame for the women, for they could not hope to be wounded, to

be disfigured. I did not know what to say but said that he underes-
timated us. He said that I was right, but that I still did not know
what I was saying, which I guessed was true. I felt bad for him, for
once he got over being out of the war he would be left without an
arm, and what could he do then? Be comforted by women, he said.
I don't know, he said. It is of no concern to me, he said. Be a good
little cousin, and bring me some nice things from the town.

●   ●   ●

I look overhead. The air is throbbing, far overhead, close by
too. I have not felt such close and throbbing heat before, not week
after week like this. In Astrakhan the land burns but it is not like
this. I look up at a large square building nearby. Big stone blocks.
More restful to look at. My head swims with nausea but I am half-
asleep anyway, vaguely dreading that Ekhtarin or someone will
come by and give me something to do. Through the uppermost
windows I can see through the blown-up roof into the sky. Some
people are moving around up there, soldiers standing on a stone
ledge. Aknyatov pats Kolparov on the back from time to time.
Kolparov grimaces faintly once or twice, not much as one hour
drags to another. There are many things on the tank that require
our attention. At last we get up and begin working on them.

In the evening the commissars show a film against the wall of
a large building. It is without human decency to show such a distraction after this morning. Soldiers watch anyway, thousands of
them sitting in the street or on piles of rubble. I cannot pay much
attention. The film runs on the wall of a building a hundred feet
high. It is about Soviet mountaineers climbing a peak in Central
Asia, the tallest mountain in the country, which has never been
climbed before. The following night we are still in Minsk and the
film runs again, against the wall of the same building. It is easier
to watch on the second night, or easier to pay attention to. A white
peak rises above a sea of other mountains, three thousand miles
away from the war. The red banner is planted on top. Russia is
unconquerable, only Russians can conquer Russia. My mind is
still wandering, even though the mountains are a beautiful sight,

and I am angry that I cannot watch this in peace. But why be angry. . . . The night is hot and dark and against a high wall we see brilliant sunlight and ice from three thousand miles away. My mind still wanders. Still, I am satisfied that I am able to watch most of it on this second night; it is good to be able to watch something like this. It seems you could lose yourself in those snowy mountains. But I start to get nervous finally, and I have smoked too many bad cigarettes already. "Tastes like food that has already been vomited once," mutters a soldier next to me, passing me a tube of majorka. I take it and stare at it and hand it back to him. He laughs quietly at his own joke, so do I. I am becoming more tense, disturbed feeling. It still seems indecent somehow, I can't help feeling it though I wish I could just relax. Finally I have to get up and walk away through the crowds of soldiers. I climb up onto a pile of rubble a short distance away, where a few other men are sitting with their backs turned to it all, still smoking, but staring off into the darkness. I sit down on a slab of concrete there.

The whole area grows darker when it is done. I don't have to turn around. I hear a great quiet murmuring in the dark back there. A few voices begin to take up the cry. Then others take it up, till there are more and more of them shouting in the dark. At length a great roar goes up into the dark from many hundreds of voices, maybe thousands of them. People shouting, shouting, shouting. Yet all the same I am aware of those who do not take part, who say nothing. Those seated smoking quietly on the rubble nearby, and those scattered in silence throughout all the shouting crowd back there. It is not like a protest or refusal or anything of this kind. I know it because I know it somehow, aware of it in the noise. It is simply the ordinary division between one kind of person and another, between those shouting or those silent, living or dead, fulfilled or betrayed, tired or easy, hungry or full, enraged or calm, man or woman, brute or saint, murdered or alive. So on, so on.

"STALIN! STALIN! STALIN! STALIN! STALIN! STALIN! STALIN! STALIN! STALIN! STALIN! STALIN! STALIN! STALIN! STALIN! STALIN! STALIN! STALIN! STALIN! STALIN!"

Sources and Commentary

Christ Asunder

The reader will note that the town of Cherkassy is barely mentioned in this story, though history has lent that name to this ordeal. Cherkassy was in fact surrounded by the Russians in December of 1943, but a relief force managed to break the ring and free the garrison trapped there.

Ironically, this garrison, along with other divisions totalling over 50,000 men, was surrounded yet again only a month later, this time in barren steppe country more than fifty miles away from the town. This second encirclement became the real "disaster of Cherkassy." The focal point of the cauldron was now the town of Korsun, and so the siege that followed is occasionally, and more accurately, referred to as the battle of the Korsun pocket.

By either name, the siege and subsequent breakout attempt across the Gniloy Tikich River became one of the most nightmarish struggles of the war. German chroniclers emphasize that nearly 30,000 men actually made it to safety, a remarkable achievement under the circumstances. The Russians were more interested in the fact that nearly 20,000 German dead lay between the Gniloy Tikich and the breakout village of Schanderowka. They liked to say that nowhere else in the war were so many Germans killed in such a small area in such a short span of time. This may be true. Only a handful of prisoners were taken.

The narrator, perhaps confused by the chaos of those days, indicates that Schanderowka was in German hands until the night of the breakout on February 17. In reality Schanderowka was overrun by the Russians before that time; the Germans then had to recapture it, before using it as the staging point for the final breakout attempt towards the Gniloy Tikich and the relief force that was struggling to meet them there.

It has been noted that the image of men emerging stark naked from the freezing waters of the Gniloy Tikich was burned permanently into the minds of even the hardened veterans of the SS Wiking Division.

A final note about climate conditions during that winter. In contrast to the Arctic temperatures of 1941, the winter of 1943-44 was one of the mildest recorded in many years. The autumn mud in the Ukraine remained until mid-December. The spring thaw then set in for good during the first days of March, and there were several temporary thaws before then. The Germans had by this time learned to cope with the extreme temperatures of the Russian winter, but the days of struggling through seas of glutinous mud, especially when followed by nights that were still below freezing, were perhaps even more demoralizing. If not for this, the breakout from Schanderowka might have happened sooner than it did, with possibly less disastrous results. It was the only period in the war when the Russians did not suspend large-scale operations during the rasputitsa, or mud season.

—*Ostfront 1944* (Alex Buchner, Schiffer Publishing, 1991).
—*Campaign in Russia: The Waffen-SS on the Eastern Front* (Leon Degrelle, Institute for Historical Review, 1985).

Demyansk

Much of this story centers around the relationship between the Graf von Brockdorff-Ahlefeldt, commander of the Demyansk pocket, and the commanding officers of the SS Totenkopf Division, Theodor Eicke and Max Simon.

I have taken a certain amount of license in creating the narratives of various lower-ranking officers. Lieutenant Nierholz of the 5th Jaeger Division is a fictional creation, as is Sturmbannfuhrer Harter of the Totenkopf Division. I have taken similar license with the commanding officers, but as the careers of such people as Eicke and Brockdorff-Ahelfeldt are somewhat better documented, I feel obliged to distinguish between fact and speculation.

Many of the scenes recreated here are based on material in Charles Sydnor's excellent history of the Totenkopf Division, "Soldiers of Destruction." Though by no means siding with the SS commanders, Sydnor does relate many of the incidents in Demyansk from their point of view. He cites numerous cables from both Eicke and Simon to SS Reichsfuhrer Himmler, in which one finds many complaints about lack of support from the regular army, varying levels of incompetence, assignment of the most difficult tasks to Totenkopf, and other diatribes in this vein.

To what extent Eicke and Simon personally blamed Brockdorff for these problems is hard to say. In such a desperate situation a high level of tension would not be unlikely, perhaps resulting in emotional outbursts that were temporary, or in grudges that were more permanent.

In general, the relationship between the army and the Waffen-SS in Russia, particularly in combat situations where close cooperation was a matter of life or death, was good. There is little evidence of the kind of anger and bickering that one sees in the communications between SS Totenkopf and Himmler during the Demyansk battles. As the war went on, men in the Waffen-SS divisions seemed to feel a closer kinship with the Landsers in the army than with the "rarefied higher headquarters swine" directing operations from a thousand miles away.

On the other hand, Eicke was widely regarded as one of the most headstrong personalities in the Waffen-SS, and in the SS as a whole. The Totenkopf Division, and particularly the senior officers serving in Eicke's command, bore the stamp of his character. He seems to have been a good leader; he seems also to have toned down his volatile temperament to some degree, as compared to the time in the early 30s when he was plotting to plant bombs in the offices of one of his Nazi party rivals. General von Manstein, one of the ablest of the German army commanders, openly admired him and the performance of his men in Russia. Eicke was nearly unique among the high-ranking officials of the Nazi regime, in that he demanded a combat assignment and forsook a comfortable desk job—at Dachau, of course—back in Germany. By and large, Nazi government leaders were notorious for doing just the opposite.

In any case, it does not seem out of character for Eicke, and subsequently Max Simon, to have engaged in a battle of wills with Brockdorff-Ahlefeldt in the Demyansk cauldron. But if such was the case, there was also out of necessity a good deal of cooperation between these men.

The main thrust of the account in this book to to turn the situation around and look at it from Brockdorff-Ahlefeldt's point of view. His personal opinions of Eicke and his men are not well-documented; thus many of the scenes as recounted through his eyes are admittedly hypothetical. It seems reasonable to speculate that if Eicke and Simon bore resentment against Brockdorff and the army, the reverse might also hold true, particularly in light of Eicke's personality.

Brockdorff did publicly congratulate SS Totenkopf for its courageous performance on several occasions. Perhaps this was motivated to some extent by diplomacy, by an awareness of the peculiar standing of the Waffen-SS divisions in the Nazi hierarchy. But it is difficult to read any lack of sincerity into these messages, when Totenkopf had indeed been instrumental in keeping the Demyansk pocket from collapsing more than once. In particular, there are no documents to suggest that Brockdorff might have considered removing Eicke or Simon from command, though some circumstances, such as Simon's direct refusal of an order during a crisis in the summer of 42, might have warranted such an action.

Brockdorff's participation in a conspiracy to oust Hitler from office before the outbreak of war is documented in Gordon Craig's "The Politics of the Prussian Army." Apparently the conspirators managed to dissolve their plot without being found out. If any head-to-head confrontation between Brockdorff and Eicke had occurred at this time, Brockdorff probably would have found himself dangling from the end of a rope. But that was peacetime. How Brockdorff's attitude might have changed during a year-long state of emergency in Russia in 1942 is part of the mystery of this story.

General von Seydlitz-Kurzbach presents a clearer picture. His leadership of the Free Germany Committee speaks for itself. It is hard to imagine that such an organization could have been created without various attempts at coercion, fraud, and treachery on the part of the Russians. Yet it is equally hard to imagine that Seydlitz's revulsion for Hitler's regime was anything but real. It was Hitler's conduct of the war in Russia that pushed him to the brink of open rebellion. His vehement criticism of Hitler after the Demyansk relief operation in April of 42 is recorded in the battle history of the 5th Jaeger Division.

From Demyansk Seydlitz was transferred to Stalingrad, moving from a merely terrible situation into a catastrophe. This was the genesis of the Free Germany Committee. Whether his decision to lead this group was an act of brave defiance or of cowardly submission to Russian pressure, only he and his captors will ever know.

—*Der Weg Der 5. Infanterie–Jaeger Division 1921-45* (Helmut Thumm, Podzun Pallas Verlag, 1976).

—*Wie Ein Fels Im Meer (Like a Stone in the Middle of the Sea, campaign history of the SS Totenkopf Division)* (Karl Ullrich, Munin Verlag, 1987).

—*Soldiers of Destruction* (Charles Sydnor, Princeton University Press, 1977).

—*Politics of the Prussian Army 1640-1945* (Gordon Craig, Oxford University Press, 1964).

The Abyss of Earthly Delights

The formation of the four SS Einsatzgruppen that went into Russia was a curious and demented business.

From evidence given in the Nuremburg trials and elsewhere, none of the four commanders wanted anything to do with this job. To despise and ostracize the Jews was acceptable, not only to members of the SS but apparently also to millions of other Germans. However, to conduct operations of mass-murder on a scale never dreamed of before was a step that many were unwilling to take. Walter Ohlendorff recounted all this at Nuremburg; his statements correspond with the statements of many other individuals; although they are clearly an attempt to rationalize his guilt, they are also, on the whole, quite believable. Yet these men went ahead and carried out these operations anyway. At no point did they declare that they feared for their lives or the lives of their families if they refused these assignments; Hitler's government, at least in its dealings with the members of its own elite, did not operate in that fashion. They were bullied or prodded in other, more mundane ways; mostly they seemed to fear that their careers in the SS would be sidetracked if they did not carry out these duties.

Evidence also indicates that almost all of the rank and file of the Einsatzgruppen were kept in the dark about the exact nature of their mission until their entry into Russia. Matthias Graf, an SS junior officer who balked at this task at the last moment, was arrested and sent back to Germany.

This kind of scenario seems fairly typical of the miasma of life in Nazi Germany. All of the commanders of the Einsatzgruppen who could be found after the war, including Ohlendorff, were hanged at Nuremburg. Others, such as Nebe, were never captured.

The facts of the events at Babi Yar remained obscure for a long time. Citizens of Kiev knew very well what had happened there, but for many years the Soviet government held to a policy of minimizing the killing of Jews in Russia, while emphasizing the suffering of Russians as a whole. The poet Yevtushenko defied this policy; the composer Shostakovitch entitled one of his symphonies "Babi Yar." The most detailed account comes from the novel of the same name by A. Anatoly (Kuznetsov), which is actually a straightforward memoir of those years. The chapter that deals with the shootings is based on an interview with one of the few survivors of that day.

Ohlendorff was not present at Kiev. He was in charge of Einsatzgruppe D, which murdered Jews in the southern Ukraine and Crimea. But the character who bears his name in this story espouses many of the same attitudes that the real Ohlendorff displayed at Nuremburg. The murders at Kiev were carried out by Einsatzgruppe C; the assistance of the Ukrainian police and other Ukrainians has been established beyond any reasonable doubt. The participation of other German units is less clear, though not unlikely. Various sources report that Waffen SS soldiers were sometimes temporarily assigned to the Einsatzgruppen as a disciplinary measure, or even as part of the "normal operations" of these groups; the evidence for this remains murky.

On the whole, these operations were not well-kept secrets. They were frequently witnessed by civilians and soldiers of the regular army. These witnesses may have been few in number, but they were enough to ensure that the word was passed around to almost every fighting unit in Russia. Perhaps uncertain rumors to some, while obvious truth to others.

—*Babi Yar* (A. Anatoly (Kuznetsov), Farrar, Strauss, and Giroux, 1971).

—*The Order of the Death's Head* (Heinz Hohne, Ballantine Books, 1971).

Summertime

Russian battlefield tactics were generally so simple and straight-forward that one sometimes wishes there were a different word to describe them. But tactics will have to do.

A Russian offensive would amass overwhelming strength at various key points. Due to the Germans' skill at defensive warfare, particularly in their mastery of the counterattack, Russian assaults at any number of points would be repelled with high losses. But if they found a weak point in the German line, all available reserves would be rushed to that area, relegating attacks elsewhere to a secondary role. Even if a weak point could be overwhelmed and exploited, the breakthrough more often than not would be met by an immediate and savage counterthrust from the German reserves, often in the form of the ad hoc "battle groups" which became one of the peculiar strengths of the German army. Thus many Russian offensives, even when initially successful, would pass through a bottleneck which the Germans would then seal off, encircling and annihilating the attackers within.

This situation was repeated again and again early in the war. The Volkhov Offensive in the winter and spring of 1942, the Timoshenko Offensive at Charkow in May of 1942, the Popov Offensive again at Charkow in early 1943, were all examples of this kind of battle. Initial rapid advances were turned into terrible Russian defeats, defeats which continued to feed Hitler's belief that the Red Army was on the verge of bleeding itself dry. Russian losses were indeed horrendous, but in terms of exhaustion, it was the German army that finally broke. Their manpower reserves were fewer and spread over much of the European continent. In the critical area of armored reserves, Hitler could never hope to match Russian industrial production, though he stubbornly refused to acknowledge this. The Battle of Kursk squandered much of the armored striking power that was essential in sealing off Russian attacks.

Thus, by the late summer of 1943, the seemingly endless Russian offensives began to gain a momentum which was never really stopped until the end of the war. The Germans no longer had the available reserves, either in armor or infantry, to carry out the devastating counterattacks which had been so successful in the past. The Battle of Byelorussia in the early summer of 1944 was the most striking example of this; in terms of casualties alone, it resulted in the greatest defeat in German history.

The Germans had only two understrength panzer divisions available to back up the 40 or so infantry divisions, also understrength, of the German Army Group Center. The armor was frittered away rushing from one point to another to stave off Russian breakthroughs. For once the Russians found, not just one weak point, but many of them, and made huge gains in territory all along the line. Hitler ordered the 5th Panzer Division to be rushed by train from the Ukrainian front. This unit was near full establishment, and in conjunction with Tiger Battalion 505, destroyed over 500 Russian tanks in two weeks of fighting. Considering the magnitude of the German defeat, this figure was remarkably high, and again illustrates the effectiveness of counterstrokes by German armor. But 5th Panzer was only able to operate in a small part of the battlefield, which stretched over hundreds of miles. Elsewhere, notably between Bobruysk and Minsk, the Russians simply poured through.

In purely strategic terms, the Russian High Command frequently displayed skill and imagination in their conduct of the war. By staging mock build-ups in other fronts, they were able to divert many of the German reserves away from Byelorussia prior to the battle; but in the moment-by-moment tactical situations that arise in combat, the Russians still favored the sledgehammer approach more than any other method. Historians like to say that their battle tactics became more refined as the war went on; there is some truth to this, but only in a relative sense. Russian casualties kept to staggering levels from the beginning of the war to the end. They showed little mastery of what are generally referred to as "small unit actions"—in other words, the ability of battalions, companies, and even platoons to cope with a crisis as an individual unit, as well as to undertake complex tasks in cooperation with other small units. This was a skill which the Germans had developed to a high degree, and enabled them to hold on in the East long after most other armies probably would have collapsed. The saga of a small squad of men in combat, so much a part of American novels and films about WWII, also has its equivalent in the German army; Willy Heinrich's novel, *The Cross of Iron*, is probably the best known example of this.

But it is interesting to note that in other German memoirs of the war, the focus on small squads and platoons is more obscure; one is more struck by the confusion of the individual soldier in the midst of huge and terrifying operations. From all available evidence, one would gather that this was even more true for the Russian soldier; such small units as a squad or platoon hardly existed as meaningful entities.

• • •

It was in the Battle of Byelorussia that Russian retaliation against German soldiers began to reach a crescendo. Vengeance is really the operative word. The war had been fought for three years with great savagery; murder of prisoners and civilians, while not universal, occurred very frequently.

After the summer of 1944, the Russian thirst for vengeance became unquenchable. They had always viewed the German invasion as a war of extermination; they now sought to exterminate the exterminators. Upon reaching the German border in the autumn of 1944, they began a campaign of atrocities against German civilians which equalled, and may have surpassed, anything suffered by Russian civilians in the preceding years. German writers, as well as other Western historians, do not fail to point this out. Nor do they fail to point out the barbaric behavior of the Soviet government against other nations, against its own citizens; before the war, during the war, after the war. All of this is true.

Yet to portray all of this as merely a Russian equivalent to Nazi atrocities is probably to distort the terrible role that vengeance can play in human motivation. The citizens of many eastern European nations feared the arrival of the Red Army in 1944 and 1945; these fears were not unfounded. Many of the citizens of the western regions of the Soviet Union also feared liberation by their countrymen; to a considerable extent, these fears were also justified, but none of these places saw the almost unimaginable wave of atrocities that took place after the Russians entered Germany. It is true that Soviet soldiers were urged on by the bloodthirsty ravings of Ilya Ehrenburg, a poet who became one of Stalin's chief spokesmen during this time; his tirades were printed in every Soviet newspaper and repeated by every front-line commissar. The basest instincts of soldiers were encouraged by the almost universal loosening of discipline once the German borders were crossed, but the men and women of the Red Army had also seen the results of three years of German occupation in Russia. Vengeance was their response.

—*Ostfront 1944* (Alex Buchner, Schiffer Publishing, 1991).

—*Hitler's Greatest Defeat* (Paul Adair, Arms and Armor Press, 1994).

—*My Life in the Red Army* (Fred Virski, MacMillan & Co., 1949).

About the Author

RUSS SCHNEIDER studied the Russo-German War for years before writing his books, teaching himself German to broaden his research. He published two collections of short stories. *Madness Without End: Tales of Horror from the Russian Wilderness* and *Demyansk: More Tales from the Russian Wilderness.* His nonfiction work *Gotterdammerung: Germany's Last Stand in the East,* was published by Eastern Front / Warfield Books in 1998 and rereleased by Doubleday as a Military Book Club main selection. Russ Schneider died in 2000 at the age of forty-three.

Printed in Great Britain
by Amazon.co.uk, Ltd.,
Marston Gate.